I0564112

SMALL TOWN SPIRIT

PATRICIA CRUMPLER

This is a work of fiction. Names, characters, places, and incidents are products of the author's imagination or are used fictitiously and are not to be construed as real. Any resemblance to actual events, locations, organizations, or persons, living or dead, is entirely coincidental.

World Castle Publishing, LLC
Pensacola, Florida
Copyright © 2023 Patricia Crumpler
Paperback ISBN: 9798891260146
eBook ISBN: 9798891260153
First Edition World Castle Publishing, LLC, August 14, 2023
http://www.worldcastlepublishing.com

Licensing Notes
All rights reserved. No part of this book may be used or reproduced in any manner whatsoever without written permission, except in the case of brief quotations embodied in articles and reviews.
Cover: Cover Designs by Karen
https://www.cover-designs-by-karen.com
Editor: Karen Fuller

Dedicated to the author John Sandford who has provided many hours of entertainment. One of his books offered part of the inspiration for me to write this novel. Mirrors that serve as windows for spirits perfectly fit my story. I hope my books will inspire other authors to write. Let us all inspire each other in a positive way.

Chapter One

An icy finger of doubt touched Jennifer Hughes, hijacking the joy she'd felt all morning. The house passed inspection, exceeding her expectations, but she had to clarify the abrupt misgiving. "Why did the sellers take my first low offer? Is it haunted or something?"

The real estate agent, Pam Caufield, nodded, shrugged, and dropped her gaze to the stack of papers she held. She lost a bit of color in her olive skin. "I should have told you this before. The sellers think it's haunted. You can back out and not sign the contracts."

Jen drummed her fingers. "It's because of that creepy dirt basement, right?"

Pam slid the stack of Jen's closing copies across the desk. "Dirt basements were common at the turn of the century. A lot of Victorians have them."

"That's it?" Jen chuckled. "I don't, and *can't* afford to, believe in ghosts. I *want* that house."

The first day Jen drove into town and passed the *Welcome to Livonia* billboard, she knew this was her chance to find herself, become independent, leave the old, weak Jennifer behind and embrace the newer, stronger woman she needed to become.

Pam's color returned. "Well, now you know the rumor. If you're okay with it, sign, and we're done."

Jen signed on the highlighted lines.

"Great," Pam said. "Why don't you go next door for a bit of lunch? I have about ten minutes' work to do. Then I'll join you. Okay?"

Accustomed to taking orders from her ex-husband Keith,

Jen berated herself for immediately rising and heading for the door. *Okay, I could use some coffee.* Hoping she could go through this post-divorce adjustment fast, she considered her actions now, not like before, jumping at Keith's commands without question.

Gold leaf words, *Carpe Foodum,* on the glass door identified the café. When the hostess approached, Jen pointed to a booth and said, "Can I please have a cup of coffee?"

She headed toward the ladies' room. In front of the mirror, she pulled the rubber band from her light brown hair and let it loose, using her fingers like a comb. She frowned at the mirror. The divorce had taken its toll on her face.

Damn that, Keith. Although not admitting it openly, she had lost her passion for him in the last few years. *The whole divorce thing has been so frickin' inconvenient.* "Oh, quit bitchin'," she mumbled and thought about the framed sampler she brought from her Baltimore house, embroidered in colorful cross stitch, *Quitcher Bitchin'.* Now it would hang in her new kitchen. She inhaled a cleansing breath, washed her hands, and returned to the table with its waiting cup of coffee.

Her waistband, loose from the *divorce diet,* gave permission for real sugar.

Before she could take a sip, Pam slipped into the booth. "Okay."

"Okay?"

"I'm done with my chore. You're the new owner. Everything's good."

Jen pictured the wooden house and its fish-scale mansard cupola with the eagle weathervane.

Pam brushed a dark lock from her forehead, put her elbow on the table, and leaned her chin on her knuckles. "You mentioned you had just divorced. I am, too, so I understand what you are going through."

Jen nodded. "Thanks. Since I left our home in Baltimore, I've felt like a vagabond."

"I hear you, sister. I haven't completely acclimated to being alone."

Jen looked at the coffee cup. "Absolutely. I need a good house, one that can be mine and not a relic of my past life. I'm thrilled to get this one and have some money left over for furniture."

"The owners said you could have the furniture if you want it."

"All those antiques? Wow!"

The second coffee came. Pam said, "Thanks. I could use a shot of caffeine."

Jen ordered a cheeseburger and fries. "Lunch?"

Pam thought for a moment. "Nah. I'm good with the coffee."

"Okay, Pam, tell me about that house. Who thinks it's haunted?"

"Some of the past owners. These last owners had it exorcised. They stayed the longest. Now only people from out of town look at it."

"Oh, come on. It's probably an old furnace. Maybe it gurgles. Gosh, a house near us in Baltimore exploded from a faulty furnace."

"The furnace works fine—upgraded ten years ago to natural gas. Funny, you should have mentioned an explosion. The original builder blew up a factory, killing a few people before he killed himself. He was involved in organized crime and all kinds of corruption."

"So, that man's the ghost?"

"I haven't a clue. That's the only thing I know about the first owner."

"There has to be a better explanation."

"Don't say I didn't warn you. You still have time to cancel if you want to get out of it."

Jen took a long sip of her brew. "No. I love that house. And I want to move in right now. I'm in a cheap rent-by-the-week place. The furniture too? I can't believe it!"

"Everything will be yours. *Everything.*"

Pam scooted out of the booth, making a scraping noise on

the seat.

"Oooh, I think that cushion is haunted," Jen teased. "Did you hear it groan?"

Pam smiled. "Ah, must be the suffering upholstery cheering the fact my big butt has lifted."Pam turned to leave. After a few steps, she hurried back to the booth. "I'm sorry. I forgot to give you the keys. Come over and get them when you're done here." She left. The little brass bell above the café door rang cheerily from her exit.

"Ghosts," Jen murmured. "A haunted house." She smiled. It couldn't be as bad as the turmoil she had been living with in Baltimore.

Her burger and fries came, along with a refill for the cup. The food tasted great, with deep flavors and perfect texture. The gloominess she'd felt in the ladies' room disappeared and had been replaced with the happies.

Stomach full and feeling like the Bliss Fairy had unloaded her wand, Jen went next door for her keys.

Standing in front of Pam's desk, she put her hand out and wiggled her fingers.

Pam leaned back in her office chair. "I hope it works out and you stay a long time."

"I survived, Keith. I can survive, um, *whoever.*"

"Here." Pam held up a dark steel ring and rattled metallic keys.

"Oh, for real? Look at those long old-fashioned things!"

"These open the front door, the side garage, and the back door. But these…." She fanned blackened finger-sized iron cylinders. "Are for the inside doors."

"Skeleton keys! Isn't that what they call them?"

Pam's left eyebrow went up. "Sounds appropriate."

Jen accepted the jangling mass.

A line formed between Pam's dark eyebrows as she handed over the garage remote control device. "Be careful."

"Don't worry. I'll be okay." Jen put the keys in her purse.

"Do you have a lot of stuff to move?"

"Nah, my clothes, keepsakes, a few linens, and knickknacks. Keith is shipping my dishes. How nice of him, eh? Maybe his new honey doesn't like my pattern. Actually, *Old Country Roses* will look good in my Victorian. Don't you think?"

Pam sniffed. "Sure. I can picture them flying through the air regularly."

"Come for tea," Jen said in an English accent.

Chapter Two

That afternoon Jennifer stopped her four-year-old Acura in front of the roomy one-car detached garage of her new purchase. She pressed the remote button. As she started to emerge from the car, a hellish screeching jarred her. She flinched, and the car door hurled back at her. She jerked her leg away to keep it from being crushed. The adrenaline rush subsided as the squeal deepened and turned into a metal-upon-metal rasp. *It's the garage door!* The wide wooden door finished its plaintive path, stopping at the top. "WD 40," she said, as if a secretary stood by making a list. She popped the trunk and cautiously got out of the car. The boxes jammed into the back had not budged for three months since she left Baltimore. She struggled to dislodge her possessions, but it felt good to no longer be homeless.

The tidy garage had a few tools hanging on one wall, and in the corner, a ladder leaned against an upright hand truck. "A dolly, just what I need," she said to the non-existent assistant. She wheeled it to the boxes sitting helter-skelter around her Acura.

Jen piled three boxes on the dolly and dragged the cargo up the cement walk to the back door. The modern door key slipped into its slot, and the door lock quietly clicked. Using her knee to hold it open, she edged the loaded dolly into her kitchen. Each box proclaimed its contents by thick black markings.

Jen looked around the kitchen. "Put plastic ware on the list." She pulled open the refrigerator door. "And food. Got to get champagne. Not Dom Perignon." She sighed. Keith would still drink that; she would have to step down to Piper Heidsieck. Nothing less, though. "I have my standards."

Opening the box marked *kitchen,* Jen removed the framed

cross-stitch sitting on top and leaned the *Quitcher Bitchin'* sampler on the counter against the fridge. "I'll hang you later." She pulled the dolly outside for the second load.

Jen put the new set of boxes at the bottom of the stairs and, one by one lugged them up. Opening the one labeled *linen*, she took out a set of sheets and placed them on the stripped bed. She pushed the box with the towels into the bathroom, next to the antique claw foot tub. The black and white octagonal tiles on the floor reminded her of beehive cells. A semi-circular stained-glass window let in colorful light above the tub. *I love this bathroom.*

On her way downstairs, she ran her hand along the dark walnut banister. The newel at the bottom sported a carved pineapple. How many little boys had their sliding plans thwarted by the threatening points of the sculpture?

Jen took a breather in the parlor and sat in one of a pair of wine-colored velvet wingchairs that faced the graceful fireplace mantel. She needed to go shopping before she wore out. Her rest lasted five minutes. She had things to do.

She searched for her handbag in the kitchen. "What did I do with my purse?" She jumped when the *Quitcher Bitchin'* frame clacked against the tile counter and hit the floor.

Her hand went to her throat. *It's only the cross stitch.* Her peripheral vision detected a movement. The back door slowly swung open. Seeing her car with the trunk aloft, she remembered where she left the handbag. *Dummy.* "Um, secretary, remind me to keep a better watch on my purse."

After she locked the back door, a thud came from the kitchen. She froze. The clacking of the cross stitch falling repeated. A scraping noise followed, the kind of sound a heavy box made by being dragged across the floor. *Must be an open window blowing my sampler over. Yeah, the wind.*

Chapter Three

Jen hurried to the garage, got in her car, and sped away. Noises forgotten, she trekked through town feeling better than she had in months, maybe years. She found a grocery store and commenced her purchasing orgy. By the final aisle, the buggy was perilously full.

Luckily, Grocer's Heaven sat opposite a liquor store. Pulling into the busy street, she made a sharp U-turn and parked in front of The Beer Cave. Saying "Beer Cahv" to herself, she wondered if the store offered a fine line of exotic beers kept at the perfect temperature for discerning customers, like a wine cave in France. Her lip turned up into a quick snarl. *I won't be around to enjoy the wines Keith bought in Beaune last year, our Europe's Finest Wines Tour.*

The liquor store did not offer a fancy, temperature-controlled wall filled with beers from around the world. In fact, the floor was bare cement.

"Welcome to the Beer Cave," chimed a young man pushing a broom. He did not say *cahv.*

Not a high-end liquor store, it still offered the usual selections of champagnes. She lingered at the Dom Perignon display but pulling away from the divine nectar, she found the Piper Heisdeick and rejoiced at the $36 price tag. She selected a set of plastic wine glasses on her way to the register, where she stood behind a black man who resembled a young Denzel Washington. He turned and smiled at her. As she smiled back, the box of glasses slipped from her grip. He caught them before they hit the floor and, with an unhurried, effortless motion, handed them to her.

"Wow, great move! Thanks," she said.

"You're welcome." He looked her up and down. "Partying alone, honey?"

Oh, no! What message did I send this guy? I don't know much about Livonia, and I'm single. This isn't my friendly, safe suburban neighborhood back in Baltimore. "Uh, no, not alone." *How do I cut this guy off?* She cleared her throat to produce a lower register. "Actually, um, I'm buying this champagne here to celebrate my engagement to my girlfriend. She said 'yes,' and we're headed to a special chapel in Aberdeen, uh…called the *Queen's Choice* to tie the knot tomorrow. Mazel tov! Eh?"

A nanosecond look of confusion crossed his face before he nodded. "Yeah, mazel tov." He turned around and took his change from the cashier. His wedding band flashed as he pocketed the change.

She paid for her purchase, reining in her usual chattiness. Leaving the store, she spoke to the unseen secretary. "New town, new people, new start. Right?"

When she pulled in to her driveway and hit the garage door opener, the door again screeched and squealed its slow progress up. *WD 40, first thing tomorrow.*

Jen spent an hour bringing in and stowing the copious purchases, then slumped into a parlor wing chair. After kicking off her shoes, she rubbed her neck and took a deep breath. "We'll have no champagne tonight. I'm dead tired and need sleep." Sandals in hand, she headed up the stairs to her bedroom.

She showered, brushed her teeth, and put on a red nightshirt. Catching her reflection in the door mirror, Jen modeled her nightwear and stroked her sides. She fluttered her eyelids, remembering how Keith liked the nightshirt. The upward curve on the side seams showing the tops of her legs turned him on, he claimed. He never failed to tweak her nipples that made slight bumps under the cotton knit. She glided her hands over her breasts. *Well, he'll never tweak these again.*

Jen opened her travel case and lined up a few bottles on the bedside table. Ever since Keith started divorce proceedings, she'd had trouble sleeping.

"What shall it be tonight? I'm so tired, I might not be able to sleep at all." She looked at the bottles. "Timed Release Ambien? Xanax?" The other bottles stood like soldiers, the guardians of her rest. "Ah, yes! I shall sleep with Prince Valium tonight." She shook the bottle of white pills. The label indicated ten milligrams as the dosage. "But tonight, sweet Prince, I shall make sure I get the rest I need for a big day of hard work tomorrow." She let two tablets fall into her palm and spun the blue top of Crystal Geyser.

Twelve hours later, she woke, stretched, and smiled.

Rested but groggy, Jen made her way down the stairs and into the kitchen. "Coffee," she said limply, waving her hand to the invisible secretary. "I need caffeine."

As she moved toward the cabinets, a glimpse of white grabbed her view. A trickle of fear, enough to bring her to full attention, guided her to a multitude of white plastic bags strewn about the floor. The pantry door gaped open.

"Hey!" Jen protested. *I'm sure I put these away. There has to be a logical explanation. Logical. Drafts? Of course, these old houses are full of drafts. But the pantry door?*

She wadded the plastic mass and shoved it into a bottom cabinet. "Make a note, canvas shopping bags. And check the handle to the pantry." She arched her back in a stretch. *Lord, do I need my cup this morning. Even if it is made from my new $15 Mister Coffee maker.*

The brew, along with two delicate croissants, fulfilled her brunch needs. Embracing the caffeine jolt, she planned to dedicate her morning to the garage. Inside the pantry, along with a few items from her shopping trip, she found the WD40 and a new speckled turkey feather duster askew on the floor. "Right. Drafts." She picked up the items. Then, lubricant and duster in hand, she headed out the back door and walked the twenty-odd steps to the garage.

Using the ladder left by the old owners, she dusted vigorously and lubed every moving part on the door opener mechanism. At the conclusion of the cleaning, the machine squeaked less, but not enough for her satisfaction. She stood in the open entry, hand on hip, and vowed to eventually quiet the damn thing. Jen, still in a defiant stance and focused on her mission, barely heard the little white Kia Rio pull up the gravel driveway.

"Hi," a familiar voice said behind her. "I see you're still here." Pam got out of the car.

Jen turned. "Yep, still here." She brought the remote from her pocket and demonstrated her minor success on the door sounds, then moved the ladder to the wall and put away the cleaning articles.

"So, how was your first night in the house? Any strange noises?"

Jen wiped her dusty hands on her jeans and meandered toward the Rio. "My first night? Great. I didn't hear a thing."

"That's good news." Pam returned to her car and came back with three bunches of grocery store flowers. "Welcome. I should have done this yesterday."

"Thanks," Jen said, pleased at the thoughtfulness. "Come in. We'll put them in water."

In the kitchen, Pam stripped the plastic from the daisies, pink carnations, and the third bunch of leather leaf fronds and baby's breath. Jen took the cellophane covers, still marked with *Three for twelve dollars,* and threw them in her new trash bin. Thinking about the overlooked price tags, Jen recognized that she and Pam had a few things in common.

"Oh," Jen's voice dropped. "I don't have a vase. I'll put that on my next list."

Pam said, "A big jar would work."

"I remember seeing some Mason jars on the shelves near the basement stairwell." Jen made an exaggerated shudder. "That basement is nasty."

Pam nodded. "I'm brave. I'll get one." She returned with a large mouth jar sporting the word *Mason.*

Jen cleaned the jar and decorated it with a paper doily, an impulse purchase from the previous night's shopping trip.

She snapped a rubber band around the jar's neck. "Voila. An Elizabethan collar for a Victorian house." They both stepped back and admired the arrangement.

"Nice," Pam said. "I took the day off. Can I help you get settled?"

Jen accepted, but before she could map out the day's labor, the doorbell rang. It was a UPS man with a large box on an upright dolly. He brought it in, and she signed for the delivery.

Jen glanced at the return address. "My dishes!" She eyed the heavy packing tape securing the box. "I need a box opener, Pam. Will you come with me to the DIY store? I also need to make a stop at an appliance place."

Pam grabbed her purse as an answer.

At the home store, Jen bought a threateningly large box cutter, hammer, nails, screwdrivers, a hose, and other DIY necessities. They walked to the nearby appliance store for the next purchase, a sixty-inch flat-screen television and a DVD player. Jen made one more stop for a rotisserie chicken and fixings after Pam agreed to stay for dinner.

As they exited the deli, a big red movie rental machine caught her eye. "I didn't know the stores still had these. I don't have Internet yet. Let's make this a true girls' night out." She rented *Gone with the Wind*.

They unloaded the home supplies into the garage. The television was lightweight but large and required them both to carry the box. As they passed the kitchen, they saw the doily-decorated Mason jar on its side, water puddled on the floor, and the flowers askew, some on the table, some in the puddle.

"Drafts?" Jen mumbled in a half-hearted excuse as she continued into the living room with her end of the box. They leaned their burden against the wall.

"Um, I'll go get the DVD player," Pam said.

"Okay, I'll clean up the flowers."

Flowers restored, and boxes opened. The two women set up the television and connected the DVD player.

"I feel really good about being able to set up all of this

equipment," Jen said. "I never plugged in a technology thingy in my life. I guess I'll have to buy a computer, too. I hope it's as easy as this stuff."

With the television installation completed, Jen cut open the UPS box and pulled the first wadding of bubble wrap from the dishes.

"Pretty dishes," Pam said.

"Thank you. I'll feel like I'm home when my Country Roses are in place."

Jen and Pam cleaned the built-in china cabinet, then rinsed and dried the dishes. One by one, the floral dinnerware went into its place in the formal dining room.

Pam said, "Break time," and returned from the kitchen holding two bottles of spring water. In the dining room, she extended the water to Jen, who sat on the floor leaning against a chair.

Pam twirled off the top of her water, squatted, and took a long drink. "How long have you been divorced?"

"Close to six months," Jen said. "How about you?"

"A little over a year."

"Did it hit you out of the blue, too?"

Pam sneered, making a noise from her throat. "I threw him out after I found a credit card receipt for a hotel room dated for the same time I attended a convention. Stupid man. He didn't pay cash when he cheated. I'm still adjusting. I know it's difficult."

Jen sighed. "One night, my ex said, 'I don't love you anymore.' And I bit the bait. I said maybe we should get divorced. He pulled the papers from his briefcase and told me to sign them. When I protested and suggested I get my own attorney, he assured me everything would be fairly divided. Our kids, Chrissy and Bobby, attend college, which he agreed to finance, and he promised to give me alimony for five years, so I agreed. It only took a few weeks, and poof! I was out the door. We met in college, and I dropped out to be a secretary so he could go to law school. Yep, Keith Hughes, Ass-squire."

Jen finished the water, stood, then pushed the empty

box outside through the back door with her foot. She washed her hands in the kitchen sink and called out, "It's six o'clock. Hungry?"

Pam came into the kitchen. "Starving."

They filled their plates with the chicken and fixings from the grocery store and moved to the couch in front of the television. Jen opened the DVD case. "The champagne! I almost forgot."

Jen came back with the moisture-coated bottle of Piper and two plastic hollow-stemmed glasses. She twisted the wire cage and eased the mushroom-shaped cork until it popped and flew across the room. They laughed, and Jen poured a liberal portion of bubbly gold.

"To your new home," Pam said.

"Down with men," Jen countered.

Their toasts stopped mid-lip to the sound of the china closet door swinging open.

"Must be a man-ghost," Jen said, sipping. She laughed at her accusation, took another long sip, and moved to close the etched glass door. "Leave my stuff alone," she teased loudly into the room. "We're trying to celebrate our liberation." Jen returned to the coffee table, where her fizzy Piper and meal waited. "By the way, I don't believe in ghosts, but did those families say they were harmed?"

"From what I heard, just frightened. I don't know much."

Jen moved her hand in the air, dismissing the thought. "Whatever. Movie time." Jen inserted the disk into the player. The room filled with orchestral beginnings, voices singing, and the scenes of the Old South. They ate, sipped, and watched. At intermission, Jen cleared the plates and grabbed a package of rich, chocolaty cookies.

"Here," Jen put the bag on the coffee table. "Enough chocolate to satisfy two almost middle-aged women not currently getting any."

"Give me two—no, make that four," Pam said.

"More champagne?"

Pam bit into the dark brown delight. "Better not. I'm easily inebriated and won't be able to drive home."

They moaned at the screen's long shot of soldiers suffering in the town square and sighed when Atlanta tumbled, burning. They cheered at the scene where Rhett carried Scarlett up the staircase. Jen and Pam reached for a cookie. Together, they sniffed when Rhett left after his famous line. Jen wiped a tear away. "I have to finish the story in my mind. I imagine Rhett doesn't get on his horse. He rushes back to her, and they have a happy ending."

Pam used her knuckle to dry her eyes. "Me too." She stood and touched her purse. "I have to go. I had a good time. Call me if you need anything."

"Okay." Jen gave her new friend a quick hug and walked her to the door. She flicked on the porch light and waited until Pam's taillights turned the corner.

She closed and locked the door, then turned out the lights. Taking the champagne, she trudged upstairs and got ready for bed.

Chapter Four

That night she chose the Ambien, washing one down with champagne. *That should be enough to help me sleep.* And it was.

The next morning Jen, refreshed, blessed the Piper for never giving her a headache. After breakfast, she put in one of her favorite CDs, Bach, cello by Yo-Yo Ma, to get her in the mood for cleaning.

The tall wood clock in the foyer had a layer of oily grit on the exposed parts. She cleaned it, and to her surprise, when she used the key lying behind the elegant curved top, she was able to wind it. With a gentle nudge, the pendulum moved in a graceful arc, and the clock began to tick.

Later that afternoon, she polished furniture. In the dining room, a drawer in the country French buffet stubbornly held its ground, unwilling to pull completely forward. Jen rubbed a bar of soap on the side rims. When the drawer came loose, it flew out, causing her to fall backward. She banged her ankle against one of the heavy chair legs. "Damn!"

But she forgot the minor sting when she saw an old photograph lying next to her foot. Her grandmother called this larger type a *cabinet* photo as opposed to a business card-sized *carte-de-visite*. The picture showed a handsome man, resplendent in his formal frock coat, a heavy gold chain stretched across the vest, and a lovely woman, wearing a white gossamer fabric dress, her hair pulled up, long curls cascading down one side. Although they didn't smile, the look of pleasure sparkled in their eyes. Jen read the neat handwritten explanation on the cardboard backing, *Miles and Virginia Hampton, 1890. Our wedding day.*

Jen stared at the photo. A flutter of envy filled her from

the couple's togetherness. *I might do some research on these people.* As she held the picture, a shadow passed over it from behind her and lingered for a second. When she turned, there was nothing there.

Leaving the memento of days gone by on the coffee table next to the remote, she went into the kitchen and heated a frozen dinner, which she brought into the living room with a glass of Coke. As she set the food and drink down on a kitchen towel, she noticed the photo was gone.

Hmm. I left that old picture right there. She searched under the couch, behind the curtains, and even the rest of the downstairs. The remote was still there, so she snapped on the news for an hour. *Jeopardy* and one detective show after another kept her entertained until the grandfather clock chimed its eleven bells.

Okay, one more night with Prince Valium. But that's it, no more. She took the recommended ten-milligram dose and slept like the proverbial baby.

Until a crash in the kitchen woke her up.

Jen scrambled to get her senses in order and away from the clutches of her favorite prince. Even when she lived with Keith, she hated the things that went bump in the night. Okay, one point for Keith—he would go and check noises. Now, alone, she would be her own hero. The bedside clock said 4:02 a.m.

She snapped the lights on in each room as she entered. Another crash sounded from the kitchen, and she really didn't want to go in there. But she pressed on, and as soon as the lights illuminated, the source of the clatter surprised her.

A large, fat raccoon stretched from the counter up into an open cabinet. Two smaller ones, maybe the adolescent children of the monstrous mother, ate the spilled cereal and oats scattered everywhere. Jen let out a howl, more of relief than anger, but there was plenty of that too. The raccoons ran from their feast and into the open basement door. Jen closed the door with a bang and wedged it with a chair from the kitchen set. *I'm going to nail that door shut.*

It didn't take long to sweep up the debris, but the whole

time she worked, a tingle tickled her spine. Accepting the sensation as the after-effects of bedtime ala Prince, she hurried to finish and hoped to get back to sleep. After an hour of lying in bed, she gave up and went downstairs to watch television.

Channel surfing produced no good old movies. To avoid the incessant infomercials, she settled on a jewelry sales channel. As she admired the offerings, she thought about the pieces she had inherited from her mother and grandmother. Keith had given her a few antique items over the years too. *Stop thinking about Keith.* She yawned. The sounds of the droning sales pitches lulled her to sleep, and she didn't wake until after nine.

Jen had dressed and made her late breakfast when the doorbell rang. She pulled back the nylon drape liners to see her visitor. A man holding an umbrella and a briefcase, dressed in a yellow golf shirt and gray pants, waited at the doorstep.

She didn't undo the chain but cracked the door. "Yes?"

"Ms. Jennifer Hughes?"

"Yes?"

He pushed his card through the door. A plain white card with black letters read *Speigal Enterprises.*

"Speigal?" She asked. "Like the real estate office?"

"That's right. The real estate office is one of our holdings. May I come in? I think you will like what I have to offer."

"You're selling something?"

"No," he said, exasperation making its way through the words. "I'm offering you a temporary job. A great deal of money for a small amount of work. It will take maybe twenty minutes of your time. Can I come in?"

"I don't know," she said, stalling while she tried to decide if he was legitimate.

"Do you know Pam Caulfield?"

"You're a friend of Pam's?"

"More like a business associate."

"Well, okay." She pushed the door closed enough to undo the chain.

The man opened the door before she could do it and

stepped inside. "I'm Sal Zemric. My mother is a Speigal. Zemric, from my father." He sat down uninvited on Jen's couch, opened his briefcase, and took out a note.

"I'll get right to the point. The Speigals pretty much run Livonia. There are three of the old families still here — the Speigals, the Ratterlees, and the Owings."

"Owings? As in Paul Owings, the police chief?" Jen had seen his name on a sign as she entered the town.

Sal's lip curled. "Yeah, he's one of the Owings. I'll skip the old family crap. You are single. You bought this house, so we know you are financially desperate. Not that I believe in that haunting sh — uh, crap, but no one would buy this heap if they weren't in some kind of trouble. Now, with that in mind, we are offering you ten bills for a small favor."

Jen recoiled, revolted by the man's approach.

"Ah, just let me finish, lady. Don't get all uppity until you hear the deal." He fished around in the case and produced an old driver's license. "See this woman? Arlene Holmes? You look like her, don't you?"

Jen studied the face. Darker hair and glasses, but a distinct resemblance. Sal brought forth another item from his leather satchel. A blown-up reproduction of Jen's driver's license had her hair penciled darker and glasses drawn on. He put Arlene's license under the large photocopy of hers. They looked alike.

"Okay, Baby Sister, ten bills if you pretend to be Arlene Holmes at the bank and get what's in her safety deposit box. Oh, yeah, we already have the key."

Jen folded her arms in front. "Why doesn't Arlene get the contents out of her box?"

Sal grimaced. "Because Ms. Holmes has something that belongs to us and won't give it up. You say you are Holmes at the bank, get the contents, give it to me, and receive thousands. How easy is that?"

"It's illegal."

He closed one eye and made an annoyed moan. "Not to worry. It's in the next town, and no one will know you or Arlene.

We have an inside guy at the bank who'll make it work. We need you for the security cameras. You'll wear a wig and glasses. It's a no-brainer, and you're making a bank deposit for your next vacation."

She shot to her feet. "Get out."

"Hey, don't be that way. It's easy. I would have used Pam, but she's too dark and would never pass."

Jen went to the door, grabbing the handle. "Pam wouldn't do it. I know she wouldn't."

Sal went to her and touched her arm. Jen pulled back and then opened the door.

"Yeah? Well, maybe Pammy wouldn't *want* to do it, but she would if we asked her nice. You know?"

"If you don't leave right now, I'm calling the cops."

Sal's lips formed a bizarre smile. The word *malevolent* came to her mind.

"What could the cops do? I'm just here selling you insurance. Your word against mine." He went to the couch, put back the things he had removed from his case, and snapped it shut."This ain't the end, Jen-ny. People don't refuse to help the families, see?"

"Out! Now!"

Sal took his time sauntering through the open doorway. He dodged the few raindrops beginning to splatter. She slammed the heavy oak door and made sure the lock connected.

Jen put her hand on her chest, feeling the rapid beating beneath. She hyperventilated for a few moments. As the weather occluded the sunlight, the room cooled. A movement in the corner caught her eye. Darkness, like a charcoal cloud, wavered. She couldn't make out its shape as it faded in and out. Although she couldn't see the shape in the shadow, when a blast of lightning flashed, a man's form stood out clearly in the blue flicker of the storm.

Jen jumped up from the couch and ran to the front door, madly fidgeting with the chain.

"Don't be afraid," a voice with fluctuating volume called

out.

She put her hands down and turned toward the corner. "You're kidding."

The murky mist disappeared. "I won't harm you." Lightning flashed through the window, and she saw the man once again. "Under the pillow."

"What?"

"Pillow," the voice repeated.

She moved to the couch, keeping her eye on the vacant corner.

"Woman!" the voice said, annoyed. "Look under the pillow."

She didn't touch any of the couch pillows. A forearm appeared sleeved in black wool, showing a white cuff held together by a gray Wedgwood cufflink. The arm threw back the small middle pillow to expose a worn, brown leather book closed with a thick rubber band.

"Call...the...police...."

"Who are you?" she asked.

"Out...of...energy. Call...police...now." The voice faded. "I...can't...later."

The first impulse was to look at the book, but all those hours spent watching the detective stories taught her the first rule: no fingerprints. Her second impulse was to get out of there. Realizing the second impulse was the wiser, she, in fitting haste, grabbed her purse and cell phone, fled to the garage, and got in her car, locking the doors. The reason she raised the garage door wasn't exactly clear to her—maybe it would assist a quick getaway. But after a few deep breaths, she called the police and stumbled over the reason she wanted their presence.

"Ah, I, uh, someone threatened me, and uh, I think, uh, I have something like evidence. Just send someone, will you?"

Five minutes gave her time to reflect on the incident. *It's my house. I can't stay in the car forever.* "So?" she asked the unseen secretary, "That man, Sal Zemric...." She shook her head at the thought. "But do I allow a ghost, a man, to run me out of my own place? Do I become independent or not?" Jen already knew the answer.

The pelting rain gave her reason to stay in the Acura. However, the time was up when a white Crown Victoria pulled into her driveway. She got out, snatched a newspaper from a stack ready to be recycled, and went to the car, holding the paper to shield her from the rain. A black man left the driver's seat, and a white man came from the other side. They showed their badges, and she motioned them to follow her into the back door.

In the kitchen, the white man said, "I'm Detective Burleigh Ferguson. This is Detective Ashton Grainger."

"Detectives? Don't regular cops respond to calls?"

Detective Ferguson nodded. "We were right around the corner."

Ashton Grainger winked at Jen and pursed his lips. "Having trouble with the missus already?" He turned to the other officer. "I told you about meeting her. Remember, Lee?"

"What?" Then she recognized him, the man in the liquor store. *Oh, God.* She ran her two eyebrows together. "Hey, you came on to me. And you're married." She pointed to his ring.

"He was on duty," Detective Ferguson said. "We had word there was a new madam in town, and supposedly she looks like a normal housewife like we'd never recognize her even if we stood in front of her. He had to give you the test."

Jen frowned. "A normal housewife? That's what this madam looks like? It's what I look like?"

"Well, you know," Ferguson said, nervously tugging at the knot of his tie. "Like a church lady."

"I look like a church lady?"

Ash chuckled. "Maybe a church lady who goes to services *in Aberdeen.*"

Jen folded her arms in front, her lips pressed together.

"Okay, Miss...," Ferguson said.

"Ms. Hughes. Jennifer Hughes."

"Okay, Ms. Hughes, what can we do for you?"

She motioned them to the living room. "A man named Sal

Zemric asked me to pose as someone else to open a safe deposit box. He threatened me. I think this is his." She pointed to the leather binder. "It might be important."

Grainger picked up the scuffed brown book and snapped off the band.

"Hey," she cautioned, "what about fingerprints?"

"We need to see it first." Grainger thumbed through the pages.

"How did he threaten you?" Ferguson asked.

"Well," Jen twisted her lip. "He didn't actually define the threat. He just said it wasn't over, and people don't refuse the families and...."

Grainger shoved the book into Ferguson's view.

Ferguson took it and read a page. "We need to call this in." He turned to Jen and pointed to the couch. "Stay here. I'll be right back."

The cops stepped outside the front to confer. She glanced at the corner for signs of the mist. Nothing had changed. Outside, the rain abated, and sunlight brightened the room. Ferguson and Grainger returned to the living room and sat on either side of her.

"Where did you get that book?" Ferguson asked.

"I'm not sure. Sal Zemric left it. I think."

Grainger leaned toward her. "It is against the law to lie."

"So, are you the bad cop." She pointed to Ferguson, "And he is the good one?"

"Watching a lot of television, are we?" Ferguson said.

"Is that book important?" Jen said.

"I think it's really important, which makes where you got it a priority. Please, Ms. Hughes, where did it come from?"

"I just bought this house, and when I cleaned, it wasn't here. Now it is." She picked up the card he left on her coffee table and handed it to him. "Like I said, Sal Zemric paid me a visit this morning and sat on the couch with his briefcase. After he left, I found the book there. It must have come from his briefcase."

Grainger looked at the card and laughed. "Lord, Lord, Sal is stupid. *They* had to know he was their weakest link. But how did you know what was in the book to make you steal it?"

Her face got hot. "I didn't steal anything."

"Well," Ferguson's blue eyes flashed. He smoothed his full hair with his fingers, a few streaks of gray moving under the stroke. "I'm sure Sal didn't leave or lose this little gem because if he did, he knows he's a dead man."

Grainger took over. "So, tell us the truth—you know, the whole truth, and nothing—"

"You want the truth? The whole truth? Fine! A ghost gave it to me."

"Right," Grainger said.

Lee Ferguson stood up. "Okay, I've heard the rumors about this place since I was a kid, but you and I know there's no such thing as ghosts."

Jen rose from her seat. "What if that Sal person comes looking for his book?"

Grainger made an *oomph* sound. "I wouldn't worry about that. Once he sees it's gone, he's headed for parts unknown. But you can call us. In fact, stay in touch." He handed her his card, and Ferguson gave her his, too.

She walked them to the door and watched them leave.

Returning to the corner where she had seen the image, she called softly, "Hey, where are you?"

"Later," a weak voice rasped. Then the house was quiet.

Later? Oh, God! What the hell? The taste of bile welled in her throat. She plopped on the couch, taking small breaths to hold back the remnants of her last meal, and with utmost scrutiny, glued her stare to the empty corner—that union of wallpaper, joined at a ninety-degree angle, where not a speck, a hair, or a bit of matter moved. *That cop Lee Ferguson said there's no ghost. Nuh-uh. I heard words coming from an image flickering in the lightning and saw a disembodied arm push away a silk pillow.* She stroked the goosebumps on her arm.

She forced herself to leave the couch and stand in the place he—or it, that figure—had been. Not a trace, absolutely nothing. *Well, what should I expect? Shoeprints?*

Mixed feelings roiled through her mind. *Fright? Hell, yes, fear. Confusion? Definitely. Anxiety? Oh, yeah. What am I going to do? Xanax?* The doctor told her in times of stress, she should take one. She slapped her knee with her palm. "No man—nope, not even a dead one—will stress me again." She tried to say, "*Come out, you coward,*" but the command piled up in her throat like a hallway rug on a slippery floor.

She smacked her knee again. *No Xanax.*

Before she became further engrossed in her thoughts, the phone rang. She jumped. It was Pam, her voice different, shaky. A knot of worry wormed itself into Jen's chest at the hesitation in Pam's words.

"Jennifer? I need to ask you some, um, questions about Sal Zemric."

Jen didn't like the sound of Pam's delivery. Sal Zemric's words played like a recording. *Maybe Pammy wouldn't want to do it, but she would if we asked her nice, you know?*

"Be careful," the unseen secretary warned.

"Who?" Jen said into the phone in her best dumb-dumb manner. "I've never heard of Hal Sendick."

After a pause and a muffled conversation on her end, Pam's voice took on a relieved quality. "Oh, okay. I must be mistaken. I'll talk to you later."

Yes, something was definitely off. But what? Why? Not hearing an answer to her unspoken question, Jen pressed the phone's off button and went into the kitchen. She grabbed a glass and shoved it under the ice dispenser on the door. Taking two cans from the fridge, she poured a mixture of half-regular Coke and half Coke Zero, then returned the half-cans to the cold shelves.

Pushing out a breath of determination, she brought her drink into the living room, sat, and pressed the remote. The new television sprang to life. One station offered an NCIS marathon, continuous delightful hours of crime investigation. Every so often, Jen's eyes moved to check the corner for activity. Seeing nothing both pleased and worried her. She fell asleep on the couch and awoke to the boob tube's early morning program, a snappy young couple hawking a countertop cooker with a chicken and vegetables turning on a spit.

The infomercial's chicken turned along its endless path, dripping juices as it moved up, around, and down. *Yep, that's me. Chicken on a spit.* She pressed the remote button, and the television's image reduced inward until gone. Staring at the blank screen, she flinched at the sound of a voice coming from the corner.

"Good morning."

Chapter Five

A charcoal-colored shimmer floated a few inches from the floor.

Jen pressed her body against the back of the couch. Terrorized, she threw a small pillow at the image, which sailed through the vapor and bounced off the wall. "Jesus!" she screamed. "Don't do that."

"What is it you would have me do?" the voice asked.

"I don't know. Hearing words like that. It's creepy. Hey, have you been there all night?"

"No," the answer came from the dark mist. "I can't bear that horrid thing."

"What horrid thing?"

"The picture frame with the moving objects."

"What's so horrid about the television? I can see your point on infomercials, but—"

"The evil opinions, why do you listen to them?"

"What evil opinions?"

"The voice that says, 'drink more beer, you need more money, take what you want, hate people who are different.'"

"The television doesn't say that. Not directly. Maybe there are subtle hints—"

"Yes, it does. Can't you hear it?" The cloud darkened. "Every so often, a voice, a high-pitched whine, says these dreadful words. I can't be in the room with that thing on."

Jen sat straight up. "Who are you?"

"Forgive me," the male voice said. The image tightened, touched the floor, and assumed a human shape.

"You're the man in the photograph."

"Miles Hampton." The figure bowed his head slightly.

"Of course. Hey, did you take my photo from the coffee table?"

The misty figure intensified and became opaque. "*My photograph.*" He coalesced into a solid form, wearing the formal frock suit like the man in the picture she had found stuck in the back of the drawer.

Jen sat back. "Right. It did belong to you."

The form clouded but maintained the man's likeness. "*I must retreat now.*"

"Retreat? Where do you go?"

The mist evaporated, his voice faint. "*I don't know....*"

"Wait!" Jen sprang from her seat and stood where she had seen Miles Hampton appear, but once again, not a vestige of him remained. "Am I crazy?"

"No," the secretary said. "You saw and heard him. And you found that book."

She hit the *on* button of the television remote, then pressed the mute button, wondering about the evil advice. *Did the mute option stop the subliminal messages the ghost heard?* Just in case, she turned the set off. While the clock chimed seven, she wanted the secretary to reaffirm her saneness but dismissed the notion. Miles Hampton might think she was talking to him. *Jesus, I'm worried about talking to an invisible secretary because the ghost in my house might misinterpret the conversation!*

Jen marched into the kitchen and made coffee. After her java and bowl of cereal, she remembered she still wore last night's clothes.

Upstairs she showered and brushed. Selecting a sweater and wool pants, Jen rubbed the pink cashmere on her cheek before sliding into the top. Loving the feel, she sighed. The sweater's softness offered some comfort, but the earlier encounter with the apparition left her feeling what her mother would have called *the willies.*

Jen usually cured uneasiness by focusing on appearance. Maybe she could feel better by looking nice. With that in mind, she plugged in the curling iron and lined makeup on the counter.

Finished with her fine-tuning, she checked her image in the mirror over the sink and approved of the result. "Not bad. In spite of all the stress." She stood sideways and sucked in her stomach. It hadn't been so flat in years. "At least something positive came from that divorce mess."

She tidied up, wondering about the next encounter. Heading for the stairs, she stifled fear as it tried to wiggle free. *Afraid? Of course. But damn, how can I have assimilated this much weirdness in so short a time? How come I haven't freaked out? Am I that flexible?*

She paused where the staircase widened into the curved broad bottom step and, placing her hand on the carved newel, entered the living room. Everything appeared as it should, the only noise being the quiet ticking of the clock and the wind chimes tinkling outside the back door. *Okay? What now?*

Lasagna. She had purchased the ingredients for the casserole, and she had yet to cook in her new home, her own Quitcher-Bitchin' kitchen. Engrossed in creating her favorite cuisine, she temporarily forgot the earlier events. She smashed the garlic in her new marble mortar. The fresh garlic aroma wafted up, and she breathed in its smell. "Garlic is friendly," she told the secretary. "Good thing I'm not going to kiss anyone." Looking at the wide windowsill over the sink, she decided she would plant herbs in small pots. Pots with foliage would look terrific against the green and red design in the stained-glass window.

As she grated the final layer of cheese, the clock pealed its melodic signal, then two bongs. The pinnacle of Italian cuisine took its place on the middle rack of the oven, and she set the timer. Figuring she'd earned a reward, she opened a bottle of Lambrusco. It could breathe as she cleaned up from cooking. Would her ectoplasmic visitor return?

On the parlor couch, she took a few sips of her second glass of wine. A white Crown Victoria pulled into the drive.

Chapter Six

Jen opened the door before they could knock.

"Hello," Detective Ferguson said.

Grainger tipped a pretend hat. "Howdy."

Jen stood unmoving in the open doorway. "Yes?"

Ferguson smiled apologetically. "Uh, I think we got off to a bad start yesterday. Can we come in and talk?"

Jen paused a moment, then moved aside. Detective Grainger sat in one of the velvet wing chairs.

Ferguson stood by the couch. "Ms. Hughes, may I call you Jennifer?"

Jen shrugged.

"Jennifer, that little leather book turned out to be a gold mine. No kidding. It will help us shut down at least a portion of a crime ring."

Jen sat on the other velvet wing chair. "What did it say?"

"You must know," Grainger said. "It was in your possession. So, tell us about it. Start with what business Zemric had with you."

Are they accusing me? A hot ripple moved from her head down through her shoulders. "He had no business with me. I don't know anything about anything. After the vile man left, that book was just there," she pointed, "under the pillow."

"Yep." Grainger directed his words to Ferguson. "We were born yesterday."

"Cool it, Ash," Ferguson said. "Jennifer, we need to know more."

Jen moved to the edge of her seat and tilted her head toward Ferguson. "First, you tell me what the book is all about."

"Fair enough." Ferguson sat down on the couch. "We knew about Sal and his activities but had no proof. That book contains details regarding Sal Zemric's extortion victims. Names, dates, addresses, amounts, and a code of what he had on them. We didn't see a name or even initials looking like yours. So, we wonder how you connect to Zemric. Maybe he had something on you."

"No, he didn't have *something* on me. There's nothing. Not now, not ever."

Grainger smiled. "You think lying doesn't count?"

She wanted to protest, but the yarn of taking her girlfriend to Aberdeen had come back to bite her. Her mother always warned her against lying. Jen wanted to cooperate but didn't know where to start. "Uh, do you know a woman named Arlene Holmes?"

"Do you?" Grainger asked, decidedly accusing.

"Apparently, she has a safety deposit box in a nearby town. That man, Sal, said I looked somewhat like her. He wanted me to impersonate her for the bank's cameras using her driver's license so I could get something out of the box for him."

Ferguson looked at Grainger, then turned to Jen. "Arlene Holmes is missing. What do you know about her?"

Jen put her hands in front of her, warding off suspicion. "Only that she has a box, and whoever *they* Sal referred to wanted what was theirs."

Grainger rose. "I'm going to call this in, Lee. We'll search the banks and get a warrant to see the box. Her folks didn't mention that. They may not know."

When Grainger left, Ferguson pulled at his chin. "Why did Zemric think you would impersonate Arlene Holmes?"

"Because I bought this house no one else would buy, he figured I was in need of money and would do a little favor, as he called it, and I could earn ten bills. I think he meant ten thousand dollars."

Lee smiled and nodded his head. "That's what it means. That slime ball, Zemric, figures everyone has something in their closet. When he finds anything advantageous, he uses it to make people pay, in money or services."

The oven bell went off, and Jen jumped at the strange noise. Because she had not heard the timer sound before, it took her a second to understand.

"The lasagna!" She hurried into the kitchen. The oven mitts, new and stiff, didn't flex as she slid her hands into them. She bent down to the oven door and sensed Detective Ferguson's watchful gaze. As she pulled out the oblong glass dish, she saw him from the corner of her eye standing in the kitchen doorway.

"Smells good."

She didn't respond and wished the secretary would whisper a clever, witty comment appropriate for the situation. The lasagna really did smell delightful. "Um, thanks." Her reply was neither witty nor clever.

So, here was this man in her kitchen, attractive, about her age, and wearing no wedding band, watching her move. *Am I supposed to offer him some lasagna?* "Idiot," the secretary mumbled. "He suspects you're involved with the mob."

Jen turned to face him. "Look, I'm not involved with Sal Zemric. I just moved here. I bought the house because it was in my price range, and I loved it. I don't know how that man got a picture of my driver's license, and if he really did check me out, he didn't find anything more than a moving violation. I've been a Girl Scout leader, for crying out loud."

"Relax. Zemric probably got your data from the real estate office. It's one of the Speigal's legitimate businesses. We ran a background check on you and know you're okay."

"You checked me out? Why?"

"Take it easy. We don't think you're involved with the Livonia Mob."

"This little town has a mob?"

"Indeed, it does, ever since 1857 when the carriage factory was built. The Irish crime bosses, the Ratterlees, moved in and ran the factory. Another mob, the Speigals, Germans, went up against them and ran the local horse trading. When automobiles started to outnumber the carriages, both businesses fell, and the families moved to new endeavors."

"Wait, Sal Zemric said, three families run this town. The third was Owings, like the police chief, Owings."

"He's right. But the Owings are the good guys. Uncle Paul keeps on top of them—"

"Uncle Paul? The chief of police is your uncle? A little nepotistic, don't you think?"

"Nice word, but inaccurate in this case. I worked for my position. Paul Owings, my mother's brother, wouldn't allow it any other way."

Jen shook her head. "This town is tiny. I'll bet there aren't two hundred businesses in the whole place. How can that support a mob?"

"Two mobs," he corrected. "I told you when the factory shut down—blew up actually—and the horse-trading business slacked, they found other sources of income. That little book you donated provided us with information on where the Speigals are operating, like Richmond, Baltimore, Hagerstown, and Lynchburg."

Grainger entered the kitchen, sniffing the air. "Smells good. We're checking banks now. Who knows what we'll find? Things happen fast in Livonia."

The secretary reminded Jen, "Don't we know it."

Ferguson smiled. "Too bad we can't stay for dinner."

Too bad? I didn't invite you.

"But we have to get going. Lots of paperwork for warrants and such. Keep in touch. Especially if you find any other books, like information on the Ratterlees."

A thought occurred to Jen. "Hey, I got a call asking about Mr. Zemric."

Grainger and Ferguson looked at each other.

"Not good," Ferguson said. "Who was it, and what did you say?"

"The call came from Pam Caulfield. I said I didn't know a Hal Semdick." She quickly added, for Grainger's benefit, "It wasn't a lie. I really never heard of a man by that name."

Grainger grinned. "Ah, lies of commission, or omission, remain lies, nonetheless. But, damn smart. You may have saved yourself a lot of grief. Caulfield, eh?"

"We looked at her when Holmes went missing," Ferguson said.

That got Jen's attention. "Pam? What does she have to do with Arlene Holmes?"

"Ask her for the details," Grainger said. "She has her reason to hate Arlene."

"Look." Ferguson handed her another business card. "Call if you think of something." He took a deep sniff. "Or if you have too much leftover lasagna."

She saw them to the door and watched the Crown Vic depart. Ferguson waved his hand from the lowered window.

Jen returned to the couch, picked up the glass of wine, and took a long drink. Her mind wandered. Holding the glass up against the arm of one wing chair, she compared the rich ruby hues. *Hues, like Hughes, my name.*

"Like Keith's name," the secretary said, breaking the reverie.

She took another sip, and the shadow formed in the corner as she put the glass on the coffee table.

Chapter Seven

The dark patch wavered and swirled.

"Okay, I see you," Jen said. "Thank you for using motion to get my attention. Do you stay in the same place?"

The image converted to light gray and stabilized into a man's shape. "Of course not. I move where I wish."

She willed her heart not to pound. "How come you go in and out of focus? That's creepy. Can't you just look like you did in life?"

"The more you can see, the more energy I use. When I become corporeal, it drains me."

"Corporeal? Wow. Great word. But would you please tell me why you are still in this house? Aren't you supposed to go *somewhere* after you die?"

"I believed that at one time, but here I am. I don't know why."

"Well...." She didn't know how to say what she thought. *Yet I am having a conversation with a dead person. How much worse can it get?* "Didn't you kill some people and then yourself? Maybe—"

The shape changed to a cloud and went from gray to black. It shimmered like heat on the road. "Never! I did *not* do those things."

Don't make a ghost mad. The indignant protests sounded genuine. Jen caught her breath. "But," she said gently, "you scared all the other owners away."

The image softened. A man's form reassembled. "Frightened, yes, but I harmed no one."

"Are you going to try to get rid of me?"

"You're different and don't frighten so easily. The first

night when I made all of my menacing noises, you ignored me and never left the bed. Even when I tried the second night, you barely moved. You're brave."

Oh, my wonderful prince.

Miles moved to the fireplace. "Furthermore, you like cello music."

Cello music soothes the spirits. Who knew?

"And," he said, turning to look at the oval carving of a woman's face on the elaborate mantel. "Your name is Jenny. You remind me of her. She played the cello."

"Her?" *The carved lady's face on the mantel?* She thought about the names on the back of the photo. "Your wife? Virginia?" *Jenny, the same nickname as Jennifer.* "I look like her?"

"You smell like her. My Jenny liked to wear a scent made for men. It suited her."

"You don't mean *Mouchoir de Mondsieur?*"

"I believe that is the name of the scent. It was our secret. I bought it; she wore it. You are wearing it now."

Spirits can smell. She put her hand to her throat in a mild panic. "Just how close does a um, spirit, um, have to get to smell perfume?"

"I noticed it when you were sleeping."

"Hey! Stay out of my bedroom."

"This house is mine."

"Not anymore, Miles Hampton. Gentlemen don't...." She couldn't think fast enough to list what gentlemen weren't supposed to do.

"Forgive me," he said. "Gentlemen, don't enter ladies' bedrooms."

"And other things." She still hadn't figured out what actions should be ruled out by proper gentlemen.

The form faded into a mist. "I feel my energy fading. I gain more each time I appear, but I won't last."

The gray mist flickered, weakened, and dissolved.

"Miles? Are you still here?"

"I can speak a little longer if I don't manifest."

"Manifest. Another great word. How else am I different?"

"You stood up to that detestable Speigal."

"The Speigals? You know them?"

"I knew the ones who lived in my time. Criminals and villains, every one of them."

"How did you know about the book? The one under the pillow?"

"I saw it in his portmanteau when he went to the door."

"His what?"

"His business case, valise. The Speigal opened it when he took out the paper he showed you. I saw the book inside and took it."

"But how did you know what the book contained?"

"I recognized it as evidence. Even in my day, the unsavory kept their information in small leather volumes such as that. I spotted his type as soon as he opened his mouth."

"I don't understand how you could know what the book meant."

"In 1900, I joined the Livonia police force and made detective within five years. Crime transcends time. Some things never change. By experience, I knew what would be in that book. But now I must retire. We will talk later."

Jen waited, but the only sound she heard was the ticking clock and the soft swish of the pendulum. She downed the wine and took the glass into the kitchen, placing it next to the lasagna. The dish scented the entire room and had cooled to lukewarm, but her appetite had diminished. Putting an undersized portion of the divine fare on a small plate, she tasted her creation. *Wonderful, but better with a little more wine. Just a slosh more. I'm not a wino.* She poured an inch of the garnet-colored fluid. As she put the glass to her lips, she heard a noise. Taking the glass with her, she checked the kitchen, then the living room. Nothing. *Always wondering about the noises in the night will be something to drive me nuts.*

"Nuts," Jen said aloud. *Living with a phantom won't be easy. Living? Interesting word in light of things. Where is Miles right now?*

Resting? How much rest do the dead need?
    Could she believe him? *Do ghosts tell the truth?*

Chapter Eight

Jen shoved the cork back into the Lambrusco and covered the casserole with plastic. With a few more hours of daylight left, she went outside to assess the yard. Two large lilac bushes flanked the sides of the house. Spindly roses badly in need of care bordered the rear of the property and around the step at the back door. The remnants of a weedy herb garden grew in an oval bed surrounded by a brick wall situated between the house and the garage.

Bending down and snapping off samples of green, she identified the withering herbs. She sniffed the broken pieces. "Sage, rosemary, and...oregano. Make a note. Forget the windowsill pots. I'll put in parsley, basil, and cilantro." She looked around again. "Maybe mustard, radish, turnips...what else?" The secretary did not offer suggestions but made the notation.

Jen took kneepads and garden gloves from the garage, purchases from her humongous shopping spree the night she moved in and went to work on the herb garden. *It will help keep my weight off.* She sucked in her stomach as a reminder of her newer, slimmer figure, claiming isometrics were as good as crunches. She worked in the garden, yanking, digging, and trimming until dark.

When Jen came through the back door and snapped on the kitchen light, she hesitated. *Maybe I should get a dog.* "I wonder how a dog would get along with...."

The glimmer of mist drew her view to the pantry.

"A spirit?" The words came from the glistening cloud.

"Um, yes. A woman alone should have protection. And

the more I hear about this town, well…."

"Evil surrounds Livonia. Obtaining a dog might be wise."

Miles's words regarding evil gave Jen a quick shiver. She changed the subject. "I've been outside weeding. The yard has great potential." *Jeez, I'm discussing gardening with a ghost.*

"I've not been outside for as long as I can remember," Miles said.

"I thought you could move around at will?"

The shimmer faded, and the voice increased in volume. "Within. A few of the past owners had the house exorcised. The last residents had a powerful spirit chaser who used potent holy water."

"Don't you guys walk through walls?"

"All the portals, the windows and doors, have been anointed. The walls have been blessed, washed with consecrated water. The blessed house keeps bad spirits out but has imprisoned me."

"You mean you can't get out?"

"I have found no egress." He took on a nearly solid form. "But look at this." He moved into the pantry. Squatting, his opaque arm pointed to a plastic flap painted the same color as the wall. "That, cut from the protected wall, is new, unconsecrated. However, it is nailed shut. Even in corporeal form, I don't have enough strength to open it."

Jen bent down and studied the flap. "A doggie door! A strange place to install one, but that should be easy for a cloud to use as an exit. Wait a minute. If spirits can walk through unblessed walls, why can't you just walk through that doggie door?"

"Strangely, I can't seem to penetrate celluloid, as I think that portal may be."

"Celluloid? Oh, yeah, plastic. Gee, I guess we all need to learn something new — that is, ghosts can't go through plastic."

She watched the thick mist move to a man's height.

"Miles, didn't you just say a blessed house keeps the bad spirits out? What bad spirits? I hope bad spirits can't get in."

"Dark Forces exist, and they can enter if invited."

"Well, I won't if you won't," Jen said firmly. "Deal?"

"Of course. But you might not recognize an evil essence in disguise."

"Would you?"

"I don't know. I have been away for so long."

"Away? Don't you live here all the time?"

"I don't know where I live. Every so often, I am sentient, like when the house gets new residents. I don't understand how this afterlife works."

"Jeez, if you don't know…. Are there others like you?"

Miles's opacity faded as he moved into the kitchen. "Yes. I have seen them. I have heard them asking to come in."

Chapter Nine

"You've seen them? Outside the windows?"

"I can only see as you do when I take solid form, but before the last owners removed the mirrors that hung on the outside walls, I could see out through them. Mirrors serve as viewing devices for the departed. The other spirits can see into the house as well. The last owners engaged a highly skilled soul-warder, who told them to remove all mirrors."

"I think my brain is full now," Jen said. "I can't process any more weirdness."

"And I grow weary from the long conversation."

"Um, Miles. If I go to bed early, do you promise not to roam around or come into my bedroom? Oh, crap! There's a long mirror on my bedroom door!"

"You have my word. I will not stir until tomorrow morning."

"All right. I guess I have no choice but to trust you."

Jen hung a bath towel over her door mirror before she dressed for bed. Even though Prince Valium tempted her, she told herself she would not lean on him but get through the night all on her own.

She did not sleep well that night.

Jen awoke later than usual the next morning, past nine-thirty. Groggy and cranky, she held the toothbrush up and caught her reflection in the mirror. The mirror hanging on an *inside wall*. Mirrors had taken on new meaning now. She would need extra attention to make-up detail this morning to erase the bags and sags from her unrestful night.

By the time she finished breakfast, Miles had still not made his presence known.

Jen cleared away the dishes and prepared for a quick trip to the local DIY store. Maybe she could snag some bargains for her garden.

As she walked through the outdoor aisles of The Home Owner's Helper, her enthusiasm for landscaping increased. The sale on daffodils, gladiolus, and other bulbs drew her like a magnet until she spotted the handwritten sign showing fifty percent off seeds of all kinds. Fate had anticipated her need for green. She thought about the lawn of her Baltimore home. "Keith and his Zoysia grass! I don't want an emerald carpet. It will be my lawn, my shrubbery, and my work."

As soon as she returned home, the white Crown Vic pulled in. Grainger and Ferguson came up to her as she unloaded the cornucopia of garden frills.

"Hi, there," Ferguson said.

Each detective took a portion of the purchases and put them in the garage for her.

Jen put down the last bag. "That was nice of you. Thanks. What can I do for you, gentlemen?"

They followed her to the back door and waited until she unlocked it. Grainger opened the door for her and held it for Ferguson.

Detective Ferguson scratched his forehead. "We need to know more about Mr. Zemric."

"Do you want some coffee?" Jen offered. She needed her mid-morning fix.

"That'd be great," Ferguson said.

As she prepared the brew, she spoke. "I don't know anything more. I promise. I told you all I know."

Ferguson stood next to her, leaning his tall frame against the counter. "How did he act when he spoke to you? Like, nervous? Angry? Frightened?"

Jen pushed the button, and the red light came on. "Demanding. Sure of himself. Rude."

"Do you still have the business card he left?" Grainger

asked.

"Yes," she said. "I expected you'd take it."

"I thought I did," Grainger said. "I stuck it in the book, but it wasn't there when I looked."

Jen left the kitchen and went into the living room. "Okay, where is the card?" she asked the secretary. "Ah, right! I remember." She had put the card in the buffet drawer after she found it sitting next to the television remote.

She returned and gave the card to Grainger. He showed it to Ferguson. Then she put cups and saucers, cream and sugar on a wooden tray. The coffee pot made a mad gurgling sound as the last of the steam propelled its way through the grounds. She thought about the fancy Delonghi machine in her Baltimore kitchen offering latte, expresso, and plain American cups of perfection. The whoosh of the steaming wand echoed in her mind. She would have to make do with microwaved milk and a hand mixer for her lattes now. She put the memories away, poured three cups, and took the tray into the dining room.

Ferguson pulled a chair for Jen and then sat himself. Grainger took his coffee with sugar. Ferguson drank it black. No one spoke for a moment.

"Great coffee," Ferguson said.

"Strong," Grainger said, "just the way I like it."

"Not strong," Jen protested. "It's rich. That's different from strong."

Ferguson sat the cup on the saucer. "You gotta learn something new every day, Ash. See? We both learned something."

It stayed quiet until Ferguson downed the last of his cup. "You ready, Ash?" He looked at Jen. "Hate to drink and run, but there's a lot of crime out there." He moved his head toward the window.

"Dark Forces?" Jen asked.

"Yeah, that's for sure. Dark Forces," Ferguson said.

"Is that a racial slur?" Grainger said with a smile.

"Aw, Ash, maybe she meant it as a compliment."

Grainger stood up. "Right. Okay." They headed for the

door. "Keep your doors locked."

"I do," Jen assured them. "Did you just come by for the business card?"

Ferguson nodded. "Be careful." They left.

While loading the dishes in the dishwasher, she sensed movement behind her. She turned. "I wondered where you were."

"I'm here now," Miles said.

"You saw the cops here?"

"Cops? Oh, yes, I remember. The shortened version of copper. Not a nice term from a lady."

"What? Cop means policeman and is used all the time. Now *pig*, that's a bad word for police."

"I will depend upon you to explain what I don't understand."

"Sure," Jen said. "If I can." She could hardly believe she had a casual conversation with a departed soul. A ghost. He wasn't scary. It was easy to talk with him.

Miles assumed the partially opaque man's form. "I can tell those detectives are well-matched as a pair. It is gratifying to see black and white working together. My father, who fought in the War of Northern Aggression, feared equality would be hard won."

"Your father was correct. What we call Equal Rights has been a terrific struggle. Surely you are aware of the events since… since your—"

"Death? Don't be afraid to speak if what you say is accurate. What is true remains true. I remember dying on my wife's birthday. I had a pearl brooch for her in my pocket. Since then, time has had little meaning for me. Up until now."

"Why now?"

"I cannot answer that, for I don't understand it myself. I have spent most of the years unaware."

"Like sleeping?"

"For want of a better word, yes. I could not tolerate anyone in my house; therefore, I made my presence known to the interlopers, and they left. Afterward, I became unaware until another disturbance brought me from my nether slumber."

"Nether slumber! You are good with the cool words."

"Cool words. I must learn the current mode of speech. Words may have changed meaning, but some things stay the same. Therefore, I must advise you to beware of that Detective Ferguson. His actions present neither a police professional nor a gentleman."

"Why do you say that?"

"In my transparent state, I heard him say things. Although I don't understand the words directly, I understood the inherent meaning."

"Tell me," Jen demanded.

"It would be untoward to speak of such things to a lady."

"Miles! Queen Victoria is long gone. We, ladies, can bear most words nowadays. Besides, if you don't understand directly, you may be misinterpreting what Detective Ferguson said."

"You wouldn't want to know."

"Oh, yes, I would. Tell me. Maybe I need to know to help me beware. Did you think about that? And maybe you would learn some new terms."

"Jennifer, it would be improper. No gentleman would—"

"Miles! Tell me this instant."

"Very well. Judge for yourself. When you left to get the calling card, he told Detective Grainger that you were a certifiable Looney Tune but adorable, and with the slightest provocation from you, he would gladly assist in the removal of your thong. It would be delightful to see the thong dangling on your ankle. Forgive me for my impropriety."

Her smile widened, showing more teeth than usual. "He really said that? I'm adorable? But a Looney Tune?"

"You aren't shocked or offended. Perhaps I did misinterpret the man's meaning. Kindly advise me on the definition of Looney Tune. And, pray tell, whatever is a thong?"

Chapter Ten

Jen thought serving as an interpreter for Twenty-First Century jargon was more of a responsibility than she wished to attempt.

"I fear I have used up my store of energy. I must leave you," Miles said.

Good.

The apparition faded into nothing.

She worked in the garden for the rest of the day. Later in the house, she clicked on the television. A consultation with the cable guide let her know she could watch *Law and Order* until midnight.

The lawn work and television combination kept Miles at bay for two days. Her victory was shallow because she constantly looked over her shoulder, checked the corners, and jumped at shadows, real and imagined.

On the third morning, she awoke later than usual. After dressing, she stepped from the bedroom door and concluded it was better to know where Miles was for sure. She called his name. Before she could say his name again, the gravel crunched in the driveway. She ran down the stairs and looked out the parlor window. The Crown Vic came to a stop with Burleigh Ferguson, its sole occupant. He stepped from the car.

"Good morning," she said, standing in the front doorway.

"Good morning to you. Can I come in? I have something you will want to hear."

"Really? What's that, Detective Burleigh Ferguson?"

"Why don't you call me Lee? Burleigh makes me sound like a species of tobacco."

Opening the door wide, she let him in and followed him to

the living room. "So where is Detective Grainger? I thought you two were connected at the hip."

"Hey. That's not nice, and I have such good news, too." Before he sat on the couch, he sniffed the air. "No lasagna?"

"Not today. What's the good news?"

"We found Arlene Holmes."

"That is good news. I'm glad the lady is no longer missing."

"That's part of it. Normally I wouldn't discuss the details of an investigation, but maybe if you heard what's happening, you might provide further information."

"Heavens, do tell. I love detective stories. I don't think I can give you any more facts than I have, but I'm interested in your progress."

"A friendly judge provided us with a search warrant based on the book and your comments. We searched the banks until we found Arlene Holmes's safety deposit box in Union Town, about a half hour away. The box contained personal mementos and jewelry. One diamond alone appraised at forty-eight bills."

"Forty-eight thousand dollars," Jen said.

"Yep."

"Good for the cops."

"Wait, there's more." He mimicked the infomercials. "In addition, we found a CD with all kinds of information regarding the Speigal's dirty laundry."

"So that's what Sal wanted. Why would they keep evidence like that on a CD? But you found Arlene?"

"I'm getting to that. We found a phone number written on one of Sal's business cards clipped inside that little leather book. It turned out to be a pay-as-you-go cell phone. Even they have locater chips in them. And that cell resided in the shirt pocket of Johnny Caulfield. We traced him to Frederick, Maryland, in a motel room with Arlene Holmes."

"She was kidnapped?"

"Kind of. Caulfield kept her there by claiming to protect her from being killed if she didn't hide, but basically, he detained her so Sal's hoods could look into her safety deposit box. And thankfully, you wouldn't participate, so we got there first. Unlike you, Arlene isn't the sharpest crayon in the box, poor little rich girl."

Jen sniffed at the last comment. "Smart enough to hide important data in a CD."

"No way she did that. Or Johnny, either. He doesn't have that kind of technical smarts. We'll lean on him and see what we get."

"Hmm. John Caulfield. Interesting. Thanks for giving me the good news."

"But," he put his hand inside his jacket pocket, "I haven't." He pulled out an envelope and gave it to her.

She read the inscription aloud, "For Jennifer Hughes," written in a woman's neat hand. She tore the end off, and a certified check slid out.

"What's this?" She counted the zeroes. "Hey, twenty-five bills!"

"Does that mean twenty-five thousand dollars?" Lee teased.

"You know it does, but why?"

"Reward. Arlene's parents put out a reward for information leading to the whereabouts of their daughter. That would be you, the one who gave us the information."

Jennifer opened and closed her mouth without a word because she didn't know what words to use. Even the secretary remained speechless.

"So, how about dinner?" Lee said.

Now Jen had something to say. "You want me to make dinner?"

"No, silly. I'll take you out. I like keeping company with rich women, especially if they're a little wonky."

"Wonky?"

"Yes, wonky. Making up a story about going to Aberdeen, asking us to believe in ghosts, and I *have* heard you talk to yourself. Look it up. It's in the dictionary. Wonky, definition: cute and strange."

"Wonky. Hmmm. You mean Looney Tunes?"

"What's that?"

"Wonky, but no thongs."

"Thongs?" Lee cocked his head and looked at her for a long moment. "Okay, maybe not Looney Tunes, but definitely psychic. Did I mention cute?"

"You may have said the word adorable."

"Really psychic. Uh-huh, I may have said adorable. So, there's a great German place called, *The Best of the Wurst.*"

"The Wurst sounds good. When?"

"This afternoon?"

"Gives me time to freshen up," Jen said.

"It's impossible to improve perfection," Lee countered.

"Do you think flattery will get you more information?"

"Maybe, but it doesn't affect what I just said. I'll pick you up at five."

Jen's gaze followed Lee as he headed for the door. She surveyed his lanky body and broad shoulders.

"Nice," the secretary said.

Jen went upstairs to redo her makeup and change her shoes. She wanted to get that check in the bank, and maybe she would cruise Livonia to get a good look at her new town.

As she brushed her hair in front of the sink mirror, a chilling breeze blew through the room. A shadow moved in the bedroom's open doorway.

"Be careful," the words came from the shadow.

"Miles, get out of my bedroom."

Chapter Eleven

"I'm in the hall, not your bedroom," Miles said. "You agreed to join that man at dinner?"

Jen put her brush down and turned to see the cloud forming outside the door. "Why shouldn't I?"

"You just met him."

"I won't justify my decisions to you. Get out of my doorway. I need to leave."

"With misgivings, I will go." The mist disappeared.

Jen grabbed her purse and the check, then left by the back. The garage door made its raucous pathway upward. She got into the car, started the engine, and backed out of the driveway. A few minutes of driving brought her into downtown Livonia.

Maryland Alliance Bank was a branch of the one she used in Baltimore. She drove slowly to look at the stores and shops around town. Livonia's commercial district had maintained its nineteenth-century charm with minor hints of twenty-first-century technology. The important buildings faced a park-like square, with other businesses laid out in an easy-to-find grid formation flanking the town's center. On one of the side streets, she passed what looked like a fifty's gas station converted into a fast-food chicken restaurant. The sign showed a smiling man holding out his finger, with words indicating the chicken was "number one" in Livonia. She waited for a red light and looked at the sign again. Something wasn't right. The hand looked amiss. Two short, polite beeps from behind prompted her to check the traffic light, which had turned green. After a few turns this way and that, she wound up on Main Street and pulled into the parking area lining the town square. Deposit in hand, she crossed the street and entered the bank.

The inside of the bank resembled a busy train station. People waited in lines for the tellers. Others sat on neutral-colored couches for their turn with the upper-level clerks and bank officers. She took a seat.

Luckily, magazines on the side tables offered detailed Hollywood gossip and kept her occupied. When it was her turn for customer service, Jen changed her account and divested Keith's name from hers. She counted the zeroes on the deposit receipt. This added to what she had left from buying the house. The healthy balance looked good, but now that she was on her own, her spending habits needed to change.

Since parking in the town square was free, Jen walked around, ambling in and out of the shops and businesses. As she walked past the Number One Chicken Place, a green neon sign flashed on, saying *hot and now*. Like a hypnotic beam, the neon attracted customers from everywhere. Once she smelled the aroma from the open door, she was hooked, too. She stood in line and ordered three wings, which turned out to be the best she had ever tasted. At three-thirty, she headed home to get ready for what was to be her first date in over twenty years.

The garage door sang its screeching song. Inside the house, she shut the back door behind her and felt a moving shadow in the doorway between the kitchen and dining room.

"Hello, Miles."

"I trust you've had a productive day?"

"I did, thank you." She headed up the stairs. Before she shut the door, Miles had assumed a dark, man-shaped shadow on the landing.

"You will be careful this evening and mindful of that man, Detective Ferguson?"

"Of course. What can happen? Livonia is a small town, and I'll be with a cop." She shut her bedroom door. Making sure a long towel covered the door mirror, she took a shower and chose her outfit from the closet. Navy blue with white stripes for the top and solid navy for her slacks. She added a thick gold chain and gold hoop earrings. For the final touch, she applied makeup and combed her hair behind her ears. Then she removed the towel from the bathroom door and checked her reflection.

As she assessed her appearance, gravel crunched in the driveway. She flew down the stairs and answered the knock at the front door.

"Hello, Detective."

He looked her up and down with approval showing on his face, like a young boy evaluating an expensive baseball bat. A smile formed. "Please call me Lee."

"Okay, Lee. On time, good start. Hold on for a minute." Jen left Lee in the living room to get her purse from the kitchen counter. As she reached for the handbag, the mist formed next to her.

"I don't like it," Miles said.

She stage-whispered to Miles, "Thank you for your concern." She threw a glance over her shoulder at Lee. "I'm a big girl."

She joined Lee in the living room.

Her date ran his finger around his collar and loosened his tie. "You were talking to yourself?"

Jen smiled and fluttered her eyelashes. "Maybe."

"So," Lee said. "Are we ready?"

"Before we leave, would you look at something for me?"

"De...pends," Lee said, dragging out the word.

"It's architecture." Jen led him through the kitchen into the pantry. Kneeling down, she showed him the plastic framed flap secured to the wall. "It's a strange place to put a doggie door, but I'm considering adopting a dog and not sure how to open it. It's nailed shut."

Lee bent down close. "It's screwed shut and painted over. I could probably get them out with my power drill. I'll put it in my car, and the next time I'm nearby, I'll take them out. How's that?"

"Thanks. I appreciate it."

"So, now we are ready?"

She quickly scanned the room. "Well, you and I are."

Lee stood and smiled at her. "Wonky."

"Whatever." She smiled back and closed the pantry.

After locking the house, Jen waited while Lee opened the door of the Crown Vic. She buckled her seat belt. "Isn't this a police car? Hey, are you on duty? Wait a minute, are you taking me out because you think I have information and I'm more likely to talk while I'm relaxed?"

"Answers in order of importance. I'm taking you out because I like you. Second, importance-wise: yes, it's a police car, but I can use it when not on duty. Being the nephew of the police chief does have some perks."

"Perks? Funny word. Percolate, perquisite, perky."

"Hmm. I rather like the word perky. Like you, perky for your age."

"Perky? My age? What does that mean?"

"Are we having our first spat?" Lee turned the key.

"Bringing up a lady's age isn't a good idea, you know."

"Sorry." He inspected the rear-view mirror. "I told you we ran a check on you, so I'm aware of your age, two years younger than me. I have to say, though, you're the youngest fortyish woman I've met."

"You're youngish for middle age, too." She wrinkled her nose at him.

He touched her nose and put the car in gear. "Even though I'm forty-three, I'm hanging on. My motto? Forty is the new twenty-five."

"Ooh, I like that. Can I use your motto?"

He nodded. "Sure. My present to you. And don't say I never give you anything."

Jen liked Lee's sense of humor.

Minutes later, they parked in the lot with a sign reading, *Best of the Wurst*. Painted beer steins flanked the words. Jen admired the German gingerbread house exterior of the restaurant.

"Herr Ferguson," the host said when they reached the front counter. The man wore lederhosen and traditional short pants. On his shirt, an enameled pin said Wolf Struttman. "Two? Follow, please, to our best table." His German accent made the place feel authentic.

Wooden wainscoting, antlers hung on the walls at regular intervals, and a stuffed boar's head over the bar gave the place an air of being in the heart of Bavaria. German music softly played in the background. The smells from the kitchen amplified Jen's appetite.

Herr Struttman pulled the chair for Jen at a small table in the corner. A starched white tablecloth and a flickering candle gave the place the final touch of Europe. The host snapped the napkin in the air and gently laid it on Jen's lap. Within a minute, he brought them small book-like menus tied with a gold braided cord.

Lee turned the plastic-coated pages of the menu. "I think you would enjoy the *Policeman's Fingers*."

Chapter Twelve

"What?" Jen's mouth dropped open.

"Oh, oh, yeah. Sorry. Uh, I can see how that could be misconstrued." Lee moved his menu around to Jen's view. "See here." He pointed to the section called *Haus Specialties*. Second from the top were *Policeman's Fingers*. She read out loud. "Long, thin sausages, lightly seasoned with garlic and herbs, our own recipe."

"You'll love them. Struttman told me the wursts are called that because of the length. Like we in the U.S. say, *the long arm of the law,* the Germans say, *the long fingers of the police.*

She thought for a moment, perplexed. "Okay, order for me. I like surprises."

"Good."

The waiter came to take their order, pilsner beers and Policeman's Fingers. Tall frosty glasses of pale gold with foaming tops came first.

Lee handed Jen one of them and lifted his. "Here's to good spirits with good spirits."

She clinked her glass gently to his. "I'm all for good spirits." Jen took a long sip. "Mmmm, delicious."

They drank without speaking for a few moments. More people came in, creating a low hum of chatter.

"How do you know the restaurant guy, Mr. Struttman? Did you go to school with him?"

"No, he married Melissa Speigal, a good friend of mine from high school."

"Speigal? I thought they were all bad guys."

"Who told you that? Maybe that was true a long time ago,

but they've spawned a few good ones over the years."

"Like the Speigals who own the real estate office I used?"

Lee held his hand horizontally to the table and waggled it. Jen didn't like to think her friend worked at a place that merited a hand waggle from a cop. Poor Pam. Jen concentrated on the chilly brew in order to clear her mind.

"So," Lee said, "Zemric's book. A ghost gave it to you?"

"Maybe we need a few more of these." Jen lifted her beer.

"Really? Drinking makes you talk?"

"No, I don't need more alcohol. Maybe you need a few to believe me."

"I'll believe you."

"I already told you, and you didn't believe it. A ghost took it out of Sal Zemric's portmanteau."

"Portmanteau? And who is *he*?"

"I'll answer in order of importance. First, *he* is the ghost, the original owner of the house. Second, it's a briefcase."

"Are you referring to Miles Hampton?"

Jen sat a little straighter. "You know him?"

"No, and you don't either."

"If you grew up here, then you know everyone who has lived in that house claims it's haunted."

"Look, I did grow up here, and as a matter of fact, I don't relish admitting it, but I'm related to Miles Hampton, some great grand uncle or something. Long gone, Jenny. Dead for a hundred years now."

"I never said he wasn't dead, Lee."

Lee took a long drink, the foam sticking to the empty side of the glass. "There's no ghost in that house. It's a myth."

"So sure, Mr. Smarty Policeman?"

Lee drank the last inch of the beer. "Yep. From the time I attended middle school until going away to college, me and a bunch of boys went there every Halloween looking for the evil ghost. If your house had a spirit, I would have seen it by now."

"Such a detective. Think about it. If you were a ghost and didn't want to be seen, would you let a bunch of pimple-faced adolescents call you out?"

"But it's okay for you to see him?"

"Yes."

Before any more conversation commenced, their wursts came, pink and skinny, looking a lot like elongated fingers. The plates included hot potato salad and perfectly seasoned sauerkraut.

Jen could not remember when she had tasted better German food and said so several times. The subject of Sal Zemric's book did not resurface. They made light chit-chat on the ride home. When they arrived, Jen fished in her purse for the keys to the front door.

Lee took the key and unlocked the door for her. "I had a good time this evening. Let's do it again sometime. Soon."

"I had fun, too. Thanks for the wurst."

He waggled his eyebrows twice. "Who knew how enjoyable policeman's fingers could be?"

"I'm not going to comment on that."

For an awkward moment, neither one spoke. "I'd like to ask you in, but—"

He stepped closer to her and didn't let her finish the disclaimer. "Then ask me in. I'll probably say yes."

"Well, just for a little while. But you have to wait here at the door for a few minutes."

She ran to the television, turned it on, volume up to keep Miles away, then returned to Lee and let him in. They stood in the living room in front of the louder-than-necessary widescreen.

"We can watch the tube for a while, but not too long, okay?"

"Sure. Did I mention I like wonky ladies?"

"Yes, you did."

He leaned closer. She knew he meant to kiss her and remembered his comment about assisting her with her thong if she gave the *slightest provocation*. She moved back a few inches. "Do you like wonky ladies who don't kiss on the first date?"

Lee scratched his nose. "If I have to."

They sat together on the couch, and Jen summoned the cable guide on the screen. "Hey, look what's on the classic movie channel. That old black and white movie about ghosts, *Topper*!"

They looked at each other and said simultaneously, "Wonky!"

A few times, Jen mentally compared the movie's portrayal of spirits to what she'd experienced. She made no comments and enjoyed the comedy. When the movie ended, Jen walked Lee out to the car. She slipped into the front seat and then shut the door.

"Going somewhere?" Lee asked.

"No. I'm making sure the light is off inside the car."

"Why?"

She moved next to him. He slid his arm around her and pulled her into a gentle embrace. She breathed in the faint scent of cologne, but more, as he brushed his cheek against hers, she could smell his skin and liked it. Jen lingered, breathing in his scent until he pressed his lips against hers.

Lee lifted her chin and whispered, "Mmm, nice. So, getting back in the car becomes our second date?"

"Yes." Jen slid away and reached for the door handle.

He grabbed her arm to stop her. "You made sure the light was off. Why? You don't want to be seen kissing me?"

She didn't want to step over the line for weirdness but sighed, knowing she'd have to explain. "You might not believe in Miles Hampton, but he doesn't like you."

"Jennifer," Lee said, in the tone of a serious lecture.

Jen gently pulled away from his grasp. "Don't forget to put that power drill in your car, okay?"

Lee laughed. "Let me get this straight. I'm invited back to *unscrew* something?"

"That's right." Jen couldn't keep from laughing and truly liked Lee's sense of humor. She thought again about his comment regarding a thong dangling around her ankle. She didn't wear them, but that didn't mean she couldn't start tomorrow.

He shook his head as she opened the door. "Wonky."

"Goodnight, Lee."

"Goodnight, Jennifer."

The kitchen door's curtain moved when Lee backed the car down the drive.

Chapter Thirteen

Jen took her time returning to the house. She liked him but might not be ready to deal with a relationship. She needed to think about this. She turned off the television and went to bed.

In the morning, when she stepped into the kitchen, Miles, the off-white cloud, swept into the room.

"Good morning, Jennifer. No ill effects from your night out?"

"No. Were you watching me out the backdoor window last night?"

"I was. In your best interest, of course."

"Of course." She pulled out the coffee and filters. "Look, the evening went well. Other than that, I have nothing to report."

"In my day, ladies didn't sit in—"

"Buggies with their dates?" She pushed the filter in the chamber with a little more force than necessary. "Come on. You know they did. I needed to, um, talk to Lee, and since I never know where *you* are, I, uh…. What's wrong with me? I don't need to tell you anything. I had a date. Nothing else."

The cloud faded, and the room went quiet. She poured the water into the coffee maker and waited for it to brew.

Lee knocked on the door ten minutes later.

She leaned against the jamb. "Coffee?"

"No thanks, I already had enough at breakfast." He carried a black plastic tool case. "I brought the power drill for the doggie door. I also brought you a lawn mower if you want it. It's self-propelled. I have two and don't need this one."

"Thanks. I hadn't decided whether to hire someone or try myself. Since I now have my own lawn mower, I'll try my hand at it."

He put the case on the small table in the kitchen, opened it, and assembled the tool. In the pantry, he kneeled and aligned the drill bit against the first screw. "I don't mind cutting your grass."

"That's kind of you, but I think I'd like to do it myself. If the mower is self-propelled, then after I start it, all I do is push, right?"

The tool made a sound, *whirp!* He handed her the first screw. "Yep. I can show you how to push."

I'll just bet you can.

The drill made its distinctive noise. She accepted the second screw.

"Does the mower take gas, or do I have to mix something with it?"

"Gas." The third screw made its last turn. "I brought a five-gallon plastic gas can for you, too. Full."

She held her hand out for number four. "Is this a hint my grass needs attention?"

Lee almost dropped the drill. "Do you really want me to answer that?"

"Probably not." Jen turned to look around the kitchen. The room looked empty, but that didn't mean anything.

Once the screws were out, Lee pushed the plastic back and forth for flexibility. "There. Now when you adopt your guard dog, he can get out. I'd put in a fence. Getting a dog is a good idea, Jenny."

When Lee said *Jenny,* the air rippled like heat waves near the sink. "I will. A fence. Good."

"I can't stay." Lee packed up his toolbox. "I'll put the mower and gas in your garage."

"Use the side door. That's easier than opening the big one." She followed him outside.

Lee popped the white car's trunk and took out a mower with a folded handle and a red gas can. Pulling the mower behind him, he opened the side door and disappeared. He returned and put the five-gallon container in as well.

"I'll stop by tomorrow." He got into the car.

Jen waved to him as he backed out of the drive and returned to the kitchen.

"Okay, Miles. Appear. I know you're here."

No answer. She called him once more but heard only the clock's pendulum.

Jen didn't like the quiet.

Chapter Fourteen

Jen worried about Miles. Why hadn't he reappeared? Had she offended him?

A noise at the front door drew her attention. The postman.

She dug into the mailbox mounted next to the door and flipped through the ads marked *occupant* until she spotted a regular white envelope addressed to her in Keith's handwriting. Jen held her breath, skipped the salutation, and skimmed to the important word, *check,* which prompted her to look at the attachment stapled to the letter. He had included a check for ten thousand dollars.

"Wow. Ten Bills."

The letter explained the amount represented four months of the agreed-upon alimony. Since she had no address, Keith had waited. *Cheapwad.* He didn't need her address. He could have deposited it into her bank account, the same bank they had used for twenty years.

She read the pleasant, friendly letter again, amazed that Keith made good on the twenty-five hundred a month. Added to the Holmes's reward, she had a tidy sum.

The thought of Arlene Holmes's return made Jen think about Pam. She got the real estate business card from the kitchen utility drawer and dialed the number. "Hi, Pam. I came into some money. Do you want to go to dinner tomorrow?"

"Good for you. I'd love to. Where and what time?"

"I've noticed our town has a great selection of restaurants for such a little place. How about that little French cafe?"

"*Live?* Great. Wonderful food."

"Right," Jen said. "Live. Good name. I'll see you there

tomorrow at 6:30."

After she disconnected the phone, Jen felt odd about Miles and wished she knew where he was. *If you have to reside with a ghost, it's best to always know where he is.*

Later that afternoon, as Jen worked in the garden, gray clouds formed. Raindrops sent her back indoors. She made a latte and sat at the small kitchen table. As she took her first sip, an explosive thunderclap detonated. The vibration rocked the house, and the wind screamed around the corners of the eaves. The little flap in the pantry fluttered with an odd scraping noise.

Lightning exposed Miles's form as he moved from the pantry into the kitchen.

"Good afternoon," he said, with a downcast tone in his voice.

"Good afternoon to you. I wondered where you were. Did you hide out in the basement?"

Another slash of lightning reflected the look of revulsion on his face. "Absolutely not. I never go down there."

She didn't want to hear his reason for disliking the basement. Maybe later.

"I've been out," Miles said. Each light flicker showed him moving closer to her. "I had to get back before someone saw me in the traces of atmospheric flashes. I'm visible in that kind of light."

"That's how I first saw you in the lightning. All that flashing light and then a see-through man. Whoa, scary. Well, you're here now."

He sighed, then pointed at the back door. "Yes, home. It's not good out there. Different than what I remembered."

She sipped her latte, allowing the aroma to precede the taste. The rain pelted the roof and smacked against the windowpanes. Low illumination did not flatter the house's interior. With the addition of Miles's flickering specter, the scene reminded her of the haunted mansion their Baltimore neighborhood set up for the kids at Halloween.

She needed a distraction from the gloom. "Tell me what

you saw today."

"No," he said somberly. "I need to think on it. But I will tell you something I learned."

"All right. Why don't you sit at this table? It's kind of creepy seeing you at different places in the storm. Can you materialize? Maybe a little?"

"I can do that." His form took on a denser appearance as he sat down on the opposite chair. "When your gentleman friend opened the pantry egress—"

"Hey, he's not my gentleman."

"I can attest to that. When I went outside, everything looked different. The light, the trees, the sky. I had difficulty adjusting. I decided to stay with your gentleman—that is, Detective Ferguson. I rode with him in his motor car."

"Gee, that must have been interesting for you."

"My dear Jennifer, I owned a motor car myself, a beautiful one-cylinder, six-horsepower Cadillac. Jenny bought it for me with an inheritance. The pleasure of ownership was marred when a few townsfolk whispered suspicions of me taking bribe money from criminals, speculating on how a policeman could own such a lovely automobile. I believe that motor car started my unjust reputation. Forgive the digression, and allow me to complete my narrative of today's travel."

"Please. I'd like to hear it."

"Detective Ferguson took his lunch at the Toad and Pond Tavern. Imagine my surprise to find that stink hole, which plagued the town in my time, exists yet today. To no surprise, the venture continues to run numbers. We, my men and I, could never catch the miscreants in the act. However, now I know their present method of eluding detection. The criminals conceal the evidence in the bottom beer keg on the hand truck. The driver of the beer truck collects the numbers from all the bookies in town and delivers them to the back of the saloon. According to the wall calendar, that's on Saturdays and Wednesdays. In my invisible state, I observed the driver take the ersatz keg into the manager's office, at which time I accompanied the brigand into the workspace. After the manager and his staff shut the door, they inserted a blade into a crack in the keg and a panel sprung open. I saw him upend the number papers upon his desk."

"Whoa, Miles, aren't you the clever one?"

"I wish my work could be more thorough. The felons at the tavern can be caught, but it still leaves the masterminds at large."

"The police can dust for prints."

"What's that?"

"You know, identify the fingerprints on the evidence."

"What do you mean?"

"People leave marks from the tips of their fingers, and no two are like. Don't you know that?"

"I know fingerprints are unique, but nothing beyond that fact."

"Oh, my. You do have a lot to learn. In this and many other countries, people have to be fingerprinted to join the military or work for the government, hospitals, and schools. Computing machines catalog and keep track of the prints. When a crime is committed, sometimes the criminals leave their prints. If theirs are on file, they can be tied to the crime."

"You don't say?"

"Yes, I do. I will tell Lee about what you observed."

Although Miles had no mass, he seemed to slump in his chair. "Does it have to be *that* policeman?"

Jen drank the remaining latte and used a spoon to get the last of the foam. "He's coming over tomorrow, so the answer is yes." She craned her neck to see out the kitchen window. The sky had begun to clear.

"You must use caution in selecting your friends."

"What's wrong with Lee?"

"At the tavern, he drank beer while on duty."

"Lunch isn't duty."

"A law enforcement officer is always on duty and always a professional. And, although I don't understand his words sometimes, I don't like his implication."

"Like what?"

"He used a hand-sized metal device to speak with someone."

"Device? Oh, you mean cell phone."

"Yes, he has a portable telephone."

"Everyone has them. I don't know how we would get along without them."

"The telephones we had in our day hung on the wall, but we didn't have to put in the long numbers to reach our party."

"Long numbers? Oh yes, the ten digits. There's a way around that."

"Suppose you have an emergency? In your excitement, you may forget the number. In my day, we turned the crank and summoned help immediately."

"Not a problem. I'll show you." Jen went to the counter and took the cell from her purse. "In an emergency, we push 9-1-1 and press the green button. That's all. It sends a signal, and the police can find the location. Even a two-year-old can do it."

"How do the police locate you?"

She shook the phone in the air. "They aren't really phones but little radios. Oh, you probably don't know about that technology."

"I know about radios. Baltimore had the first telegraph line strung before my birth, and because telegraph lines couldn't go across the ocean, some bright fellow invented wireless transmission for ocean-going ships. You know, dot, dash, dot."

"Morse Code. I suppose you speak fluent Morse?"

"In my day, every policeman in Livonia knew the code. In fact, we each had a special leather-handled knife, wherein, during a crisis in outlying regions where no telephone existed, we knew how to climb the poles and send an emergency message by tapping the wire with the knife."

"Quite impressive. But I'm glad we have cell phones. Not too many people these days could shinny up a telephone pole."

Miles nodded his transparent head. "True. I'd like to see your detective Ferguson try that."

"Yes, that would be interesting. But, what has he said lately you didn't understand and didn't like?"

"Using the portable telephone, he told someone that he and two clerics would join together this weekend to slay Orcs and, by significant and lucky rolls of the dice, would find the gold and finish the mission."

Jen bit her lip. "What do you think that meant?"

"He and two corrupt clergymen will gamble for gold and kill a man named Orcs."

Chapter Fifteen

Jen placed her hand next to Miles's shadowy palm. "Miles, I'm pretty sure Lee indulges in role-playing games for adults, meaning imaginary expeditions played with dice and complex mapping boards. No one gets hurt or gets any gold."

"Pretend? Adults don't do that."

"Yeah, they do. It's a form of amusement."

"Then *some* adults have too much time on their hands."

"I can't argue with that. Um, you've been talking with me longer than usual."

"Each time I materialize, I get stronger, and my transparent state lengthens. My corporeal time, though, is still quite limited. I can't control when I fade. It just happens."

"Learn as you go, my grandmother used to say."

"I'm learning." He started to diffuse. "And now, I'm going."

Miles faded until the room looked empty.

"Are you still here?" Jen asked.

"Yes, but I won't be for long. I recognize the feeling before I slip away."

"Okay, then. Slip away and get your rest. Oh, I plan to watch my favorite crime shows on television until I go to bed."

"In that case, I won't be here until morning."

Jen suppressed a chuckle. She had used the television to occupy her children when they were young, and now she used it for privacy from a spirit. She still wondered about the subliminal messages Miles mentioned earlier.

Jen expected to hear from Miles during breakfast, but the sounds of the hissing coffee pot and the rich aroma of the brew were the only company she enjoyed.

At ten o'clock, Lee arrived to show her how to operate the lawn mower. He brought the mower and the gas can from the side of the garage. "Don't pour gas into the mower while in the garage. You need plenty of ventilation."

"Why don't you let me do that, Lee? I need to learn, and you might get your nice shirt dirty from the grease or something."

"Grease? Not on my mower. I assure you I keep my tools in perfect order. All my tools," he said with a naughty grin.

Jen squatted next to the mower and carefully poured the gas into the tank, not spilling a drop.

"Good work." He put the gas can aside. "Now, push this lever back and pull the cord." He demonstrated, and the mower started up with a roar. Then he turned it off. "Your turn."

She followed the steps, and the machine started. "Thanks. I'll do a little mowing later."

Lee handed her a folded red mechanic's rag from his pocket.

She wiped her hands. "Do you know Morse Code?"

"Me? Why would I know that?"

"You didn't learn it when you were a Boy Scout?"

"Nah, that's what the good little boys did in Livonia. I hung with the delinquents."

"Until you grew up?"

He took the rag from her and wiped his hands. "That's right."

"So now you only hang around with clerics and kill Orcs for their gold?"

"How do you know about that?"

She tapped her temple. "I know things."

He leaned against the side of the garage. "I think you do."

"I know you eat at the Toad and Pond, and the managers run a numbers racket."

"Okay, tell me something I don't know."

"You know about the numbers?"

"Of course. We've never been able to nail them on it."

"They keep the evidence in the bottom beer keg on delivery days. They pry open a flap on the side."

Lee stiffened and came to his full height. "The beer delivery? We never checked the beer kegs." He regarded her for a moment. "I couldn't just show up and search. But the health inspector could, and Grainger and I might be there enjoying lunch. They do make the best corned-beef sandwiches. If we closed them down, I would miss the food."

"Is number running so awful? No one gets hurt."

"The numbers racket isn't bad in itself. Some local yokel wins a few bucks and buys the missus roses and candy. It's what the money funds on the larger scale, the unseen crime under the surface. Picture a big spider web with a whole bunch of wrapped insects stuck on the web. The numbers game represents just one of the poor insects waiting to be devoured to feed that spider."

Jen shuddered. She could picture the spider web with its prey bound and frightened.

He looked directly at her. "How do you know about this?"

"I can't divulge my sources."

"Yes, you can."

"You wouldn't believe me anyway." She didn't want to alienate the friends she had in her new life with stories about talking with ghosts.

"Yeah, okay. Maybe it's better, I don't know."

Jen waved goodbye to Lee as he backed the big white cruiser out of the drive. After a quick lunch, she worked in the yard for several hours before returning all the implements to the garage shelves and giving the gas can lid a tight turn for safety. In the house, she installed a hasp on the basement door. Pleased with her do-it-yourself work, Jen brushed her hands together with satisfaction.

After showering, she studied her closet, taking time to select an appropriate wardrobe for her dinner with Pam. The midnight teal wool crepe surplice slipped over her head easily. She removed the towel from the full-length mirror and allowed herself a good look. "Wow," she said and turned for a back view.

"I'm looking fine."

Black Ferragamo pumps and her thick gold Omega necklace completed the outfit. She recalled the hefty price she paid for the shoes several years ago. Even with the reward money, her clothing budget would have to be reduced with a single income. *I don't need Keith or his paycheck. I'll take care of myself and buy clothes with my money. I have my own life.*

"Yep," the secretary said, "and a great house with a ghost."

At six-thirty, Jen found the *LIVE* café on one side of the town square. Despite its diminutive size, the cozy place had all the trappings of a genuine bistro. The tuxedoed host escorted her toward a booth where Pam waited. Lights from outside shone through the window, causing the restaurant's name to shadow across Pam's forehead. Her friend smiled, rose from the seat, and opened her arms wide for an embrace.

A waiter brought them water and a plate of tapenade, ground black olives heavily seasoned with garlic and olive oil surrounded by crusty bread rounds. Both ladies dug into the appetizer.

Edith Piaf's voice sang in low volume. Jen closed her eyes for a moment with the memory of the last time she and Keith had been to Paris. When she lifted her lids, a server stood waiting to give her the menu. He recited the specials *du jour*.

Pam shrugged, then put her finger against an open page and pointed to *Coquilles St. Jacques*.

Jen asked for *Steak Au Poivre,* then ordered Margeaux wine for them both.

As dusk set in, the café mellowed and relaxed in the light of the flickering candles. Pam's skin glowed like she was painted with gold dust. The soft, muted illumination skimmed over her face, airbrushing away lines of worry and making her appear a decade younger.

Keith said candlelight made all women beautiful. *Lord, he could be so full of shit.*

"So," Pam said after popping the last bit of appetizer into her mouth. "It's great to see you. Things seem to be good. You've come into money. How wonderful. Tell me about it."

"Idiot," the secretary said. "What are you going to tell Pam? That you found Sal Zemric's book and gave it to the cops? You remember not knowing Hal Sendick? How will you explain the money without lying? And Grainger said they looked at Pam for Arlene Holmes's disappearance."

"Keith made good on his alimony."

Pam's eyebrows arched. "I thought he gave you a lump sum, and that's what you bought the house with."

"Oh, he did, but when I complained I hadn't worked since he graduated from law school, he agreed to supplement my income until I became able to support myself. I'm temporarily rich. Did you get alimony when you divorced?"

The waitress brought their wine. Pam took a big swig of her glass.

"Pam? Are you all right? You look pale all of a sudden."

Pam quaffed another guzzle and quietly choked. "I got nothing from the divorce. And I just heard...." Her words came out slowly, like she did not want to cry or make a scene in a restaurant. "Johnny's in jail. This time I think he's in deep trouble."

Johnny Caulfield. That's who Lee said kept Arlene Holmes away from Livonia. Whoa, this is getting tangled. "Johnny, your ex-husband? What did he do?"

"I'm not sure," Pam put the linen napkin to her eyes and dabbed at her lash line. "He's the bad boy type that women can't keep away from. But I know it has something to do with that bitch, Arlene."

Double whoa! The secretary nudged Jen's shoulder. "Careful, now, keep your mouth shut."

"Who is Arlene?" Jen said in fake surprise.

"The woman Johnny cheated on me with, a stupid, ignorant bimbo who has more money than sense. She's had most of her body stuffed, sculpted, and scraped. Her credit card's a bottomless pit."

"It seems as if what your ex does still bothers you. Aren't

you better off without him? Especially if he's in jail."

Pam sniffed twice. "Yes, I guess I am, mostly. But there's no explanation why I sometimes go nuts when I think of him and Arlene."

"There is an explanation. You aren't over him."

"I don't handle things very well. I've always been the emotional type. I want what I shouldn't have."

"What kind of work does Johnny do?"

Pam's face blanked as if someone from behind a curtain pressed the off button. In a second, her poor-me expression returned.

"Odd jobs, whatever he can find."

"Like construction?" The secretary nudged Jen again as a reminder to be careful with her questions.

Pam ran her fingernail along the fine edge of the wineglass. "No, more like running errands or messenger services."

Jen already knew Johnny had mob ties. How much information did Pam have? How much did this woman know about her ex-husband?

When the dinner came, it brought tantalizing smells that sailed on the curling steam from the plates. Time took a back seat until the plates lay clean on the tabletop. After the waiter cleared the dishes, Pam drank the remainder of the wine. Following a long sip, the tears reappeared. Pam wiped her eyes after each sip.

"We need *crème brulee*," Jen said, hoping to lighten the mood.

Pam managed a smile. "Okay. Thanks for listening to me, Jen. I felt like I knew you the minute I first saw you. Since the divorce, I don't have many friends to choose from."

Jen summoned the waiter and ordered two desserts. "Would you go back with Johnny if he straightened up?"

Pam stared at the tablecloth. "Arlene knew Johnny was married but started an affair anyway." She inhaled a large swallow of wine, clearly ignoring its subtle bouquet of pears. "She could have any man. Why did she have to steal mine? I don't know if I could take him back. I'm lonely. And Johnny is good where it counts, you know what I mean? Maybe I just need a man in my life. A nice one with a good job who comes home every night and isn't afraid to talk about work. Isn't that what most women want? Don't you want to meet someone too?"

Jen frowned. She had been slipped a leading question. Keith used to do that to her when he wanted information instead of just asking. She didn't like it then and didn't like it any better now.

The newly born rebel in her took control. "Not really," she said in the dumb-dumb voice. She held up the glass of water. "Down with men!" She slurped to show her seriousness.

"Yeah." Pam picked up her water glass. "Down with the miserable bastards." She slurped louder.

They both laughed and then *ahhed* as the waiter brought the crème brulees.

Jen rapped the hard sugar crust sharply. "This is a man's head."

"Use a bigger spoon," Pam said.

Both ladies sighed with sugar-laden contentment when the waiter took the empty dessert dishes away.

The waiter came with the bill.

"On me, remember?" Jen put her credit card into the fancy leather wallet and closed it. After the waiter brought the wallet back, Pam and Jen walked to the parking area.

Jen said, "Want to go to a movie? Or come back to the house, and we'll rent one?"

Pam shook her head. "My car is a disaster. I've got to get it washed and vacuumed before my early client appointment tomorrow morning. Thanks for the dinner and the ear."

"Any time. Call me, and we'll do this again."

They slipped into their cars and drove off in opposing directions.

As Jen neared her driveway, she timed hitting the remote so the garage door would be aloft enough to pull the car in without stopping. The light in the garage was out. The door lifted, dancing to its squeaky melody. She guided the Acura forward to its place, stopped, unfastened her seatbelt, and opened the door. A flash of adrenaline raced through her as the garage door creaked its way down, and darkness surrounded her. She hadn't touched the remote.

A hand on her arm whipped her from the seat. Everything faded to stygian blackness.

Chapter Sixteen

Winding her way through a long dim tunnel, Jen reached consciousness amid sirens, flames, and tinny voices saying, "Roger that." She coughed, and acrid smoke in the phlegm choked her on its way up and out her mouth.

"Be still for a minute, miss," a gentle voice said. A strong grip held her wrist. Jen's eyes flew open when a sharp needle pricked her hand. Two medical techs bent over her, one flicking the plastic tubing in place connected to the bags of clear fluid held up by the other.

Her head throbbing, she looked around. She lay on a stretcher on the back-porch step. Flames licked the top of the garage. Men moved swiftly, readying a thick hose. At a fireman's sharp command, a stream of water gushed and pounded against the flames lapping the side of the garage.

"What's happening?" Jen said weakly.

"Relax," the man with the gentle voice said. "Ready?" he asked the other tech. "One, two, three."

They lifted the stretcher. She tried to turn her head to see, but her neck was strapped to a stiff board. Just before they closed the ambulance doors, she saw another ambulance, techs crowded over something on the ground. Firemen hauled a heavy object from the side door of the garage.

Jen's head hurt as the vehicle moved, and once again, she drifted away to a dark and quiet place. She awoke in a hospital bed, drowsy and claustrophobic. Her one mobile arm moved a mask hissing cool, sweet air from her face.

A nurse appeared at the bedside and settled the oxygen mask over her nostrils again. "You probably ought to leave that mask on. You got a snootful of smoke."

Jen pulled the mask aside. "I don't know what happened."

"You escaped a fire. You're lucky to be alive."

The nurse worked silently on a roll-about table with a laptop as Jen checked the clock on the wall for the time—three a.m. The door made a slight whoosh as it opened.

Lee stuck his head into the room. "Decent?" Before the nurse could object, he walked in with his badge in hand. "Is she okay?"

"Smoke inhalation and a contusion on the back of her head. Nothing life-threatening."

The nurse left, and Lee scooted a chair to Jen's bedside. "Hey, Smoky. How are you doing?"

"Lee, what happened?"

He pulled at his chin. "I hoped you could tell me. What do you remember?"

"I drove into the garage." She searched her memory. "The light in the garage was out, and the overhead door started to close. That's it."

"So, you don't remember your two friends in the garage who weren't so lucky?"

She shook her head and wrinkled her eyebrows. "Who? What?"

"Strangely, you managed to clobber two very large fellows with your garden spade before making it to your back step."

"Clobber?"

"Big time clobber. Did I mention this activity occurred *after* you sustained an assault from a clay pot? Then you called 911. All as your garage burned so very brightly."

"I got hit on the head?"

He reached over and pulled a tiny bit of orange from her tangled hair and showed her the minute shard. "In addition to psychic, we have to add Wonder Woman to your resume. You defended yourself. Strong, like bull," he said in a poor Russian accent.

"What about my garage?"

"Needs some work."

"My car?"

"Oh, needs a lot of work." He rubbed her forearm above the taped IV. "But *you* are okay. The other stuff can be replaced."

"You don't think I'm replaceable?"

"Not in a million years." He bent over and kissed her cheek. "You need to rest. I'll check on you tomorrow, okay?" He rose. "By the way, name the last person you saw."

"Pam Caulfield. But we parted after having dinner together."

"Okay. Easily checked."

"You don't suspect Pam?"

"We check everything. You know, eliminate the impossible...and, crap, I forget the rest of the saying."

"Whatever remains, no matter how improbable, has to be the truth." she yawned. "Arthur Conan Doy...a...l."

Lee made a gun shape with his forefinger and thumb and gave her a shot in the air. "Right, cowgirl. See you tomorrow."

Feeling happy and relaxed, warmth and well-being spread its pleasant wings.

Then she thought about Miles. And the two men.

Chapter Seventeen

In the morning, a nurse removed the IV. A young doctor came in, examined her and signed her chart. "You can go home."

Jen had already called Chrissy and Bobby. She tried to keep in touch with her kids every few days. Now she used the bedside phone to call her homeowners insurance company, then called Pam. "I'm in the hospital, and I need a ride home. Will you be available sometime this morning?"

"My client rescheduled for the afternoon. I'll come right away. What happened?"

"I can't talk about it right now." Her voice quivered.

"Please, Jen. This is serious. I want to know."

"I'll tell you on the way home. Thanks."

As Jen's wheelchair entered the lobby, Pam came through the doors. A nursing assistant helped Jen get into the little Rio.

Pam slid into the driver's seat, turned the ignition, and left the hospital parking lot. "Do you need to stop at a pharmacy? Groceries? Anything?"

"I'm good, thanks. I want to go home."

"Okay," Pam said. "Start from the beginning."

"I don't really know what happened. I can't remember anything after pulling into the garage, which caught on fire. I managed to get out and call 911. Pam, two men died in my garage. It's horrible."

"You don't know what caused the fire? Or who the two men were?"

"I don't remember anything. Oh, those poor men."

Pam's mouth formed an *O*, and she let out a loud breath. "Firemen?"

"I don't know who they were."

"That's awful. At least you seem okay."

"Right," Jen said. "It's so horrific. I don't want to think about it. My head hurts." She opened the little plastic bag the nurse had given her and took a pill, spit-assisted.

At her house, yellow crime scene tape held by stakes encircled the garage.

Pam parked on the street parallel to the house. She helped Jen out of the car and gently looped her hand around Jen's upper arm as they stepped toward the door. Not having her purse and keys, Jen fumbled under a smooth rock in the planter for the spare key.

"Great security," Pam said.

"What can I say?" Jen mumbled, unlocking the door.

Inside, Jen plopped on the sofa.

Pam followed Jen into the living room. "Can I make you some tea or coffee?"

"No, I think I'll just rest and then go up to bed."

Pam didn't sit. "Can you manage the stairs?"

"Sure. Don't worry. I'm good—physically."

"Sorry. I can't stay. I'll check on you later."

The doorbell rang, and Pam answered it. "Hello, Detective Ferguson, Detective Grainger." Her greeting dripped with acid.

"Hello, Ms. Caulfield," Lee said.

"Howdy," Grainger said, not cowboy friendly.

The two men avoided Pam as she headed to the door. They moved together toward Jen.

"We'd like to ask some questions, Ms. Hughes," Lee said. "Are you up to it?"

Ms. Hughes?

Pam took her keys from her purse. "I'll see you later."

The detectives exchanged glances. Grainger went to the window and pulled the curtain aside. In a few minutes, he let the curtain down. He approached the sofa, where Jen reclined. "Feeling better?"

"Yes."

"Glad to hear it. I want to take a look around your yard. It might be a while. Ta." He exited out the front door, his footsteps clomping on the porch and steps.

Lee sat on the couch next to her. "Wow, who did you piss off?"

"What?"

"The two guys who croaked in your garage were hit guys from Philly. Bad, bad dudes."

"Lee, I don't see how I—"

"Killed those guys? Yeah, me neither, but the evidence suggests—"

"Oh, God, Lee. Am I going to get arrested?"

"Some formalities, but nothing dramatic. The now-deceased torched your garage and hit you with a flowerpot. You foiled their plans by not dying of smoke inhalation. I suspect they were going to try to make it appear like your gas can spilled and a spark from somewhere ignited."

"How do you know they did all that?"

"We found the gas can outside the garage undamaged, with one of the perp's fingerprints. That would be Tony Marcello. The broken pot made its way out next to the gas can, too. Prints on that piece belonged to the other slime ball, Gus Hansson. Your prints showed up all over the garden spade handle, and what looks to be their smeared blood matted on the blade. Cut and dried case. No problems. Right?"

"Oh, Lee."

Lee moved closer and took her hand. He kissed the bandage where her IV had been. "Relax, Jenny. You're okay. But I wonder who put out the hit on you."

"Hit? Oh! Maybe it's Sal Zemric because I gave you the book."

"Nope, guarantee it's not old, Sal."

"How can you be sure?"

"Because Sal took a water nap in the Shenandoah River near Harper's Ferry." He put Jen's cell phone in her hand and gently closed her fingers. "We found this next to the pot shard and the gas can." He brushed her cheek with his fingers. "I need to talk to Ash, and then we have to boogie. Keep your cell with you everywhere. I programmed my number into it. Hope you don't mind. Call me if you get scared or any other feeling that may require my services."

"Thanks. I appreciate it."

"Try not to worry. We, your friendly copsters, have it under control. I'll check on you later." He left.

The back door closed. A movement in front of the fireplace caught her eye. Like a movie in slow motion, Miles appeared in solid form, wearing his dress blue uniform.

Jen smiled. "Miles! What a great uniform. Were you wearing it when you saved my life?"

He didn't answer.

"Come on, I know you rescued me."

"You suffer no after-effects, Jennifer?"

"I'm okay, but I need to find out what happened last night."

"As you will. I have taken notice of your *modus operandi* upon arriving home. That is, when the garage door opens, you park your motor car, then walk to the back-porch step, turn, and shut the door with your signaling device. Last night the door came down without you. I checked the garage and saw those dregs of humanity, one assaulting you, the other picking up the gas can. I became solid and used your garden spade to render them *hors du combat*."

"Render them what?"

"Out of commission. By then, the fire had caught, and smoke billowed about, so I pulled you to safety. I would have pulled them, too, but I expended my energy accomplishing more important objectives."

"Making the 911 call and securing the evidence?"

"Yes. Showing me the emergency measures regarding your portable telephone proved providential. Your innocence could easily be established by displaying the evidence. Having accomplished those tasks, I faded and did not return until just now."

"My hero! But why wear the uniform?"

"Because I can."

"I don't understand. Don't you usually appear wearing the suit in the photo?"

"I didn't plan on that mode of dress. Perhaps it is related to the photo you saw. I've not appeared to another."

"I'm the first to see you?"

"Yes. I recently learned how to summon my choice of dress. I chose to greet you thus."

"And a mighty handsome hero-greeting indeed."

Miles made a bow. "Your humble servant, dear lady."

"I don't know what to say. Thank you can't be enough."

"Quite sufficient, truly. If you don't think it rude, I will depart for a while. As much as I don't savor visiting the outside world, I must. I take my leave." Miles headed for the pantry.

"Invite him into the house," the secretary said.

"Um, Miles. Wait. You need to leave by something more dignified than the doggie door. Remember when you said spirits could not enter the house unless invited? Go out one more time through the flap, and I will invite you inside."

Jennifer went to the back door and opened it wide. In a moment, a slight blur progressed up the walk. She curtsied and swept her hand across her body. "Why, Miles Hampton, do come in. I bid you welcome."

The blur brushed over the threshold.

Miles materialized in his frock coat from the photo. "I believe I have observed a fine rendering of strategy. Well done, Jennifer."

"How did you know it worked?"

"In my non-corporeal state, the walls appear to me as gray monoliths, and when you issued your invitation, an opening shaped like a door appeared. Shall we prepare the front door as well?"

Jennifer walked through the kitchen, stopping to adjust the Quitcher-Bitchin' sampler while she waited for the telltale blur on the front step. "Come in, Miles. Come into our house."

Miles solidified as he entered. "I've not walked through that door in a very long time. Thank you. I believe we have evened the scoreboard."

"No way we're even."

"Keep vigilant until I return." Miles's form faded as he moved toward the closed door. The mist melded into the wood.

"Damn," she said. "My life has become one weird fantasy story."

Before she could think too deeply, a car stopped by the sidewalk. She pulled in a quick breath. Soon a knock on the door sounded.

Chapter Eighteen

Jen opened the door. "Why are *you* here?"

"Are you okay? Can I come in?"

"I don't know — you might be one of the Dark Forces."

"What are you talking about? I'm blond."

"Although," she pulled the door open and backed away. "They can have any hair color. Your disguise *is* rather thin."

Her ex-husband, Keith, walked into the living room. "Nice place. Maybe I gave you too much money."

"Very funny."

"Our daughter called me and said you had been in the hospital. Chrissy was very worried. What's up with the crime tape?"

She was in no mood for long explanations. She especially didn't want to talk about the men who perished. "The police are investigating the fire. I didn't want to worry the kids, but I thought I should tell them I inhaled smoke when my garage burned. I'm okay."

"Small-town cops probably don't have that much to do and can investigate a garage fire. A bit of bad luck for you, but these things happen. At least you're okay." Keith sat on the couch and looked around. "Here, come sit by me."

Jen hesitated. He could no longer tell her what to do.

He patted the cushion. "Please, I want to talk with you."

The secretary punched Jen's shoulder. "Miles said to be vigilant, so watch it. I'll bet he wants to alter the alimony or worse."

What could be worse?

Jen sat on the couch as far from Keith as she could sit on

the same piece of furniture. "What do you want? You had to drive a hundred miles to get here, so it has to be important."

"I wanted to see how you were. Is that so unusual?"

Jen opted for non-verbal vigilance.

"You know," Keith said, "maybe this divorce happened a little too fast. Twenty-some years of marriage down the drain in six weeks. Since you left, I've had some time to reflect."

The secretary yelled, "Run! Don't let him say another word. He's way out of our league in manipulation."

Keith put his arm along the couch back. "I've been doing a lot of thinking. By the way, Jen, you look great. You lost weight and got a tan."

"Look, Keith—"

He slumped, spreading his knees, and dropped his head lower. "I made a mistake. It hasn't been the same without you. I miss your quirky little ways and the funny things you do. You know, you can be so…."

"Wonky?"

He lifted his chin and locked her gaze. "Yeah, wonky. I miss your eccentric personality and your clever comebacks. I never knew what you would say next. No one has your…charm."

"I know. I'm adorable." She rolled her eyes.

"I don't have a clue what came over me."

"I have a clue. You had an acute attack of gonad-o-citis. Most probably contracted from that Ukrainian office clerk with the six-inch cleavage. What's the matter? Didn't it work out?"

Keith's head fell back against the couch.

"I don't care. You can admit it." She remembered what Miles had said. *Don't be afraid to speak if what you say is accurate. What is factual remains factual.*

"Nothing to work out, Jen. I don't know what happened. I only know the house is really lonely."

"I'm not going to discuss it."

"Okay. I understand. Just out of the hospital and your garage and all. Before I go, I'd like to see your house."

Jen shook her head. "You need to vamoose. I just got over

a scary event. I can't handle guided tours right now."

"Vamoose? I hoped you would invite me to stay over. I mean, this being so far away from Baltimore and all. I could look after you. How about dinner out? I noticed some nice places on my way here."

"No dinner or overnight visit. Take a quick look around. Then you'll have plenty of time to get back to Baltimore."

Keith scooted closer to her. "Isn't that kind of cold?"

"Yep, guess so." She rose from the couch and went into the kitchen. As she tidied, Keith moved through the house.

In a few minutes, he joined her. "What's that door?" He waved at the door with the hasp.

"The basement. Help yourself."

Keith unfastened the metal bar and went down the steps. He wasn't gone long before a crash and a commotion came from the depths of the dark. Keith yelled and ran back into the kitchen.

"Jesus H. Christ!" He slammed the basement door, his chest heaving and his breaths coming in rapid pants.

Chapter Nineteen

Jen didn't move from her spot near the counter. She closed her eyes and swallowed. *What did he see down there?* After a moment, she forced herself to speak. "What happened?"

He gained his composure and straightened up. "You should have warned me." Keith stomped past her on his way to the front door. "A goddamned raccoon jumped on me. You'd better do something about pest control."

He slammed the front door so hard the Quitcher Bitchin' sampler jiggled on the wall. *A raccoon frightened him? Ha! If he only knew.* She laughed. After the assault, the fire, and the hospital, a territorial raccoon sounded like cookies and milk.

Jen made herself a latte and received a call from the insurance company saying her rental car would come that afternoon. She was lucky to have that company. When Keith had been so eager to get rid of her, he offered to keep the Acura insured until the next renewal. The same company wrote her new homeowner's policy as well.

Not too long after the caffeine bestowed its magical gift, two cars parked outside alongside the sidewalk. Jen opened the front door as far as the chain permitted. Two men in golf shirts sporting the insurance logo held clipboards and toted computer bags.

After checking their ID, Jen allowed them to enter.

When all the paperwork was signed and one man handed over keys to a fancy Chrysler Town and Country, they left. Fatigue set in. Jen's headache returned with a vengeance, forcing her to take a pain pill. Relaxing on the couch, she picked up the remote, hoping she could watch the TV for a few hours without offending Miles. She flicked through the channels and, finding no crime shows, switched the thing off. The medicine made her drowsy, and succumbing to droopy eyelids, she napped.

Sunset rays cast soft stripes on the wall when she awoke and sat up. "Miles?" she called out, but the house remained quiet. Her cell phone's loud ring made her flinch and knock the device onto the floor.

"Everything okay?" Lee asked.

"Sure. I have my rental car, and the adjuster for the garage will come tomorrow. My head hurts a little, but other than that, nothing to complain about."

"Want some company?"

"Only if you bring a pizza."

"Deal. Beer?"

"No, better not mix the pain pills with alcohol."

"True. I'll see you in a little while. Keep the doors locked."

Upstairs she showered and put on makeup. As she combed, little bits of the flowerpot came loose and plinked onto the counter. The nurse said she couldn't wash her hair for a few days, but she needed to see the wound. Holding a mirror to show the back of her head, a white patch that looked like a bullseye where they had shaved and used six stitches to pull the now bruised skin together. The mirror shook in her trembling hand as she thought about the two men who attacked her. Having no memory of the assault did not block the fear of someone trying it again. Her heart rate increased, and the queasiness in her stomach ratcheted up a notch.

At the sound of a car in the driveway, she pulled back the curtain in her bedroom to see the white Crown Victoria. Lee got out and took a pizza box from the passenger side. She headed down to unlock the door.

"I'm scared," she said.

He followed her into the kitchen. When she put the box down, he pulled her close and hugged her. "I put a car on the end of your street all day. But, if an emergency calls, the guy on watch will have to go. Livonia doesn't have that many patrol cars."

"There's a cop on watch?"

"Not now. I'm here. You have to be careful. You've had a bunch of visitors today, including your ex-husband."

"You know about that?"

"Uh-huh. Plus, we took note of the guys who brought you the replacement car. Look, those two could have been criminals, and you let them in."

"I made them show their IDs."

"IDs can be faked. I want to be here when the property adjuster comes."

"The insurance office called and said he would be here tomorrow at ten." She put two plates next to the pizza box.

"So will I, and I'll take down the yellow tape tomorrow too." Lee reached for a napkin from the holder on the table. "I'd save a cop a lot of trouble if I stayed over, you know."

She gulped a breath. A shot of warmth quivered inside her. Lee's suggestion made her feel good, wanted, and needed.

"Don't respond," the secretary said.

They sat at the table and ate, saying little. After the second slice, a hazy form took shape behind Lee in the doorway. Miles was back.

"Lee, do you think you could take the crime scene tape away now while there still is a little light? It embarrasses me when the neighbors drive by and stare at it."

Lee finished his pizza. "I can do that."

Just as he left, the doggie door opened. The noise made Jen look. A roiling golden iridescent cloud moved in and stopped near Jen's legs.

"My God! What's this?"

Chapter Twenty

Miles's essence thickened into semi-transparency and stood next to the golden mass. He bent down and put his hand into the material. "It's a dog."

"What? How is that a dog, and what's it doing here?"

"I saw him earlier today, but I didn't invite him in." Miles petted the pearly bulk. "Hey, boy." As he stroked, the golden matter formed, and the shape of a dog appeared. "The Innocents have a golden aura. They go where they want."

"Innocents?"

"I've been learning some things."

"I have company, Miles. You've got to get rid of this... dog, spirit, innocent, whatever. I don't want to have to explain this to Lee."

"I understand. Come, Rex."

"Rex? Is he your dog?"

"No, I don't know where he came from. I picked a common name."

Miles disappeared just as Lee walked through the back door with his arms full of tangled yellow tape. "You were talking to yourself again."

"I think I need to rest now."

"Head hurting?"

"You have no idea." *Spinning is more like it.* "Thanks for the pizza."

"Sure. I'll see you later."

The doggie door opened and closed. Lee looked toward the sound in the pantry. "You know, you ought to get a watchdog. Not one of those tiny yippy things, though. One that gives bad guys second thoughts."

"Right. I'll do that; get the kind of dog that frightens people."

Lee kissed her forehead. "I'll be here tomorrow before ten. Don't let anyone in, and call me if anything strange happens."

As Lee departed, the golden cloud tumbled into the kitchen, rolling and turning until a dog shape formed. The Innocent solidified into a four-legged creature and sniffed the floor around the table where the half-eaten pizza sat.

"Miles!"

He appeared at the doorway between the kitchen and living room. "Ah, your company has retired. Finally."

"Look, I love dogs, but, like, living dogs, see? Please! Get rid of this *thing*."

The dog had made his way to Jen and sniffed her leg. She pulled away when a hefty tail wagged enthusiastically. A thin rope circled his neck, and a short tether dangled down his front shoulder.

"Look, Rex likes you. Innocents recognize goodness." Miles, half-transparent, squatted and stroked the dog. "They go where they are supposed to be."

"What does that mean?"

Rex trotted over to the small kitchen table and curled up into a ball underneath.

Miles stood. "Here's a bit of what I learned. Innocents, although rare, are the spirits of animals and children. The Dark Forces can't affect them, and they wander at will, usually searching for something. Maybe Rex thinks he will find what he seeks here with you."

"Well, he can't stay here. How do I make him leave?"

"I do not know."

Someone rapped on the back door. Jen's hand flew to her chest.

"It's me, Lee."

Miles went transparent.

"Jen?"

"Hold on, Lee."

Jen searched the room, looking for something to cover the sleeping dog. Rex shifted from solid to smoke. She grabbed a pile of dishtowels, but then he faded to invisibility.

"Jen?"

She rushed to open the door.

"I left my cell on the table." He came in and picked it up. "Can't leave home without it. Plus, I get to kiss you goodbye again." He kissed her cheek. "You look a little peaked. Is your headache getting worse?"

"Pains. Worse. Yes, indeed." She walked Lee to the door. "See you tomorrow."

As soon as the door closed, Rex materialized, black spots first, followed by the white body and then his brown head. This time his thick tail remained mysteriously absent. He reminded her of the description of the Cheshire Cat from *Alice in Wonderland*.

Wrapping the remaining pizza in aluminum foil, she put it in the fridge and placed the dishes in the sink. "I'm going to bed now, Miles. Do you suppose Rex will be here in the morning?"

His words floated somewhere above her head. "That I cannot tell you. But, do retire. I will be on guard."

"Curiouser and curiouser," Jen groaned, shaking her aching head.

"Indeed," agreed Miles's voice. "Good night."

Jen pushed against Rex with the toe of her shoe. His scrawny body felt solid.

Rex looked at her with large, sad, brown eyes. He threw back his head and gave a mournful howl.

Chapter Twenty-One

When she awoke the next morning, Jen checked the house for Rex. "Rex! Here, boy."

"He left this morning," Miles said, materializing in the kitchen.

"Oh, good." Jen let the words breathe out in relief.

"Like me, I'm afraid Rex is a discouraged outsider in a hostile world."

"Hostile world?"

"Extremely so, dear Jennifer. Yet, I believe Rex will return. The Innocents know when to appear; therefore, try to dismiss your apprehension."

"Which apprehension is that?"

"That someone who shouldn't shall see us."

"An insurance adjuster and Lee will be here this morning."

"I do not relish inactivity but will conduct myself in invisibility as events require."

"Thank you."

Within an hour, Lee arrived, and after coffee, they examined the charred remains of the garage. For the first time, Jen got a good look at the damage.

The entire back of the structure was blackened and looked as if a strong wind would bring it down. The smell of burned wood and wiring hung in the air like a curtain surrounding the small building.

A car pulled up close to the intact part of the garage exactly at ten. Two men in suits approached them.

"Ms. Hughes?" said the shorter man.

"Identification?" Lee said.

The taller man stepped closer. "You are Mr. Hughes?"

"No." Lee whipped out his leather holder and let the flap open, exposing the gold shield.

"Ah, yes," the tall man said. He produced a laminated badge with his picture proclaiming him the lead adjustor for American Liberty Insurance. The other did the same. Lee shook hands with the two men, after which they donned their yellow hard hats and began poking around the garage.

"I should go with them and explain what happened," Jen said.

Lee put his hand on her arm. "Why don't we wait on your back steps? It won't do you any good, and you might get in their way. Besides, you'd need a hard hat, and that wouldn't be good over the stitches."

Jen and Lee sat on the steps. He patted her back as she leaned forward, staring at the blackened shell. After a few minutes, the two inspectors came back. They said the tear-down would start tomorrow, and as soon as they could get a permit, a contractor would be there to rebuild.

"I hope the neighbors don't mind the smell and the disturbance. I haven't even met them. Welcome to the neighborhood, Jennifer, you-cause-trouble Hughes."

Lee rose and took her hand. "You have a kind soul. Kooky but kind. When the neighborhood knows you, they'll adore you."

She angled her head. "Because I'm adorable?"

"That's my story, and I'm stickin' to it. You want to go to lunch?"

"Thanks, but I want to do some research on this house and the history of Livonia."

"Well then, you should go to the town's library. That place will provide way more than any computer, *and* you will get to meet my Aunt Mildred. She's been the librarian here since the invention of dirt. You won't find a more complete collection of local history in any other town. I guarantee it."

"Your aunt?"

"Maternal. My mother died a few years ago."

"So, your aunt tries to take her place?"

"Oh, God, no. She's all business, believe me. In her other life, she must have been a Roman general. You'll see. I can't think of anyone more efficient or organized than Auntie Millie. And don't you dare tell her I called her that. She still scares me."

"I guess I'll see you later then," Jen said.

"That sounds like a kiss-off to me."

"I'd like to think of it as more like you're getting paid to detect crimes, and sitting on the back steps with me is wasting taxpayer's hard-earned money."

"Ow! Harsh, Jenny. Okay. I know when I'm not welcome." Lee bent over and kissed her quickly on the lips. "Be careful. Don't get involved with strangers. Try to get home by dark. My patrolmen will be worried if they don't see your car in the drive or lights indoors."

"Yes, dear."

Inside the house, she found Rex under the table. Miles didn't answer her call. She took her purse, went outside, and sat in Town and Country. She started the car and paused to survey the remains of the half-burned garage and its blackened timbers. *I move to a small town, and my life goes from routine to wild. What's next?*

Chapter Twenty-Two

Jen's phone navigated her to her destination. The red brick building looked like a library from the Victorian era. Climbing roses attached firmly to white trellises over the entryway. Windows with leaded diamond shapes sparkled as they flanked the front steps. Two stone lions guarded the bottom steps, smaller but more imposing than the famous New York City library lions.

Inside, a wooden panel foyer gave way to a rounded lobby with an oak desk. The antique brass sign on the desk read: *Information.*

How can I get information since no one occupies the seat? Maybe the library has an information ghost, and the ghost is presently in a transparent state. It had been a joke, but Jen got a little chill because she *did* have a ghost.

From behind her, a voice said. "Welcome to the library."

Jen jumped. Turning, she encountered a woman who looked as much like a librarian as the building looked like a library. The lady stood tall, regal, and slender, with gray streaks in dark blond hair pulled back in a bun. She stepped closer, at least an inch into Jen's personal space. A minor detail but a powerful message. This self-assured woman took charge of her surroundings. Half glasses perched on the tip of her nose, and to complete the look, she wore large pearls, matching pearl stud earrings, and a grey suit. No doubt, the low-heeled black shoes offered great comfort as the imperious woman walked about her realm.

"Are you Mildred?" *She has to be Lee's aunt.*

"I am. Mildred Owings. And you?"

Jen stuck out her hand, and after an awkward pause,

Mildred Owings clasped her fingers in a brief but brisk shake. "I'm Jennifer Hughes. I'm new to Livonia, and—"

"Yes. I understand. You want to read the newspapers headlining the explosion of the carriage factory, plus the inquest and verdict regarding Miles Hampton."

"Lee Ferguson told you?"

"Why would my nephew Burleigh have anything to do with this? I have been expecting you. Word travels fast in Livonia. You're the new owner of the Hampton House and, like every owner before you, curious."

"I am, but not necessarily about the explosion. I want to know about the family."

"The family? There's not too much. Engagement and wedding announcements, births, Mr. Hampton's accomplishments, commendations and advances, and our humble philharmonic originating with Virginia Hampton."

"Oh, cello?"

"You've already done some research, I see."

"Ah, some. Do you have microfiche?"

Auntie Mildred's face took on a *my dear, please* look, starting with her eyebrows and ending with the set of her mouth. "We have the original newspapers. You can read them yourself."

"The newspapers? How can they last that long? What kind of retrieval system do you have?"

"Up until maybe the beginning of the twentieth century, newspapers were printed on cotton bond paper, strong and durable. We laminated a few of the popular ones, like the explosion, but most have held up quite well. Regarding the library's retrieval system, ever since Livonia founded this library, it has been fortunate to have more volunteers than work to keep them busy. Our newspaper section of the Reference department is spotless and organized. Come with me."

Soon newspapers piled on the table next to an upholstered chair, and Jen traveled through the cotton bond reporting of Livonia's past, including engagement and wedding notices. She paid particular attention to Miles's police appointment and an engraved photo displaying a line of men in their uniforms swearing an oath to protect and serve. Virginia Hampton's picture showed her sitting at her cello. Other newspapers announced concerts in the gazebo of the town square with a large advertisement for the May Day festival. Jen discovered a fine image of Miles when he made detective.

Aunt Mildred came by. "Find anything interesting?"

"All of it. How can I get copies? Do you allow photocopies?"

"No, bright light may damage the sheets. Anticipating the need for reproduction, we had them computerized on a staff-dedicated device. From that version, you can purchase copies. I'll get you the request forms."

Mildred returned with a stack of forms and a pencil. "You can get eight by ten-inch copies by selecting what part of the newspaper you want. We divide each page into six sections numbered one through six. Fill out the forms and pay fifty cents each."

As she scanned the papers, Jen found one of interest. The headline read, *Livonia Detective Receives Commendation*. She glanced at the article adjacent to a photo of Miles, so handsome, looking straightforward and unsmiling as he stood next to the mayor and the police chief, who held a box displaying a certificate.

A volunteer brought another newspaper to Jen. "This was out of sequence, so I missed it."

"Thank you." Jen flipped through the pages. At the bottom of the first page, the title, *Madame Zelda, Gifted Seer, predicts mayoral race. Mayor Owings to be the winner.*

Jen read the few pages and turned to the classifieds, where she found an ad in the back listing Zelda's services with a catchy Egyptian Eye of Horus as her symbol. Jen reread the prediction article, and in her photo, Madame Zelda wore a gypsy outfit, looking like a Halloween character.

Jen became engrossed in reading about Livonia of the past. The news informed her, but the advertisements on the back pages fascinated her. By the time Jen looked up from her page, her stomach complained loudly. She handed the forms and her money to a volunteer and waited for her stack of copies.

After thanking Aunt Mildred and her numerous volunteers, Jen headed home. Hunger induced her to stop at the fast-food chicken restaurant she had seen on her tour of Livonia. She remembered the sign showing a smiling man holding up his finger—Smith's Fried Chicken. Number One! On her way to the chicken restaurant, a sign caught her eye in front of a quaint white house. *Madame Zelda, Gifted Seer.* The Eye of Horus overlooked the expensive sign.

Madame Zelda? Eye of Horus? What's going on? Jen pulled into a parking lot, flipped through the copies from the library, and read the one-hundred-year-old article about Zelda, Gifted Seer. Then she drove into the drive-through at the restaurant and ordered the three-wing box. On the road home, the aroma emanating from the box overcame her fear of being tacky. Armed with paper napkins, she wolfed down that chicken with the speed of a dry sponge thrown into a bucket of water. Satisfied, hunger took a back seat when she arrived at her driveway. Even though the front of the garage seemed intact, the memory of the blackened back gave her a sick feeling.

Entering her kitchen, she called out Miles's name, but the place stayed quiet. A dog's tail attached to nothing thumped from under the table. "Hi, Rex." She sighed, bent down, and flailed in the air, trying to find the rest of the animal. Rex's head appeared, and Jen's hand made contact. "Good boy. I did say I wanted a dog. And here you are. I hope Miles is correct and you know when you are supposed to show up." Jen put her library copies in a folder and, bypassing the television, went upstairs. After dry-washing her hair, doing her nails and toenails, and having a clay facial, she went to bed at nine, early for her.

In the morning, the insurance adjusters arrived, accompanied by the crew hired to fix her garage.

"Ms. Hughes," the shorter man said, "This is Dave, the foreman of the crew."

She shook Dave's hand. He gave Jen a description of the work and an estimated time of completion. Jen walked around the garage and choked up at the damage, not only to the structure but also to her garden. In the exposed sand, tiny footprints suggested raccoons.

Jen caught up to Dave. "Would you be interested in fixing my basement?"

"What's wrong with your basement?"

"It's made of dirt." She led Dave to the door and undid the hasp. Turning on the switch for the hanging light, she said, "You see why I call it *the pit?*"

"Not a big deal," Dave said. "We'll pour concrete on the floor, use block for the walls, and reinforce them with rods. Twenty thousand, and I'll drywall, too. You could have another room down here."

"Twenty thousand? You'd write that on a contract and keep to the price?"

"Yes, ma'am."

Being called ma'am made her feel over forty. "Would you take the deductible for the garage out of the price?"

He shrugged. "Okay."

"Then we have a deal."

"I'll have a contract for you later this afternoon."

Jen had seen no sign of Miles since the prior day. Around three, teatime she liked to call it, she made her latte. As she sat back to enjoy her afternoon addiction, Lee knocked at the back door. She invited him inside. "Latte?"

"Nah, I'm a straight black coffee kind of guy. I want to let you know how much I appreciate you."

She stopped mid-sip. "Um," she hesitated. "Appreciated for what?"

"Grainger and I are receiving commendations for work resulting from the evidence you provided—that is, Sal's book, Arlene's CD, and the tip on the beer barrel at the Toad and Pond. It's been a bumpy ride, but the town seems to be just a little cleaner."

"Commendations? Really?"

"Thanks to you and your psychic powers." He kissed her

forehead.

"Psychic powers? Oh, that."

"I'm still having difficulty with accepting parapsychology, but, well, the proof is in the pudding, they say."

Lee wouldn't accept the truth about Miles. Hardly anyone would, so psychic power would have to do.

"Lee, do you know Madame Zelda?"

"Zelda Silverstein? Sure. She reads futures, but in case you're wondering, she never gives us crime tips."

"How long has Zelda been in business?"

Lee scratched his thick hair. "She's an old lady. Like, she's been around forever."

"Forever?"

"As long as I can remember. A bit eccentric. Must be worth millions. She does the crystal ball thing for kicks. Owns half of the commercial properties downtown."

"Really? Anything else?"

"She's some kind of city planner, although you'd never figure her for a politician. She's into preserving the historic parts of Livonia. Actually, I think they tried to tear down this house once, and she knuckled enough of the big guys to squelch it."

"Maybe I need to visit Madame Zelda and get my palm read."

Lee pulled at his chin. "You're going to offer to trade secrets?"

Jen didn't find his comment amusing and frowned.

"Whatever," Lee said. "I shouldn't question the wacky things you do or say. I mean, look, I'm getting praised based on what you provided. So, have at it."

"When is the ceremony for your award?"

"In the morning, the day after tomorrow, but no ceremony. It's just an office event. Grainger and I dress up, and Uncle Paul and the mayor give us certificates, and the rest of the staff applauds, that kind of thing."

"May I attend?"

"Nah, it's not that earth-shaking. But I'd like to take you to a nice lunch afterward. How's that?"

"You'll be in uniform?"

"Sure, I'll keep it on for lunch." He raised his eyebrows a few times. "You dig uniforms? Turns you on?"

A large bang came from the backyard. Jen ran to the window. A huge yellow beast of a tractor pulled down one wall from the garage.

Jen's eyes watered. "My garage. It's gone."

He slid his arm around her. "But you remain." He tightened his hold into a hug. "I'm sorry."

"I know," she said.

"I don't want to leave you like this, but...."

"You need to go. I understand."

He kissed her cheek. "See ya."

The diesel engines of the large machinery groaned as the crew coordinated the wrecking and removal of what had been Jen's garage. After an hour of clamor and clattering, the crew left.

She pulled her cell from her pocket. "Now," she said to the secretary, "for Madame Zelda." Jen scheduled an appointment for the next morning and then chose her favorite frozen dinner, meatloaf, from her freezer's selection. She put it in the oven, set the timer, then sat down. While waiting for the timer to ding, she reviewed each event that had occurred since she bought the house. It seemed like a lifetime, especially with all the weird stuff going on, but it had only been a few weeks.

The buzzer rang. She took the hot tray to her place at the table, and as she took the first bite, a familiar thumping sounded near her feet, Rex's tail hitting the floor with its rope-on-wood noise. He raised his head and, with the tail in a slow wag, ambled to the back door. A cloud turned into a shadowy figure. Miles emerged through the closed door.

"Good evening, Jennifer." He stooped and gave Rex's head a double-palmed caress. "Have you been guarding our mistress?"

"Some guard dog," Jen said. "I suppose the head and tail would be enough to make a criminal go screaming."

Miles stood, almost solid. "He does guard you. I don't know what, but something builds. As the Dark Forces become bolder, perhaps the blessed walls won't be enough. No spirit will come in while I'm here, but they might breach the wards when I'm absent. Neither will a spirit bother a place occupied by an Innocent. Therefore, Rex is the centurion while I'm away."

"What do you mean when you say something builds?"

"I don't know enough to explain it all. The time will come when I will understand enough to apprise you of the other world." He pointed to the door. "Out there."

Chapter Twenty-Three

At eleven the next morning, Jennifer struck the gong on Madame Zelda's front steps. *Nice touch, that gong.*

The door creaked, of course, as it opened, and a petite woman dressed in gypsy garb peeked out. A charge surged through Jen as if she had touched a battery. The woman from the picture in the old newspaper stood in front of her. Jen backed away.

"Jennifer Hughes?" The small woman took a stride forward. "My eleven o'clock appointment?"

Jen retreated a bit farther.

Madame Zelda grabbed Jen's wrist. "Come in, honey. You shouldn't be afraid of Zelda. Zelda knows all things. You bought the Hampton House." The woman, stronger than she looked, pulled Jen forward through the door and cackled.

"I've changed my mind," Jen said. "I'll reschedule."

"Nonsense. You're here. I'm here. Come in and sit."

Zelda led Jen to a small room off the entry hall. The darkened room looked like a gypsy's lair. Heavy curtains shadowed a small round table draped in blue cloth stamped with planets, stars, and suns. A crystal ball completed the décor.

"Like it? Come into my parlor, said the spider to the fly." Zelda chuckled and flung open the curtains. Light shining into the room entirely changed the mood. "Did I scare you?"

"Um, well." Jen pulled out the photocopy of Madame Zelda from the old newspaper. "You?"

Zelda slid a chair near the table. She waved her hand toward it, indicating Jen to sit. The woman took the photocopy and wrinkled her forehead into deep furrows. "I'm not *that* old.

That's my grandmother."

"Your grandmother?"

"Oh, honey. I guess I went too far. I have a little fun now and then with the newbies. My grandma had a good thing going, and I took up where she left off. I go to great lengths to look like Granny. She raised me, and I keep this little business up to honor her memory. I have fun, too. You just moved to town, right?" Zelda sat and put her hands around the crystal globe. "So, you want to know your future?"

"Not really. I read an ad in the old newspaper and then saw your sign. I hoped you could tell me some things about Livonia."

"Usually, folks come to me for the future, but you've come for the past. I like that. You might call me the town historian, so you're at the right place."

Hmm, I thought Queen Mildred was the town's historian.

"I'll start with the first Zelda. My grandmother was a capable and shrewd woman. In fact, as a young woman, Granny admired Miles Hampton."

"Really?"

"They had a relationship, but both knew it couldn't go anywhere. Back then, the differences between religions were like different species. Christians didn't marry Jews, so they remained good friends. Zelda's folks arranged a marriage for her to an older man, a pharmacist, and they lived over the drugstore. When her husband died, Zelda had to support her three kids, so she sold the drugstore and bought a duplex, renting out one and living in the other. She supported her family on her palmistry and saved every nickel to buy real estate. By the time she was old, she owned a lot of property in Livonia. My mother didn't care for mothering, so I lived with Grandma Zelda. Jeezy, I called her; you know G. Z., get it? I inherited most of her property."

"Do you know anything about the explosion of the carriage factory?"

"The explosion happened during the only time Livonia had not elected an Owings for mayor or police chief. Miles had made enemies because of his skills as a detective, and he wouldn't take bribes. Jeezy believed Miles had been framed and said it regularly and publicly. Poor Virginia, Miles's wife, was never the same after that."

"Do you know what happened to Virginia Hampton?"

"I do. Miles's boyhood friend, Damon Cisco, felt it was his duty to help the family. He, a recent widower, eventually convinced Virginia to marry, but Damon couldn't bear living in that house and moved them away. Um...." Zelda rolled her bottom lip. "He took them to Pittsburgh. Yeah, I'm pretty sure. Jeezy talked about it all the time. She thought Damon put the moves on Virginia and couldn't understand why Virginia let him adopt the teenage boys, Christopher and Timothy."

"So, the boys would have used Cisco's last name."

"You're going to research those boys and find out what happened to them."

"How do you know that?"

Zelda tapped her temple. I have a little gift. It's not *all* smoke and mirrors."

"So, you're a psychic?"

"More of a seer."

"What's the difference?"

"I see into the future. For example," She took Jen's palm. "I'll give you a freebie, you being interested in the town's history. Let's give it a shot. Yes! I see it! You and a tall shaft of fine tobacco. Er, um. No, I see you and the tall, handsome police chief together, married."

"Me and Chief Owings?"

"Ha!" Zelda gave out a hardy laugh. "Have you ever laid eyes on Paul Owings? He's short and definitely not handsome. Come on, girl. Tobacco...Burley? Burleigh Ferguson?"

"Oh, you mean Lee? *Lee*?"

"Yes. You, my dear, have the hots for Lee Ferguson."

Jen's eyes expanded until she blinked them back to normal. She tried to think fast, to whip out a denial or at least a deprecating remark to show she wasn't interested in Lee. Instead, she said, "You can see that?"

Zelda clapped her hands. "No! That's not from a vision. I'm a mathematician. That is simple math, like two plus two. When you pulled out the photo of my grandma, I saw enough of Lee's card to know you met him. And what normal red-blooded woman wouldn't wet her pants over that bachelor hunk?"

"Wet her pants?"

"Yeah. One good thing, and there are so few, about being old is you can get away with saying inappropriate things. You know what I mean? I can say things people think but wouldn't say out loud. When you're my age, you'll do it, too."

Jen didn't deny it. She began to think of Zelda as an older version of herself. "You know Lee?"

"Quite well. His mother, Bertha, Bertie, and I were best friends. BFFs—see, I keep up. I sure miss her. I kind of watch over Lee. He visits and thinks he's keeping track of me."

"Oh."

"Now you want to know about Lee. But you won't ask because it's not proper. So, the old lady excuse is going to come in handy. You aren't asking. I'm just mouthing on."

Jen clammed up.

"Okay, then. Have you heard about the Currier School?"

Jen shook her head, afraid it would be this old lady's load of crap.

"Well, right after the Civil War, Mr. and Mrs. Winston Currier started a school for wayward girls. The Curriers had money and fine Arabian horses but no children. They hired tutors and riding instructors. Pretty soon, the graduates were not only highly educated but also knowledgeable about horses and fit for the aristocracy. About this time, a lot of low-lifes from the big northern cities came into money from post-war industrialization. New money, but none of the graces derived from the wealth of established families. Their daughters looked like fools in high society. These *nouveau riche* tried to enroll their darlings in the Currier School, but the Curriers held the spaces for underprivileged gals. Finally, the school was bought by a rich New Yorker, and from then on, it became exclusive, very expensive, and very hush-hush. Sheiks' daughters, along with European princesses and mobster offspring, got their education and horsemanship skills from the Currier, and it is still the finest school unknown to most people."

Jen sat quietly, hoping this discourse would go somewhere.

"That's where Marjory Ferguson, nee, Dix attended, and one day on her way out of town in her little convertible sports car, newly hired patrolman Ferguson pulled her over for speeding. Bertie and I knew the relationship would never survive. Margery worked in the bank Daddy bought so his daughter could have a good job. They lived in a house they bought with their own finances, and two kids later, they traded Marjorie's convertible for a minivan. Poor Marjorie couldn't handle being middle class. After fifteen years, she got the kids and split. That was six years ago. Anything else you'd like me to see?"

"How about the library?" *Crap, couldn't I do better than that?*

"The library." Zelda made a face. "Old Maid Millie? Isn't it funny that even now, Mildred, Paul, and Bertha are still referred to as the Owings kids? Paul and Bertie were fun, but Mildred.... Never had it and never will. Not at her age now. Up-tight; always was."

"Um, Zelda, what do you mean by *it*?"

"It, girl. It! That which makes the species survive. That which drives men to war makes them crazy. Makes us happy! That which, sadly, I no longer enjoy. Oh, don't get me started."

Jen did not want Zelda to lament over her lost sexuality. "Can you tell me some history about Livonia?"

"Of course, I can. My grandmother's grandmother moved to this area in the early nineteenth century. Not too many white folks lived here, mostly Indians. My ancestors lived in harmony with the native people and respected their traditions. One important tradition regarded the sacred burial ground. When the Indians were torn from their lands, white people moved in and farmed. No one really knows where that sacred spot is, but the medicine man put a curse on the spot, and a legend says one day the Evil One will ascend, take charge of the world, and reap revenge."

"Are you making this stuff up?"

Zelda's eyebrows raised, followed by a grin. "Yeah, but it sounded good, didn't it? My ancestors didn't settle with the Indians because the whites ran the Indians out of Maryland way before the Revolution. However, the curse hurled by the Indian chief several hundred years ago is well known. Supposedly, an ancient evil will ascend to conquer the world. You can ask Chilly Millie about it the next time you go to the library, or you can trust Zelda."

"Do you really have your grandmother's first name? I didn't think Jews did that."

"I am Zamilia, but that's close to Jeezy's name, so in order to carry on the tradition and keep the same business, I use Zelda, too." She stood and put out her hand. "I am glad to meet you, and I've enjoyed our little session."

Jen rose. "Thank you. Nice to meet you, too. How much do I owe you?"

"Free. Hang in there. Lee might just give up his role-playing games and take another chance on love."

"Do you always hold back like that?" Jen said.

"Yeah, by now, you must have noticed my shyness."

Is this me in thirty years?

Zelda accompanied Jen to the door. "Come back anytime."

Jen sat in the car for a few minutes sorting through what Zelda had said. She turned the ignition. *An ancient evil?*

Chapter Twenty-Four

Jen left Zelda's house perplexed. It would take a while for all of that information to soak in. She had no trouble identifying the other feeling—hunger. The *hot and now* sign of the nearby chicken place called her name. The box holding her three-wing order dispensed an aroma in the car better than little cardboard trees hanging from a rearview mirror. She ate the wings while she drove. At home, she parked on the street to avoid the construction materials in her driveway. A stack of yellowish lumber gave off the pleasant smell of newly cut pine. The crew had torn down what had been her garage to the cement slab, where years of oil stains mixed with unknown substances formed a design reminding her of a Jackson Pollack work in shades of gray. Eerie, ghostlike. *Well, there's a surprise.*

After entering the kitchen, Jen threw away the box from her lunch and heard the familiar thumping of Rex's greeting. "Hey, Rex," Jen said as she put her purse on the counter. A tail appeared, swishing to and fro as it made its way to her. She bent down and waited with her hands extended. By the time Rex arrived, he had almost formed. She rubbed his ears. "It's nice to have a pet, even if you're not always complete. My mother used to say half a loaf is better than none. I should coin a new phrase about half a dog, shouldn't I?"

Jen scratched the dog under his chin and then stood. Rex returned to his place under the table and disappeared. Movement caught her attention. The Quitcher Bitchin sampler straightened of its own accord.

"Good afternoon, Miles."

"Good afternoon, Jennifer." Miles, in his half-state,

flickered.

"Miles, I met someone interesting. Zelda...oh, I don't remember her last name."

He went solid instantly. "You met Zelda Rothberg? Her spirit remains?" His voice pitched higher. "Where?"

"Oh, sorry. I didn't meet your Zelda. I met her granddaughter."

"My Zelda. Ah, thinking of her...." He made a short, derisive sniff. "Until you brought me forth, actual *thoughts* have eluded me."

Jen found the library research and held the papers out. "Look. I have newspaper copies about you." She spread them out on the kitchen table. "Here is a picture of you getting a commendation."

Miles bent over the copies. He picked up the engagement article and then the wedding notice. He put them down and ran his finger over Virginia's name in the May Day announcement.

Jen held the paper showing his commendation. "Why didn't you smile? You look so snappy in that uniform. You don't have any expression on your face."

"Be assured, I was not without sentiment. I received the award for killing two dregs of humanity who murdered, extorted, and committed acts too vile to describe. I did not then, or now, enjoy taking lives, even for the good of society."

"I guess we all do things we don't want to out of necessity. I'm sorry you felt bad taking the award when I know you saved many innocent people. Just as I know you didn't cause the explosion of that factory."

"So," Miles said. "You had an audience with Zelda's granddaughter. Please tell me about her."

"Exceptional." Jen scooted the chair out and sat. "Her grandmother spoke often of you. She proclaimed your innocence for years."

"How like Zelda to exhibit grace and respect toward my good name."

"I believe your Zelda knew in her heart that you were a

decent man. I feel that way, too."

Miles put his hand on her shoulder. "Thank you for your kindness. Let us dispense with this subject. It does neither of us any good. I shall leave for a time this afternoon. Rex will keep you safe."

"Miles, may I ask a favor? Can you give me some kind of sign of your presence? Unless you materialize, I don't know your location."

"I understand. I won't lurk. I shall announce my presence in an unobtrusive way. I came back to check on you. Now I have things *out there* that need my attention. Good day."

Miles traveled through the closed back door. *Will I ever get used to that?* Shaking her head, she looked around for something to do. Kitchen work waited. As she pulled the strings of the trash bag, she noticed the chicken box contained a remnant of meat. She removed the small piece and offered it near where Rex ought to be. His tail made a few thumps, but the meat remained in her fingers. *I guess ghost doggies don't need to eat.* "You're the perfect pet, Rexie-boy. You don't eat or poop, and you disappear at the right moment. Too bad I can't tell anyone about you." The thump-thump against the chair leg indicated Rex knew she had addressed him. "Good boy, Rex. Very good boy."

She took the bag outside to the garbage container. One of the truck drivers who delivered construction materials headed toward her with his own empty box from Smith's Number One.

"Good chicken," Jen said, holding the lid open for the man.

"Yep, The Finger makes the best."

"Finger?"

The man cocked his head as if her question was silly. "Oh. New to town. That place, see, Smith's Number One, opened in the sixties. Since the couple didn't have enough money for a sign, the lady painted it herself and didn't get the hand right. Everyone thought it looked like the hand shot a bird.... Oh! Excuse me, ma'am!"

"I know what a bird is. Tell me the rest."

"Well, people called it The Finger, which made everyone

want to see the sign, and the food was great, so it became a hit. The big fried chicken franchise down the street couldn't compete and went out of business."

Jen smiled. She identified with Smith's Number One and mentally shot Keith, her own bird. She returned to the kitchen. The phone in her purse rang, and she hurried to get it. The caller was Lee.

"How did your visit with Zelda go? Did she tell your future?"

"That and a whole lot more."

"I'd like to stop over this evening if it's okay."

Where will Miles be? She was uncomfortable about her resident ghost when Lee visited. The word *lurk* stuck in her mind. But didn't *she* own the house? Okay, Miles had a right to it as well. Or did he? She knew she felt safer for his presence. Great, a phantom made her feel better. *Go figure.*

"Jenny?"

"Oh. Sure. You can come by."

"See you later." Her life with Keith seemed deadly dull compared to living in Livonia. *Deadly dull.* Then she thought about the attack in the garage. *More like, dull but alive in Baltimore versus spine-tingling death here.*

As she busied herself around the house, thoughts regarding food crept into her mind so often that she admitted she needed something sweet. Flipping through the recipe cards, one sang to her with a siren's call. *Gingerbread with Rum Cream Sauce.*

Later, spicy, dreamy aromas filled the kitchen, permeating up the stairs and into her bedroom. She had enough time to refresh her makeup and comb her hair while the cake cooled on the counter. She breathed in and savored the essence of spices, powerful even in her bathroom. She hurried downstairs.

The sauce would only take a few minutes to make. When the mixture turned into a pearly white gloss, it took its place atop the mahogany-colored cake.

Rex made a sound not exactly unlike a bark.

Chapter Twenty-Five

Lee had arrived.

Before going to the front door, she crouched down to look under the kitchen table. "I hope you stay invisible, Rexie-boy. Miles promised you'd know what to do. Remember, only appear when the bad guys come around." She hoped the two thumps meant Rex would behave.

As soon as she let Lee in, he sniffed the air. "What is that wonderful aroma?"

"Gingerbread. Would you like some?"

I think I've died and gone to heaven." He inhaled deeply and fluttered his eyelids. "Oh, yeah."

"You think that's where you'll go?"

A puzzled look washed over his face. "I've been a good boy. Why wouldn't I go straight up?"

"Maybe we make a lateral move for a while, like in a business."

"This aroma has gone to your head, Jen. We die. We pass on. Like a promotion or an advancement to the executive department. That's all."

"If you say so." They entered the kitchen. Seeing no sign of the Perfect Pet, she let out a sigh of relief. She tapped the back of one of the chairs at the small table.

Lee nodded and sat down.

Jen cut a piece of cake. "Would you like some tea or coffee?"

"Ooh. Got milk?"

"Sure."

Lee lifted his nose and sniffed in deep. "This reminds me

of my boyhood. In fact, if I close my eyes, the smell takes me back to my grandmother's kitchen."

"Great. Now I remind you of your grandmother?"

"In a good way. Except, Granny used to make me eat oatmeal for breakfast."

"What's wrong with that? My grandmother said oatmeal keeps you regular."

"Well, neither one of us seems like regular folks. That's why we like each other."

"That's not the regular I meant."

He bobbed his head. "I know what you meant."

She put the dish of gingerbread and glass of milk in front of him and placed her own plate opposite.

"Thanks." He reached over and touched her hand for a moment. "Forget regular. You're special." He took a bite of the gingerbread and sipped the milk. "Tastes even better than it smells. You know what they say. The way to a man's heart is through the stomach."

"Is that true?"

"Well, there are other paths, of course. Shall I call you the Pathfinder?"

"Pathfinder? Not very romantic. Sounds like someone you go camping with."

"Jen, I'm not sure I can deal with these mixed messages."

"What do you mean?"

"You've been playing footsie with me, rubbing your ankle against my calf since you sat down. You're a cool one, too, not showing any of the playfulness by your facial expression."

Footsie? What is he talking about? Jen felt a nanosecond of confusion followed by panic. *Rex!* "Don't put any meaning into it, Lee. I'm not sending messages, mixed or otherwise."

"Well, you must know what calf-rubbing means in Livonia." The corners of his mouth broke into a smile. "It means you have to kiss me."

"It doesn't mean that."

"I had to try. I figured you might buy it."

Jen needed to do something to manage this awkward situation. "More cake?"

"Hard to resist—like you, Jenny."

A warm ripple of pleasure coursed through her at Lee's compliment. The feeling stopped short when she felt Rex's tail thump against her foot. That could mean Miles had returned. "Would you like some cake to go? I can wrap it up for you."

"Is my time up? I guess I came on too strong. Sorry about that. And, yes, I'll take a care package. I might get hungry later on tonight. Alone, in my house."

Jen quickly cut and wrapped a large piece in aluminum foil. As she put the foil back in the drawer, she saw the Quitcher Bitchin' sampler tilt, signaling Miles's return.

Jen put the foil package in Lee's hand. "I'll walk you out."

Dusk settled in as the pair approached the big white car. Had Lee noticed the curtain on the door pull slightly aside? Like the time before, she opened the door and slid into the passenger side.

"So, it's my car you like, eh? And I thought my sparkling personality charmed you."

"Fifty-fifty." Jen laughed.

He pulled her close. "Let's see if we can up the percentage."

"On which side?" She moved nearer.

"Bless the bench seats in the cop cars!"

They kissed gently. After a few moments, the kissing became serious.

He put his lips against her ear and whispered, "I feel like I'm a teenager on a date, and your father might come from the house and haul you out of the car."

"Me, too. Exciting, huh?"

"I'm excited, all right. I guess I don't care *why* the cop car has an effect on you."

"You know girls can't resist a car in uniform."

"You're funny, smart, beautiful, and unpredictable. I just don't know about you, Jenny."

"What don't you know?"

"My heart says you might be the woman of my dreams. My brain, the part I'm supposed to listen to, says those dreams might involve a few nightmares."

"Which body part do you think has the right advice?"

"Well, if body parts could talk, there's one hollering right now."

"When your parts have settled the debate, let me know."

"Jen, you're delightful. You make me look at things differently. Like life."

"How about the Afterlife?"

"See. That's you. Enchanting."

"Adorable?"

"Absolutely."

"Thanks for saying that." She hadn't felt that good about herself for years. "You receive your commendation tomorrow?"

"At eleven. I'll pick you up at one for lunch, okay?"

"In uniform?"

"Oh, yeah."

She leaned in and kissed him. He touched his tongue against hers, and a tingle shot from her shoulders downwards. In the middle of their next kiss, the car's radio cackled.

"Attention units, respond to Quiet Valley Cemetery."

"Gotta go, dream girl."

Jen scooted out of the car and stood in the driveway. Lee put a magnetic strobe on the top of the Crown Vic as he backed out. The light flashed a blinding blue, easily seen until the car vanished down the road.

In the kitchen, Jen called for Miles.

"I'm here," he said and formed almost solid. "Detective Ferguson's departure had a distinguished flair."

"His radio directed him to the cemetery. Do you know anything about that?"

"No. I've not been there. Not recently."

"I thought the cemetery would be Spirit Central."

"If you mean a place for souls to congregate, then you would be wrong. The graveyard is the last place a wandering soul wishes to visit."

"Is there such a place? I mean, a place where you, um, spirits, go to meet each other?"

"The most wicked and corrupt souls, known as the Salients, unite for their foul purposes. I know little of them and avoid them as much as possible. Some Innocents roam, searching for that which will allow them to pass over."

"Pass over? Where do they go?"

"I have yet to find out. The Innocents know those answers. However, Innocents are rare, and then only a few, like young children, are able to communicate their knowledge."

"Do you know why you remain here?"

"No, but I believe the reason can be discovered. Each day I learn more, which assists me to arrive at a solution. Fortune seems to have favored me, for I think you are part of the answer."

"Lucky me."

"Yes, perhaps to your sorrow."

"I'm sorry. I didn't mean—"

"Do not apologize, gentle lady. You are entitled to fear. You have endured danger, and I hope to render a good account of myself on your behalf."

"You're not responsible for the fire in the garage; however, you did save my life. That's a pretty good account."

"I fear you honor me with more than I deserve."

"Oh, Miles. I can truly say I've never met a man like you."

"On that note, my dear, I shall retire for the evening. Rex and I stay ever at your service." As he walked away, he became transparent until he winked out.

Jen went into the living room. Aiming the remote at the big screen, she broke the evening's silence with a *Law and Order* marathon. After a few hours, she went to bed.

Promptly at one the next afternoon, Lee knocked at the front door.

"Oh, my. Don't you look nice in that uniform," Jen said, purse in hand.

"I'm striving for sexy or stimulating, actually."

"You look dashing. The style hasn't changed for a hundred years. Even the cap."

"And you know that, how?"

"Old photos from the library."

"You really do like uniforms."

"Yes, I do." She pulled out her house key, and he saluted as she locked up.

Lee held the car door open for her. "I'm taking you to a fun place for lunch."

"How long do you have?"

He slid into the seat. "All afternoon. Uncle Paul gave me and Grainger the day off."

"Don't you work? You seem to have a lot of free time on the taxpayer's nickel."

"It would be a lot better if I did work nine to five. I'm on duty twenty-four, seven. You don't know about the times I'm called out in the wee hours. I take what time off I can. The work commitment caused my divorce."

"Really?"

"That and the fact she didn't take to small-town life."

"Margie?"

"Marjorie. She wouldn't be called by a nickname. Zelda told you, right?"

"She told me a few things. I hope that doesn't offend you."

"I warned you she'd talk your ear off. She's a harmless but wonderful old lady."

"The complete opposite of your Aunt Mildred."

"Oil and water. They never mixed."

"Zelda said you visit her often."

"I check on her now and then. She makes me tea and reads my future in the leaves. By the way, she's an incurable matchmaker. Beware."

Jen bit her lip, saying nothing, but Lee turned his head away from the road to look at her. "I see. She's already predicted your love life, eh?"

"Tall, un-dark, and handsome."

He looked at her and smiled. "Two-thirds of it sounds like me. Gotta love that Zelda."

"Since you've checked me out, you already know my history. Tell me about your kids. Do you see them often?"

"I don't see them as frequently as I'd like, but I try to talk to them as often as possible. They live in Cape Cod with their mother and grandparents," he said.

"You are on good terms with everyone?"

"I'm okay with the kids, Sally and Peter. Sally goes to nursing school, and Peter is a computer genius. My ex-mother-in-law still likes me."

"Do they know about the commendation?"

"They probably know about the award. Mr. Holmes would have mentioned it."

"As in Arlene Holmes? You knew Arlene?"

"I still do. She and Marjorie shared a dorm room at the Currier school. That's a joke — dorm room. Those rooms rival any five-star hotel suite. The stable has a chandelier. Can you believe it?"

"Zelda told me about that school. I'd never heard of it before."

"That's the point. It stays under the radar. The girls who attend live at the top of the food chain. Security up the ying-yang and the finest education money can buy, pretty much individual tutoring. Their big deal each year has a catchy name, The Fox Hunt."

"With a real fox? Is that legal?"

"It is when six governor's daughters participate. It's coming up soon. You'll know when you see the Bentleys, Rolls, and Maseratis glide through town."

"I'll bet the local motels are thrilled during The Fox Hunt."

"No way. Money like that doesn't stay at Worst Western. The school has *accommodations* for visiting royalty, foreign or domestic. You should see that place."

"Unless I hit the lottery, I guess that's not going to happen. You've been there?"

"Once, when Marjorie and I attended Fox Hunt. Disgusting."

"The poor fox?"

"The moral values. Shallow conversations about servant problems, travel plans, and nothing regarding real life. I didn't fit into that box. But, enough about Currier. It's not our world, Jen. Let's talk about something we have in common."

"Okay, what happened last night at the cemetery?"

Chapter Twenty-Six

"Oh, that. Kind of funny in a sad way. Mr. Lowe, a nice old guy, lost his wife after being married a gazillion years. He visits her grave every day. When he saw a solar-powered ornament in a catalog, he ordered it. After charging it in the sunlight yesterday, he brought the heart-shaped pink and white LED light gadget that says *beloved* and put it on Daisy's grave."

"Solar powered?"

"Remember the time I got the call yesterday, just at dark? Well, Mr. Eiler, *not* a nice old guy, walks his dog every evening, and on his return walk, he passed the cemetery. Just as he got there, the sign switched on. The grave ornament started to glow on Daisy's headstone, and he thought he saw a ghost. Eiler had a heart attack, and his dog went nuts. A driver heard the barking, stopped, and called 911. That dog saved his life. Unfortunately, Eiler wants to sue poor Mr. Lowe."

"A night light for a headstone? Doesn't the cemetery have rules?"

"Not this one. It's privately owned."

"I've never heard of a privately-owned graveyard in a city."

"There are a few. Grandfathered in. There's still room, too, if you know the right people."

Jen wrinkled her nose. "Lights on the headstone, kind of tacky."

"To each his own. Poor Mr. Lowe, he just wanted to honor his wife, and now he's facing legal action."

"Even small towns have plenty of excitement."

"Sometimes more than others." Lee turned the car into a

small parking lot. The plain building had a single sign with the words, *The Rasta Pasta*, in large letters, and under that, in small letters, *Where Italy and Jamaica Collide, Mon.*

"I like it already."

Island music blasted as the waiter showed them to the table. Lee asked if they could turn down the volume.

"Yes, sir, officer, sir," the waiter said in mock servitude.

Lee turned to Jennifer with a smug look. "Maybe I should wear the uniform more often." He handed her one of the menus sitting upright between the bottles of sauces.

She read the offerings. "One side of the menu lists their Italian food."

"And, the other side offers Jerk."

"I'll bet the jokes never quit."

"So," he said, eyes twinkling, "what will it be? Italians or Jerks?"

"I've never tried Jerk, but if an award-winning Scottish-American detective recommends it, I'll give it a shot."

Lee ordered the jerk pork for both of them.

"Tell me about Arlene Holmes," Jen said.

"Why?"

"I'm curious. Indulge me."

"She's a nice gal. A little short on smarts, but nice. She liked Livonia, and after graduating from Currier, she stayed. Mr. Holmes, Daddy, bought her a horse farm in the boonies and stocked it with the finest Arabians. She bred and sold them like crazy but never made a dime. Then she got involved with the wrong sort."

"Johnny Caulfield?"

"Uh-huh. I can't figure it out, though. Johnny Cee, his street name, is a minor hood, not in the same strata as Zemric and the Speigal Family. I don't understand why they let him inside."

"What about Pam? How does she fit into all of this? I can't imagine her involved in anything illegal."

"She's a transplant from New York City. When she took up with Johnny Cee, we checked her out. She's clean."

"Like me."

"Yeah, but not nearly so cute. Anyway, I can't explain the attraction. I know Pam Caulfield hates us, the cops, for harassing Johnny, but she divorced him. What does she care?"

"That I can explain. She still loves him."

"Big mistake."

"Is it so hard to fathom a person falling in love with someone not suitable?"

"No, I guess not." Lee scratched his head. "Love is blind."

Jen nodded. "The ancients explained it by saying a mischievous god shot a magic arrow, and then you fell in love with the next available person you encountered."

"That's as good as any theory I've heard. Oh. Here comes our jerk."

The music volume slowly increased, but Jen and Lee focused on the zesty food, barely speaking, so the loud island rhythms were not a problem.

After lunch, as Lee escorted Jen out of the restaurant, he took her hand. "You want to go somewhere? We could ride out to Currier and see the place."

"No, I ought to get back home. The construction crew needs my supervision."

"Do you really think the construction guys require your presence?"

"My life has changed. Keith, my ex, always called the score. I intend to take control as much as I can. It's my house, I love it, and I want to participate."

"I can understand that."

"Did you know the garage had been built as a garage rather than a stable? Miles Hampton owned a Cadillac."

"No, I didn't." Lee stopped waking and seized her gaze. "Now that I have been amply accoladed by my superiors, I'll need to shine again and not rest on my commendation today. Put that gifted noggin of yours in gear and see if you can come up with some ideas as to how a prostitution ring operates in this town right under the nose of the law without so much as a smidge of proof."

"You want me to find out about prostitution?"

"Why not? You gave us the data on Zemric's extortion victims, the whereabouts of Arlene Holmes, and the number-running at the Toad and Pond."

"Um. I'll see what I can do." *I know just who to ask.*

When Jen arrived home, two men were measuring the concrete slab with metal tapes. The supervisor, Dave, recorded the details and checked his clipboard frequently.

Lee pulled the car along the sidewalk and put it in park. "I had a fun time at lunch. Let's do it again soon." He pulled her gently to him and kissed her. "I could stay a while?"-

"Thanks, but I want to speak with the construction manager, and you would be a distraction."

He slid out and opened her door. "Thank you for a fun lunch." He hopped back in and rolled down the window.

"Thanks for inviting me," she replied.

The car skittered a few bits of gravel as he left, and she headed to the construction site.

Dave nodded in agreement as Jen told him her ideas for the garage. "All within the parameters of the remodeling." He assured her. "We've got just about everything we need to start the building tomorrow."

Lunch with Lee and now smooth sailing with the garage rebuild energized Jen. When she entered the kitchen, a few spots floating in mid-air meant Rex was there. He greeted her with his wagging disembodied tail accompanied by a low woof.

She patted where his head should be and felt the softness of his fur. "I hope those construction guys don't hear the barking. They might ask questions."

"They don't hear him. Only the initiated, such as you and I, can hear his sounds."

"Miles!" She looked around the room but saw no sign of him.

"I beg your pardon," he said, taking shape. "I didn't mean to startle you. I thought you addressed me."

"That's okay. Can you appear in your uniform? Hat, too."

"Certainly." Within a second, Miles became solid, dressed in his navy-blue uniform with brass buttons.

Jen retrieved the photocopies of the newspapers from the drawer in the country French buffet. "Look at this." She pointed to the shield on the hat and then at the emblem on his jacket. "You wore these in the picture, but you don't have them now. And Lee's uniform included the two items."

Miles took off his hat and checked the brim. He looked down at his chest. "I can't explain it. The buttons are here, and the collar pins." Running his hand under the jacket, he added, "No belt buckle top. I haven't been able to materialize my gold pocket watch or diamond shirt studs, either. How odd. I must investigate this further."

"While you explore the mystery of the missing items, will you see if you can find out anything about a prostitution ring operating in Livonia?"

"Jennifer! Ferguson must have a hand in this. Such repellent activities should not concern a lady."

"Times have changed. Many subjects unacceptable in your day can be discussed freely in mixed company now."

"Times may have changed, but obviously, crimes have not. What do you wish me to do?"

"Can you can find out about the, uh, illegal activities I mentioned?"

"As you will. I may be able to uncover information since I have advantages not available in my earlier career. I will report what I find and shall be careful not to offend your dignity."

"My dignity will remain unharmed. Your detective skills will benefit Livonia, and I will manage to bear what information you uncover."

"Then I go forthwith. I take my leave, dear Jennifer."

"Yes, go forthwith."

Once again, Miles melted through the kitchen door. *I never get tired of seeing that.*

As the last of Miles disappeared, the phone rang. The

caller ID indicated Pam Caulfield.

"Jen," she said. "Can you please come over here? I really need to talk to someone."

Chapter Twenty-Seven

Jen cast a glance at the grandfather clock. "Now?"

"Would you mind? Do you know about panic attacks?"

"Of course. Had a few of them myself. What's going on? Are you all right?"

"I am now, but I don't want to be alone."

"I'll be over right away. How do I find your condo?"

Jen wrote the directions and took her purse from the kitchen counter. *Panic attack? Pam didn't seem the type.*

She found the place easily. The New Beginnings Condominium, brick with white trim, blended into the Victorian charm of the town. Jen pressed the unit number button at the entrance. Pam answered immediately as if she had been hovering over the intercom.

On the second floor, a door was cracked open with a figure pressed against the edge. She didn't need to read the door number. It would be 223.

Jen slowed as she reached the door. "You okay?"

Pam dropped her chin for a second, then looked up with tired eyes. "Not really. I'm so glad you're here."

"I brought something for you." Jen gave her an aluminum-wrapped piece of gingerbread.

"Thank you." Pam put the gift to her nose. "It smells good even in the foil."

"Old family recipe. Heavy on the spice. You'll love the frosting. Put enough rum in something, and it will taste good, right?"

"You're so nice. Not only do you come here last minute, you bring me a goodie. I'm so glad you moved to Livonia." Pam's lip quivered for a second. The words cracked, and the last two squeaked out, "You're my only friend."

"You know that isn't true. Anyone who meets you would want to be your friend. Is there anything I can do for you?"

"Just spend some time with me. I don't want to be alone."

"What happened?"

"Stress. I really don't want to think about it right now. I might get upset again. Can we talk about it later?"

"Sure. Do you have any games? Do you like Scrabble?"

Pam's lip twisted in a quick sneer. "Scrabble? No. I couldn't concentrate on anything like that. Maybe there's something on one of the movie channels." Pam checked the listing. "How about *Casablanca*? After that, *Jezebel*? If you don't mind watching the old ones not in color."

"I love both of them. Let's send out for Chinese. My treat."

Pam hugged Jen. "I knew you'd come through for me. Thanks."

Jen ordered from her cell, and twenty minutes later, the deliveryman buzzed the entrance. While Jen paid the check, Pam made tea.

Jen left the kitchen and looked around the condo. Italian Renaissance prints, surrounded in fancy gilt frames, hung on the living room walls. The vanilla-colored leather couch set featuring buttery soft grain, accented by pillows with an olive branch motif embroidered on the fabric, displayed the definite touch of a high-end decorator. Jen thought it odd there were no photos on the mantle, only ornate brass candlesticks with tall, slender tapers and a sleek clock.

Pam brought the food and tea out on a tray. They watched the classic movies and ate out of the little white containers with chopsticks, and by the time the credits rolled on the second film, Pam's panic had waned. She was relaxed and calmer.

"Look at the time," Jen said, pointing to the clock on the mantel. "I need to get home for my beauty sleep."

Pam smiled and walked her to the door. "Thanks again, Jen. I would have had a terrible night if you hadn't come over."

"My pleasure. Promise me if you have another bad spell, you'll call me."

"I promise."

When Jen entered her darkened home, she heard the reassuring sound of Rex's tail. Light revealed Rex's head moving to her. "Hello, Rexie-boy, you smart dog. You materialize what you want me to pet." She scratched his ears and patted his head. His hind end appeared. "Okay, a butt-scratch for you, too, old boy. I wonder how old you really are." After a few seconds of vigorous fur ruffling, Rex's head and tail returned to under the kitchen table and disappeared.

"Miles?"

Jen only heard the sound of the grandfather clock and the tinkling of the outside wind chimes. She checked the locks and went to bed.

Loud voices outside awakened Jen in the morning. She ran to the window. Two men in jeans and chambray work shirts conversed. A truck pulled next to the Town and Country, and two more men emerged. She recognized Dave as he put on his yellow hard hat. Jen dressed and went downstairs. While she made breakfast, she thought about Pam. *I wonder what stress caused her to have a panic attack? I guess she'll tell me when she's ready.* The best she could do for Pam would be to listen and keep her company.

Coffee in hand, she sat at the small kitchen table and sensed a presence. She checked the Quitcher Bitchin' sampler for movement. It didn't move, but Miles announced his attendance by knocking softly on the doorframe between the kitchen and living room.

When she turned her head to the sound, he became solid. "Good morning, Jennifer."

Miles wore trousers woven in a small gray checked pattern, the pants held in place by black suspenders. His white shirt sleeves rolled up to the elbows and showed muscled forearms.

"Hi, Miles. I've noticed you appear in full...um, flesh now."

"I've mastered the craft of materialization, expanding my

time. I have learned things."

She took a sip of coffee. "Ghost college?"

"Higher learning to be sure. A form of college, perhaps."

"You can materialize for longer periods. What else?"

"I have advanced. When first we met, I would be called a Floater."

"Like floating around on air?"

"Meaning not grounded in knowledge of my purpose. Staying in nether sleep, having low power and no motivation. The weakened state means vulnerability, easily taken over by the Dark Forces."

"Dark Forces." She shook her head. "Sounds scary."

"Quite. But because of you, I have changed."

"From Floater to what?"

Chapter Twenty-Eight

Miles took a step closer. "Soldier, one who learns, trains, and awaits orders."

"Who gives the orders?"

"I do not yet know."

"Soldier sounds better than Floater."

He nodded. "Better. Yes. Some souls remain Floaters. I see them roaming, asking directions, not knowing where they are or what they should do. Something needs to occur to shake them out of their oblivion. Like you did for me."

"Wow. I shook you out of oblivion? Go figure."

Miles bowed his head in a gesture of respect. "Perhaps I can return some of what you have done for me by giving you information regarding the subject which we discussed."

"The prostitution ring?"

"Yes."

"Well?"

"Quite a sophisticated set-up. One must admire the complexities and ingeniousness of the operation."

"Miles. Out with it."

"You may tell the police the activities transpire within the confines of the Currier School, all day, seven days a week, even on Sundays, with the solitary exception of Fox Hunt Week. The constables should go to the north wing, the guests' accommodations. There the police will find the miscreants engaging in illicit activities."

"The Currier School! Are you sure?"

"Of course. I traveled there myself to see. And I did see. All those years in Livonia and I get my first view of Currier after death. Ironic, no? The police will not be disappointed. They just have to burst through the doors."

She tilted her head. "Police can't do that anymore. They must have a warrant or reasonable suspicion."

"A warrant?"

"You were a cop. Don't you know about warrants?"

"Certainly. However, if the law enforcers already know felonious activities take place, why can't they just arrest the villains? Barge in and subjugate them."

"This may be difficult to understand, Miles, but if not done properly, the police might violate the rights of the perpetrators."

"What? The rights of perpetrators? Does this apply to all crimes or just the…aforementioned offense?"

"All crimes, even the worst murderer. More than one criminal has beaten the legal system because the police did not follow procedures."

Miles stomped his foot. "Incredible. What about the rights of the victims?"

"It defies logic, but our constitution extends rights to all people. You must know, innocent until proven guilty."

"I recognize the concept, but it sounds like the law has been turned around."

She downed the last of the coffee. "I can't debate this with you because I agree. However, for the police to legally enter the Currier, they need something more concrete in the way of proof, probable cause. How do the men find out about this service? How do they make the arrangements, and how — ?"

Miles put up his hand. "Go no further. I will obtain additional evidence, enough for modern-day procedural minutiae."

"Good. Then the prostitutes can be arrested."

"Jennifer, do you believe the fault lies in the women who sell themselves?"

"I don't know. I've not really thought about it."

"Whose crime surpasses? The one who sins for pay or the one who pays for sin?"

"Do you think the men who visit should be arrested as well?"

"I do, indeed, along with the financial backers and anyone associated with the business."

Jen ran her finger around the rim of the empty cup. "It's considered the oldest profession. Who does it hurt?"

"The crime alone hurts no one. It has to do with the corruption of society's infrastructure. I doubt anyone would complain about funds earned in this manner used to survive. However, money from prostitution usually supports a malevolent program which ultimately hurts the innocent."

"Lee—um, Detective Ferguson—said something similar. The criminal element exists like a huge spider web, and all the players resemble the insects bound with a web waiting for the spider to consume."

"Your detective friend can be eloquent. I'll give him that."

A loud noise distracted them from their conversation. The sound of a board hitting the cement and the subsequent swearing of the worker drew them to the back door.

Miles pulled back the curtain. "Those men should watch their tongues. They know a lady lives here."

"As long as they work, I'm pleased."

"I have been out there checking the site, watching the men begin their labors."

"Really?"

"While observing them in my invisible state, I have become greatly interested. They have a machine that drives nails and extremely effective electrical saws."

"I guess I take modern-day improvements for granted. You went outside to inspect the progress, eh? Does that explain your rolled shirt sleeves?"

"It does. When they took a break, I examined their tools. I can get dusty in my corporeal form."

"Ah, another mystery bites its dust!"

"You can be quite amusing, Jennifer. Speaking of mysteries, I have solved the enigma of my missing emblem and nameplate."

"And?"

"I can materialize only that which has been destroyed, meaning, somewhere, my cap shield, jacket insignia, belt buckle, and nameplate exist."

Interesting. Treasured items of a lost husband or father? I'm going to see if I can find out what happened to Miles's family after they left Livonia.

As Miles stood in the light of the kitchen window, his close-cropped fair hair glistened. The backlighting caused a halo-like glow emphasizing his face, notably the perfectly groomed mustache and sideburns.

He bent and stroked under the table while Rex materialized enough of his head for a good petting. "Good dog. Stay alert, my friend. Remember whom you protect, this woman, our ally, so much like a precious jewel."

Miles stood and took Jen's hand in both of his. He lightly bent her fingers and brushed them under his lips in a weightless kiss. "I take my leave of you, dear lady, and defer your safety to our most estimable fellow, Rex."

The phone rang, redirecting her attention, and when she again looked to where Miles had just been, no sign of him remained. She answered on the next ring.

"Jen," Pam's voice said. "You told me to call you if I needed to."

"Right," Jen answered.

"I need you. Please come over. I don't know what to do."

Putting all thoughts of research at the library away, she agreed to come to Pam immediately. This time Pam was waiting for Jen in the lobby. Pam held her lips tight in the elevator, but as soon as she entered the apartment, she let loose and cried, allowing tear floodgates to open fully.

Jen guided Pam to the couch. Magazines and newspapers lay strewn on the floor. A few dishes and glasses on small tables gave the feeling of distress and inattention.

"What's wrong?"

Chapter Twenty-Nine

Pam brushed the moisture from each eye with the back of her hand. "I wanted to tell you last night, but I couldn't. I don't know where to start. I'm in trouble."

Jen gave a quick shudder. "In trouble. The old-fashioned type of being in trouble, or...?"

"I pissed off the Speigals, which might be the same as being black-listed by the Mob."

Although Lee had said something similar, Jen shook her head. "The Mob? Here in Livonia?"

Pam looked to the floor. "Maybe not *the* Mob, but just as bad. It's hard to believe this charming little town, so full of refinement and elegance, has a dark side. But it does, and now I'm part of it."

"What do you mean? You'd better start at the beginning."

Pam's shoulders hiked up and then drooped down. She hung her head and slumped for a second. Sighing, she sat up straight. "All right. I'll tell you everything. In fact, I need to tell someone."

"Problems shared become problems halved, my grandmother used to say."

Pam looked to the kitchen. "I need wine. How about you?"

"It's not quite lunchtime, kind of early, but, sure, I'll have some."

Pam left the room for the kitchen and brought out two tulip-shaped stem glasses along with a huge jug of Gallo rosé. She twisted the metal cap and poured the pink wine.

Jen tasted. "Okay, take a few sips and then get this weight off your chest. Unload, girl."

Pam took a long draw. "I met Johnny at a New York bar. I don't know what happened. I don't usually like his type, but…. I spent the night with him and…. Oh, my God. Incredible. Something about him…I…." She took another drink. "I gave up my job as an accountant and came here. I didn't want to lose him, so I insisted we get married."

The room stayed quiet for a short time. "I thought I could help him, you know, better himself. Maybe I could be a good influence. Get him to go to school or learn a trade. He made money sometimes, but he didn't elaborate on his source. One of us needed regular work, so I got a Real Estate license. Johnny introduced me to the Speigals, who hired him for odd jobs, and they offered me a position at the real estate office. I bought this place and let Johnny play. And he played."

"With other women?"

"Only that bitch Arlene Holmes. I meant he played games—gambling, drinking, and drugs. He liked destructive entertainment, blowing things up, and messing with fire. I doubt if he would hurt anyone, but he'd torch a building for cash. When I found out he cheated with that, that, disgusting, ignorant, greasy…."

Jen didn't understand the words after greasy. Pam sobbed a few garbled epithets and wiped her nose with a tissue she pulled from her pocket.

"Well," Pam said in a slightly calmer tone, "I went nuts and divorced him. He promised to be good, but I wouldn't change my mind. Without me, he became an easy target for some of the seedier types." Pam took a long sip and locked eyes with Jen. "Like Sal Zemric."

Jen felt a prickle on the back of her neck. She rolled her bottom lip under her top teeth for a think-second, then said, "Who?"

Pam put down her glass. "Some awful man. I'm glad you don't know him. You're better off."

"Do you want to get back with Johnny?"

"Yes and no. I miss him. He wants me to get an expensive

lawyer and bail him out of jail. I think he's going to take the rap for a whole bunch of crimes. I know he's no angel, but he doesn't deserve that. I don't have the kind of money a good criminal attorney demands."

Jen sipped the wine. "Why don't the people he works for help him?"

"They will under a few conditions. They offered me a deal. I do some of the jobs Johnny would have done, and they'll take care of his defense expenses."

"What kind of things, Pam?"

"A lot of it involves picking up clients in Washington and driving them around."

"Where to?"

"To places of entertainment in Livonia. No details until I agree to do the work. They also want me to *run errands*. I'm not sure what that means either. I refused, absolutely not. Then Johnny called me. He said they had pictures of me and Johnny and then mentioned the Internet."

"So what? Why do you care if your photo goes on the Internet?"

"Jennifer. *Pictures.* Pictures Johnny took for fun. Just for us to look at. I think he sold them." Pam broke down sobbing and ran into the kitchen. She came back with a whole paper towel sheet.

"Pull yourself together, Pam. How bad can photos be? Nude pictures? Hardly anything to worry about. Call their bluff."

Pam went into the bedroom and returned a minute later with a plastic folder. She handed the folder to Jen.

Jen looked at the first photo of bodies intertwined and let the others slide onto the floor. "Oh. My. God," she said between breaths. "Jee-ma-nee Christmas." That particular expression handed down from the family had always been saved for the absolute worst situations.

Pam picked up the other photos and gave them to Jen one by one.

After letting the images of a man and woman pleasuring

each other take hold in her mind, Jen shook her head. "I don't suppose you want to go to the police with these? You know, claim blackmail."

"No one blackmailed me. An insinuation isn't a threat. I don't know what to do. What do you think? Suppose I picked up some gentlemen in Washington and brought them to Livonia for their business meetings or delivered them to places of entertainment. How bad do you think that would be? Mr. Speigal said all I have to do is use the navigation device and take them to the address on a letter. I don't even have to talk to anyone. What do you think?"

Places for entertainment. Although Jen had never seen the Currier school, she envisioned high iron gates decorated with a shield showing horses and a Latin motto. *The men receive acceptance letters to get into the Currier. I wonder where they get the letters.*

"What would *you* do?" Pam demanded.

Jen bit her lip for a thinking minute. "So, let me get this straight. Mr. Speigal, your boss at the real estate office, wants you to drive to Washington DC."

"In a Lincoln or Cadillac," Pam interrupted.

"You pick men up, where?"

"I think he said it's a private club that's been there since Abraham Lincoln ran for office. Someplace with the word 'League' in its title. I don't exactly remember, but the men are members."

"Okay. You bring them to Livonia and deliver them to an address in a letter, like a letter of reference?"

"Yes, but I don't think I'm supposed to know details. I just deliver the men, pick them back up, and take them to D.C. sometime later. Maybe days."

"So where do these gentlemen stay while they're in Livonia?"

"I think they stay where I take them. I didn't ask too many questions. I want to know what you would do. Advise me, Jen."

"A lawyer should give you advice. Look, if Johnny or you travel out of Maryland to do illegal business for the bad guys, the crimes become Federal offenses. Maybe Johnny knows something he can trade for immunity. You and he can get witness protection and live happily ever after."

Pam shook her head, her face hard, her eyes flinty. "You watch too many stupid detective stories on television. That's not real life. Besides, how would I know an honest lawyer, not on the take with the Speigals?"

"Well, then." Jen took a hefty sip. "Consult a priest. That's the best advice I can give. Lawyers or holy people. For both you and Johnny."

Pam stood and brushed at her dark wool pants. "Thanks for coming over and listening to me. I'll think about what you recommended. You won't tell anyone about the photos?"

Jen had been asked to leave. "I won't tell anyone about the pictures. Try not to worry." She started to say *something will come up* but thought better of it. "Call me if you need to talk again."

When she started her car, her mind raced. *Poor Pam. How could she be so stupid to pose for those pictures?* The secretary nudged her. "Keith talked you into some photos, remember?"

Jen remembered. They had just married, and she quit college to get a job. Wanting to look nice for an interview, she let a hairdresser, Mr. Jose, talk her into a new hairstyle. Showing Jen a photo and claiming she looked a lot like Princess Diana, Jose cut her hair in the Princess's style. To prove how much she resembled the royal lady, Jen took the picture home to show Keith.

"Let's get some real pictures," Keith said.

Okay, I posed for some snapshots, as Keith called them. I wouldn't want them on the Internet. Wow, next to Pam's photos, I look like Little Miss Muffet.

Jen thought back on the conversation with Pam. It didn't take too much of a leap to guess where the gentlemen would go for a few days in Livonia. With the exception of Fox Hunt Week, of course. *I hope Pam doesn't do any chauffeuring. Between Miles's investigation and the information about the letter and the Washington men's club called "League," around since Honest Abe, Lee might have enough to break up that business. Jeez, Pam might be up to her ears alongside Johnny.*

Jen had not had a single day of boredom, not one, since moving to this sleepy, classy little town. In her mind, Jen reviewed Pam's pictures. *I see how Pam became attracted to Johnny Caulfield. What a hunk. Johnny's back muscles perfectly rippled in the right places and smoothed out where the tan line met his hips.* She had to admit that his face had been the minor attraction in the photos. Johnny's face reminded her of Lee. She wondered how much of the rest of Lee looked like the captivating Mr. Caulfield. What six-pack undulated beneath Lee's shirt? Did he have a tan line meeting the white of his lower regions? The image of Johnny's lower regions popped up in her mind. *Popped up. Jee-man-nee Christmas!*

Her jeans grew tight in the crotch. She moved around in the bucket seat, hoping to ease the discomfort. Jen focused on the road ahead in time to see the light turn red and slammed the brake pedal. She looked around, feeling a wave of guilt for the screaming stop, and hoped no cops lurked in the vicinity.

Words and images surged through her mind. *Photos. I wonder if Keith still has those photos of us. Sooner or later, I'll hear from him again. Maybe I'll ask him to bring the photos.*

Jen laughed to herself, thinking how amusing those old photos would be. *Old photos. Miles.... Oh, my God, what if Miles saw those photos!*

Chapter Thirty

Once again, the next morning, men's voices in her yard brought her from her slumber. She made breakfast, noting Rex's presence, and wondered where Miles was. At mid-morning, Jen checked her watch. She had enough time to drop by the hospital to get her stitches removed and perhaps research for a few hours at the library. Maybe Library Millie or one of the minions would give instructions on how to do a genealogical search.

Going through the outpatient entryway, she checked in at the desk. Jen liked the friendly and informal way the hospital functioned. The day she had been discharged, the nurse told her to come back in a week or so and she didn't need an appointment. Within a half hour, she left, stitch-free, making the library her focus.

With no sign of Mildred Owings, Jen asked a welcoming young man at the checkout desk if someone could help her. A volunteer named Ralph quickly came to her aid and escorted her to a bank of computers. Jen strained to grasp the basics of the Ancestry program and frequently had to call Ralph to answer questions. Just about the time she became comfortable, an announcement stated the library closed early on Thursdays. Her luck. Would she forget what she had struggled to learn?

I need my own computer.

On her way home, she stopped at the Finger for chicken. When she came into the space left in her driveway, the garage rebuilders were energetically picking up the mess they had made in their rush to go home. In the kitchen, Rex howled a low song at her arrival, but she still saw no signs of Miles.

While finishing the last chicken wing, the phone chimed,

and, trying to remove enough grease from her fingers in order to pick up the cell, she almost missed the call.

Caller I.D. said, *Keith*.

"Hello, Keith."

"Hey, Jen. On the mend, I hope. I've been worried about you. How's your head? Everything okay there?"

"I appreciate your concern. I had the stitches out today. I have a question for you. You liked the laptop computer you bought right before we, um, split. Can you tell me the details? I need a computer. I've been using the library, but I need the convenience of my own."

"Look," Keith said. "I feel really bad about what happened between us. Let me buy you one, and I'll bring it over and set it up for you. No strings attached, just something I can do for treating you so abominably. Besides, we should talk about the kids. Chrissy called me the other day all upset about having a patient die under her care."

"I didn't think many people die while having their X-rays taken."

"Heart attack."

"I can see why she's upset. But why did Chrissy tell you? Why not me?"

"She said with all the excitement lately, you didn't need her problems."

"Really? Now my kids think they can't count on me?"

"Of course not. You're a good mother. You've taught them respect and concern. So, can I come over and bring you a computer? How about I bring Chrissy with me on Saturday? Maybe Bobby can squeeze a visit into his busy schedule."

The chance to see her children and get a new computer presented more temptation than Jen could resist. "Okay. I'll fix dinner for us."

"Mmm. Can I request roast pork loin with the browned potatoes?"

"Sure. I haven't had that myself for a long time. Sounds good. Bring wine."

"How about the wine we bought from Beaune last year?"

"Great." She smiled to herself. Miss Boobs-from-Ukraine hadn't been offered the high-class vintage after all.

Later that afternoon, as Rex thumped his tail against the chair leg, Miles's cleared his voice in a kind of "Ahem."

"Hello, Miles."

He walked to the table and gave a nodding bow. "Jennifer."

Jen pushed the chair out with her foot.

Miles sat. "I have more information about the illicit affairs at the Currier."

"Excellent! Do tell."

"Difficult as it may seem, a number of students, not the class of ladies one expects to have enrolled at the Currier, serve as the dispensers of pleasure to wealthy, and sometimes famous, gentlemen. The person in charge, I knew the title as Madam, surprisingly turns out to be the headmistress named Stella Anderson. The gentlemen arrive in long black shiny automobiles. I know not from where. The length of stay varies for each guest, but I do not know the remuneration details."

Jen nodded. "I think I have a few of the missing pieces. A gentleman's club in Washington, D.C., with the word 'League' in the title, may be the business center of the operation."

"The League of Learned Lawmakers?"

"That might be it. Were you a member?"

Miles sat up straight and gave a haughty sniff. "I doubt my pedigree would have been good enough to gain entrance into the humidor room at the League."

"What's that?"

"That would be a room with wooden lockers for each member to store his private selection of cigars and pipe tobaccos. Each cabinet had the owner's name engraved on a brass plate, and when the member retired to the smoking parlor, he ordered an attendant to fetch his desired smoke. Ah, the thought of a fine Cuban brings back memories."

"You smoked cigars?"

Miles nodded. "And a pipe. Perhaps you would be good

enough to acquire a Cuban for me?"

"I don't think it's legal."

"Cigar smoking?"

"Not the cigar smoking. The United States has an embargo against Cuba since that country went Communist."

"How interesting. I recall when the United States under President McKinley rallied millions of dollars to help the insurgents withdraw from Spain, especially after those dastardly Spaniards blew up the *Maine*."

Jen shook her head. "Spain didn't really do that. The ship exploded from the ammunition cargo."

"Ah, now. I find that truly remarkable. We make a good team. I give you information, and you supply me with significant facts."

"I think what you give me means a whole lot more to society, Miles."

"To Serve and Protect." He sighed. "No Cuban cigars. Such a pity. I wonder if the tobacco blend I enjoyed in my pipe is still available."

"What do you mean by blend?"

"Ah, Golden Cavendish heavy with cherry and vanilla, imported from Denmark. Virginia liked to watch the smoke feather from the bowl. She called them fingers of smoke curling in the air. And she enjoyed the aroma."

"You could smoke a pipe now?"

Miles leaned in closer. "In my full form, I may enjoy all of the stimuli of a living man."

Jen blinked a few times, digesting the disclosure. "I'll see if I can find some Cavendish for you."

"Perhaps you would enjoy the scent as well."

The secretary nudged Jen. "And enjoy explaining the scent to your guests, like Lee."

"I wonder if my sons liked smoking when they matured," Miles said.

Jen thought about her library mission of researching the Hampton boys. "Miles, after the explosion, do you remember anything happening here in the house with your family?"

"I don't know how long I had been dead, but I awoke to cello music, a sad Bach. I saw Jenny playing, her fingers moving, pressing the strings hard against the fingerboard, and she sawed the bow like a blade. Her tears splashed, and I so wished to comfort her, but I knew not how to move or touch. I was but air and could not speak. Furious, I wanted to scream, to strike something, to let her know I stood next to her."

"I'm sorry," Jen said.

"The frustration became so unbearable I dissolved until another day when I awoke and heard soft music. I still couldn't affect my surroundings. I had no control over my awakenings or movement. The boys were older. Then I saw *him*, her suitor, Damon Cisco, my best friend in life. By the time I had mastered the skills I needed to reach her, they left. My boys, my wife...I know not where they went. In my despair, I dissolved and nether slept until I heard noises in the house from each successive owner. My powers have gradually strengthened since you, Jennifer, brought me into fullness."

"Fullness. You can be so creative with your words."

"You have given me back my *raison d'etre*. Thank you for the opportunity to practice my career skills."

"By the way, Miles, how did you get the information on the Currier?"

"The same way I have learned many things since you have awakened my being. I asked Brad."

From the side of the house, a voice yelled, "Son-of-a-fucking-bitch!"

Chapter Thirty-One

Miles slammed the tabletop. "Profanity! I'll not have it!" He ran to the kitchen window.

Jen joined him. Near the construction site, four workers bent over a kneeling man, wincing in pain and clutching his lower leg.

"I'll see what happened." Jen went outside and approached Dave, who bent over the workman.

He turned to Jen. "A nail from the air gun hit his leg. I think we better get him to the hospital. I'll take him in my truck. I know it's early, but do you mind if I give the rest of the day off to the other men?"

"No problem," Jen agreed, and the work ended for the day.

When she returned to the kitchen, Miles no longer sat there and did not answer her call, but the thumps under the table meant she still had at least one companion. She took her cell phone from its charger and sat on the chair. Feeling around with her foot under the table, she made contact with fur. "Good boy, Rexie."

Armed with her new Currier information, she called Lee.

"Ferguson," he said.

"Lee, I have something you might want to hear."

"Terrific. Shoot."

"I have information, but I'll squeeze a lunch out of you before I deliver. A lunch without Ash Grainger."

"Sounds like a business lunch. Why can't Ash be there?"

"My information, my terms, buddy."

"Okay," he said. "But you don't need to squeeze it out of

me. I'll do lunch any time or dinner, and I'd especially love to eat breakfast—"

"Tomorrow, then?"

"Breakfast? That would mean—"

"Lunch, you bad boy."

"Aw, come on now. Don't you like a bad boy once in a while?"

She kept quiet. Words that could change everything hovered on the tip of her tongue.

"Fine, then," he said with mock exasperation. "I'll pick you up promptly at twelve. Alone."

She called Dave for an update on the injured workman, and he assured her the fellow would be fine, only requiring a bandage, a tetanus shot, and a few pain pills.

Jen's mood shifted. The workman would recover. Keith had promised her a computer. She would soon see her daughter, Chrissy. Miles had delivered valuable information. And she was scheduled to have lunch with Lee on Friday.

She searched the refrigerator for dinner. She had all the ingredients for meatloaf, and she hadn't made that dish for a long time. She would even peel a few potatoes for real mashed. How could her day get better? Maybe she should invite Pam over. As the meat baked, Jen called her.

"How ya doing?" Jen asked.

"Better, thanks."

"Would you like to have dinner with me? It's just meatloaf, but—"

"No. I'm going to do my hair tonight. I think I saw a few grays. Can't have that."

"I yank mine. Don't have enough strands to color, not yet."

They both laughed. Pam's tone sounded like she had taken a turn for the good.

"Okay then, if you change your mind, just pop over. It's pretty quiet here. One of the men working on my garage rebuild got hurt, but they'll be finished soon. Then they can start my basement."

Pam's voice became more serious. "Your basement? What do you have planned for that?"

"Cement blocks and a poured floor. In other words, a real basement."

"Sounds great. Well, have a nice night. I'll see you later — without any gray hair!"

Later Jen took her dinner into the living room. With no sign of Miles, she watched television until eleven. When she said goodnight to Rex and got ready to retire, her spectral roommate still remained unseen and quiet since the afternoon.

That night, Jen tossed and turned. She moaned and thrashed against the blanket and grasped the pillows. Half awake, she heard the knock at her bedroom door. "Jennifer! Jennifer! May I come in?"

"Yes," she said in a strained cry.

Miles walked through the door, materializing as he approached. He snapped on the bedside light. Miles pushed the second pillow behind her back and, moving the blanket aside, he sat on the edge of the bed. He took her hands in his. "I heard you call out. What is wrong? What is it? Tell me."

"I had a bad dream." She sucked in a staccato breath. "It was so scary, so awful."

"There, there," Miles soothed. "What happened in your dream?"

"I don't want to talk about it."

"If you describe the fear, you can face it, and it won't bother you again."

Her mother had advised the same thing years ago. "Awful, sooty smoke-fingers surrounded this house. They tried to get into the windows and doors and the chimney too. I could see it outside, but then I hid under the covers so they couldn't touch me. Since the fingers couldn't come in, they started to scream and shriek for me to open the doors."

Miles's voice dropped a register. "Dark Forces. But they *can't* hurt you. The blessed house and Rex keep them at bay."

"Dark Forces? For real? Not a dream?"

"You dream because the Dark Forces have influence in this town. For some reason, they want into our house."

"Why?"

"I don't know. I search constantly for the answers. You must not let it affect you. The good forces battle the evil for you and others who have no stake in the conflict." Miles brushed an errant tress from Jen's face and stroked it behind her ear. "Lie down and return to your slumber. Nothing will hurt you. Not while I stay my watch."

Jen reached to the side table and broke a Xanax in half.

Miles stilled her hand before it reached her mouth. "You truly need that?"

"It will help me sleep."

"Very well." Miles gave her the glass of water she kept on the table.

After she took the pill, Miles moved a chair across the room. She turned off the light and lay back. Within a few minutes, she drifted off to sleep.

After falling asleep for the second time, her dreams after the nightmare made her feel protected and warm, like a comforting blanket cradling her with strength. She was wrapped in shielded security, so the horror of the sooty fingers no longer threatened her safety.

Chapter Thirty-Two

The next morning Jen limited her breakfast to coffee and looked forward to lunch with Lee. The eleven o'clock debate began in the bedroom closet. *Something a little slinky? Soft and silky? Or maybe basic black.* Jen pushed laden hangers back and forth until the mental light turned on. *My royal blue sheath and red scarf held with a gold mermaid pin. Perfect! Dark stockings, low Bruno Magli pumps.* She went to the bathroom mirror, where she lined up her make-up in order of its use. *Just a touch of blue eye shadow for the dress and red lipstick to match the scarf.*

At twelve, Lee knocked, and when she opened to door, he stepped back with raised eyebrows. "Gorgeous! Oh, man, aren't you something? And ready on time."

"I can say the same for you. Prompt."

"You'll love this place we're going. Great food, great décor."

As they drove through town, Jen pointed to a small store. "That's a tobacconist!"

"Why would you be interested in that?"

"I believe I would like to try a blend of pipe tobacco." She recited the ingredients.

"If you wish to partake of tobacco, don't forget my name — Burleigh."

"What does that smell like?"

He touched his neck. "Help yourself to a whiff."

She strained the seatbelt to put her nose close to his shoulder. *Skin perfume.* "Nice."

"Here we are." Lee pulled the car into the parking lot of a diner. From the outside, it appeared as common as any diner Jen had seen before. The sign over the door read *Salvador Deli,* which didn't mean anything to her until she went in and saw Dali prints hanging on the walls. As they waited to be seated, the parody of Dali's *The Persistence of Time* affixed to the cash register made her laugh because instead of melting clocks and watches, the melting objects were dollar bills, coins, and credit cards.

The menus sat between the tall colorful salt and pepper shakers on the tabletop. She studied the sandwich names and smiled. Each sandwich made fun of a notable artist.

"How's the Rubens Sandwich?" Jen asked.

"Good," he said. "I recommend the Eggplant Sub, though. See," he pointed to the title on the card. "It's called Eggplant De-gas."

"I'll steer clear of that one, then. I prefer food with no gas. How many of these funky-named restaurants does Livonia have?"

"It started with The Finger. You know about that story, right?"

She nodded.

"And then Struttman opened the Best of the Wurst. After that, most of the restaurants had to keep up with being different."

"Are there any regular ones with ordinary names?"

"Yep, but I'm trying to impress you. How am I doing?"

Warmth tingled down her neck as she looked into his slate-blue eyes. "Just fine."

The waitress brought small plates and a metal stand with three bowls containing sweet pickles, dill pickles, and coleslaw, plus a basket of fresh rolls. They each ordered Rubens.

Lee stabbed two small dill pickles from one of the bowls and put them on Jen's plate. "Try these. Best I've ever tasted."

She bit into one of them. "You're right!" After finishing the gherkin, she said, "I'm glad Grainger's not here. I don't think he likes me."

Lee took a bite out of his pickle.

"You aren't going to challenge my statement?"

He took another bite, a big one.

"What's Grainger got against me?"

"Let's just enjoy our lunch."

Jen gritted her teeth. "What's his problem?"

"I don't want to go into this."

"Why not?" She stared at him.

"Grainger's a worry wart. He warns me about getting involved with you. Frequently."

Jen frowned. "What does he warn you about?"

"He thinks you're a nut case."

"Why does he think that?"

Jen forced her head to nod. Maybe she didn't want to hear it. Yes. She did.

"Ash has done some...digging. Your mother was hospitalized in an institution for six months because she heard voices."

She gasped and clasped her hand to her throat.

"And your father did some time for conning."

"My mother had a head injury and suffered from hallucinations. My father lost a huge investment. In trying to recuperate his loss, he got into hot water working with a con artist. My dad didn't even know what was going on but took the fall for it anyway."

"I'm glad you're not claiming that a ghost helps you. But honey, you have to admit that if your mother heard voices, you might see or hear things as well."

Jen's chest rose and fell. Her lips parted, and she gained control. "Grainger shouldn't have snooped. It's illegal to dig into other people's lives."

"It's not illegal."

"It should be."

"Probably should. I'm sorry, but on the other hand, Ash believes you have strong psychic abilities and thinks that should be enough reason for me to steer clear of a relationship."

She sat straight and looked Lee in the eye. "Screw Grainger."

Lee smiled. "Why him and not me?"

"Not the right time for a joke, Lee."

"Wrong. It's the perfect time for one."

"I'm not a bad person."

"I know that. Don't worry. It doesn't matter what Grainger thinks, anyway. It's what I feel that counts."

"You trust me, don't you?"

They stopped talking while the waitress placed their plates on the table.

When she left, Jen ignored her food. "Well? You trust me, right?"

"Well?" Jen said, her voice pitched higher.

"You must know how I feel about you."

"In spite of Grainger?"

"In spite of everything that could ever happen in the universe."

"You don't think I'm crazy? A nut job?"

"I think you're adorable, and I don't care about any of the rest." He pointed to her sandwich. "Try it. Delicious."

After eating half of his sandwich, Lee moved his plate aside. "Okay, we've dispensed with the niceties. Tell me what you know."

Anything in the universe. A smile crossed her lips. She couldn't help it. "Ah, the old *tell me ze plans routine*, eh?"

"Exactly. Now spill."

Jen lowered her voice and leaned toward him. "The hookers work out of the Currier School—"

"What the fuck!" Lee shouted, causing everyone in the diner to look at them with disapproving frowns.

Jen leaned forward and lowered her voice. "Yep. The madam is the headmistress, Stella Anderson. The customers belong to a men's club in D.C. that has been around since the Civil War and may be called the League of Learned Lawmakers."

Lee swiped his hand across his mouth. "I've heard of that club. You must be kidding."

"Let me finish. Members who want services receive a letter of recommendation and get taken by limousine to the Currier.

The ladies of the evening, also bona fide students, make their client's dreams come true."

He narrowed his eyes at Jen. "You're sure?"

"Pretty sure. I trust my sources."

"Sources? I thought it was all up here?" He tapped his forehead. "Name your other sources."

"No. You wouldn't believe me anyway."

Lee tilted his head and stared for a moment but remained silent.

After waiting several seconds, Jen asked, "Are you going to check out the men's club?"

"Yeah, that's where we'll start. Damn! The Currier! Sweetness, I hope your information works out. You're really something." Lee looked at his sandwich. "I may have to get a doggy bag. I'm not sure I can eat right now. The Currier School!"

"I'm hungry, and you," she said firmly, "are going to take time to eat, too."

"Yes, ma'am, my favorite and most lovely psychic darling!"

After lunch, Lee drove her home. He hardly talked in the car, only answering her questions with one-word replies. With a quick peck on the cheek at her door, he hurried to the car and peeled off, making the workmen stop their activities as he squealed the tires.

Chapter Thirty-Three

Jen entered a quiet and empty house—Miles still hadn't returned. She spent the remainder of the day cleaning and preparing for her dinner on Saturday.

Keith arrived around ten the next morning with both of their kids, Chrissy and Bobby. Chrissy had cut her honey-colored hair short, and Bobby looked more like Keith than Jen remembered. After some initial awkwardness, the four of them lapsed into their familiar routines, just like in the old days. Chrissy and Jen made dinner together. Bobby and Keith set up the computer and installed the software. With the computer task completed, the two men watched NASCAR racing, switching to various sports shows during the commercials or the dull racing moments.

Chrissy pulled a kitchen chair from the small table and sat down, leaning her elbows on the scratched top. "Might you and Dad work this thing out?"

"No, sweetie. We talk and get along, but I don't want to go back. For the first time in my life, I have total control. You can't appreciate the freedom because you already have it, but I didn't until your dad kicked me out of the nest. Now I enjoy my life. Don't you love my place?"

"It's uber-cool. Mom, do you have a boyfriend?"

Jen hesitated. "Do you?"

"Okay." Chrissy laughed. "I'll show you mine if you show me yours."

"Christine Marie!"

"So...do you have a boyfriend?" Chrissy repeated with raised eyebrows.

Jen turned back to wrapping potatoes in buttered foil.

"Ah ha! You do have a boyfriend. Does Dad know? Even though I love him, I admit he wants things his way and doesn't like to lose."

Jen looked at her daughter and smiled. "You really have grown up, my little girl."

"Yep. And when Dad did his *thing*, I saw life in a new way. By the way, you handled it really well, Mom. I admire you for it."

"Thank you for saying that."

"You're welcome. You haven't become bitter or bitchy, but you are still my fun and wacky mom, like always."

Jen rolled her eyes. "Oh, yeah, the wacky component. I've been told that, too."

"Never change. It sets you apart."

"Not too far apart, I hope."

Chrissy shook her head. "Yep! That's my mom."

Chrissy didn't press for the boyfriend report, nor did she elaborate on her own relationships.

Jen enjoyed the rest of the day, including dinner with the exquisite wine. When Chrissy told Keith she had an early class in the morning, he agreed to leave.

At the front door, after Jen hugged her daughter and son, Keith said, "You kids wait in the car, okay? I want a word with your mother."

Bobby and Chrissy waved as they headed to their father's car.

Keith closed the door and, putting his hand on her shoulders, turned Jen to face him. "I had a wonderful day, honey. Thanks. The dinner was marvelous, as always. Look. Come to Baltimore next weekend. Stay with me."

"What?"

"Come on. We'll go shopping, carte blanche. You know, the Cashmere Store? I'll take you dancing. You love to dance."

"Keith!"

"Seriously." He touched her collar and ran his finger

around it, then raked his hand through her hair. "I'm betting you've got some horns growing up here. I know my horns need trimming."

"You have a lot of nerve," Jen said, clenching her teeth.

"Oh, baby. I know you. You must be higgly-jiggly by now. Couldn't you use a nice weekend of shopping, dancing, and you-know-what?"

"Look, don't assume just because *you're* horny—"

"Jen-doll, I'm pretty sure you're horny, too. We can take care of that problem quite nicely."

"Unbelievable! You just ruined the nice day we had together."

"Oh, come on, now. Listen, if you change your mind—"

"Good night, Keith. Thank you for the computer and for saving the good bottle of wine." She pulled back as he tried to kiss her.

"Hey, just a kiss on the cheek, Jen. How can that hurt?"

Jen put her cheek towards him. "Be careful on the drive home."

"See, you care about me."

"I care about your passengers, too."

Keith nodded and left.

Oh, God, I am needy, and Keith knew. So, how long has it been? She recalled lovemaking with Keith and remembered the details. Instantly the image of Johnny Caulfield's photos came to mind, especially the region below his waist. She pictured Keith in comparison and snickered. Keith was *not* Johnny Caulfield!

"Something amuses you?"

She turned around at the familiar voice. "Maybe. How long have you been home?"

"The better part of the day. You have a lovely daughter."

"Thank you. Eavesdropping?"

"In my position, it can be difficult to avoid. Most of the time, I stayed upstairs with Rex to permit your privacy."

"Thank you. You liked Chrissy. How about Bobby?"

"Of course. He appears to be a polite young man. You did

a good job in their upbringing. In spite of the father."

"Not impressed with Keith, I see."

"Not any more than I fancy Detective Ferguson. My dear Jennifer, I have a question for you."

"Yes?"

"Define horny."

Chapter Thirty-Four

"You know what, Miles? I'm awfully tired." Jen stretched her arms and moved her head from side to side. "I think I'll just go to bed." As she headed up the stairs, she said, "You'll be here tonight?"

"I will. Rex and I maintain our guard."

"Thank you."

Jen fell asleep without the aid of medicine. It had been a long day, and when her head hit the pillow, she dozed off immediately.

With ten hours of sleep, she awoke rested and clear-minded. After coffee, she took her purse and drove into town, hoping the small stores in Livonia were open on Sundays. When she returned to the kitchen, Miles materialized at the small table.

"Perfect," Jen said. "I have something for you." She handed him a gold foil box.

"A gift? For me?" Miles removed a smooth brown pipe and a small bag of tobacco.

"I hope that's the blend."

"How splendid. I am touched by your thoughtfulness." He pinched a bit of the thin leaves, put them to his nose, and nodded. "Yes!" He packed a small wad into the pipe's bowl. Jen demonstrated the Zippo lighter. He pulled on the mouthpiece until smoke curled around his face.

"That smells nice," Jen said. "Much better than nasty old cigars."

"You don't mind this?" Miles tapped the bowl.

"Within limits."

"Understood." Miles moved his chair to an open window.

Miles looked complete with his white shirt and gray checked pants, the wide mustache and the way he held his pipe against his cheek, like an old habit.

"I heard the man offer to take you dancing last night. What kind of dancing do you enjoy? Waltzes? Mazurkas? Polkas? Two Step?"

Jen covered her mouth to hide the grin. "None of those, actually. I'm thinking of Boogie, the Pony, or just slow dancing."

"I am at a disadvantage regarding those names."

"Oh, I couldn't live with myself if I didn't show you how dance has evolved since Queen Vicky's day." Jen waved him into the living room and turned on the XM radio. She searched until the seventies and eighties music played.

Miles tamped out his pipe.

"Keep your pipe and tobacco in the buffet," Jen said. "The drawer where I found your photo seems fitting."

By the time Miles stowed his gifts, Jen was moving about the room shaking her hips and swaying to the beat. She glided toward him with arms outstretched.

"Mr. Hampton, may I have this dance?"

Miles put his right arm over his abdomen and his left in the back and bowed stiffly. Jen jiggled and stepped lithely around him as he stood in place. He tried to copy a few of her moves but shook his head at the failure.

"I'm afraid my inability to perform modern dance insults my dignity."

"Nonsense, Mr. Hampton. When one dances the pony, one has no dignity."

Miles bobbed his head and tried to learn the music's tempo. "I'm helpless, indeed. This is impossible."

"Go for it, Miles!"

"You challenge me? Force me to display my cowardice?"

"Fear has nothing to do with it. Move to the beat!"

"Perhaps I should take a different approach."

"Try this," she said. The oldie music changed into a slow dance. Jen moved closer and put his right hand on her shoulder and the left on her waist. "Here's your new approach. I know you can do this. Travel around slowly. Glide."

Miles relaxed and stepped gracefully. "I am pleased to have the attention of my fair companion."

"No talking. Concentrate. Although I think what you just said was probably cool."

"Do you hear something?" Miles asked.

Over the music, the sound of the front doorbell chimed. Miles disappeared as Jen ran to turn down the radio. Coming to the door, she looked out the window and saw Lee standing on the front steps. Jen opened the door.

"What were you doing?"

"Dancing," she said, holding the door wide.

Lee stepped inside the foyer. "Who were you dancing with?"

Jen shut the door with more force than necessary. "Do you see anyone else here?"

He lifted his nose in the air and sniffed. "Were you smoking a pipe? You weren't kidding about wanting to buy tobacco, were you?"

"Did you ever hear of calling before coming over?"

Lee scratched his nose. "Are we having our second fight? Besides, do I have to call first? I was in the area and thought I'd check on you. I don't want any more fires or assaults." He leaned toward her and gave her a quick kiss. "Especially to you. Remember what I said about anything that happens in the universe?"

"I remember. You can come over whenever you like. But it wouldn't hurt to call first."

Lee smiled. "So, you like dancing? There's a place in Union Town, about thirty miles from here. They have dancing every Sunday night. Want to go there tonight? I haven't danced since Grainger's wedding."

"Okay. What's the dress code?"

"Beer and popcorn." Lee kissed her on the cheek. "See you at seven."

When Lee's car left the driveway, Miles appeared. "Perhaps I can join you at that ballroom now that I have the basics."

"No way. Don't you dare."

"Very well. I bend to your command."

"You'd better." Her stomach growled. "I'm hungry for lunch. I think I'll make a salad."

Jen assembled items and placed them next to her wooden cutting board. As she struggled to cut a ripe tomato, Miles appeared at her side.

He shook his head. "A dull knife is an enemy. Always keep your blades honed."

"I'm not good at knife-sharpening. Keith used to do it for me."

Miles looked in the utensil drawer and took out the sharpener. "It's my turn to teach. Observe. Hold the handle tightly and bring the knife over the rod." He stroked the blade over the cylindrical sharpener. "You try."

Jen rubbed the blade up and down.

"How you dishonor your blade. However, no fine thing can be made without toil. Imagine the sharpener as an onion from which you slice a fine portion. Push the blade away and picture the slice. Now do the same in the opposite direction."

"I don't know what you're talking about."

Miles stepped behind her. He put the knife in her right hand and the sharpener in her left and, with his arms over hers, showed her the motion to achieve an edge.

Jen inhaled. Miles smelled of leather and tobacco. His warmth brushed against her neck. The firm muscles of his chest pressed into her. She pushed her shoulders back. He tightened his grip on her knife hand and pushed slightly forward.

Something else pressed against her backside.

Chapter Thirty-Five

Jen breathed in small gulps. "Uh…Miles?"

"Forgive me." He dropped the knife and sharpener on the counter, turned, and left the house through the back entrance.

She stood motionless for a moment, then moved to the kitchen table, no longer interested in a salad. The quiet of the house put her on edge. *I need something to do.* She ran through some options. Watch TV. No. Listen to the radio. Definitely not. Do laundry. Not enough for a full load. Bake a cake. No, she wasn't in the mood for cooking. Nothing appealed to her. As she mentally ticked off what she wouldn't do, Rex's tail hit her shin. He banged it harder and faster. Then he let out a mournful howl. It made the hair on her neck stand.

"Rex! Stop that."

The dog took solid form and ran to the front door. He howled, but the mournful sound turned into a happy chord. Between the notes of the dog song, Jen heard a voice, and it was getting closer.

A young voice called. "Lad! Lad, boy, where are you?"

Jen rushed to the front door and opened it. A thin, small boy approached her front porch. He carried a piece of rope in one hand.

"Lad!" he said, and the dog bounded out to him.

The boy looked up at Jen. "Hello. You been keeping Lad for me, ma'am?"

"We call him Rex. Who are you?"

"Oh," the boy said, and hung his head. "My bad manners." The child's clothes were soiled and torn. "I'm Billy Parker. Me and Lad was borned the same day. We always stayed together. I been looking for him for a long time now.

"Where are you from, Billy?"

"Johnstown, Pennsylvania. The dam broke, and me and Lad got separated in the flood water."

"When was that?"

"On our sixth birthday, May 31, 1889. I couldn't cross over without him. So, I been wandering around looking everywhere. I knew I was getting close."

"You've been searching for over a hundred and thirty years?"

"I guess so, ma'am. But now we can go where we're supposed to be." Billy bent down and started to tie the end of his rope to the piece still on his dog's neck.

"Wait a minute. Do you know what's on the other side?"

"Sure, I do. Come on, Lad.

"Billy! Tell me."

"Well," he began and pulled the knot tight. "You see...." He picked up the lead. The boy and his dog disappeared.

Jen closed the door. A feeling akin to numbness overtook her, and she sat down hard on the couch. She jumped when the phone rang.

"Hey, baby. I'm calling to thank you for dinner and to reciprocate with a good dinner — in Baltimore."

Jen let out a long sigh loud enough to carry over the phone.

When she didn't answer, Keith also sighed. "Okay. I got the message. But keep it in mind. Bye."

Jen crumpled on the couch. The ticking grandfather clock with its pendulum sounded like the swishing of a blade reminiscent of Poe. Chimes hanging from the tree outside no longer tinkled but tolled. The house's atmosphere became tomb-like, eerie.

Jen trudged upstairs, lay down on the bed, and closed her eyes. *A ghost and I danced today, then I gave him a woody for the first time in over a hundred years. A boy who died in a horrific natural disaster arrives to take his pet, my companion guard dog, into the afterlife with him. To top it off, my philandering ex-husband wants me to go to Baltimore for a booty call. Can things get any worse?*

"Things won't get worse if you don't let it." the secretary said. "You need the music, the activity, and the company."

Jen napped, and when she awoke, it was five-thirty. The house had not changed its sensation of silent emptiness.

She sorted through the closet. "Beer and popcorn attire. Okay, gray linen pants and a black sweater."

Once dressed and satisfied with her makeup and hair, she waited downstairs at the small kitchen table with a cup of tea. She moved her foot around underneath. No Rex. A ripple of sadness for the dog made her choke on the next sip of Darjeeling. Rex had been with her for a short time, but long enough for her to love him and depend on his protection. *Jeez, from what?* More than that, wagging his disembodied tail fulfilled her need for pet company. Was Miles right about Rex? Did his status as an Innocent make him so powerful even the most evil spirits avoided his environs? What would that mean for her and this house now?

She tidied the kitchen, checking several times for an indication of Miles's return. Keeping busy helped shake the goosey feeling of being alone in the empty house.

Lee arrived on time, dressed in jeans and a red print cowboy shirt.

"Is this your Clint Eastwood look?" Jen said when she opened the door.

"Yes, ma'am," Lee drawled as he stepped inside. "I'll have to check my six guns at the dance hall door."

She laughed. The day had been a series of ups and downs, and she wished she could tell him about Miles, Rex, Billy Parker, Keith, and the Dark Forces she had been warned about. How would this man, who claimed to care, react to her extraordinary life? Considering Ash Grainger's intrusive scrutiny of her, she decided now was not the time for show and tell.

"You okay?" Lee asked. "I hope our discussion about Grainger didn't upset you too much."

Why did he bring that up? It didn't matter. She still stung from Grainger's actions and snorted a puff of air. "Upset me? Of course not. Why should snooping and meddling in my family's troubles bother me? Everyone loves having their dirty laundry aired."

"Don't let it get to you."

"As long as it doesn't affect you."

"Nope. It's too late to prevent me from being caught up in your life."

"What does that mean?"

He pulled her close and whispered in her ear, "It means I love you."

"I'm not ready for that, Lee," Jennifer said.

"I know. I'm not either, but *because* I'm trained to see clues and draw conclusions, I can't deny my feelings. I'm going to be careful. I screwed up one relationship. I don't want it to ruin this one, too."

Jen reached for his hand. Neither spoke the rest of the way to Union Town.

The sign on the building Lee pulled into said: *Dance Hall.* Its style resembled an old-time Western Saloon. Painted on the wall was a saloon girl with her gloved arm pointing to the entrance.

"Now I see why you're wearing the Western get-up."

"It's a Christmas gift from Uncle Paul." Lee reached into his pocket and took out a wad of dollar bills.

"Are you trying to impress me with your wealth?"

"Not unless you're impressed with singles. The DJ charges a dollar per request. No dollars, no music. I plan on a lot of slow dances. The place requests small bills, so I came prepared." He removed two tens from the stack. "For the cover charge."

The entrance consisted of two large swinging doors faced with metal. Jen thought it must be aluminum because the texture showed machine designs in circles, like the dashboard of her father's antique Studebaker. At eye level, each door had an egg-shaped glass window placed at an angle.

Lee pushed one door forward.

She stepped through. "I love these doors!"

"Me, too," he said, increasing his volume to compensate for the loud music from slightly off-register speakers.

It took a few seconds for Jen's eyes to adjust to the dark. Lee paid the cover charge to the hostess waiting at a stand.

The smell of beer and popcorn greeted her, obviously the reason for Lee's dress code description. Self-serve popcorn machines flanked the funky doorway. Neon beer signs made up the reigning décor, doubling as the libation menu. At one side of the room stood a concession stand. As her eyes adjusted to the dim lighting, she silently read the food offerings in big lettering.

Music reverberated from the walls as Lee looked around to select a table. He chose one edging the parquet wood flooring half-filled with dancing couples.

Lee held her chair, and Jen sat. He leaned toward her. "What would you like to eat? They've got burgers, chili dogs, pizza slices, and chicken nuggets. The potato choices are French fries and chips."

"Nuggets, uhm, honey mustard," she said. "And chips, with a Miller Light."

He left and placed the order at the stand. When he returned, he put a number card on the table to alert the server. "Excuse me," Lee said, taking out his wad of singles. "I need to pay the piper."

He approached the DJ, who handed Lee a booklet. After a few minutes of reading, Lee selected and paid for his requests. Just as he returned to the table, a waitress brought their tray. They had enough time to eat before Lee's music choices played. He rose and scooted out her chair, extended his hand, and led her onto the dance floor. One slow song after another kept them close, with small breaks to eat and drink. Dancing with Lee was more of a moveable embrace than exercise to music. Jen relaxed into his arms. Their motion, slow and close together, made them each half of a single, undulating unit.

They left when the dance hall closed at midnight, filing out to the parking lot with the other patrons. In the car, Lee pulled Jen close, crushing her in his arms and kissed her. She held his face close to hers, pressing her lips against his. Their ardor surprised her.

"I know you dig my cop car," Lee whispered, pulling away from her caress. "I hope some of your reaction is from me."

Jen placed her face in the curve of his neck and shoulder, nestling close. Lee nuzzled her ear and cheek. They kissed again, losing track of time until someone knocked on the windshield. Lee rolled down the window.

"Hey, buddy, get a room." The DJ jangled his keys and made a clucking sound before walking to the only other car left in the empty lot.

Jen scooted to her place on the Crown Vic's bench and buckled her seat belt. Lee cleared his throat as he turned the ignition and put the gear in reverse. He entered the two-lane highway connecting Union Town to Livonia. The middle lines on the highway blurred as he accelerated.

"You're speeding," Jen said.

"I'm in a hurry."

"Aren't you worried you'll get pulled over? Besides, you've been drinking."

"This is a cop car, honey. Union Town boys won't bother me. Plus, I only had a few beers. I doubt my blood alcohol exceeds the limit. Relax. I'm fine. We'll be at your place in a few minutes."

Lee parked the car in front of her house, and as soon as he shut down the engine, he moved over in the seat and pulled her close. Kissing her, he touched his tongue to hers. Still tingling from the passion in the Dance Hall parking lot, she whimpered softly. Lee slid out of the car and quickly came to her side. He helped her from the seat and put his arm around her on the way to her front door. She handed him the key, and he opened the door.

Inside the house, he put his lips to her ear. "I want to have breakfast here when we wake up."

"Here?"

"Yes," he said.

She thought about Miles. "No, not here."

He put his hand on her shoulder and turned her. "Why the hell not?"

"Uh, well, no, not here."

"Son of a bitch." The lock clicked, and he opened the door. "Don't tell me you won't sleep with me because of some damn ghost."

She protested, but the words came out as indistinct, guttural sounds.

Lee barged into the living room. "All right, Hampton, show yourself."

Chapter Thirty-Six

Jen followed him into the room. "Lee! What are you doing?"

"I'm calling the bastard out. Do you hear me, Hampton?"

"Don't! Don't call him."

"Why? Do you think he could take me? Hampton! Cowboy up."

"Lee!"

"I'm going to kick his ass. Get rid of him once and for all."

"But you don't believe in Miles."

Lee turned, bringing his face close to hers. "But you do, and I want you to be free of that notion."

Jen put her hand to her throat. "But, Lee—"

"Okay! Hampton! I don't see you. Show yourself."

"He's not showing himself because he's not here right now."

Lee's words came from between his gritted teeth. "He's not showing because he's not here at all. He's dead, long gone. Why do you think an arsonist and a suicidal murderer would stick around, keeping *you* from enjoying life?" He turned away from her. "Come on, you coward!"

Jen pushed him. "Get out!" She shoved against his back. "Get out of my house. Right now, and don't come back."

"Jenny."

"Go!"

"Shit," Lee stomped away, and the front door slammed shut.

Zombie-like, Jen moved to the couch. "Call him back!" the secretary screamed.

"No! I won't." Jen sat down hard as the engine of Lee's car

roared. Her angry pride dissolved, leaving her confused, hurt, and saddened. Tears escalated into sobs. After several minutes, Jen inhaled and swallowed to clear her clogged throat.

Jen felt almost composed when Miles rushed to the couch. He sat next to her but kept enough distance not to make contact.

"You weep. That scoundrel Ferguson. Curse me for a fool for not returning earlier. Tell me what transpired. You may count it as truth that I shall appear to him as a man and make him pay for his misconduct."

She swiped at the tears rimming her eyes and smiled. "You'll call him out?"

"Most assuredly."

"You'll take him on? Kick his ass?" She raised her eyebrows.

"If that be the colloquial term, yes. You find that amusing?"

"Uh-huh. You and Lee have more things in common than you know. But it's not necessary. He didn't do anything worthy of violence. I became upset for another reason."

"Rex? As I got close to the house, I saw he has left."

"How could you tell?"

"His golden aura covered the house like a dome. His glow, the one that sent out its warning to the Dark Forces, no longer exists. Where did Rex go?" Miles frowned.

"A little boy, his owner, came for him so they could pass over." Jen shrugged one shoulder. "They were gone before I had to chance to ask him about the other side."

"I see."

"Now that Rex has gone, what about the evil trying to enter my house?"

"The blessing remains, but it won't guard against one whom you might have invited in. I must think on this."

"And I need to go to bed. Miles, you will be here tonight, yes?"

"Right outside your door. You have but to call."

"Thank you."

He reached out to take her hand but pulled back. "With

your permission, I would like to check on you now and then."

"Of course. I'll rest better knowing you keep guard."

"With my life, Jennifer. Or what substitutes for my life now."

After trying to fall asleep for an hour, Jen broke a Xanax in half and swallowed it. The next morning, she recalled a dream in which the house was bathed in a golden light, but as the light faded, a black cloud descended over the roof, hovering but not touching. Another dream was a repeat from a few nights before. She was wrapped in a blanket of warmth and security. She stretched and smiled. *Dreams, like ice cream cones, came in many flavors.*

In the morning, as she prepared breakfast, the sound of the buffet drawer opening in the dining room pleased her. Soon the aroma of the Danish blend filled the house.

Miles entered the kitchen. "Good morning. I trust you slept well." He moved a chair from the table and opened the window facing the garage outside, the noise of the workers unloading their tools carried in on a breeze.

"Very well, thank you." She pushed the button on the coffee maker. "The insurance company said they will bring my Acura back today. After that, I'm going to the Currier."

"Why there?"

"I want to see what it looks like."

"You won't see the building, for it is surrounded by acres of wooded terrain. Although the gatekeeper's house remains, no one mans it. One must call by a summoning button and get permission to enter. I doubt you will be admitted."

"I still want to see what I can."

"I shall accompany you."

"You'll ride with me in my car?"

"How else?"

Within an hour, her Acura pulled up with the two men from the insurance company. One rep examined the rental car she had been using while the other had her sign paperwork. They left with the loaner Town and Country. Jen juggled the Accura key in her hand as she entered the house.

"You ready?"

Miles tapped the pipe ashes in the trash and stowed his smoking items in the drawer. "I am."

He directed her through town and onto the road that meandered into the countryside. Jen stopped at a traffic light at the intersection of the country road. She rolled down her window and waved a dollar at a man holding a *Will work for food* sign.

As she started up again, Miles reappeared and mumbled. "Exceedingly shameful. That man looked healthy."

"It's sad. So many people have to rely on handouts. I can spare a dollar to help."

"Quite the contrary to the ethics of my day. One can work if one truly wants to."

"Don't lecture me on encouraging laziness. I got enough of that from Keith."

"Then I shan't align with *that* man, for it delivers me into a disagreeable situation. But, of these many who beg for their income, I say the more ignorant, the more susceptible to degeneration. Soon every city will have the same."

"Maybe you shouldn't travel into a big city, Miles."

"I should like to remain in Livonia."

"Until you discover your purpose?"

"For numerous reasons," he said.

After Jen drove several more miles, Miles pointed. "There. See the gate?"

She slowed the car as it approached huge stone walls connected by a tall iron gate with a motif of graceful horses racing toward each other. Roses and curlicues wound around twisted irons bars that towered to spearhead finials creating an arched top. A sign set into one of the walls, sandblasted and gilded, proclaimed, *Currier School for Young Ladies*. It might well have said, *Only the Rich and Snobby Need Apply*.

To Jen's surprise, the wheels of the iron portals slid inward on curved cement pathways. She released the brake pedal and steered the car away from the opening metal barrier. A massive gray Rolls Royce rolled past her car. She glanced up to the top of the stone wall.

"I wonder if the camera is focused on my license plate number."

Miles gaped at her. "What do you mean? A camera?"

Chapter Thirty-Seven

Jen stopped the car and turned to see the plate on the Rolls. She whipped out the pad and pen she kept in the console and wrote down CHS356. "Okay, got it. Check out the iron gate. See the little black square above the end finial on the left?"

Miles disappeared for a few minutes and returned. "I saw what you pointed out. It didn't look like any camera I've seen. Are you certain?"

"It's a security camera. We should go. I don't want to look suspicious."

As they drove, Miles came into and out of solidity, depending on their location. Near other cars, at intersections, and at stop signs, he disappeared. When they reached town, and to avoid a small jam caused by a delivery truck, Jen turned onto Clematis Street, where traffic was light. They passed the library, The Finger chicken restaurant, and the Eye of Horus sign, on the home of Madame Zelda, Gifted Seer.

Jen pointed. "See that place? Zelda, your Zelda's granddaughter, lives there now."

Miles nodded. "That's Dr. Lambrigger's house. I remember him."

"Your Zelda bought it after she sold the pharmacy when her husband died."

"Ah, yes, the druggist. I remember him, too. Nice fellow. Older than Zelly. He was a good man."

Miles returned his scrutiny to the small Victorian structure until they made a turn on the next road. Soon Jen pulled the Acura in front of her own house, where the construction crew worked on her garage. With her companion now invisible, Jen waved to the workmen and unlocked her back door. Miles appeared inside the house.

The grandfather clock sang its melodious Westminster tune and gonged four times. Jen set her purse on the counter. "I think I'll make my latte."

"Jennifer, I am loathe to leave you for fear a follower of Darkness might intrude, but I must see to things. I must learn what to do to safeguard you."

Jen put water in the coffee pot. "Explain what you mean by learn."

"I must ask Brad."

"You mentioned that name before. Who is Brad?"

"An important entity and the means to insure your welfare."

She pushed a filter into the holder. "Is he the ghost leader?"

"You might say that. I don't know exactly how the hierarchy works, but Brad's great power has helped me advance."

Jen touched the start button. "Can I meet him sometime?"

"I labor toward this purpose. Brad will know how to conduct us to the right path."

"This Brad must be special."

"He knows naught of fear and demonstrates how to recover from despair. He displays a kind of chivalry that teaches how to become a champion of the weak and helpless."

She folded her arms over her chest. "You think highly of him."

"It was he who rescued me that first day I ventured out after meeting you."

"Why did you need rescuing?"

"As a Floater, I was doomed to fail in the milieu of roaming spirits. Shortly after going on my primary foray from the safety of this shelter, accomplices of the Dark Forces besieged me. After I left the Toad and Pond, they surrounded me and attempted to invade my essence. Brad charged to my rescue, driving the fiends away. He then accompanied me to a safe place, beneath the high school stadium bleachers, where the soul of an Innocent maintains a haven for those who take cover from harm."

"An Innocent. Another dog?"

Miles shook his head and cast his gaze to the floor. "A newborn, abandoned by her mother."

"Oh. How sad. Can the baby communicate?"

"No more than Rex could. Nonetheless, her power is unassailable by all evil. If spirits, like Brad of the Stalwart class, find a lost Floater, he can lead them to safety under the stadium seating."

"How did you get back here that first day?

Miles shook his head. "That day during my time spent with Brad, I learned how to shield from the Salients and their minions. Through him, I became a soldier, strong enough to journey out on my own searching for lost souls in peril."

"So, when you leave here, you go to the high school?"

"Not always. I help Brad in many places, each day gaining strength and knowledge. I must go now. Although I still grapple with time awareness, I will endeavor to return before you retire."

"Miles, can you...um...die again? Be eliminated?"

"Much worse. My essence can be drawn into a malevolent spirit to be used against those I care about." He caught her eyes with his. "And those I love."

"Be careful, please."

Smiling, he pretended to touch a sword to his nose, waved it with a flourish, and bowed. "Let whoever seeks nothingness try to impede me."

"Touché!"

He bowed again and, at the bottom of the movement, disappeared.

Alone, she savored the foam from her afternoon latte. By the sounds from outside, the workmen were picking up their equipment before quitting for the day. The trucks started up and backed out of the drive.

Once more, the house, in its stillness, seemed large and engulfing. She deliberated on stopping the pendulum in the big clock, but then the house would be stupendously quiet. The phone rang, and she jumped at the sound.

"Hi, Sweetie."

"Hello, Keith." Her voice was flat and unemotional.

"What's happening?"

"Nothing much."

"Okay, now, this is no pressure, but would you enjoy going to lunch, just lunch, not an overnight date? Just for a few hours. Anywhere you want. Baltimore, Livonia, Washington, even New York, if we can get an early start."

Her nostrils flared. The secretary interceded. "He said anywhere, like Washington."

Washington!

"Keith, have you ever heard of the League of Learned Lawmakers?"

"Sure, some stuffy old rich farts' club. It costs like fifty grand a year or maybe more to belong."

"I want to go to lunch there."

"You're kidding."

"Nope. I believe you said anywhere I wanted."

She pictured him biting his lip, then scratching his ear, and finally looking side to side. Twenty-two years with a man produced an indelible picture of his mannerisms.

"A member must sponsor guests. I could ask Judge Bantan. He belongs. Being retired, he'd probably like some company."

"I remember him. Nice guy. So, call me when you've arranged it. Bye."

Inwardly, Jen smiled, and soon the smile made its way onto her lips. It felt good to call the shots. It was damned empowering! A pinch of guilt stung her. Did she just manipulate Keith? "Of course, you did," chimed the secretary. "And don't you allow one iota of remorse to tread on your triumph."

Jen sat upright. "Yeah. This time it's me. I'm going to check out the League. Maybe before Lee gets around to it."

With Miles absent, she could watch television.

While a rerun of *Law and Order* played, her thoughts strayed to the mysterious Brad. Jen wondered what his solid form looked like. Miles said Brad was powerful, smart, and a defender of the weak. Was he a departed military hero, or a powerful past prime minister, or an ancient king?

The phone interrupted her spirit speculations. "Hello, Keith. That was quick."

"Judge Bantan will be delighted to host us for lunch at the League. How about Thursday at noon? Do you want me to pick you up? I could come early, and we'd do breakfast and—"

"No. I'll drive myself to Washington."

"You should drive here to Baltimore, honey. The parking is dreadfully expensive in DC. No sense taking two cars."

"That's okay. I'll look up the League on the internet and find a parking lot nearby. See you in front of the League at noon. Thanks."

Jen pressed the end button. She liked calling the shots, especially with Keith. Had taking control pissed off Lee? Too bad. Her house, her rules. Moreover, he insulted Miles. She wished she could prove Miles's innocence. After what happened the other night, she doubted Lee would help her. Would Miles even want Lee involved, and would Lee ever even speak to her again?

Chapter Thirty-Eight

Jen waited late that night for Miles to arrive before going to sleep. When he didn't show up by midnight, she checked the locks and went to bed. Knowing that evil spirits surrounded her home, trying to pierce the blessing, scared the crap out of her.

The next day she shopped, did laundry, paid bills, and washed her hair. Miles was conspicuously absent.

On Wednesday morning, Dave, the contractor, knocked at the back door. "We'll probably finish the garage tomorrow. I'll ask you to sign off when I'm done."

"I'll be gone most of the day Thursday. I'll sign on Friday. How's that?"

"Fine. I have another small job, and then I'll start your basement. Most likely Monday or Tuesday. I'll need five thousand to start. I listed the incremented payments on the contract, remember?"

"I remember. I'll have your money Monday."

"Super," Dave said. "I like that smell. I smoke a pipe, too. Do you mind telling me the blend? I'd like to try some."

She found Miles's tobacco pouch and brought it to the back door. Dave examined the bag and pinched a bit. He sniffed it and tasted a thin shaving. "Okay, I taste cherry and vanilla. What's it called?"

"Golden Cavendish Blend from Denmark. I got it from the Pipe Dream store in town."

"Thanks," Dave said, handing her back the bag. "I'm going to buy some. See you later, Ms. Hughes."

Jen went to bed that night without seeing Miles.

On Thursday morning, he still had not returned. She

worried. In preparation for her Washington lunch, she pulled a dark green wool suit from her closet. She added her heavy gold necklace with the emerald slide and the emerald dangle earrings Keith bought her when they traveled to Colombia. No doubt, Keith would point out his generosity when he saw the jewelry.

It was chilly outside, so she slipped on her St. John's coat with the thick beaver collar.

At noon, she pulled into a parking garage three blocks away from the League. Keith waited for her on the corner.

He kissed her cheek. Running his hand along the plush black fur collar, he smiled. "I've always loved this coat. What do you have on underneath?"

"My dark green suit."

Keith put his lips to her ear. "Nice. I like the way it feels to the touch."

The secretary punched her. "Don't let him get away with that."

"You gave up the right to feel my clothes a while ago."

Keith's eyes expanded. He opened his mouth. "Oh," he mumbled. "O-kay."

They headed for the League.

In the lobby, Judge Bantan sat on a red velvet sofa encircling a stand holding one of the largest flower arrangements Jen had ever seen. The room's dark wooden paneled walls screamed old money. She imagined Mary Lincoln gliding her tiny feet upon the patterned carpets, her satin dress swishing under immense hoopery.

"My boy," the old judge said, clasping Keith's hand. "And your wife. Good to see you, Jessie."

Jen hugged the elderly fellow. "Jennifer."

A tuxedoed staff member appeared. "May I take your coat, madame?"

"Sure." The staffer slipped her St. John's trophy off her shoulder. "Do I get a number or something?"

Without a perceptible facial expression, the man said, "No, ma'am. No one steals coats here. I'll remember which one is yours when you wish to have it returned."

"Oh," Jen said, feeling like one of the *gens pauvres*, the great unwashed.

Judge Bantan took Jen's arm. "Shall we go to the dining room?"

The judge bypassed the curved wide marble staircase in favor of the elevator to reach the second floor. Upstairs the elevator opened into a broad hall. Double glass doors fitted with lace curtains hid the interior of rooms as they headed down the corridor.

"What's in that room?" Jen asked of the first set of double doors.

"The Reading Room." Judge Bantan stopped and opened the doors so Jen could peek inside. Old men in high wing chairs read newspapers and sipped from cut glasses in the paneled expanse.

"What's that?" She pointed across the hall.

"The library." Again, he opened the doors, showing desks with green hooded reading lights and ceiling-to-floor bookshelves with a tracked ladder.

"Is there a Humidor Room?" Jen asked.

Judge Bantan smiled. "Ah, yes! We have a special cigarillo for our lady guests. I'll take you there after lunch."

"Wonderful. I've taken an interest in fine tobaccos," she said.

The judge covered his mouth with his hand and spoke softly. "One of our emissary members brings in first-rate Cubans. I could snag you one if you like."

"I would love one! I'd like to try the cigarillo first. Would it be terribly rude to take the Cuban back with me?"

"Absolutely no problem. I'll get you two. How's that?"

Keith touched her arm and gave her a cockeyed stare.

"Lighten up, Keith."

The secretary nudged her. "Atta girl! Sticking up for yourself."

At the end of the hall, a door opened, and the judge

escorted them into the dining room.

A woman in a gray-jacketed dress with a badge welcomed Judge Bantan. *Meg* showed them to the table in the sparsely attended room. Three ornate cut glass chandeliers radiated soft light. Windows all along the outside wall let in the natural sunlight. Fresh, rarified air Jen knew had been separated from the earth's atmosphere and saved just for the League's members, circulated, smelling like an Alpine mountaintop.

"May I order for the three of us?" Judge Bantan asked.

"Please," Jen said. Keith nodded.

The judge chose salmon, thin-sliced sauteed potatoes, and asparagus with Mosel wine. Jen protested against the chocolate mousse for dessert, but she could not resist. Coffee was served after the meal.

"I'd like to know a little history of the place, Judge," Jen said.

Chapter Thirty-Nine

Judge Bantan continued his discourse of the exclusive club to Jen and Keith. "Of course. Lincoln's supporters built this place, and members proudly proclaim that from the start, the League allowed Jews and blacks membership."

"Were there a lot of Jews at that time?" Jen asked, thinking of Zelda's family.

"I'm not sure. Did you know one of Jefferson Davis's cabinet members was Jewish? Secretary of Treasury, I believe. Frederick Douglas refused a *gratis* membership to the League because one of his German mistresses had been insulted by a board member."

Jen's eyebrows went up. "One of his mistresses?"

"The gentleman had a very understanding wife. After the Civil War, the League continued as a men's club. No party affiliations were required. They just had to be rich and well-known. All members must pass close scrutiny."

"Blacks and Jews," Jen said. "How about women?"

"Well," the judge shrugged. "Women have been allowed since 1984."

She forced a smile. "Ladies in the eighties. Go on."

"Right, then. The organization bought the hotel next door in 1915 and attached it as suites for members only. In recent times, although the board has tried to keep it a secret, we members know the League was purchased by new owners who have made changes. For one, although we are an exclusive club with closely scrutinized membership, one can buy a temporary membership with no background check."

"What do you mean?"

"Take, for instance, if a rich European comes into town, he can stay at any of the finest hotels D.C. has to offer. If the visitor wishes to stay here, he must pay two hundred dollars a day for the temporary membership and five hundred a day for the room. Even though the accommodations are beautiful, the most illustrious of the old guard members balk at commercializing the League and having strangers in our midst. Wealthy, but unknown."

"Does that happen a lot?"

"It must because lately, they have been doing extensive remodeling. I've been a member for forty years, and during that time, every repair or improvement required an assessment on our dues. The new management hasn't asked for an extra dime, but the money has to come from somewhere."

And I'll bet I know where. "Judge, do you think it's possible for me to see one of the glorious rooms while I'm here?"

"Of course. We'll pay a visit to the front desk. Besides, it gives us time to digest our lunch before we enjoy the cigars."

Judge Bantan escorted Jen and Keith to the front desk of the hotel. While the judge made the arrangements, Keith took out his cell phone.

"Jen," he said, motioning his hand for her to move. "Stand next to the statue of Lincoln. I want to take your picture."

"Okay. It might be nice to have a memento of this place." She posed next to the statue, in front of the fountain and sitting on a plush velvet couch.

A uniformed bellman accompanied Judge Bantan, who extended his hand with a gesture to follow. The bellman led them to the fourth floor and unlocked a door to one of the rooms. Jen oohed and ahhed as she walked around the splendid high-ceilinged sitting room, the all-marble bathroom, and the bedroom. The mahogany bed sported a carved canopy jutting out three feet over the top, with high, carved posts at the end.

"Wow, what a great trysting place this would make," Keith said.

Judge Bantan harrumphed. "Absolutely not! You won't

find any improprieties here. Even with the temporary, albeit rich rabble, the members won't stand for any hanky-panky. No scandal allowed under this roof."

Jen scoffed. *No scandals here? Except maybe money laundering and pandering for prostitution. The scandalous action does its business end here under the noses of lawyers, judges, and congressmen. They puff their tobacco in the Smoking Salon while rich men ride the limousines to the Currier, where the hookers ply their trade dressed in little plaid skirts and school ties.*

"Would you like to see more of the hotel?" Judge Bantan asked.

Jen took a last look at the luxury suite. "No, thank you, Judge. I've seen enough."

He led them to the Humidor Room, which sat behind a lounge, referred to as the *Bar.* Although having had a hundred years of cigar smoke, the place didn't reek or offend, smelling serenely good.

They sat in leather seats facing a small round inlaid topped table, and the judge placed an order. They'd chit-chatted for ten minutes when a tux-uniformed young man brought two nipped-end cigars, a thin, plastic-tipped cigarillo, and two uncut cigars all on a napkin-lined silver plate.

Tux-boy lit Jen's cigarillo first and then the two men's cigars. She drew in the cigarillo and blew out. The smoke left a tang on her tongue reminiscent of spicy molasses. She acknowledged her approval to the young man, and when the judge nodded, the employee took the tray and left. He reappeared with a parchment-wrapped package the size and shape of a burrito. Jen put the wrapped cigars in her purse. *Miles will be surprised with the Cubans.*

After the smoke, Keith thanked the judge. He offered to pay, but the judge adamantly refused. Judge Bantan kissed Jen and gave her his card, insisting she return often as his guest. In the lobby, the coat man, complete with his disapproving attitude, appeared with Jen's fashionable coat and held it open for her to slip into the sleeves.

Keith walked Jen to her car. "I hope you've not started smoking, Jen. First of all, it's a disgusting habit, and second, cigars?"

Jen couldn't resist. "I'm afraid wearing thongs has changed me. I have developed a few new habits since I've been alone."

Keith, usually ready with a comment, sputtered.

She kissed him on the cheek. "Thanks for a lovely day."

With fighting heavy traffic around the Capital, the drive home took her three hours. She was surprised to see tools and construction debris around the newly completed garage. *I was told they would be finished today.* The design matched the house better than before, with more emphasis on the Victorian style. Dave had even added a bit of gingerbread on the corners of the roof. *I love it!*

When Jen entered the kitchen, her cell phone beeped. Keith sent a text with the photos from the League. As she examined each shot, the pleasant smell of Danish blend tobacco became stronger. Miles stood behind her and radiated his warmth.

"Good afternoon, dear lady. The photos on the screen show that you were at the Currier School. I thought you were to spend the day with *that man* in Washington at the League."

"What are you talking about? These photos come from the lobby of the League."

"Then why, pray tell, does Miss Stella Anderson, Head Mistress at the Currier, stand behind you?"

Jen turned to Miles. "Stella Anderson?"

He touched the screen, which made a slight wiggle. "If not she, then her twin."

"This is a photo of the League's General Manager? Could you be mistaken?"

"I don't believe so. I have been trained to observe. Most certainly, the woman I see before me is closely related to the headmistress of the Currier. I'd bet my — Well, I cannot do that, now, can I?"

"Don't bet your second life, Miles. I have become accustomed to you being here."

The League and the Currier. Of course, they are the two players. The headmistress would stay at the Currier, so she wouldn't be the same woman behind the desk at the League. But according to Miles, they look alike. Sisters? Jen brought her laptop to life and brought up the League's website. The site showed a photograph of a smiling middle-aged woman, Stephanie A. Vargas, the general manager. Jen wished she had paid more attention in the lobby, but the coat man had given her a temporary inferiority complex, so she watched her own behavior rather than her surroundings.

Judge Bantan said the League had been secretly purchased in the last few years. Lee said the Currier would now accept any rich girl, bypassing the old policy of acceptance through special need. That sounded a whole lot like the recent new standards of the League. The Money-Above-All aspect, in spite of social standing, allowed scoundrels to mingle with the world's finest under the guise of respectability. The lily-white reputations of the League and the Currier shielded sleaze and corruption. She wanted to talk to Lee, but the fiasco after the dance date left her raw and vulnerable. She couldn't call him. Not yet.

"I must leave you alone for a time tonight," Miles said. "Its importance supersedes my wish to keep you company."

"That's okay. I think I'll turn in early, anyway. The traffic wore me out driving home. Rush hour in Livonia is only five cars waiting at the four-way stop. I had hoped to forget what Washington travel could be like."

Miles's voice became serious. "Do not let anyone in the house tonight. The blessing continues to hold, but an evil presence can intrude by invitation. We no longer enjoy Rex's power to prevent unwanted visitors. I will return as soon as possible. Good night."

Jen retired early. She slept on her side these last few nights inviting the warm cozy dream that frequently rewarded her rest. She thought of it as her favorite flavored dream, referring to it as chocolate. That dream made her feel safe and secure, providing an enveloping feeling. Luckily, the chocolate dream occurred again.

Her peaceful sleep was interrupted when her body contorted into a face-up position and heaviness pressed upon her. A rough hand squeezed her breast and rubbed at her neck. Tight bonds engulfed her, pulling taut until she couldn't move at all. Struggling for breath, she could not draw in enough air.

"Stop! Please!" she begged. "No, let me go! Miles!" She sat up and grabbed at her throat. Leaning to the side table, she snapped the light on. In an instant, Miles stood beside her.

"What is it?" Miles said.

"I had a nightmare. It felt like I was bound, unable to break free. I couldn't breathe, and something had me in a tight grip." She narrowed her eyes at him. "Did you do that? Was it you?"

Miles knelt to eye level. "Certainly not. If fortune had bestowed to me the closeness you described, I would never waste the opportunity by frightening you." He stood and moved her arm gently so he could sit next to her and took her hands in his. "Jennifer, you experienced a dream. The evil surrounding the town uses every tool to inspire fear and distrust. Many people wake up from their rest, alarmed and terrified. Try to return to sleep and rely on my protection and concern, or the evil will have gained a victory this night."

"You'll be nearby?"

"Where I remain each night, just outside your door in nether slumber."

"Can you hear me when *you* sleep?"

He pressed her wrists, one at a time, to his lips. "You have but to say my name." Miles rose, squaring his shoulders. "You need only to call out." He shook his head slightly. "But, please, precious jewel, I pray you do not call...." He walked to the door and touched the handle. As he opened the door, he turned to look at her.

The touch on the door handle meant he promised to no longer melt through the doors but exit like a whole, living man. Trusting Miles's guard, she relaxed and returned to sleep.

When she awoke again, a sense of longing, the need to be caressed and held, engulfed her. Perhaps Keith had been correct.

Maybe she had a good case of the higgly-jigglies. She missed feeling the closeness of a man's body.

After dressing, she headed to the kitchen for her much-needed coffee fix. Even if Miles did nether-sleep outside her bedroom door, he usually greeted her in the kitchen each morning.

As if on cue, he said, "Good morning. You slept well?"

"Yes. Thanks to you."

"At your service. However, I must leave shortly. Brad and I have much to accomplish today. Keeping track of time is difficult while I am in the invisible state, but I improve steadily and have almost mastered the ability to determine nighttime. Therefore, I can, with some accuracy, promise to be home before you retire."

"No spirit, Rolexes? Spectral pocket watches? Oh, dear."

The coffee rumbled its way down into the glass pot when she heard a sound in the driveway. Miles pulled aside the lace curtain on the back door. He made a low throat snarl. "It's *him*, Ferguson. Perhaps," Miles said with a scowl, "I can manage to stay a little longer this morning."

Jen answered the knock at the front door. Lee stood on the front step, accompanied not by Grainger but by a medium-sized dog, white with brown and black patches. Saying nothing, she stepped back from the opening, allowing Lee access to the living room.

They both stood silent and looked at each other. The dog sat down, and the leash fell across Lee's shoe. After another few moments of silence, the dog made a soft woof.

Lee cleared his throat. "Um, Jen. I only have a few minutes, but one of our guys found this poor fellow stuck in the middle of the interstate, scared to death. He didn't have a collar or tag, and the vet found no chip, so I guess he's homeless. You said you were thinking about getting a dog. Before he takes a one-way trip to the pound, I thought maybe you might want him. He's a nice dog."

Jen knelt down and petted him. The dog responded with a quick lick to her cheek.

"Oh, you're the kissing kind, eh?" He reminded her of

Rex. She missed the ghost pet's companionship.

"See. He likes you," Lee said. "But who wouldn't?"

Jen took the leash from the floor and stood. "I do need a dog. You said a vet checked for a chip?"

"Uh-huh. I'm old friends with one of the vets in town. She gave the dog all of his shots and checked him over just in case you would take him." Lee squatted in front of the dog. The animal locked eyes with the man. "What do you want to name him?"

"How about Rex? It means king."

"Great."

Jen stroked Rex Number Two's head. "Ah, Rex. I need to remember that you're the kind of dog that needs feeding and walking and hands-on care, aren't you?"

Lee's eyebrows squished together. "Did you ever know a dog that didn't need feeding and walking?"

Jen and Lee looked at each other for another few moments; then he rose, brushed at his knees, and picked a white dog hair off his pants. "I've got some things for him in the car. I'll go get them." He took two steps away and turned back. "Jen, I'm sorry for the other night. I was way out of line. I didn't mean to get so…pushy." He rotated his palms. "All I can say in my defense is when I get close to you, I forget everything and want to get even closer. You were right to throw me out."

Jen nodded, then picked up Rex's leash and unsnapped it from the collar. Lee turned to the front door.

When Lee left the house, Miles materialized next to Jen. "I guess Detective Ferguson and I do have a few things in common after all. I can tarry no longer. Hopefully, our animal-loving detective will hasten to his assigned task as well. Good day, dear lady."

Miles walked to the front door and reached for the handle. By the time the door fully opened, he had disappeared. Lee walked in. When the door at his back closed behind him, he jumped, nearly dropping the items he held. "What the hell?"

She shrugged.

Lee put a metal bowl set and a bag of medicines on the coffee table. "I left the vet papers at home. Sorry."

"I can get them later," Jen said.

"Jen?" Lee ran his fingers through his hair.

"Would you like some coffee? It's ready."

"I'd love some."

Jen hung Rex's leash on a hook by the door. The dog's new license jangled against the metal ring of his collar as he walked around the living room, sniffing the furniture. Lee followed Jen into the kitchen. She took an extra cup and saucer from the cabinet. After pouring two cups of coffee, she stood behind Lee and put his cup in front of him.

Lee was freshly shaven and dressed in a suit. He smelled of a crisp citrus scent.

"You're wearing cologne?" she asked.

"Yeah. Grainger's Secret Santa gift from last year's station party. I decided today might be a good time to try it out. What do you think?"

She leaned over the small tabletop and inhaled.

"Not too close," the secretary warned.

Jen smiled. "Very nice. I like it." Then she sat in the chair across the table from him.

"Thanks."

A surge of heat coursed through her loins. She smiled weakly at Lee and took a sip of coffee. He lifted his cup to lips she knew kissed with unrivaled excellence.

"It's good coffee," he said.

"What? Oh, yeah," she answered

"Get a hold of yourself," the secretary admonished.

"Jenny, don't get mad at me, but what in the *hell* were you doing outside the Currier School on Monday?"

"Were you following me?"

"No. We got you on camera."

"No way."

"Remember when you generously gave a bum a buck?"

Jen thought back on the events of that morning. "The I'll-work-for-food guy?"

"He's one of our undercovers. We've been watching the school."

"You have?"

"You need to let us do the detecting." He softened his tone. "Please. I don't want you to get hurt."

"But I never got out of my car."

"The camera, hidden in our man's sign, showed you alone when you gave him the dollar. But the photo of your license plate showed someone was with you in the passenger seat. Was someone hiding in your car?"

Jen gave a dismissive wave of her hand. "I can't account for your faulty equipment."

Lee finished his coffee and checked his watch. "I've gotta go. Um, maybe you could come over to my house this afternoon and pick up the rest of the dog items."

Absolutely I can! Your house! Right! "I don't know. I have a lot to do today. Besides, I haven't a clue where you live."

He took a business card from his jacket pocket and wrote on the back, *1715 Clematis Road.* "Go a mile past the library. I'm the last house on the left. Brick with white trim and a carport. I should be home around five."

"I'll see if I can make it. I did plan on going to the library this afternoon. Of course, now that I have Rex, I'll have to fit his feeding and walking into my schedule."

"I hope to see you." He got up from his seat

Rex trotted into the kitchen and put his front legs on Lee's thighs.

"You stay here, Rex, and take care of your new lady, now." He cast a smile at Jen. "She's very important to me." He winked at her. "See you later."

Jen stayed seated. "Be careful out there."

"Don't worry about me."

Chapter Forty

At noon, Jen slid into her Acura, ready to visit Livonia's library. Her garage showed no signs of the construction workers. She hoped Dave would come by and clean the assorted bits and pieces still strewn about. The fascia and soffits remained unpainted, and the new garage door controller box lay unopened near the side door. For the few days Spirit-Rex had been gone, the raccoons chattered in the night, telling her they had once again set up camp in the basement. Maybe the new Rex would chase the critters away, but she would feel better once the work under her house started.

Okay, the garage was not finished, and the raccoons returned. Not a perfect life, but Lee had come over, and life moved a bit closer to perfect. If she had a few hours to use the Ancestry program at the library, maybe she could find out what became of Miles's sons.

At twelve-thirty, she pulled into the parking lot of the town's library, the Empire of Mildred Owings.

A young woman sitting at the information desk greeted Jen with a bright smile.

Jen looked around the room. Every desktop computer had a head bent over the keyboard. She flashed her library card. "I see all of the computers are busy, but I'd like to reserve the next one available. Until then, can you direct me to a book with information on this county?"

The young lady took a long look at Jen's card. "Oh, you're Jennifer Hughes. Ms. Owings would like to see you. She's in her office right now." The young librarian pointed across the room to an alcove near the bathrooms and a drinking fountain. "Past the bathrooms, at the end of the hall."

"Thanks," Jen said with a strained smile. Being sent to Library Millie's office felt akin to going to the principal's office.

Jen had that pleasure twice. Once when she was told her mother had been in an accident and a cousin waited to take her to the hospital, and a second time when she had a scuffle with Alison Farth. Jen had reached her teasing limit following her mother's commitment to the state mental hospital. To avenge Alison's mean comments about Jen's crazy mom, Jen called her classmate Ally Fart. The kids laughed, and several called out, "Ally Fart!" Alison flew over three desks, pulling Jen down to the floor in a rollover melee. The kids shouted "Fart! Fart! Fart!" instead of the usual "Fight!" The teacher called for help to disengage the two wrestling hair-pullers. Both young ladies seethed and quivered while escorted to the principal's office.

Fortunately, Jen's punishment coincided with her father's early release from prison. His parole had been granted for special circumstances, namely his wife's hospital admission. Jen's father didn't care about her five-day suspension. Jen heard that Ally-Fart's alcoholic father had given his daughter got a good licking when pulled from his personal stool at the Tuna Bar during the World Series to pick up his scrapping brat from school. Even better, in Jen's view, from then on, the name Ally Fart stuck.

Jen knocked on the portal with the brass insignia designating the realm of Mildred Owings, Head Librarian.

The word "Enter" penetrated the antique oak door. Inside, Mildred sat at her desk, looking through a large leather-bound book. "Be with you in a minute." She did not look up from her study.

Jen stood in front of the desk. As she waited, she surveyed the room. Dark bookshelves lined the back wall. Interspersed between attractive bindings, carved wooden African animals sat as bookends. Jen had seen similar ones on her family's one vacation to Busch Gardens in Tampa. She had wanted a handsome foot-high giraffe and begged her father for it. The price tag was too high for their vacation budget. But here in Mildred Owings's office, not only the giraffe, but two graceful antelopes, a leopard, and a zebra flanked rows of books.

On a side wall, muted green bamboo print curtains hung

on a single window overlooking the back parking lot. The wall on the other side only contained a triangular shadow box with Old Glory folded the way veterans' families received them at a funeral. A member of Mildred's family must have been in a war.

Finally, Mildred shut the book with a loud clumping sound. She stood. "Ms. Hughes."

Once again, Jen noted the lady's tall, straight stature. Her beauty had not completely faded with age. She must have been exquisite in her younger days.

Mildred walked around her desk. "My nephew called and asked if I would personally assist you."

"He did?"

The librarian pointed a militant finger in the air. "I don't pry into my relatives' lives. Nor do I wish to hear details. However, Burleigh asked this favor of me, and I will honor it. What can I help you with?"

The tone of Mildred's words sounded as if the woman offered a wondrous gift, and Jen should damn well use and appreciate it.

"I would like to know if you have books or magazines or anything with the history and pictures of Livonia in the late nineteenth and early twentieth century. You know, information about the old families, businesses, goings-on in the community — things like that."

The librarian walked out of her office without a word or gesture. Jen followed.

Mildred spoke over her shoulder. "In our facility, we have a comprehensive compilation of Livonia media. As an archival collection, I doubt it has a parallel in any other library. We are proud of our archives."

You mean you are proud.

They walked across the main floor to the other side of the building toward conference rooms. Over one of the doors was the inviting sign: *Welcome to Livonia.*

"This," Mildred said, opening one of the doors, "will have everything you could possibly need. For the last thirty years, I have been in charge of the collection, like the librarian before me and the one before him. We've made it our goal to accumulate and preserve our town's past. Frequently, when long-time residents pass, we get old books. Any books appearing to belong in the archives are routed to me. I read them, and if they meet the requirements, they are added to the Livonia Archive shelves."

"So, you know all of the books in this room?"

"I've read every page. When bequeathed items arrive, I check for notations and possible graffiti, ready with an eraser or white-out to take care of any inappropriate or stray marks."

I'll just bet you do.

"Tell me what you're looking for, and I'll direct you to the proper media."

A flash of coat-man from the League insinuated itself in Jen's memory. Did Mildred intend to supervise Jen's research? Did she think Jen would make errant pencil marks on the sacred relics of the town's past?

"Miss Owings," Jen said with firm politeness in her voice. "These books have public access, right?"

"Yes. They can be checked out two at a time."

"Then I would like to browse and study at my leisure. I'm sure you have important things to do."

The head librarian's eyes bored into Jen's. "Am I being dismissed?"

"Um, why, yes. I guess you are."

The woman turned without a sound and left the Livonia Archival collection.

Chapter Forty-One

Mildred Owings had not exaggerated the extent of the Livonia collection. An abundance of books, magazines, diaries, scrapbooks, and newspaper clippings showed the town from its beginnings to the heyday of the railroad and carriage factory days up to the present year. Jen spent three hours looking through the assorted offerings. She viewed the town as Miles, Virginia, and Zelda Rothberg had known it. The town had modernized, but many of the homes and buildings looked the same in the old photos, except cars and trucks replaced the horses and buggies.

Jen focused on historical data. At three o'clock, the young library clerk notified her that a computer had been vacated. She left the Livonia Collection and fired up the ancestry program. Utilizing every avenue she could think of, she found no record of Christopher and Timothy Cisco other than the courthouse notation in Pittsburg of their adoption by Damon Cisco, Miles's best friend and second husband to Virginia. The only household members noted on the 1920 Census was Damon and Virginia Cisco. What happened to the two boys? Had they been killed in World War I? They must have been old enough to serve, but when she searched the war records, no soldiers by that name had been listed, killed or otherwise.

At four-thirty, she left the library and headed home. The new Rex barked as she approached the back door and waggled happily when she entered the house.

"Good boy, Rex. No puddles, no piles, no damage. Maybe this will work out for both of us. How do you feel about nasty basement coons?"

She clipped his leash and took him for a walk around the yard. As if in answer to her query, Rex dug with furor at the side of the house. She pulled him back, worried he would dig into the dirt chamber below. The basement remodel was a priority. She needed to call Dave and rattle his cage about getting the job on his schedule.

After feeding Rex, she refreshed her makeup in the master bathroom. Downstairs, she checked her purse for the card Lee had given her. With the giddy feeling of attending her first school dance, she hopped in the car and drove a little faster than she should. A brick house with white trim and the house number printed on the card sat at the end of the road. A red Porsche, sleek and shiny, resided in the carport. Jen stopped in front and wondered if this was Lee's house. She pulled out her phone to call him when in her rearview mirror, she spotted the Crown Vic. The sedan pulled behind the red sports car. Lee got out and sauntered to her car.

"Whose Porsche?" Jen asked as he opened her door.

"Mine." They walked toward the fancy wheels. "It was a gift from my father-in-law the day I signed the papers agreeing to let the kids move out of state and live with Marjorie's folks. A kind of a thank-you gift for not giving them a hard time."

Jen put her hand on her hip. "So, why didn't you give them a hard time? I wouldn't want my kids to move away."

"I didn't want them to move either, but they were teenagers and wanted to go. Both kids knew the difference between the lower middle class in Livonia and the wealthy privilege in Massachusetts."

"Weren't you afraid they'd be spoiled by rich permissive grandparents?"

"Not really. George Dix is a stern disciplinarian, and he's home every day to keep on top of things. Caroline, Marjorie's mother, could apply for sainthood as far as I'm concerned. So, I had no good reason to keep my kids from a better life. I can see them whenever I like. I have been consulted with every major decision, and now they're in college."

"But what about the car?"

"I don't like it."

"Oh, come on. What man doesn't like a Porsche?"

"A man who has traded his two kids for one, maybe?"

"Yet you kept it?"

"Yeah," he said, escorting her to the front door and turning a key in the lock. "I thought maybe I'd score a hot chick with it." Inside the house, he laid his jacket over a chair in the small living room. "But there it is, seven years later and has two thousand miles on the odometer. I fire it up now and then and take it for a short ride."

"No hot chicks?"

He raised his eyebrows. "You certainly qualify."

"I was snagged by your hot cop car."

"Make yourself at home. Have a look around. I'll be right back." He opened the front door and lifted the lid to the mailbox.

Although Jen knew little of the previous Mrs. Ferguson, the house had a woman's stamp with brocade chairs and sofa, plush carpet, heavy silk drapery, and *mirrors*. A huge gilt-framed mirror hung over the couch between the windows. Another nautical-type mirror with a convex lens decorated the kitchen. As Jen walked around, she realized Marjorie Dix Ferguson loved mirrors. Every room in the house had at least one.

Most of them hung on *the outside walls*. Windows for spirits to peek through.

Lee met her in the hallway with envelopes in his hand. "Did you see the whole house?"

"You've got a lot of mirrors."

He put the mail on a decorative table sitting under a mirror-framed mirror. "Is that bad luck?"

"It is for you." *And a disaster for me. I won't put on a show for the spirit world, no matter what.* "Can I have Rex's vet papers, please?"

"What?"

"The papers. You said you forgot to bring them this morning. That's why I'm here."

He put his arms around her neck. "I hoped you came because you like my company."

"I do like your company, but I'm not comfortable in your house."

They locked gazes.

He withdrew his arms. "Not here. And not at your place either?"

She moved away a few steps and looked out the window at the Porsche and Crown Vic. *Automotively worlds apart. And he prefers the gunboat.*

"Wait a minute," Lee spun her around. "The car works for you?"

"Huh?"

The secretary gave her a shove. "He thinks you're looking at the cop car with lustful thoughts."

Jen couldn't resist leading him on. "Why not? You know the car affects me. It's where we've done the best kissing. So.... Give me one good reason."

"How about I give you a few good reasons? For one, that's the mobile office I share with Grainger. Second, if I got caught, I'd get fired, even if the chief *is* my uncle. And...it's just not right."

"Aw, just once wouldn't hurt. What do you say?"

His cell phone rang. He reached for his pocket like a drowning person grabbing a lifeline. "Ferguson." He listened, then nodded. "Okay. I'll check it out."

"You're taking a call?"

"Nothing dangerous. We get this every year or so. The cheerleaders at the high school claim they hear a baby crying under the stadium bleachers."

Chapter Forty-Two

"Oh!" Jen said. "Can I go with you?"

"Not on an official police call. But you can drive your own car."

"I know where the high school is. I'll see you there. Don't forget Rex's vet papers."

Jen sat in the Acura until Lee, a folder in hand, got in and fired up the Crown Vic. She followed him for ten minutes until they reached Zachary Taylor High School, the one she had seen in a photo at the Livonia library collection. The Federal style two-story brick building had changed little from the date of its 1850 dedication, proudly inscribed over the entrance.

She followed Lee's car to the back, where they both parked. Lee led her past the cafeteria to the gymnasium and just beyond to the stadium. Football players practiced, and the cheerleaders clustered in an area at the far end. As they walked, Lee explained the nature of the investigation.

"In the middle sixties, a student—"

"A girl named Abigale had a baby and abandoned her under the bleachers?"

"Good news hangs around, doesn't it?"

Jen smiled. "Or maybe I'm psychic?"

"Is that how you know?"

"Um, no. Someone told me about it, and I checked it on the Internet."

"I'd forgotten the student's name and can't remember if I ever knew the baby was a girl. Anyway, it's public knowledge, and every so often, we get a call from people claiming to hear cries."

"Reliable witnesses?"

"Preachers, judges, and schoolteachers. When we get a call, we have to check it out but never find anything."

"What do you think it is?"

Lee shook his head. "Imagination. I told you I don't believe in ghosts."

"So, you've said."

Lee scanned the area. "Why don't you take a seat somewhere? I need to interview the witnesses. It might take a few minutes, then I'll look around."

"Okay," Jen surveyed the array of empty seating in the bleachers. She selected a seat in the middle of the wide-open area. Lee strolled over to the clot of under-dressed cheerleaders. The girls spoke with flailing arms and pointing fingers. Her daughter, Chrissy, had been a cheerleader, and Jen thought back to the days when her minivan became the cheerleader bus for the team. Engrossed in her motherly memories, she detected the faint aroma of familiar tobacco. Jen couldn't see him, but before he spoke, she knew Miles was nearby.

"What are you doing here, Jennifer?"

"Lee is investigating the cry from Abigale's baby."

"The Innocent does not cry. The child did not live long enough to develop much consciousness. She makes no sound."

"Rex made sounds. Why wouldn't the baby?"

"Rex made sounds only you could hear. Rex could make limited choices. He chose to appear and be heard by you."

"Are you sure, Miles?"

"Absolutely."

"You don't know everything. You told me each day brings new information. Maybe she does cry, and you just don't know it."

"Jennifer, I assure you, in this case, I am certain."

"Why don't you find Brad and ask him? He knows so much. Maybe he can answer the mystery."

"I don't need to find Brad. He is here, on your left."

Jen turned but saw nothing. "That's pretty creepy. How

about a proper introduction?"

"Not now," Miles said. "Go home. You can do no good here. In fact, you can cause trouble for us."

"You think you can tell me what to do? Think again, Mr. Hampton." She turned her head to the left. "And you too, Mister…. Mister Brad."

"We don't want to have attention called to this place," Miles said, his voice emphatic.

"How much more attention can there be? The cops are investigating where the cheerleaders heard the sounds."

"Good. Just so they don't come over here."

"Why not here?"

"Because just below where you sit is the place our Innocent inhabits."

Jen got down on her knees and peered through the wooden planks. Paper bits, wrappers, a few soda cans, and other detritus littered the ground. Dusk had set in. She was unable to find any evidence of the occupancy in question.

"Go home," Miles said sternly.

"Listen carefully. First, don't take that tone of voice with me. Second, don't tell me what to do. Third—"

"Who are you talking to?"

It was Lee. She jerked, bumping her head on the seat. She got up and brushed specks from her knees. Still annoyed with Miles, she answered before giving the response enough thought. "It was Miles, damn it. He—"

Lee's nostrils flared. "For crying out loud. Isn't it enough you think you have the ghost of Miles Hampton in your house? Now he follows you around to public places?"

"He's here." She turned right and addressed an empty seat. "Miles, say something to Lee. He needs to hear you."

"I have nothing for him to hear," Miles said. "I wish to withdraw. Go home, now."

"Mi-les!"

Lee slid his hand over her elbow. "So, he said for you to F off?"

"He wouldn't use that kind of language."

"Come out, come out, wherever you are," Lee sang. "If he's real, he's a coward, Jen."

"He's not here now." Jen picked up her purse and headed for an opening in the row. Lee followed her. "Jen, stop. I'm sorry. Wait."

She walked faster, taking two steps for each of Lee's long strides.

But he caught up and grabbed her waist. "Hang on. Don't go. Please."

She turned to face him. "You don't believe me."

"You know what? I don't care. Really. I've never met anyone like you, and if you are happy having a ghost buddy, then I'm happy, too."

She opened her mouth to speak, but before a word came out, she saw the sign behind him. Signs from local supporters lined the stadium fence, and this one looked familiar. The Eye of Horus, *Madame Zelda, Gifted seer, platinum supporter.* It seemed Zelda dug deep into her pocketbook for the school. The wind picked up and blew a cool zephyr. The Eye of Horus moved as the sign waved in the breeze. Another gust drove Jen's hair into her face, and an errant receipt from The Finger took flight. The sign danced, making a strained, flapping sound. Jen and Lee looked at each other. A third blast of wind moved Zelda's platinum supporter marker almost horizontal with a noise like the cry of a baby.

Lee pointed to the sign. "I know what the sound is. They need to fasten Zelda's contribution sign and give it some oil." He took her hand. "Would you like to come to my house? We can order Chinese and have a cozy evening." Lee pointed to another donor's sign, hanging three places down. "Or we can go to that place for a bite."

The sign's artwork caught Jen's attention. She read the advertisement twice. The drawing depicted a large dark pie with a hovering fly and a swiftly charging flyswatter. The words *Chu Phly Pi's Asian Kitchen* took her a few seconds to understand.

"Shoo Fly Pie! Now, *that* is funny."

Lee chuckled. "It's the owner's name, and you will love the food. He even has Shoo Fly Pie on the dessert menu."

"How can I refuse?"

"I knew it would appeal to your unique sense of humor."

Jen touched his arm. "Speaking of sense of humor, I was teasing about doing it in the cop car."

"I thought so."

"You did not. You were considering my offer."

Lee winked at her. "You'll never know for sure, will you?

"Did you forget? I'm psychic."

"I'll keep that in mind. Look, Chu's is a quarter mile away. Next street east of Clematis, on Rose Drive. Turn right on Main. Meet me there?"

"Okay."

Five minutes later, Jen pulled into a small strip mall parking lot next to the Crown Vic. Chu Phly Pi's Asian Kitchen sat in the middle of a four-unit building next to a laundromat, a shoe repair, and an antique store. Smells of ginger and chicken wafted about the air. A tinkling of bells heralded their entry and rang again when the door shut.

A tall man, bald with a Fu Manchu mustache, dressed in a gaudy red Chinese outfit, bowed. "I feel safe already. Welcome, policeman."

"Jennifer Hughes, please meet Chu."

"Hello, Mr. Chu." Jen could not take her eyes off the cascading mustache.

"So," Chu eyed Jen up and down. "This you new squeeze?"

"I'm trying my best."

"Come. I give you best table."

Lee followed the large man. "How long have you been in this country?"

"Many years."

"And you still have your heavy accent?"

Chu stopped short and turned. "You not come to Chu's to talk. You come to eat! So shut up. This you table. Nice. Quiet.

Not by kitchen."

Lee held the chair for Jen. Within a minute, a small Asian girl dressed in black brought them a pot of tea and tiny china cups without handles. Behind her, another girl brought crunchy noodles and a slender dish that held small metal cups containing sauces of many colors.

Chu returned, put his hands together, and gave a short bow.

"May I see a menu, please?" Jen asked.

"No menu. You not need. You get chef's spesh...chef's... spech."

"Chef's special," Lee said. "That sounds great."

Jen looked up at Chu. "What's in it?"

Chu pursed his lips, causing the mustache ends to flap. "Don't ask. That's what's special."

Lee winked at Jen. "Trust him."

Chu held up his forefinger. "Not nice you always tease Chu."

"I'm not the one who teases you. That's Grainger."

Chu waved his hand in the air and turned away. "You cops all look alike to me."

"All right for you, Mr. Chu! You give it to him." Jen laughed. She thumbed over her shoulder at the retreating Asian. "I rike him arot."

Lee took her hands in his. "I rike you arot, too."

"Enough for a ride in that Porsche?"

"If you want to, okay."

"You take the lady vet out in it," Jen said. She selected a crispy flat noodle and studied like a scientist looking at a new life form.

"How do you know that? Oh, yeah. I forgot, psychic."

"In fact, you date her when either she or you get lonely, kind of an old established friendship that can get temporarily intimate. She's your fallback squeeze."

"I neither confirm nor deny." He dipped a noodle in a bright red sauce and chomped it whole. "Jealous, I hope?"

"Maybe. A bit. Ask me after the ride." She took another noodle and tried the red dip. "Lee, I went to the League of Learned Lawmakers a few days ago."

"Don't do that. You can't possibly find anything, and you might get into trouble."

"I was with Keith. No trouble."

"From the little you have said about him, he must be an idiot. I doubt he could defend you if something came up."

"That wasn't very nice."

"I didn't mean it to be. That imbecile let you leave him. He didn't even try to keep you."

Jen sighed. "Keep me? He's the one who sent me away. He had a mid-life crisis."

"He'll be sorry when he realizes what he's lost."

She smiled at him. "Already happened. Keith has his uses. He knows some members of the League and got us a lunch invitation. And it so happens that I did find out something. The general manager is a dead ringer for the headmistress at the Currier. You should check them out."

"Have you met the headmistress at the Currier?"

"No, I haven't seen her, but I have it on good authority."

"Good authority?"

Jen's face warmed. She got mad so easily these last few days. She threw her hands in the air. "Haven't I given you good information so far? I'm giving you some more. Do you want my help or not?"

"Hey, hey, don't get riled. And, yes, you've given us terrific leads. I'll look into it for sure." He picked up a noodle and pointed it at her. "Don't go to the Currier or to the League. Promise me."

Jen looked away. *Another man telling me what to do.*

"Jennifer. Look at me. Promise."

"I'm trying to help you."

"Then help me by staying put. Rest on your couch. Close your eyes. Allow the magic or vibes or whatever it is to work. Then tell me the information you get so we can arrest the bad dudes. Okay?"

"Well, I—"

"Honey, it's not safe. If I could be with you all the time, I wouldn't worry so much. Think about it. A few weeks ago, some thugs burned your garage and tried to kill you."

"I try not to think about it, but I'm scared."

"You should be scared. Stay out of harm's way. I'd like to think you'd be safe in your house, but—"

Chu came to their table, interrupting the conversation. "You have some of these." He put down a dish with puffy dumplings surrounded by a dark brown liquid.

"Mr. Chu," Jen said. "I love the way you've decorated the restaurant. What do those symbols mean at each table and over the door?"

He got closer to Jen. "Call me Chu. My mother paint those. In old country, she boss chief. She chant when she get up each day and drive the evil spirits away with symbols."

Lee rolled his eyes. "Do you think it works?"

"You see any evil spirits around?"

Lee picked up his chopsticks. "I guess it drives away elephants, too. I don't see any of them, either."

Jen touched Chu's hand. "Thank your mother for the symbols and her chanting. It's nice knowing we are safe from evil in here."

Chu nodded. He stared at Jen for a second and bobbed his head slightly. Then he walked away.

"Don't egg him on, Jen."

"He may be doing us a favor." She thought about the Innocents. "Evil spirits can be driven away by symbols and chants."

"Sure." Lee pushed the dish of dumplings toward her. "Try one."

She arranged her chopsticks in her fingers. After a few attempts, she took the fork sitting in a holder and stabbed the thing.

They ate quietly for a while until Chu brought a sizzling

platter to the table. Steam danced from the myriad of vegetables and the postage-stamp-sized pieces of steak nestled in a clear sauce. Bits of red, yellow and purple made the dish look like an abstract painting. One of the girls brought a covered dish of white rice. From the aroma, Jen noted a hint of curry, jasmine, and hot pepper in Chu's chef's special. After two bites, she could identify some of the flavors as each one presented itself on her tongue. The steak practically melted away while the essence of charcoal bloomed with each morsel of meat.

"This meal is wonderful," Jen said, taking a sip of tea. "I've never had anything like it."

"Unique?" Lee asked.

"Absolutely."

"Like you," he said, almost whispering. "Jen, I've been doing a lot of thinking. I don't want to be alone anymore. I want a normal life, and I want it with you."

She put down her fork. "Normal life?"

"It could be. I want you with me in the morning when I leave and there at night when I come home." He lowered his voice again. "I want you next to me while I sleep. I want to kiss you…everywhere you can be kissed."

Chapter Forty-Three

Those hormonal urges she had captured and securely imprisoned during her library research shook the bars and escaped. The marvelous meal had just been trumped by the vision of Lee kissing her in the many places now screaming for kissage.

Jen fidgeted in her seat. "Jee-man-ee Christmas! We need to slow down."

"Why? We're in our forties. Young enough to enjoy life, but not so young we can waste time. You could still have kids."

"Kids? I don't want to even think about that."

He leaned toward her. "I'd like another chance at happiness."

"I would like a chance for happiness too. I'm afraid to rush into it." Jen ate a few more bites before she pushed the dish away. Chu came with the little white cartons carried by the wire bale and filled them with the leftovers. Instead of a red pagoda on the sides, the boxes had the same evil-warding symbols guarding the doors and tables.

"Nice touch, Chu," Jen said, admiring the cartons. "Thanks. And do tell your mother to keep up the good work."

Lee said, "Check, please."

"On me tonight, Detective. You have good taste in companions. You bring this squeeze back to Chu's soon." He bowed and left.

"How about that?" Lee said, holding Jen's chair and picking up the doggie bag. "He's never comped me."

"Nice guy," Jen said. "Like you."

"Nice guy? Is that what I am to you?"

"Nice. Dependable. Handsome. Sexy. Honorable."

"Great. I sound like a Boy Scout. All those qualities, but you're not interested in spending your life with me?"

Jen swallowed hard. The electricity from his comment about kissing all her places still pinged around her body. What kind of an answer could she give him? Where was that advice-giving secretary? "I need some time."

Lee nodded and walked her to the car. He pushed her gently against the door and kissed her. She wanted more. She knew he wanted more, too.

"Take some time, but not too long, okay? Good night," Lee said. "Drive carefully. Give Rex a pat for me."

Jen's body tension subsided when Lee drove off. They both needed time to think. On her way home, she stopped at the pet store and bought a dog bed and chew toys. A very real-looking stuffed raccoon caught her eye, and when she pressed on its belly, a nasty-sounding squeal enticed her to add the item to the basket.

When she got home and walked Rex, he headed for the spot he dug at the foundation. She handed him the squealing raccoon for diversion. It didn't divert as well as she had hoped, but she pulled on the leash and brought him into the house.

In the quiet of the house, Jen reflected on the day. Lee practically proposed to her. In addition, she didn't feel good about her exchange with Miles in the bleachers and wished they could talk about it. He said he would be home before she retired. By ten o'clock, still alone, she enlisted the aid of her favorite prince, Valium, and fell asleep. No dreams of any flavor visited her.

In the morning, she found Rex curled up on the end of her bed. She slipped into a robe.

"Okay, Rex. Time to pee."

Rex followed her down the stairs and waited at the front door, where Jen had looped his leash on the antique hall tree. She clipped the lead and took him for a stroll to the backyard. It was nine a. m. and no sign of Dave or his crew. She would definitely have to get on his case.

Back in the kitchen, Miles sat at the table reading the

newspaper.

"Good morning, Jennifer." He put down the paper. "And Rex."

"I guess it's good." Jen headed to the coffee pot.

"My dear," Miles began.

She turned and held up her hand. "Not until after my coffee, okay?"

"Very well." He went into the living room and made sounds of loading and tamping his pipe. Next came the twang of the lighter and the smell of lighter fluid. Soon the bouquet of sweet Cavendish mingling with her favorite morning aroma, coffee, gave her a secure, cozy feeling.

She brought her cup to the table. Miles entered the kitchen, sat, and folded the paper into a neat rectangle.

"You were rude to me last night, Miles."

"I regret you construed my interaction as rude. You did not respond to my first request. Therefore, I resorted to a different tactic."

"Yes, different—rude. I don't care for your policeman's voice."

"That is an interesting description. In fact, we were trained to give commands in such a way to make people listen and cooperate."

"Why didn't you want me there? I wasn't hurting anything."

"You could have caused a great deal of trouble by asking questions. Brad fears journalists claiming to be ghost hunters will come to Livonia. The legend of Abigale's baby may be just the thing to bring them here. They possess powerful cameras and sensitive equipment that might interfere with the souls who prepare to battle against evil."

"A battle?"

"The tension builds. We do not know what will happen, but be assured, some great encounter awaits us. Ghost hunters! The sound of their name bespeaks incalculable havoc."

"Ghost hunters have shows on television. Have you

thought that maybe bringing your efforts to public attention will help?"

"It would be disastrous. Have you not felt the negativity brewing about you? The evil enveloping Livonia disseminates suspicions and hostilities. At first, the malevolence impinged on the population's consciousness in dreams or in vague suggestions. But I see the misery expanding. Imagine the confrontation in our town should strangers invade and expose our spirit dwellers. Some people would believe, and some would not. Some would rejoice while others become fearful, angry, or mad."

"You're right. It would spook a whole lot of folks, for sure."

"And interfere with the good works Brad has commenced."

"I'd like to meet this Brad and have a real conversation with him. He sounds like a hero."

"He is."

"Okay, I'll downplay the whole spirit world thing. No one believes me anyway."

"There are those who believe."

"A lot of us?"

"No. And it should remain so."

"Gotcha."

"And I will take care not to use my policeman's voice on you." He picked up the pipe and took a strong draw. "Unless, of course, I need to." He blew a series of perfect smoke rings in her direction and smiled.

The smoke rings amused her. The comment did not. "You will never need to."

Miles stood from his seat. "I regret I must take my leave now. In my absence, please think on this, my dear lady. Police are trained in certain skills. When those skills benefit an individual, he praises the law enforcer. When the same skills are not directly favorable, frequently the person complains about them as a nuisance."

Jen thought about his comment as he put away his smoking items. Miles paused on his way to the back door and kissed the top of her head. "Keep safe."

Like my father used to kiss Mom goodbye each morning. He'd say, keep safe. Lee's words in the restaurant about being together morning and night sifted into her mind. "Miles, you leave in the morning and return at night. We act like an old married couple chatting over breakfast before the man leaves for work."

"Parts of your observation seem quite pleasant to me. I will see you this evening."

"Wait. What do you do when you leave here?"

Miles turned the door handle. "Soon, I shall explain in detail. It is about time you knew."

Chapter Forty-Four

Unnerved by Miles's remark, Jen mentally mapped out her day. First stop would be the bank to deposit Keith's monthly check. She would ask him to have it electronically transferred the next time they talked. Then visit the library to use the ancestry program for obituaries. Perhaps she could find out more about Timothy and Christopher Cisco. After that, a stop at the grocery store.

The Maryland Alliance Bank on Broad Street didn't have a guard. That struck her funny, considering the evil lurking in the nooks and crannies of the town. *I guess this town's brand of evil doesn't include robbery.*

Standing third in line, she hardly noticed the small woman in front of her until the woman turned around and smiled. "Good to see you again, Jennifer."

Jen strained her memory for recognition. The lady sporting dark hair streaked with gray looked familiar. The wool suit with black and white checks threw her. The face. Yes, *Zelda Silverstein – the current Madame Zelda.*

"Hi, Zelda. I didn't recognize you out of uniform."

"Uniform. That's cute. So, how's things?"

Jen smiled. "You're the Seer. You tell me."

Zelda grabbed Jen's hand and peered upon it. "Yes, it's all here. Your existence takes twists and turns daily." She lowered her voice to almost a whisper. "And your sex life sucks."

"Wow. You do have the gift."

"Nah, I say that to everyone. It fits most people. Even me, especially the sex life part." *Oh, no. Here we go again with Zelda's lack of action.*

Zelda gave a one-shoulder shrug. "Don't worry. I'm not

going to bore you with my lackluster love lustings."

"Wow, maybe you *do* have the gift!"

"Next!" the cashier called out. Zelda took her turn at the window.

When Zelda concluded her transaction, she stepped aside and waited for Jen to finish her business. Zelda jerked her head in the direction of the lobby. Jen followed her. Next to a potted palm, Zelda said, "I like you. Lee likes you, too. Come see me. How about today?"

"Today? I'll check my social calendar." She closed her eyes and opened them. "Okay. I can fit you in, say lunch-ish. How's that?"

"Sounds great. Eat before you come. The Great Zelda doesn't cook. See you."

Zelda left the bank, speaking to practically everyone on her way out.

Having completed the first chore on her list for the day, Jen focused on the next, which turned into a bust because the library's computers were down.

With extra time on her hands, she filled her car with gas, then browsed through the Goodwill store, searching for affordable cashmere sweaters. What had been fun hunting while married to Keith might now turn out to be an action of need. No cashmere, Ralph Lauren, or Donna Karan. At least she managed to bag an apparently unused pair of black Bally pumps for $9.99. After a visit to The Finger, she headed for Zelda's house.

Zelda, now in her official gypsy uniform, let Jen in. "What can the Great Zelda do for you?"

"You invited *me*."

"Right. While you conduct your Hampton Family Tree search, maybe I can save you some time and give you something you won't find on ancestry software."

"How do you know I'm searching the Hampton Family?"

"I'm the Seer, remember? Also, the young library clerk lives next door, and I asked her what you were doing. Didn't Lee warn you about me being nosey?"

"He didn't use that term, exactly."

"Don't I just love that man. If I was forty years younger... mmm. What information are you looking for?"

"I want to know about Miles Hampton's wife and children after, you know —"

"After his demise? I've already told you what I know about Virginia and her children after the explosion. Why do you care?"

"I want to find out about the family, what happened to his kids and grandkids. I saw a picture of Virginia and Miles. I'm curious. And I agree with your grandmother. Miles couldn't have done those things."

"You base your feelings about his guilt on an old photo?"

"That and..." Jen put her hand in the middle of her chest. "What I feel here."

"What will you do with the information? Write a juicy expose or magazine article? You aren't going to invite a television crew to film your house and claim ghosties?"

"Zelda," Jen said, with a crack in her voice. "No ghost hunters."

"Nah, I didn't think so. I trust you. Based on what I feel," Zelda put her hand in the middle of her sagging breasts, "here. But I can't see what good it will do to know the history of people long gone."

"For my own satisfaction. I look at the furniture that Virginia probably picked out. I wonder who ordered the stained-glass window designs. Who chose the fish scale shingles? Lots of little reasons. You don't have to tell me if you don't want to. I can research and maybe find out bits of information. But since you offered, it might be more fun to hear it from you."

"Didn't Lee warn you not to pay attention to what I told you?"

Jen couldn't hold back the smile. "Of course, he did. But I think there might be a few nuggets of truth in your tales."

"More than nuggets, sweetie. I know stuff that'll knock your socks off. Want some tea?

"Yes, please. Um, regular tea, right?"

"Hmm, I might throw a dash of something in mine, but your cup'll be straight up."

Jen waited at the table covered with the sun, moon, and stars cloth while the older woman moved around the kitchen. The kettle whistled. A few minutes later, Zelda entered with cups and a plate of Oreo cookies on a tray.

They sipped the tea without speaking. Zelda pulled her Oreos apart, licked the filling, and dunked the cookie wafers. Jen envied the woman's *joie de vivre*. Jen accepted the thought of being wonky but couldn't bring herself to enjoy Oreos like a kid in front of another adult.

After Zelda cleared the dishes, she came back to the table with a shoebox. "Jeezy's father was the town's photographer. He developed pictures for the newspaper, too. You might enjoy some of these images."

Zelda dumped the box on the tablecloth. As Jen picked them up one at a time to view, the Gifted Seer sorted through and selected a handful of pictures. She put two wide-angle photos aside.

Jen turned over each photograph Zelda selected and read each caption aloud. "Town Hall. Library. High School. Police Department. Stanton Owings, Police Chief. Railroad Station, Ratterlee Buggy Factory. Is this the factory?"

"Yep." She put the photo down and picked up another one. "Now, look at this." Zelda held a photo of a teenage girl, long flaxen sausage curls tumbling over her shoulder. A lovely cameo centered on the neck of a pin-tucked blouse. Unlike other poses of that era, this young lady smiled at the camera.

Jen took it and turned it over. "Oh. Zelda Rothberg. She's beautiful."

Zelda nodded slowly. Then she handed Jen another photo. The young man, clean-shaven, had bright eyes and golden hair. A slight smile bespoke his inner nature.

Jen didn't have to turn it over. "Miles."

"Jeezy helped her father in the dark room. She produced a

lot of these pictures herself secretly from the glass negatives. She told me a lot about her life and gave me her stash of pictures." Pointing to the two wide photos, she gave a short whistle. "Check these out."

Jen held the first one of a baseball team. Her gaze followed a hand-drawn arrow. Miles stood proud in his uniform, just as handsome as the newspaper photo of him with the police squad. The second wide-angle shot showed a group of young men stripped down in he-man undershirts and work pants, digging what could have been a basement. Perhaps a photo for the newspaper, the caption on the back said: *Young men volunteer their services in building the new Presbyterian Church.* Taking a magnifying glass from Zelda, Jen viewed the image close-up, revealing Miles's rounded, muscled shoulders rippling as he pushed a shovel into the turned earth. The invisible secretary gave Jen a shove and said, "Ooh, ooh, Miles! You brawny, strapping cutie, you."

Jen cleared her expression lest she be caught drooling. "Do you think we'll find photos of Miles's children?"

"Some of them."

"Uh, what do you mean by that?"

"Got your socks on tight?"

Chapter Forty-Five

Zelda left the room and returned with an old Whitman's Sampler box. "Jeezy excelled in her studies, but when she turned seventeen, her grandfather in New York sent for her. The story was she went to help with their fur business because some of the relatives got the flu. She dropped out of school and came home a year later. But Jeezy really went to New York to have her child."

Jen sucked in air, making a whistling sound. "Oh! Miles's baby!"

Zelda nodded. "She broke up with Miles while she stayed in New York with her relatives."

The older woman's candy box showed folded, yellowed letters. Zelda held up one letter. "Miles would have done the right thing, but Jeezy knew it would have ruined him. He couldn't have succeeded in any career with the reputation of moral turpitude, and she doubted he would have converted to Judaism. So, Grandma Jeezy sent Miles a *Dear John* letter saying she wished to end their relationship. Would you like to read Miles's reply?"

The words were written in the calligraphic style of the day and spoke of his love for the young woman. No begging, for she knew Miles wouldn't beg, but the letter told of his disappointment and the advice to think it over. "Poor Miles."

"My grandmother knew she couldn't keep little Emma, so she let her aunt's neighbors—a childless couple, Mr. and Mrs. Charles Caulfield—adopt the baby." Zelda riveted her eyes on Jen for a moment.

The name sunk in. "Caulfield! As in Johnny Caulfield?"

"The very same. Jeezy returned to Livonia and helped her

father in the studio while he searched for a suitable husband. One day a young lady came into town and had her portrait done. As soon as Jeezy met her, she knew Virginia Carvelle would be perfect for Miles." Zelda shuffled through the photos and handed Jen a three-quarters view of another young lady.

Jen had seen that face before. "Virginia." She turned the photo and read, "High School Graduation, 1888. She's pretty. I like the pose."

"Jeezy called it right on. Miles fell like a brick, and they married. Meanwhile, Granny got her own man." A new photo emerged from the pile. "Here, look at this."

The picture showed lovely young Zelda and an older, obese, bearded man. Jen turned to the back. "Zelda and Abraham, Wedding Day. Oooh, poor Zelda. He's old and *gross*."

"But," the Gifted Seer said, "in those days, the list of men who would marry a fallen girl had to be a short one. Abe's wife had died, his children were grown, and he had a good profession, a pharmacist. He had enough money to provide well. Jeezy said he was nice to her and gave her more freedom than a lot of other women of the time."

Another photo of Zelda, Abraham, and two children came from the stack for Jen's inspection.

"Jeezy did what good wives do and gave Abe a few more kids." The modern-day Zelda touched the picture over the girl's head. "That's my mother, Sylvia. Sylvia didn't take well to motherhood. Demons tempted her."

Jen experienced a flash of fear. "Demons?"

"Drink and sex. I guess I inherited a bit of her appetite. But not for alcohol. Sylvia — I never called her Mother — abandoned me, and Jeezy raised me. I didn't know Abe. He died before my birth."

"Too bad Sylvia turned out so wayward," Jen said. "Must have been hard on you."

"I fared much better being raised by Granny. The family lines must have had bad genes because not only Sylvia fell from grace, but Emma turned out to be a hellion. Sylvia's brother,

Herman, became a zombie."

"What?"

"He turned out okay if you like people who have stones for hearts. I suppose you want to hear more about Emma."

"Uh-huh, please."

"You see, even though the adoptive parents did their best, Emma was a wild child. Jeezy kept track of her, and somehow Emma found out her birth mother lived in Livonia. At sixteen, Emma came here searching but never discovered who her mother was. By then, Jeezy had become a widow and made her living by palmistry and renting rooms. Can you guess who she rented a room to?" Zelda fished out another photo. "Behold! Emma Caulfield."

The photograph showed a beautiful teenager with wild curly hair and a defiant expression. The resemblance to Miles was evident.

"There's more," Zelda said. "Emma hooked up with Marcus Ratterlee, and she got pregnant. The girl went home to her adopted momma, dropped the kid off, and returned to Livonia, where Marcus did his thing again. After that, Mr. Caulfield came and forced Emma to return to New York, where she stayed with her parents and two kids."

The gong outside bonged.

"Oh." Zelda put her pointing finger to her cheek. "I must have a customer. Maybe I forgot an appointment. I think this is enough for today anyway."

"You've told me a lot. Why?"

"Didn't you want to know?"

"Yes, of course. But—"

"Then quit asking foolish questions and enjoy the history. I have my reasons." Zelda quickly gathered up the photos and returned them to the box. "I'll call you some time for the rest of the story."

"There's more?"

"Indeed. And next time you come, wear tight socks!"

Chapter Forty-Six

Jen walked to her car in a state of shock. If what Miles said upon leaving that morning almost unnerved her, Zelda's revelations finished the job.

"Get it together," the secretary demanded.

Jen put the car in gear and headed for The Green Way, the upscale grocery store that played Vivaldi and offered small cups of wine and little cheese cubes. Maybe a stroll through the hanging plants and the strains of soft music would clear her head.

At the corner, she hit the brake to avoid a white Kia backing out of a driveway. The same kind of car Pam drove.

She read the sign in the drive where the white car had been.

"Blakely Construction, Licensed Contractor." The building was an older home converted into a business office. *David Blakely! The name on the contract for the garage. This is Dave's office!* His green double-cab truck sat in the driveway.

Jen pulled in behind the truck. Her mobile phone rang.

"Hi, Jen. It's Pam."

"Speak of the devil!"

"Excuse me?"

"I just thought about you not ten seconds ago."

"Oh. What did you think of?"

"How are you? Any more panic attacks?"

"I'm good. Can we get together? I've got some things to tell you."

"I'd like that. Dinner at my house tonight? Six?"

"Super. Don't go to too much trouble."

"I need to. Cooking fixes me. What do you hate to eat?"

Pam laughed. "Almost nothing. Papayas, beets, and cranberries. Surprise me. Bye."

"See you later. Bye." *Pam sounded better. I need some girlfriend company.*

The slamming of the office front door caught her attention. Dave walked toward his truck, his head down. Jen jumped out and blocked his way.

"What's going on, Dave?"

"Oh, Ms. Hughes." His shoulders sagged. "Sorry for the delay. We'll come over tomorrow and install the opener and paint the trim. I'll make sure we leave everything nice and clean."

"Good. When do you start my basement?"

"About that...."

"What about that, Dave?" Her words formed angrily, anticipating trouble.

"It can't be done."

"Wait a minute. You said it would be easy."

"I was wrong. I can't finish your basement."

"Oh yes, you can," she said. The amount of rage generated by Dave's refusal surprised her. "We have a contract, remember? You deferred the insurance's five hundred deductible toward the job, remember?"

Dave walked around her and got in his truck. She followed and stood next to him to keep the door open.

"I'll give you the five hundred back."

"I want my basement built." Her teeth clenched, and the words, normally controlled by her *reasonable* brain, rushed forward at light speed. She pointed her finger at him. "I know a very good lawyer. If you don't finish my basement and soon, I will *so* sue you. I will kick your ass in court." *Wow, where did that come from?* But she had said it and couldn't take it back.

Dave put his forehead on the steering wheel. "I'm sorry." He spoke so softly she barely heard him.

When Dave wouldn't look up or speak, Jen, trying to sort out anger from embarrassment, returned to her car. Miles, Zelda, and now Dave. What could happen next? She didn't mean to, but the tires squealed at her gear change from reverse to drive.

At the Green Way Store, fall decorations were placed on the shelves, complementing the aroma of mulled cider available at three stations throughout the store. Jen ambled through the aisles fighting the desire to fill the cart with everything she saw but buying only a round roast, a bottle of burgundy wine, carrots, mushrooms, potatoes, onions, and wide egg noodles for *beef bourguignon*.

As soon as Jen got home, she walked Rex. After assembling the ingredients, she put the covered roasting pan in the oven. While it cooked, she prepared the table with her one good tablecloth, candlesticks, and her good china.

Two hours later, Rex wolfed down his kibble as Jen ladled the roast beef and sauce into a covered tureen and spread the noodles on a platter. Pam's car crunched in the drive at six on the dot. Jen tilted the Quitcher Bitchin' sign. Miles would know to straighten it to signal his presence.

Rex barked, and Pam warily entered through the back door into the kitchen. Jen introduced the dog to her friend. He growled, a low, threatening rumble.

"When did you get him?" Pam asked.

"The other day. He's good company." She admonished the dog. "Rex. Stop growling. Lay down." The dog quieted but didn't move from his spot.

Pam sniffed. "Something smells good," Walking slowly past Rex while maintaining a careful eye on him, she handed a bottle of wine to Jen.

Jen read the label. "Whoa! *Neuf Chauteau du Pape*. Big spender."

"It's a gift from last year's Christmas party. Besides, we're celebrating."

"Celebrating? Do tell," Jen inserted the corkscrew and slid the stopper up noiselessly.

As Pam left the kitchen, she adjusted the Quitcher Bitchin' sign. "I can't stand tilted wall hangings."

Jen brought food dishes from the kitchen and placed them

on the table. Then she removed glasses from the dining room hutch.

Pam poured the wine and held her glass aloft, smiling.

"Okay," Jen said, grabbing her glass and clinking the rim with Pam's. "What's the occasion for the toast?"

"I turned the Speigals down!"

Jen took a long drink. "Good for you. How about those photos?"

"I visited Johnny in jail yesterday. He admitted he didn't give the pictures to the Speigals. He just told me that so I'd cooperate with them, and they would spring him. But after thinking about it, he knew he was wrong and told me not to do anything for them. Johnny's not brilliant, but he's not a bad guy, either. He said the slammer isn't so bad, and he knew it was just a matter of time before he'd get into trouble. A good lawyer can get him off. He wouldn't even need a good one if it wasn't for that damned Ferguson."

Chapter Forty-Seven

That got Jen's attention. "What does Ferguson have to do with Johnny?"

"Some age-old feud between Johnny and Burleigh Ferguson. I don't remember the details. But the cops, meaning *Ferguson*, urged that dog-dirt bitch Arlene to press charges."

"Say how you really feel, Pam. Don't hold back."

"Her rich parents have her stashed away, not allowing any calls. Johnny said if he could talk to her, he could get her to drop the whole thing."

"You think Ferguson told them to keep her out of sight?"

"I think that ugly booger has some link to the dumb slut's family."

Jen took a drink. "You don't think Detective Ferguson might be a little attractive?"

"Not in the least. He has connections, and he's setting Johnny up."

Jen placed a serving onto her plate. "That's not the vibe I get from Ferguson. Why would he want to railroad Johnny?"

"In high school, Johnny beat the crap out of him." Pam buttered a slice of French bread and bit into it. "Ferguson has hated Johnny ever since."

Jen sat quietly, sorting out this bit about Johnny and Lee. She needed to hear about this from Lee himself. The new information damaged the rest of her appetite. "You know, Pam, if Arlene Holmes stays sequestered, you'd have another chance at Johnny."

"What good is that if he's doing ten to twenty?"

The conversation eased, and toward the end of the meal,

Rex came from the kitchen, barked, and wagged his tail.

"What's that about?" Pam asked.

"He does that from time to time."

"Maybe it's your ghost. They say animals can see them. Any problems with your so-called spirit? I've never heard you say anything."

Jen put down her fork. "Not with ghosts. But raccoons. That damn Dave Blakely is trying to back out of doing my basement. I want that basement fixed. I can't stand having the raccoons down there."

"Should have got yourself a good old-fashioned coon dog. That would take care of your critter problem."

"Maybe Rex will take them on. I have to keep him from digging at the foundation when he's outside. There's one more reason to get that basement finished. My dog may dig my house into the ground." Rex came over to Jen and wagged his tail. Jen stroked the soft fur on his head. "Rexie, why don't you turn into a coon dog and get rid of them coons?"

Rex wagged his tail again.

"Don't stress over it. This house has been around for a long time. Maybe you should just let it go."

"More wine?" Jen asked.

"No. I'm, driving, and the cops might see a taillight dim or something and pull me over. I'd better not have wine on my breath. I hate the cops."

"How about dessert, then?"

Pam felt around her belly. "Uh, yeah, I have room—right here."

Bringing Rex back into the kitchen, she assembled dessert. Jen scooped vanilla ice cream into glass dishes and opened a can of cherry pie filling. She mixed a slosh of brandy into the cherries and ladled it over the ice cream. In the dining room, after pouring an additional tablespoon of brandy on each dish, its azure flame glowed.

"Oh! Red, white, and blue! Spectacular." Pam proclaimed the dessert scrumptious. "I'm going to do that the next time I have someone to dinner."

After dessert, Pam helped bring the dishes into the kitchen.

Jen stacked them in the sink. "How about a movie? We can see what's on television."

Pam shook her head and cast a glance at Rex. "I think I'll go now. You're a good friend. Thanks for everything." Pam kissed Jen's cheek and left.

Jen shut and locked the kitchen door.

"I thought she'd never leave," Miles said, taking form.

"You don't care for Pam?"

"I'm annoyed by anything that takes time away from your company. I want to spend as much time solid with you as I can."

Jen surveyed Miles as he approached the small kitchen table. "New outfit? I like it."

"I remembered these trousers." He pinched the velvet-like brown corduroy. "Quite comfortable."

"Perfect match with the shirt."

He held out his arms covered with a brown and tan Tattersall print on white cotton.

"I love the suspenders, too."

Miles titled his head. "On occasion, dear one, I suspect you have fun at my expense. Is the love true for the suspenders?"

"Now that I've had a moment, I call back the sarcasm. I do like the suspenders. The fashionistas wear them even if the straps don't really suspend anything.-

"Explain fashionista and why their suspenders don't work."

Jen waved her hand in the air. "Never mind. It would waste my time and yours. Tell me about your day."

"Brad and I traversed the streets searching for Floaters, vulnerable souls we can lead to safety in sheltered havens."

"What's a sheltered haven? Like a church?"

"Some churches offer protection. In my invisible state, I see the world from a different perspective. Havens project a blue light. The stronger the light, the stronger the haven. The strongest light, a golden one from the Innocent, comes from under the bleachers at the high school. That light is a beacon in a dark landscape. You already know about that. The blue lights form a dome over the havens, but the newly oriented must know how to read the beacons."

"You said some havens are churches. The biggest church here is St. Mary's, and Catholics are the ones who do exorcisms, so their light must be strong."

"The Catholics do exorcisms, but it depends on the efficacy of the preparer and on what he believes. Saint Mary's light, unfortunately, does not shine so brightly."

"Really?"

Miles raised his eyebrows in reproach. "The church I belonged to for years hardly glows at all. Actually, the strongest church light beams from the tiny All Faiths Christian Church at the end of Broad Street. I have seen Detective Grainger there with his wife."

"Oh, great. A star for Ash Grainger. Skip the churches. What else can be havens?"

"A few businesses who have had their doors blessed and who keep up their guard. A strong light glows over the restaurant you dined at the other night with—"

"Lee? Chu Phly Pi's? Hey!" She glared at him. "How did you know I was there?"

"That's the restaurant. It's a great haven, well placed in an emergency. The woman who blesses the place understands our needs."

"Do you talk to her?"

"We don't need to."

"Okay, so, say you are out in the street, and a poor Floater comes by. Then what?"

"Brad and I approach the soul and offer an escort to the habitat under the bleachers, or if that isn't possible, to one of the havens. Just as I was naive the first day I ventured out, we find new souls who know naught of the dangers lurking about."

"I didn't think a lot of people in Livonia are dying. How many souls are walking about?"

"The spirits aren't necessarily from this area. Many of them have been in nether sleep like I was and are waking up. I still don't know why they are coming *here*. Perhaps Brad can enlighten me on that question. He is a most potent force. I become stronger each day through his teaching. He came to the Spirit Plain already a Warrior, learned on his own, and has attained the rank of Paladin, the highest level a spirit can realize."

"There's nothing higher?" Jen raised her eyebrows. "Like God?

Chapter Forty-Eight

"I don't know. Nor does Brad. I know about the division, the evil and the good. There must be leaders, but we work using what we know. I believe our actions come under the concept of Free Will. It is our will to save the living against evil."

"You frighten me, Miles."

"I am regularly frightened, dear woman."

Jen had enough of Spirit 101. "Tell me about Zelda Rothberg."

"Why?"

"I want to know. I've seen photos of her. Stunning."

"Zelda was a rare rose, an incomparable beauty, her loveliness surpassed only by her kind sweetness. She possessed an intelligence encountered once in a lifetime." Miles caught Jen's eye. His face became serious. "She broke my heart."

Jen reached for Miles's hands. "I'm so sorry. Tell me about her."

"We loved each other. She ended it. No more to tell."

"No, no, no. There's plenty to tell, and I want to hear it. Let me guide you on this trip down memory lane. You and Zelda obviously met in school, and when you reached young adulthood, you fell in love. Now don't give me a difficult time about this. Back in your day, young people didn't have the same opportunity for…closeness. Nowadays, we mothers tell our daughters not to give it out too quickly, or the guys won't respect them. I would think mothers in the nineteenth century told their daughters not to give it out at all."

"Gentlemen don't discuss these things."

"Uh-uh. I think you two had assignations. I don't need the

intimate details; just tell me how you accomplished the logistics."

"Jennifer," Miles said in a voice close to the policeman's tone.

"Come on. I don't need the spicy stuff. I'm curious how you managed."

Miles tugged at his carefully groomed mustache. "I said Zelda was clever."

Jen moved closer and leaned in toward him. "Yes, you did."

"My mother had an elderly aunt who lived on the other side of town nearby the Rothberg's photographic studio. Ever since I was a little boy Aunt Olive favored me, and my mother constantly brought me over there to visit. When I got older, I learned not to mention I was going to the ballfield, or the chemists, or to that side of town because the next thing I knew, Mother had something I needed to bring to or retrieve from Aunt Olive. My aunt was deaf, and so was her only companion, Lily, the old servant. The two of them resided in a huge house with front and back staircases, but the ladies only lived on the bottom floor."

"Ooh, I see where this is going."

"The Rothbergs stayed in quarters above their studio. Zelly helped her father and became an accomplished photographer. What a shame that malingering brother of hers inherited the business. Zelly had regular rounds, picking up the chemicals at the chemist, delivering the photographs, and conveying mail to the post office. I knew her time schedule. On the days I could get free, I used visiting Aunt Olive to my advantage. I told Mother I was headed to the ballfield, etcetera. As predicted, she would produce some reason I should stop by my aunt's house. Naturally, I protested, but Mother would kiss my forehead and say I was such a good boy. Didn't I want to please her and Aunt Olive? I would then relent."

"So, you've been manipulating women for over one hundred years now?"

Miles pulled at the other side of his mustache. "I hadn't quite thought of it in those terms. Thank you for opening my eyes to more personal guilt."

"Whoa, whoa, don't stop talking because of guilt. Being a man, the guilt won't last long. Get over it and finish the story."

"It's finished."

"No, no, no. How did you and Zelly communicate your little trysts?"

"Telephone."

"No way."

"Mr. Rothberg was a successful businessman, and my father was the town's doctor. Both of our households had telephones. To keep the nosey exchange operator in the dark, Zelly invented our code. I'd call, and since her mother usually answered, she'd summon Zelly with a reminder the phone was for business. Zelly would say hello, and I'd ask how her father's bursitis was, the code for can you meet me. If she said his health was excellent, then she'd ask about my father. I'd say something like he's had ten patients already, or one man came in with a broken arm. That code gave her the time. I'd visit with Aunt Olive and Lily, and when Zelda climbed the back stairs, she'd stomp on the floor to let me know she waited. Aunt Olive's dog, an Alsatian named Duke, would bark when he heard the stomp, but Auntie didn't hear it, even with her hearing device."

"What kind of device?"

"A brass horn she stuck in her ear. I shouted into it when I'd leave and gave her a kiss."

Jen smiled. "Zelly *was* a clever girl."

"I didn't doubt her love for me. Look at the chances she took. I loved her, and I wanted to marry her. I even talked to my father about giving me an operation to make me more suitable in the eyes of her family."

"An operation to make you more suitable?" Jen thought for a minute. "Oh! Do you mean circumcision?"

"Yes."

"You weren't already snipped?"

"Why would I be? It's cultural, performed as a religious custom."

"Now there's a visual for you," the secretary said.

And it was. Jen had never seen a soldier at attention with a helmet before and searched her little gray cells for an image.

"It's done routinely now," she said. "I didn't want Bobby to have it when he was born, but Keith insisted, so he wouldn't be different from his dad."

The thought of Miles's uncultured condition seeped back into her gray cells. She shook the image out of her mind in time to see Miles's pained expression.

"I never understood it, Jennifer. How could she forsake me? Zelda dropped out of school and left for New York City to help relatives in an emergency. While there, she wrote me a letter saying it would be better not to continue our love. You should never experience that degree of misery. There is no pain like that of a broken heart."

"Oh, Miles. I'm so sorry."

"If she didn't love me enough to marry, then so was it decreed. I trusted Zelly's judgment above all others. About a year later, I met Virginia. And Mr. Rothberg arranged a marriage for Zelly, the pharmacist who bought out the chemist and made a good living for them. Abraham was a nice man. I liked him."

I wonder if Abie knew about you, Miles.

"Zelly seemed content. I don't think she was happy." He slouched in the chair. "If ever I was to be wrong, I prayed it was with that notion. If nothing else in the world, I wished Zelda true happiness."

"Miles, were *you* happy?"

"Virginia was the perfect wife and mother. I cared a great deal for her."

Jen, saddened by Miles's story, went into the kitchen. The few inches left in Pam's wine bottle offered solace. She brought back two glasses. "Would you like to try some? Can you taste the wine?"

"Of course, just as I taste the Cavendish. My tongue is fully functional," he added in a serious tone. "I'll have some wine."

She downed the bit of rosy solace and stood. As she passed

a glass to Miles, she leaned in and put her cheek on the top of his head. "I'm sorry. Life wasn't fair to you."

"I had twenty good years with Virginia and my sons."

"I'm so glad. Thinking about your happiness is important to me."

He reached upward and rubbed her arm. "Your words provide food to my hungry heart."

"Goodnight, dear Miles."

"Sleep well, precious Jennifer."

Jen readied for bed, selecting her red nightshirt. Sleep eluded her as she mulled over the day. The wasted time at the library, that damned Dave and Zelda Silverstein, had certainly given her a lot to think about. Some of it must be true because Miles had confirmed parts. But Lee had warned her about Zelda's embellishments. *What about Emma? Did Zelly leave to have a baby?*

The secretary stepped in. "Sort through the verifiable facts, meaning the only thing Miles can confirm is that Zelly left town, and she wrote him a letter."

I saw a picture of Emma.

"You saw a picture. How do you know the identity? Even if you could confirm the name, there's no way to know if she was sired by Miles."

She looked like him.

"And you look like Princess Di, remember? Coincidence."

Why would Zelda show me that photo, then?

"Because she's wonky? What fun for someone to feed a new hunger for the town's dirty laundry. You can be a sap, you know. Keith worked you all the time."

Thanks.

"Only because I care."

So, what do I do?

"Keep this stuff to yourself until you know more. Go to sleep."

Chapter Forty-Nine

Jen drowsed off. That night no chocolate dream slipped in to cuddle her. The dream *du jour*, startling and vivid, presented tall pink soldiers, each with soft helmets on their non-faces. Changing, the soldiers lost arms and legs, becoming sleek tan monoliths retaining the slouching hats. Marching in formation, they drilled back and forth until they turned and headed straight for Jen, who watched from her seat on the high school bleachers. Closer and closer, the faceless, erect sausages progressed toward her. The first row jumped onto the bottom seating and advanced to the second stage, as the following row took their place behind them. They swarmed the bleachers. Jen's pounding heart woke her.

"Miles! Miles!"

Her bedroom door flew open. Miles turned on her bedside table light and sat next to her. "What is it, my dear? Another bad dream?" He helped her sit upright.

She closed her eyes firmly. "Not exactly a bad one." She moved closer to him until she was able to put her face against his neck.

Miles put his arm around her. "Frightened?"

"Not exactly frightened." She cuddled closer, laying her nose against his skin.

"Are you all right?"

"Not exactly all right." She touched her lips on the warm apex of his neck and shoulder.

"Jennifer," he whispered.

She didn't respond, drinking in the masculine bouquet of skin, the Cavendish, the wine, and that scent belonging to the man himself.

Miles kissed her hair, gently moving to her ear and cheek, then along her neck. Jen breathed a little groan. Miles pushed her down and moved next to her, placing kisses over her neck and chest, moving up to her mouth. Miles's fully functional tongue proved his claim. Jen moaned quietly. He moved his hand over her breast, making Jen's quiet moan increase in volume. She ran her hand over his corduroy pants. Solid. She wanted him. The hormonal urges recently subdued and abused took over.

"Oh, Lee," she cried.

Miles halted and moved away.

"Miles! Don't stop."

"You called me Lee," he said icily.

"No, I didn't. Did I? Don't pay attention to that." She tried to pull him close, but he didn't move. "Oh, God. Between you and Lee...you're driving me crazy. Miles!"

"It is just as well. This can't be."

He stepped away from the bed. His hand went to the crotch of the corduroy trousers. He pulled the seam away from that which was solid, very solid.

Jen put her hand over her lips, hoping her fingers were wide enough to hide the sides of her mouth.

Miles looked furious. "And what, pray tell, do you find amusing in this situation?"

Jen couldn't hold back. "It just occurred to me that ball adjustment transcends death."

Miles scowled, obviously not appreciating her observation.

"Come back, Miles."

"It's wrong."

"Seems to me, whatever reason we are together, we have the means of enjoying our good luck. Should we miss the opportunity? You said the other day that if fortune bestowed the gift of closeness, you wouldn't waste it."

"I was wrong."

"I have never begged for sexual attention in my life—"

The secretary scolded, "And you're not going to now

either."

"And I'm not going to beg now."

"It would not become you."

Yeah, no becoming for Jennifer tonight.

Miles headed for the door.

"What are you afraid of, Miles?"

He turned his face toward her. "The only thing I fear is that Detective Ferguson won't be so noble."

"I can pretty much guarantee he won't."

Miles put his hand on the doorknob.

"Miles, I want to tell you...your kisses are divine... wonderful...indescribable." She could see the unspoken question on his face. "Yes, better than Lee."

"Liar," the secretary said.

Equally good. Leave me alone.

"Goodnight, Jennifer." Miles left.

Chapter Fifty

Rex woke Jen the next morning by licking her hand.

"Well, at least one male around here appreciates me." She kicked off the covers. "Hold on, boy. I'll get my robe."

Rex paced in front of the door, telling Jen to hurry. At the hall tree, she grabbed the leash. After she unlocked the door, Rex ran to the nearest bush. When he put down his leg, he barked and pulled Jen around the corner of the house. A work van turned into the drive. Jen brought her robe together closer and tied the terry belt.

Two men got out of the van. One walked around to the van's back door and opened it. The other approached Jen.

"You Jennifer Hughes?"

"Yes. Who are you?"

"Dave sent us to install your garage door opener. It'll take us a while, and then another guy will come and paint the trim. Oh, and the paint guy will put in the lock set, too."

"Thanks," Jen said, and walked the dog to the side of the house, where he sniffed vigorously at the foundation. "Is this where the coons get in, Rexie boy? Are you going to roust them out like a good ole coon dog?"

Rex dug, and a stream of soil shot from under him.

"No digging. I don't want the basement to cave in. Come on, we'll take a stroll around the yard, and then it's time for my coffee."

When she brought Rex into the house, Miles sat at the table.

"Good morning, Jennifer," he said, looking up from the newspaper.

She didn't answer and avoided eye contact, embarrassed after the events in the bedroom.

Miles looked toward the window. "Workmen?"

"For the door opener. Another workman will come to paint and install the side lock." Jen squirmed and looked away. "Um. We should talk."

"Dear lady. Please do not fret over our late-night *contretemps.* Worry is a destructive force, precisely what the Evil Side would have. You are a victim of the detrimental atmosphere set forth. As the town fortifies against the wickedness, the Dark Forces must attack in other ways. You and many others suffer the results of emotions orchestrated to wound society."

"What does *that* mean?"

"Have you not experienced strong emotions lately? Feelings contrary to your usual amiability?"

"Like—"

"Rage, envy, pride?"

"Yeah. Add lust and gluttony." She looked at the sink full of dishes left from her dinner with Pam. "But not sloth! I'll fight that one. So, you're saying I'm being affected by what we call the Deadly Sins?"

"Yes."

"You said many others. Does that include you?"

Miles looked down at the paper for a moment. "No. My lust cannot be blamed upon the Dark Forces but from which grows inside as I become corporeal for long periods. I offer no excuse, only that after one hundred years, I am in close quarters with one whom I find nearly irresistible." Miles folded his paper and stood. "I must go. Be careful. Don't let anyone in." He kissed her forehead. "Stay safe." He turned the handle, and by the time the door had fully opened, he disappeared.

Jen touched the spot of his kiss and let out a soft breath. She made her coffee, put two slices of cinnamon swirl bread in the toaster, gave Rex a cup of kibble, and ran upstairs to dress.

As she sat down for her breakfast, she heard a faint mechanical sound, letting her know the garage door apparatus functioned. Looking out the window, she smiled as the door went up and down and then cycled again. This device sounded smooth and quiet, not at all like the squeaky contraption preceding it. She waved and smiled. The workmen waved back and departed.

A few minutes later, Rex barked. Jen checked through the window but didn't see anyone. "Coons? Is that what you hear?" She undid the padlock on the basement door and, carefully stepping on the treads, made her way down, pulling the cord from the light that hung adjacent to the third step. "Come on, Rexie. Find those rascal varmints and scare them away."

Rex passed her and went along the packed dirt walls sniffing at the dusty shelves, stopping to smell patches here and there on the floor. She hadn't noticed it before, but a crack ran most of the way along the middle of the soil floor. She had only been down there a few times and didn't have a recollection of anything but the nasty furry fat coons she knew to be hiding somewhere. Rex came back to her at the bottom of the stairs, and she interpreted his facial expression as his doggie *all clear.*

"Okay. You earned your keep for the day."

They returned to the kitchen. Rex stopped, came to attention, and growled.

Jen checked the back and side through the windows. She saw no cars, no workmen, no one walking dogs, nothing. Rex continued his odd snarly rumble.

"Quiet, Rex."Jen resumed her breakfast.

Rex moved to the back door, emitting low growls.

"Hey, enough. There's nothing there."

The dog's lips quivered over his teeth.

"Okay, when I'm done with the dishes."

Rex put his paw on the door, his threatening rumble increasing.

"All right, we'll check it out now."

Jen opened the back door. Rex raced for the garage. When she opened the side door, she stood face to face with a man, ruddy-skinned with uneven whisker growth. "Oh! You scared me. Are you here to paint?"

The man nodded as he put on work gloves. Rex moved stiffly, in slow motion.

"It's all right, Rexie. Relax. Sit!"

The dog sat. "Good boy." Jen turned and opened the cabinet, picking up one of the small cans of paint. When she turned back, the man held a gun.

"Get in your car. We're going to take a little ride."

Chapter Fifty-One

She backed out the open door a few feet from him. A flush of anger ran through her. "No, we're not."

"Well, I could just shoot you right here then," he said in a gravelly voice.

"You won't shoot me. I have neighbors. And, most likely, there's a cop nearby. Get the hell out of here before I start screaming."

"You won't have time to scream," he raised the gun toward her head. "And no one will hear the shot."

She ducked to the side, heard a slight whoosh, and a puff of air moved her hair under her ear. A bullet! She threw the paint can at him, and it struck his elbow. He moaned and dropped the gun, grabbing his arm. She froze.

He retrieved the gun. "Goddamn, sonofabitch." He trained the gun on her. Staring at the barrel, she moved backward.

Before he could pull the trigger, a blur of white flew at him. Rex's teeth bared and dug into his arm. The gun flew aside. The man fought, but Rex tore at his flesh, snarling at top volume. Jen heard screaming and realized the sounds had come from her. The cacophony of Rex's vicious growling, her screaming, and the thug's yelling echoed from the side of the garage. While Rex did his best to mutilate her attacker, Jen picked up the gun and dashed to one of the trash cans lined against the wall. Moving its lid, she dropped the gun into it and slid the top back.

Rex wouldn't stop. The mauling continued while Jen screamed and the attacker yelled in pain. Time stood still until a black and white patrol car screeched into the drive. A uniformed cop and his partner flung open the doors and ran to the excitement.

"Help me!" the man said. "Call this monster off."

"Ma'am, call off the dog."

"That man tried to kill me."

"Call off the dog," the officer said in his control voice. "Now."

"Rex!" Jen said, responding to the command. Rex lowered his level of intensified maiming but didn't let go.

"Ms. Hughes," the officer said, "I'll have to shoot him."

She stepped close and pulled Rex off the man. Shreds of skin stuck out of the dog's mouth. The man's arm had bloody gaps, with drippy red patches staining his clothes.

Sirens squealed in the background. Before Jen could speak, the white Crown Vic shrieked to a stop along the street. Lee dashed from the front seat.

Lee looked to Jen and to the other cops. "What's going on?"

She put a shaking hand to her cheek. "He tried to kill me."

The bleeding man stomped his foot. "That fucking fruitcake tried to kill *me*. I came here to paint, and she sics Cujo on me." A slight accent punctuated his words.

"Lee! It's not true. He pointed his gun at me and said we were going to take a ride. He shot, and I threw a can at him."

"Gun?" Lee said.

More sirens sounded from a distance.

The man wrapped his gloved hand around his bite wounds. Blood oozed through his fingers. "She's nuts! In fact, yesterday, she threatened to kick my boss's ass." His accent became more apparent.

"In court!" Jen argued. "I said I'd kick his ass in court!"

"Gun?" Lee repeated.

Jen turned to the trash can and opened the lid.

"Not my gun. It's hers, the one she pointed at *me*," He added a groan as he pulled his arm close to his jacket.

"We can test it for fingerprints," said Lee.

The man flexed his gloved fingers. "You won't find mine on it."

Lee stiffened. "Will we find your prints, Jen?"

Jen's face burned. "Yes, because he dropped it when Rex bit him. I didn't want him to get it again. If it hadn't been for Rex, I'd be dead." She stroked Rex, who lay at her feet. "Wait! Can't you check his gloves and jacket for gunpowder residue?"

Lee ran his fingers through his hair. "Maybe."

The man sneered. "Not my gun."

"Let's see some identification," Lee said.

"I can't let go of my arm."

The ambulance maneuvered around the cop cars. Emergency techs hopped out and ran to the man.

Lee pointed to one of the uniforms. "Destry, go with them. Get his I D. Grab the jacket and gloves as soon as they come off." He turned to the man. "What's your name?"

"Ivan Rodovich," he said, allowing the Russian accent its full range.

Lee backed away to let the EMTs help Rodovich to the ambulance. "Destry."

The uniformed cop turned. "Yeah?"

"Get his info. I want to know what happened after his fifth birthday up until two minutes ago."

"Right, Lieutenant."

As Rodovich stepped into the ambulance, he shouted, "Arrest that crazy bitch before she goes on a killing spree. And give that monster dog a needle!"

Lee pressed his key to open the Crown Vic's trunk and took out gloves and a plastic bag. Retrieving the gun from the trashcan, he held it up. "Silencer."

Jen looked at it and put a shaking hand to her throat, remembering. "That's right. I didn't hear a loud bang. But how did the police get here so fast?"

"I have them park around the corner to keep an eye on you when they can. A neighbor called in a dog attack." Lee gave the bagged gun to the other uniform and took her by the elbow into the house. They stepped into the living room. "So, tell me from the beginning what happened."

After escorting her to the couch, he moved the burgundy wing chair a few feet opposite her.

Jen put her hands to her face. Tears slid down her cheeks. The magnitude of the event settled, and within seconds, she started to suck in air, followed by loud sobs.

Lee grimaced. He leaned toward her, then sat back. "Jennifer," he said in the policeman's voice.

She looked at him, took a big sniff, and dabbed her cheek on her sleeve.

"Jenny," he said softly. "It's okay." He went into the kitchen and brought back a few paper towels. "Tell me what happened," he said in a tone, part police professional, part champion.

She blew her nose and wiped her face. Gaining control, she recounted the morning with the workmen and added her confrontation with Dave.

Rex rubbed his snout against Jen's knee. "What would have happened if Rex hadn't jumped that man? You believe me, don't you?"

"Yes. And I believe Rex." He moved from the chair to the couch next to her. "And, when my men arrived, there wasn't a vehicle. If he was there to paint, he'd have his ride. That doesn't sit right. We'll get to the bottom of this."

A car screeched to a stop outside. A door slammed, and footsteps sounded on the porch steps.

A voice called from the porch step. "Hey. It's me, Grainger."

"Great," Jen said, not concealing her annoyance.

Lee opened the door.

Grainger nodded his greeting to Jen and spoke to Lee. "I just talked to Robinson. He and Destry got here pretty quick."

Lee sat in the wing chair. "They were parked around the corner."

Grainger eyed Jen. "This, uh, incident. It's a he-said-she-said thing." He pointed to her. "I'd like to hear the *she said* part."

Without invitation, Grainger pulled up the second velvet wing chair to face the couch. Jen told her story.

Grainger shook his head several times during the account.

Anger built inside her. "Why are you shaking your head? You don't believe me? That man pointed a gun at me and fired. He tried to kill me. What else do you need to know?"

"A lot more than that. You know," Grainger's eyes narrowed. "Strange things seem to happen all around you. Enough strange things, then, well, one could conclude—"

Jen jumped from her seat. "Conclude? What does *that* mean?"

Grainger pointed his finger at her. "I take the direct approach, meaning cause and effect. If B always follows A, then I, as a detective, conclude A caused B. That's how I work, and it usually turns out to be sound."

Jen turned to Lee. "Do you agree with that?"

Lee gave a quick shrug and slanted his head. "Usually. Yeah. I do."

She paced in front of the chairs. Her anger banished the shakiness. "And just where did you two get that load of crap?"

Grainger sat back in the chair. "From our classes at John Jay University."

"Never heard of it," she grumbled.

Grainger rolled his eyes. "That doesn't surprise me."

"You learned that from classes in police work? Hmm." Jen pulled at her chin with exaggeration. "Then night must cause day since B follows A *every single time!* Thanks for the illumination. I've been wondering for years why it happens every twenty-four hours."

Jen returned to the couch. She caught Grainger's scrutiny as she sat. "I know you don't like me."

Grainger's eyes looked like pieces of onyx. "Who said I don't like you?"

"I can tell."

"It has nothing to do with like or dislike."

She folded her arms under her breasts. "I don't want to debate your feelings, Grainger. I want you to believe the truth."

"That's Detective Grainger to you," he said.

She uncrossed her arms and touched her knuckles to her

waist. "All right, *Detective Grainger*. You two need to talk to Dave Blakely. I think this has something to do with him not working on my basement."

Grainger took out his palm-sized notebook. "What's going on with your basement?"

"Well, *Detective,* I hired Dave to replace the dirt with concrete and steel."

"Why do you want to do that?"

"What's it to you?"

Grainger clicked his pen in and out. "Why do people have to change things that work? Hasn't that basement been dirt for over a hundred years?"

"Maybe it has, but I don't like coons in my house."

"What?" Grainger's eyes flashed. His jaw made clenching movements, and his chocolate-colored skin showed red undertones.

Lee stepped in between them. "She didn't mean it like that, Ash."

Jen turned to Lee. "Mean it like what?"

Grainger sneered. "I don't appreciate that racial slur." He stood and stomped toward the door.

Jen put her hand to her mouth. *Oh, God!* "Grainger! Detective Grainger! Wait!"

She sprang forward, stopping in front of him. Putting out her hand, she pushed her palm against his chest. "I didn't mean that comment as a racial slur. I wouldn't insult you that way. Not that I have any qualms against insulting you because you have earned a few, but I wouldn't do it like that. I meant raccoons, noisy, dirty mammals that live in my basement. I want them gone."

Grainger's nostrils flared, but he didn't move farther toward the door.

"Damn it!" Jen said. "I almost got killed. Why are we debating racial slurs?"

Grainger bit his lip. He let out a long breath. "You're right. I don't know why I reacted like that."

Maybe the evil air in Livonia has gotten to you, Detective.

Returning to the chair, Grainger looked at his notes. "I promise to give this my utmost attention, Ms. Hughes."

"Detective Grainger, please call me Jennifer. I don't want bad feelings between us."

Lee sat down. "Neither do we, Jen. Ash and I will get to the bottom of this."

Grainger's cell phone played. After a brief conversation, he closed the phone and stood. "Gotta go. For some reason, Rodovich's gloves and jacket disappeared from the hospital."

"Oh, no," Jen said.

Lee touched her hand. "Don't worry." He looked at Grainger.

"I'll take care of it," Grainger said, his tone kinder, more sympathetic. "What about the dog?"

Lee petted Rex, who sat quietly on the floor next to the couch. Traces of Rodovich's blood still dotted the white fur around the dog's mouth. "I'll vouch for him. I had him for a while before bringing him here. I don't think he's vicious." He turned to Jen. "I think he's protective around his owner."

Her anger slackened. Jen began to cry. She wiped her eyes with a crumpled paper towel.

Grainger pointed at Jen. "We're going to need your clothes for gunshot residue."

"I didn't shoot. I just picked the gun up to throw it out of reach."

Lee turned to Jen. "You said Rodovich stood a few feet away from you?"

She nodded. "Even when I backed up, I'd say about the same amount as between us right now."

Lee shot a glance at Grainger. "She'll have residue from the close range."

"Test my hands," Jen said. "I haven't washed them. You'll see. No nitrates. Probably in my hair and my blouse. I didn't fire, so no nitrates on my hand."

Grainger cocked his head at an angle. "You watch a lot

of cop shows, don't you? All right. The van is on its way. We'll need your clothes to test. Stay right here. Don't do a thing until the tech completes her tests. Lee?"

"I'll tie her up if I have to," Lee said with a smile. "No hand washing until the test."

Lee walked with Grainger to the door. They talked in low tones before Grainger left.

"Lee," Jen said, coming toward him. "I don't understand any of this."

No longer the policeman, he rubbed her shoulder and gently moved her back to the couch. "I don't understand it either, but crime isn't always logical."

"Do you think it's because I am providing information?"

"I don't see how. The only people who know are Grainger, Uncle Paul, and me. I have to tell you, Uncle Paul doesn't buy into psychic clues, but he lets me run down your leads. He's happy with the results. We found out the headmistress Stella Anderson's sister, Stephanie, works as general manager at the League. Furthermore, those ladies have mob ties. Uncle Paul seriously enjoys the pressure from the Feds to turn the case over to them. He's taking ten phone calls a day from Washington and New York."

Jen blew her nose.

"There's not much we can do until Grainger checks out Rodovich. Try to relax." Lee moved closer. He guided her head to his shoulder. "Feeling better?"

She touched the tissue to her nose. "A little."

"Good. Let's drop this mess for a minute. Maybe I can help cheer you up. Do you enjoy live theatre?"

"Plays? Musicals?"

"How about *Oklahoma*?"

Jen smiled. "I was Ado Annie in high school. Beat out that nasty Ally Fart for the role."

"Fart? What a name. Hey! You're smiling. So, next Saturday afternoon, I'll pick you up for a play and a nice dinner."

"Another funky-named restaurant?"

"It's a surprise. Be ready at four."

"That's kind of early. Why — ?"

Lee put his finger to her lips. "No questions. Just say yes."

"Okay. Yes. But I have some questions for you about something else."

"What's that?"

"Did you know Johnny Caulfield in high school?"

"Uh, yeah."

Before he could reveal further memories, the crime scene van arrived. Lee introduced Jen to the lady tech who accompanied Jen upstairs. The tech bagged Jen's clothes and swabbed her hands for residue testing.

When they came down the stairs, Lee was closing his phone.

"Swell," he grumbled. "Not only did Rodovich's gloves and jacket disappear from the hospital, but now Rodovich himself is gone."

Chapter Fifty-Two

Lee stiffened. "Destry has the hospital security tapes for us to examine."

"Lee? This all looks so bad. Are you sure, Grainger—?"

"Ash is one of the good guys. Everything will work out. Let us do our job." Lee pulled Jen's chin to his face and kissed her, holding it long and pressing hard. "Until later. Keep Rex close."

Jen followed him to the door and watched him leave. She sat on the couch. Rex put his chin on her knee, looking up with sympathetic eyes.

"My brains feel like scrambled eggs, Rexie. By the way, thanks for saving my life." She scratched him behind one ear. "I guess I should give you a bath. Wash away every trace of that horrible man." Jen switched to Rex's other ear, massaging the soft flap.

The notes of the phone interrupted the ear rubbing. Jen groaned, seeing Keith on caller ID.

"You should answer," the invisible secretary advised. "Perfect time for a diversion. Ask your questions about suing Dave."

"Hi, Keith."

"What's going on with you?"

"Everything's just peachy," she said, thinking a description of the morning's events would prolong the call.

"Can I come to see you? I'll bring the kids. Maybe Saturday? We'll go somewhere nice?"

Don't commit to anything yet. "Maybe." The secretary tapped her shoulder. "Keith's brother is an architect." *Architect. Basement.* "Heard from James lately?"

"My poor little brother. He and Mona just finalized a divorce. She's demanding substantial alimony."

"That's a shame. Do you think he would like to join us for dinner sometime?"

"I'll bet he'd love it. Can he come with us this weekend?"

"I have plans for Saturday, Keith. Check if the kids and James would like to come over Sunday for a visit. Give me a call." She clicked off.

Rex seemed to know the conversation ended because he trotted up next to her, putting his ear near her hand.

"Such a smart doggie," Jen told him, resuming the scratching. "Such a good boy, too. I hope we don't have trouble over this. Good thing Lee knows you, fellow."

After a few more minutes of canine affection, Jen sat back on the couch, and Rex curled under her feet.

The grandfather clock chimed noon.

Jen's head fell back on the couch's upright cushion. She unclenched her teeth and rubbed her knotted stomach. Closing her eyes, she said, "Oh, Lord, who is trying to kill me? And, please, let the rest of the day be boring." *Is it too early for wine? It's never too early for Xanax. Maybe I should take a nap. Like I could really sleep.* When her mind completely jammed, Jen stared at the wall.

After a quiet, blissfully boring fifteen minutes, the back door squeaked open, and Rex wagged his tail. Miles entered the living room.

"Today is just full of surprises," Jen said.

Miles sat in the wing chair, still near the couch. "Your words are at variance with your appearance. What has happened?"

"A man shot at me this morning."

Jen told Miles her account. She added the fact that not only had the man disappeared from the hospital, but her fingerprints would prove she held the gun, in addition to the powder residue. She hoped the cops would find the bullet and it would have prints. At least *hers* would not be on it.

Miles reached for her hands. "Twice now, you have been in jeopardy. Do you know why this brute sought your death?

We must learn the motive, for when we know the source of the illness, we can seek the cure."

"I don't have the faintest idea. I hope Lee and Grainger will find some clues."

"As much as I wish not to bestow glories upon Detective Ferguson, I am in his debt for bringing Rex to you." Miles patted his knee. "Excellent animal," he whispered to Rex.

"Almost as good as an Innocent?" She leaned over and petted the dog again. "Aren't you home early? Did Brad give you the afternoon off?"

Miles nodded, his serious look increasing. "Yes. In a manner of speaking."

"I said it as a joke."

"I must insist you stay here in the house the rest of the afternoon. Please cancel any plans you have made."

"I should ask you why you want me to stay put, but truthfully, I'm sure as *hell* not going anywhere. I doubt I'll even walk Rex. I'll let him out and call him back." She eyed the dog. "Just to pee, now, Rexie. You have to stay close."

Miles stood.

"Okay, so what's so important? You're home early and insist I don't go anywhere?"

Miles headed for the front door and opened it. "Brad, outside, awaits your invitation."

"Brad? *The* Brad?" She moved to the doorway, looking left, then right. "I don't see anything."

Miles stepped outside and stood on the doorstep. "I assure you, Brad is here. Invite him in."

For the second time that day, Jen crossed her arms under her breasts. "I'm not inviting anything in I can't see."

Miles stiffened. "Jennifer. For what purpose do you insult the being who may ultimately save Livonia?"

Jen tightened her grip against her ribs. "Savior or not, if he doesn't show himself, he doesn't get invited in. If you want the Invisible Man to pop in for a chat, then you invite him."

Miles pulled at his mustache. "Only you can extend the

welcome."

"What happened to Miles Hampton's house?"

"I don't have the time to explain the intricacies of the spiritual realm. Suffice it to say what is considered as truth by common thought becomes the truth. This house belongs to you." Miles adopted his policeman's voice. "Invite Brad into the house."

"Oh, well, since you put it that way, then. No."

Jen heard a distinct chuckle from the porch step.

Chapter Fifty-Three

Both Miles and Jen looked at the empty space beyond the open door.

"Jennifer," Miles said.

"If he wants to come in, I need to see *something*. I'm creeped out as it is, and I refuse to screw around with *anything* or *anybody*."

"I do not understand your actions. Scarce a dozen steps from you awaits a soul of unusual abilities and knowledge."

"Scarce a dozen steps?" Jen took four strides and slammed the door. "If he wants to meet me, he needs to materialize."

"Jennifer, why do we quarrel? Brad does not materialize." Miles opened the door.

Instead of a chuckle, the sound on the front steps increased to full laughter. "Dude," a voice said. "Yep. I see why you like her so much. She's all that!" A glow formed in the open doorway. "How's this? Can you see me now?" The light increased. Colors flashed. "Can you see me now?" Sparks flew in all directions. "Can you see me now?"

"Stop! The neighbors will freak out." She cleared her throat. "Look here, Mister, um, Brad. Go around to the back door, and we'll talk. I've had enough male intimidation to last a lifetime. I don't care if you're Laser Show Jesus. If you want to meet me, it's my way."

"Or the highway?" the light display said, finishing her sentence.

"That's correct."

Miles said nothing. His humanized solid body became more rigid. His handsome face paled. He didn't move.

"Oh, what's wrong with you?" Jen said to Miles.

"Paralysis of perplexity."

"Whatever," Jen mumbled.

The light show dimmed to a small glowing sphere, which moved outside toward the back. Jen ran into the kitchen.

"Okay," Jen said, opening the back door. "I see a ball. How about something closer to human?"

A luminous figure of a man formed.

"Miles, you better be here. Now."

The glowing man-shape laughed. "What a woman!"

"Jennifer," Miles said, coming next to her. "I vouchsafe Brad's earnest regard for our wellbeing. His integrity lies beyond question."

She sucked her teeth in a quick sound. "Oh, that's enough, Miles. Come in, Brad."

"Thanks," a young man's voice said. "I can do some really cool light effects if you want to see."

"Why not just corporealize?"

"Dude! You been spending too much time with this lady. She's using big words."

Jen put her hands up, palms out. "You know what, Brad? I've had a really bad day. Why don't you come back when I'm feeling nice and you look like a person?"

The phone rang.

"Damn!" Jen cringed at the second ring.

Miles bent over the phone, eyeing the caller ID. "It's the detective."

Jen pulled the phone from its holder. "Hi, Lee."

"I'm checking on you. Everything okay?"

"I'd feel better if you had news for me. Say, like, you found Rodovich, and he confessed and then told you who is trying to do me in."

"I wish I could tell you all that. I've got a few leads now on Rodovich, but if you need me, I'll come over and stay for as long as you want."

"No!" She realized she sounded too emphatic. "No. I want

you to put all your efforts into cleaning up this scary problem."

"Call me," Lee said. "I'm number four on your cell speed dial."

"I know. I'll be okay." She looked at Miles. Her eyes moved to the glowing figure next to him. "I've got Rex."

"I'm glad. Ring me later so I'll know you're all right. Grainger and I'll be at the station all night."

"Thanks, Lee. Thank Grainger, too."

"Protect and Serve. Bye."

She replaced the receiver and then looked at Miles. "I don't know what to say. This is the first time a ghost has introduced me to another ghost. I'm not sure of the protocol."

"The what?" the young man's voice said.

"Miles. Are you *sure* this is the astounding Brad you've gone on and on about?"

"Dude!" the young voice said, the pleasure ringing in the word. "You been bragging on me?"

"He has, indeed, Mr. Brad. I expected Superman."

"Nah, not Superman. If I had to choose, though, I always thought Wolverine could be pretty cool. You know," he said, putting a glowing hand in the air and brought down blazing fingers. "Snickety snick!"

"My son, Bobby, had Wolverine posters all over his room. Of course, that's when he was a teenager."

Miles made a little noise in his throat like a prompt to get back to the point.

"Oh, yeah," Brad said. "He has a mission. Ma'am…. Um, can I call you Jennifer?"

"Okay. I should call you Brad or Mr. Brad?"

"Brad's good. So, Jennifer, do you mind if Miles splits and we yak for a while?"

Miles touched her hand. "It's important, or you know I wouldn't go."

"Um, Miles," Jen said, "may I have a word with you first?"

He nodded and held her elbow as they walked to the front door.

Jen touched his corduroy jacket. "What's going on?"

"I will be gone overnight. If all goes well, I'll return late tomorrow. I have asked Brad to look after you."

"Is Brad a kid?"

"I don't know. I have never seen him. In fact, until just now, I hadn't heard his voice."

"But you've spent so much time with him."

"In the spirit state, we don't speak or see as you know it. Whatever he was in your world is irrelevant. For now, he is a mighty power. One I trust implicitly."

Miles pulled her close. He kissed her lips, holding the kiss long, pressing hard. He left. She flinched when he shut the door. Turning to the glowing figure, she said, "Would you like to sit down?"

Brad's gleam increased as the radiant light moved through the house toward the couch. "It would be more like a hover."

"Oh, God," Jen mumbled.

"Yeah," Brad said. "I guess this is pretty weird for you. It's whacking me out, too. You're the first living I've talked to."

"Really?"

"Us spirits don't usually talk to Breathers. Oh, uh, excuse me. I didn't mean to insult you. Hey, I just thought of something. How's this?"

Brad's light dimmed.

Chapter Fifty-Four

As Jen watched, he took a form from the bottom up, completely covered with black boots, red and black leather pants, a matching jacket, black gloves, and, to top it off, a shiny red and white helmet with a blackened face shield. "It's my old leathers. I should have done this first."

Rex trotted over and sniffed the solid Brad, who took a seat on the couch. He petted the dog's head, and Rex lay down at Brad's feet.

"So," Jen said carefully. "You're a biker?"

"Was a biker. It's how I met my end." He tapped his gloved finger on the shiny white dome. "The time I didn't wear the helmet."

"I'm so sorry." She sat on the couch.

"Nah." He put both hands on his knees. "Don't be. In life, I was a piece of work. I've been given a second chance."

"Piece of work? What happened?"

"I didn't have a father because my mother didn't know or care who he was. She stayed drunk most of the time, even when she worked the *night shift,* if you get my meaning. I didn't go to school half the time and supported myself by breaking and entering. One time I hit the jackpot. Some idiot had thousands of dollars hidden in a box under his bed. That's how I got my bike. After that, it was me and my wheels. No school, no parents, no friends. Just the way I liked it. A few days after my seventeenth birthday, I was cut off by some old fart on the interstate. I hit a light pole."

Jen reached over and patted his gloved hand. "Poor boy."

He shrugged. "It's okay."

Jen swallowed twice in the silence. "Do you know what's on the other side?"

"No. My only connection is an occasional message from a Lingerer—someone who stays near the entrance and won't go over. Lingerers wait for loved ones. They throw out messages aimed at the loved one, and some of us spirits can hear them. In fact, before I came here, a soul named Daniel Shoemaker sent a message."

"Why don't the Lingerers just come back as spirits and speak to the loved ones?"

"Because they can't come back. We don't get a choice. But, once at the gate, spirits don't have to cross over, so some wait outside. Lingerers can hear the thoughts the living directed to them, like when a person visits a grave and speaks to the departed. The only way a Lingerer can answer is to call out and hope one of the resident spirits will hear. One of us can carry the message."

"What kind of message?"

"Daniel Shoemaker said he knows she still loves him and has been faithful after these many years apart. He wishes her to wear the ballerina slippers on his birthday."

"Strange message," said Jen. "Who is it for?"

"I don't know. I didn't hear that part. And getting the message to the Breather poses a problem. If the, uh, living person doesn't believe in ghosts, hearing the message from thin air freaks them out. Sometimes we appear while they sleep and whisper in their ear. That's the best way. They feel the answer, and it isn't as scary. But, even if I find out who should get the message, someone else needs to deliver it because I'll be leaving Livonia."

"Why?"

"Because I must complete my purpose. I got to make amends for all of my thieving, lying, and disregard for people. I know what I got to do."

"Do you know Miles's purpose?"

"Yeah, actually, I do."

"Tell him."

"That's not how it works. He has to get it on his own, see? It don't work right unless the spirit figures it out."

"He needs to clear his name?"

"I can't tell you."

"Can you tell me why some souls, like you, become powerful after death?"

"Kind of. Who we are in the spirit world is who we were in life. See, I did my own thing. Nobody told me what to do or when to do it. I guess you can say I had a strong personality. I'm like that now, too. But it doesn't mean we can't change. We should change to be better."

Jen nodded her head vigorously. "That should apply to Breathers, too."

Brad's tone became serious. "And some of us didn't cross over because of our oaths."

"What do you mean by that?"

He spread his leather-clad arms, extending gloved fingers. "Oaths, them things we say when we're all heated up and making promises to ourselves. When we yell things like 'I swear I will get you for that,' or 'I'll come back to haunt you,' or 'I promise to wait for you forever,' can come back on us. That's the biggest reason for the Lingerers. They made promises, and they have to keep them. Daniel Shoemaker must have made an oath with his loved one, and he's waiting for her. He's heard her speak to him, and he wants to let her know he's kept his word."

A chill ran down Jen's spine. "Do you mean the things we say actually affect us in the afterlife?"

"Well, it's more like the after-death because you don't go to the afterlife until you keep your promise. So, yeah, the things we say come back. When I was little, my grandfather told me the chickens always come home to roost. He said the things we do come back in some way. Like if we tell a lie, it goes out into the universe and bounces back at us, maybe in a different way. Say, we burn our finger on the toaster. We don't connect the two, but the pain is the backlash of the lie."

"You mean something like the wages of sin?"

"Yeah, I guess. I never went to church or nothing like that. That's what makes the Innocents so strong. They didn't do bad stuff to bounce around the universe, so when they die, they have a lot in their account. The more you do bad stuff, the smaller your account gets. Man, I had zero minus zero. But I'm going to take care of that."

"You're referring to your purpose."

"Yep. But I'm not quite ready yet. I gotta finish with Miles and some other souls."

Jen touched his gloved hand. "You will tell me before you attempt your purpose?"

"Okay. Don't say nothing to Miles. Let me tell him when it's time. It won't be too much longer before I go."

"Go?"

"Yeah, I have to travel a long way to fulfill my purpose. But that's enough of that, okay?"

"Sure. I didn't mean to pry, but it's so interesting and tempting to want to know more. You understand?"

"Yeah, I understand. You're a nice lady. I know why Miles likes you so much."

Jen bit her lip at the compliment. "Speaking of Miles, can you tell me where he's going?"

"Union Town. Something big is brewing here in Livonia. We need to know what's happening nearby to see if it's here or everywhere. He'll be traveling. He's become a Paladin. He won't admit it because he doesn't want to leave you."

"Me?"

"He thinks his purpose involves protecting you."

"It isn't?"

"Yeah, some. Miles's purpose has a few parts. But that's all I want to say about that, okay?"

"Sure. Can you tell me about the Dark Forces?"

"I don't know too much, only that they're here. And hopefully, they don't know too much about us. It's like a war, see. Them, the evil guys, against us, the good guys. It's harder for us because we have to protect the living from the bad dudes. The first time I saw Miles, he was surrounded by the Dark Forces, but now he can fight them."

"Can the Dark Forces hurt the living?"

"Not physically. Miles brought me back to protect you, but he didn't need to. He wanted to make sure you *felt* safe. You are safe here because this house is amazing. It's a fortress. Blessing barriers surround the house. The holy water and the prayers the former owners used to safeguard this place."

"I have to go out sometime, though."

"True. They can try to invade your personality, but for someone like you, they would have to try hard. They go for the easy ones. I think you're okay. But I know there is someone living in Livonia who hosts a really bad spirit, and that's the *person* you need to be careful with."

"Who is it?"

"If I knew, I'd be out whomping up on him or her. I hope me or Miles finds out before something big happens."

"Something big?"

Chapter Fifty-Five

Brad's helmet moved up and down.

Brad spent the night on the couch, and Jen slept with Prince Valium. And Rex.

In the morning, Brad said goodbye and disappeared through the back door. After her morning regimen, she headed for the library.

As Jen paused at the checkout desk, she exchanged a brief stare with Mildred Owings.

"May I help you?" Mildred said, her voice as cold and crackly as breaking icicles.

Jen laid her library card on the counter. "I'd like to use a computer, please."

Mildred picked the card up and put it into a small filing drawer. "Use computer four."

"Thanks," she said, hoping to warm the chill.

"You are welcome," Mildred answered, stern and chilly.

That lady doesn't like me. Maybe she's the Evil One. She'd be a good candidate.

Jen summoned the Ancestry program and began her search. After an hour of not finding what she wanted, she searched for Miles's sons. She had seen the adoption record, so Timothy and Christopher Hampton later acquired the last name of Cisco. She got hits. Both young men served and returned from their service in World War One. They reverted to their original name after age eighteen.

A wave of tenderness spread through her. It meant the boys were not ashamed of their father. Energized by positive feelings, she pressed on. At the end of the second hour, she found their obituaries and names of surviving children. Further, she found the addresses of two living descendants of Miles Hampton. Both of them resided in Virginia. Armed with the printouts, she collected her card at the checkout desk. Was the young lady at the desk the chatty neighbor of Zelda Silverstein?

As Jen ambled through the library parking lot, she noticed a man leaning against the car next to hers. His back was to her. Jen stopped. She considered going back into the library when the man turned around. He looked familiar, dressed in a blue golf shirt and tan pants. It was Chu Phly Pi but without the drooping mustache. He approached her.

"Good morning, Jennifer."

Jen hesitated. He looked different. He sounded different. She pressed the door unlock on her key. "Fancy meeting you here."

"I waited for you."

"Hey, what happened to your accent?"

Chu smiled. "I don't have one. I'm a Harvard Business School graduate. The accent and the appearance work like expensive advertising. The patrons love it."

"Tricksy, those Harvard grads," she said.

"You bet."

"How did you know where I was?"

Chu stepped closer. "Zelda told me."

"You consult Zelda?"

"Absolutely not. She has no gift for Seeing. But she knows everything that goes on in Livonia. You weren't home, so I took a chance Zelda might have made your acquaintance, and by now, she knew minute details of your life."

Prickles shot up her spine.

Chu smiled. "She told me to try the library. So here I am. And here you are, too."

Jen swallowed. She took a short breath. "What do you want?"

"My mother desires to meet you. She saw you when you and Ferguson ate the other night. Mom says you have the purest aura she's ever seen."

"I have an aura?"

"She said you connect with spirits. The color of your aura means you keep close contact with a powerful spirit."

"Wait a second. Does this aura mean I go around with a light blinking over my head welcoming ghosts?"

"I don't know if spirits can see your aura. Mom is a sensitive. They can see and read auras."

Maybe I'll write a dictionary for the spirit world. Sensitives, Innocents, Lingerers, Paladins, Warriors, Floaters, and Salients.

"Jennifer?" the man said.

She'd been staring into space while she processed this new information.

"Uh, yeah?"

"Will you visit with my mother? She has many questions."

"I have no answers. I don't know anything."

"My mother senses the change in the town's atmosphere, the bits of evil being released. She thinks the evil is being focused on you, and she wants to help."

I need to get home to my fortress.

"My mother studied under a powerful seer in her village. Mom has spiritual gifts and desperately wishes to speak with the spirits, but none have ever contacted her. She thinks you can connect her. Plus, she knows she can help combat that which attacks you. Please, let her help."

"Look, Chu Phly, I can't...I'm not.... Please don't—"

"I'm not Chu Phly Pi, either. I'm Harold Chang."

"Thank your mother for her high opinion of me, but I can't deal with this right now."

A lady passed them on her way to her car.

Harry Chang bowed his head. With his voice loud enough for the passerby, he said, "Chu happy to be you friend. You come to shop soon. Yes?"

Jen opened her car door and slid behind the wheel. Chu grabbed the handle before she could shut herself inside.

"Please think about it," Harry Chang said softly. Then in

a louder voice, he said, "Come soon, Miss Jennifer." He shut the car door and walked away.

Jen reached for her mobile phone and pressed number four on speed dial.

"Hi," Lee said. "How are you doing?"

"I'm okay. I needed to hear a friendly voice."

"Why? What's going on?"

"Oh, nothing dangerous. I'm about to leave the library. What's happening with my, um, case?"

"We've been working since last night. Rodovich is a criminal rock star. He was whisked out of the hospital by an unidentified man dressed as a doctor. Two men started a fight in the Emergency Room waiting area as a diversion. When everyone focused on the trouble, Rodovich and John Doe split. We're looking at bank cameras and various security images in the area. We think we have a license plate."

"Did you talk to Dave Blakely?" Jen asked.

"Gone with the wind. Neighbors said he pulled into his drive like a madman and fifteen minutes later squealed his truck out with the whole family and the dog."

"Thanks for your good detecting, detective. Thank Grainger…uh, *Detective* Grainger for me, too."

"Sure. Honey, be careful, okay? I'll call you later."

The second tender wave for the day passed through her. "Okay. Thanks, Lee."

As she put away the cell, it rang. She didn't recognize the number.

"Jennifer? This is Zelda. Are you free for the afternoon?"

"How did you get my cell number?"

"I'm the seer, remember? I don't give out my secrets. Can you visit?"

Why not? Let's see if today can be as bizarre as yesterday. "I'll come over after lunch."

"Oh, hey, bring me three chicken wings from The Finger."

Coincidence? Did the seer know I'd go to The Finger?

"Is that a 'yes, I'll bring lunch,' Jennifer?"

"Yes, I will, Zelda. See you later."

A quick trip in the drive-through produced three wings and fixings for Zelda and a chicken sandwich for Jen. At Zelda's house, before Jen could ring the gong, Zelda opened the door and waved for Jen to come in.

"Thanks," Zelda said as she took the box and escorted Jen to the kitchen table set for two. "What do I owe you?"

"Some truth," Jen said and sat in one of the chairs.

"What does that mean?" Zelda asked, opening the box. "Oh, goodie! Biscuits, too!"

Jen put her sandwich on the waiting plate. "It means if you have more to tell me, make sure it isn't stretched, padded, embellished, or — you get the picture."

Zelda broke off a piece of biscuit. She regarded the piece and then looked at Jen. "You think I don't tell the truth?"

Jen put a paper napkin next to the dish and locked eyes with Zelda. The quiet between them spoke a whole conversation.

"Okay, okay," Zelda said, flicking her hand in the air. "I have some interesting things for you. I have evidence to back them up, but it might take me a few days to locate what I need."

They ate in silence for a few moments.

"So," Zelda said. "How's your research going? You know, at the library."

"Pretty good." Jen related her discovery of Miles's sons' name change.

"Do you ever see Mildred Owings at the library?"

Jen gave a little sigh. "Yes. I see her there. She's not very friendly. I think she lives inside a hard shell."

"Hard shell. Good description. Hard to penetrate. Ha, ha. Yes, indeedy do. There's one who needed major penetration."

"I guess you've known the Owings for a long time."

"Uh-huh. Mildred Owings. I know her well. Her mother had difficult pregnancies. To help out, I used to babysit Mildred. Even back then, she was an Ice Princess. At five, she insisted we call her Mildred, and she was the most serious kid you ever saw. I'm twelve years older, so by the time she was in high school, I was married with my own family. In school, the students called her *Chilly Millie* behind her back. Or maybe to her face. Her one chance at a thaw was Danny. They were an item. She sure missed her opportunity. Maybe if she had just banged the guy at least once, she would have developed some emotions. They planned to get married. He went off to the service. Meanwhile, Mildred went to college so she could help support them when Danny returned. But he never came back. He was part of an *advisory* group that went to a little-known area of Asia once called Indochina, but we know it as Vietnam."

"Mildred's boyfriend was killed in the Vietnam War?"

"Sadly, yes. Mrs. Shoemaker was a military widow herself and gave the folded flag to Mildred. If you're ever in her office, check it out. She has it in a triangular glass frame on the wall."

"I was in her office. I do remember seeing…. Shoemaker! Daniel Shoemaker?"

Chapter Fifty-Six

Zelda cocked her head. "Yeah. Why?"

"Oh," Jen said, backpedaling in her excitement. "I've heard the name before."

Zelda stared at Jen for a moment. "Since I want to give you evidence with my future disclosures, come back in a few days. I'll call. Thanks for the *Finger-food*."

After lunch with Zelda, Jen hurried home. The new garage door glided quietly down. In spite of the violence associated with the garage, she smiled, pleased at the new look and the new sound.

Inside the house, she sat at the kitchen table and stared at the printouts from the library. *I'm going to call them. I just don't know what to say.* She said the names aloud, "Carvelle Huron and Winslow Hampton."

On the back of one printout, she penned her little speech. *All right. That will be my lead-in. Now what?*

"Take it from there," the secretary said. "Wing it."

Jennifer dialed Carvelle Huron. "Hello. May I speak to Carvelle Huron?" The woman who answered asked her to wait.

Carvelle Huron came to the phone. "Hello?"

Jennifer consulted her speech notes. "My name is Jennifer Huges. I recently bought a house in Livonia, Maryland, and I believe it was built by one of your ancestors. Would you mind if I asked questions about the house and your relatives?"

Carvelle agreed to speak but only in person. Jen then called Winston, gave the same spiel, and mentioned she would be in the area to speak with Carvelle. Mr. Winslow Hampton sounded eager to talk. She arranged meetings with both of them for the following week. Luckily, they lived a few hours apart, and if she got an early start, she could be back home by the evening.

Still smiling from her success, she answered her chiming cell phone.

"Hey," Lee said. "Everything okay?"

"So far," she answered. "You're still working?"

"Yes, ma'am, and we've made headway. We tested the gun and sent the photos off for analysis. There's an APB on Blakely and the license number we saw from the bank security footage."

"How long does it take to get the results?"

"Usually a few weeks, but Uncle Paul put it to the Feds to get this done immediately. They're jumping through hoops for him because of the mob investigation. And, let's face it, *you are* a priority."

The third wave of tenderness spread through Jen's body. "Thanks, Lee."

"Do you want some company?"

"I think you should get some rest."

"I really do need to get some sleep. I *could* kill two birds with one stone."

"Go home. Save your birding skills for another time when you're at full speed."

"You're so cute," Lee said in the middle of a yawn. "Some other time then when I'm at top performance." He yawned again. "I'll call you later."

In the late afternoon, the doorbell rang. Checking the peephole, she saw a leather-clad, helmeted motorcyclist.

"Yes?" Jen said, chiding herself on the suspicious sound of her voice.

"It's me, Brad."

She opened the door and then looked around through the doorway from left to right. "No motorcycle?"

"Nah," Brad said, stepping into the living room. "Someone else must have it or its parts. I tried to materialize it, but no go."

Jen walked to the kitchen to finish making her supper. "I thought Miles said you couldn't materialize."

Brad followed her and sat at the small table. "He said I *didn't* materialize."

"Oh," she said. "But here you are."

"Yep. Here I am. I've never needed to get solid before. I had to promise Miles I wouldn't scare you, so I can't show my body. He won't mind if I'm covered."

Jen stopped her work and turned toward him. "Um, are you all zombied and decomposed?"

Brad laughed. "Most corpses are decomposed. We can appear how we want, how we were at any time. Miles told you about only being able to bring back solid what is gone, right?"

"He did. That's why he couldn't have his badge or insignia on his uniform."

"Right. Remember when I said I hit a light pole? I didn't die right then. I became aware when I floated over my body in the hospital. A doctor brought my mother in and said I would never recover. He requested her to donate my organs. She asked how much money she could get. When he told her it was a donation, no payment, she said I hadn't been worth a damn in life, maybe I could do some good dead and to take whatever he wanted. As soon as the doctor pulled the plug, I knew I was gone. While they took my organs, eyes, skin, and bone marrow, I roamed the hospital. I stopped and listened to a man crying in a waiting room. I found out he cried for me! Even though his wife would live because of my heart, he wept because I died. Someone cared about me. I knew then why I hadn't crossed over. I had to make up for my former life."

Jen could only manage the words, "Oh, Brad."

"I look whole," he said. "But under the leather suit, I'm in pieces."

"If you were whole, I'd hug you."

"How about this?" He rolled back one sleeve and took her hand. A crude tattoo below his elbow proclaimed him to be *Bad Ass Mean*. She put his forearm to her lips and kissed it.

"If you had been my mother...or Miles had been my father..."

Jen brushed a tear from her eye. If she said anything, she would choke.

"But," Brad eased his tone. "If I had been brought up like the lucky kids, I wouldn't be here where I'm most needed."

Jen nodded, allowing a few seconds to calm her emotions. "What makes you so special? So powerful?"

"A couple of things. For one, I'm not intimidated by anything. Meeting up with evil couldn't compare to my years as a little kid. And, I know things, with no clue where the stuff came from. I mean, I have instincts. Like somehow, I knew I should come to Livonia. When I got here, I already knew how to fight the Dark Forces."

"Are you like the Innocents?"

"Different. I came to the spirit plane as a Warrior. Without thinking about it, I started defending helpless spirits and teaching skills for protection. Innocents don't defend or teach. They are so pure they repel evil. The Dark Forces can't stand to be near them."

"What happens to helpless spirits if Warriors or Innocents aren't around?"

"The Dark Forces suck the essence of a weak spirit, leaving nothing but a hollow shell."

"A hollow ghost shell? Ugh."

"When I arrived in Livonia, I saw the shells lying around. They look something like shed snake skins."

Jen shuddered from the mental picture. "So, ghost snake skins lie about the town?"

"Not anymore. I gathered them and left them with the Innocent under the school bleachers."

"Can the spirits ever get back to their shells?"

"It's possible. But Miles and I have a long way to go before we start restoring spirits."

"Why is Miles in Union Town. What for?"

"Assessing damage. Looking for shells."

Jen rubbed her forehead. "It's all so sad."

They sat at the small kitchen table in silence until Jen's

phone rang.

"I'm coming over," Lee said.

"Good."

"Then we're going out to dinner. Mexican or seafood?"

"Let me think about it. I'll tell you when you get here." Jen put the phone back on its cradle. "I'm going to have a guest."

"No problem. I can be invisible."

"You can be outside."

"I guess this means your guest is the detective Miles gets so perturbed over."

Oh, yes, it is. "Hey, you…don't read minds, do you?"

Brad's voice became playful. "What if I said I did?"

"Well?"

"My powers are limited to Evil Spirit fighting. Don't worry. I can't hear your thoughts. Maybe I'll just come back later. Miles wanted me here so you'd feel protected. You don't really need me all the time. And there's always the dog."

"And the detective," Jen added.

"So, it *is* him coming."

Jen laughed, welcoming the release of emotion from the previous subject.

Brad stood. Rex trotted to him and put out his paw. Brad bent to pet Rex. "Dogs can see us, you know. In our invisible state, I mean."

"I figured that out. Rex wags his tail at Miles even when I can't see him. Can cats see the spirits?"

"If they can, they don't show it. Cats are pretty worthless."

"I guess they work for witches, not ghosts."

"Witches?" Brad shook his head. "No such thing." He stiffened. "I've got stuff to do. I'll check on you later."

Jen nodded. Brad disappeared.

She ran upstairs, showered, and selected going-out clothes. Where they ate didn't matter, she just wanted to have an evening with someone normal.

Normal. What does that mean?

After putting on the last touches of makeup, she heard Lee

pull into the drive. She ran downstairs in time to open the door, his hand in mid-air, ready to knock.

"It's really good to see you," she said, shouldering her purse handle.

He stepped over the threshold, pulled the door behind him, and drew her close.

She backed up from the kiss. "Um, not here."

He shook his head and escorted her to the car. When he slid behind the wheel of the Crown Vic, he reached over to her.

She shied away. *Brad might be outside.* "Um, not here."

"Where?" he said, nostrils flaring.

"Around the corner. Pull into the gas station."

Within two minutes, Lee put the car in park at the BP station. He scooted next to her. Before he could embrace her, she moved her arms around his shoulders. She kissed him and put her head into the crook of his neck.

Lee gave her a gentle squeeze. "Have I ever told you I think you're wonky?"

"Yes. Isn't that why you like me?"

He pressed his nose against her cheek. "No. It's why I love you."

Chapter Fifty-Seven

Jen moved her lips against his and enjoyed a prolonged, heat-surging kiss. It felt good to be in his arms.

When they both needed to breathe, Lee separated from her. "Mexican or seafood?"

"Wow," Jen soothed her hair in place. "You change gears fast."

"I have my priorities. Kissing you, then feeding me. I've hardly had anything to eat for the last few days."

Because you've been working hard for me. "Fish and chips?"

Lee started the car. "Excellent choice. It's six o'clock, and my stomach demands dinner."

On the other side of town, past the high school, past the remnants of the old drive-in, now a weekend flea market, Lee pulled into the parking lot of an art deco-style structure that had once been an old ice house. The restaurant owner left a painted sign on the side of the building that advertised "Ice — Ten Cents a Pound." On the long side of the building, faded and almost unreadable, the word *Ice* seeped through the coats of paint attempting to cover it.

Jen loved the art deco style almost as much as Victorian. After they parked, Lee took her hand and walked her around to the front. A sign over the door showed a drawing of a fisherman, but instead of a pole, the figure wielded a whip, causing fish to flee in all directions. The name over the fisherman said: *The Marquis de Cod.*

Jen halted and pointed to the name.

Lee grinned and pulled her hand as they entered. "I thought you'd get a kick out of the place."

"Livonia! Never a dull moment," Jen picked up her step.

"Not lately, for sure," Lee said as they headed for the nearest booth. "I don't know what's going on here. We've always had some crime. Hell, the mob operates here." He nodded. "A little less now that we took down the Toad and Pond numbers racket. But, the residents. We've been getting calls complaining that the neighbor's dog is peeing on their azaleas or that Joe Blow doesn't like that John Doe is looking suspiciously at Joe's new boat. All kinds of weird things. And, the complaints we get about kids parking…"

"What's wrong with parking?"

"Parking. Making out, back seat mambo-ing."

"Teens have always done that."

"They're doing it more, and parents are going nuts. They want us to do something. Not much we can do except tell them to go home when we see the steamed-up windows."

Jen nodded. "Lust. And rage. Envy?"

"That pretty much covers it." He reached over the table and took her hand. "The lust part sounds pretty good."

Jen searched her brain for a snappy comeback, but the invisible secretary had been silent since the description of the ghost snake skins. Jen didn't reply.

The waitress shoved menus in their faces. After they ordered, Jen leaned in toward Lee. "What's happening with the Rodovich investigation?"

"He's vanished, but we're looking. He's wanted for a whole string of assaults along the East Coast. He's obviously for hire."

"Hired by Dave Blakely?" She gulped. "To kill me?"

Lee ran his fingers through his hair. "I know Dave from Little League when my son played on the same team with his kid. I just don't see Dave doing that. He's a real family man, a hard worker."

"But didn't he take off right after Rodovich got snagged?"

"Yeah. That's incriminating. Maybe he ran for another reason. That gun — um, the one with only your fingerprints — "

"Lee."

"I'm just jerking your chain. We heard from the FBI that the gun can be traced to a few murders. They got back to us really fast. They can cooperate if they want to. And they want to. Officially you're not off the hook—"

"Lee."

"You need to stick around."

"I'm a suspect?"

"Nah, not to me or Grainger. I want you to stick around. You're still on for Saturday, right?"

"Of course. You said live theater, but I haven't seen a playhouse in Livonia."

"All theater mysteries will be revealed Saturday afternoon."

"Okay. I'm pretty much done with mysteries and strange happenings in Livonia, anyway. I want a nice quiet evening."

"With the man of your dreams," Lee added.

Jen smiled.

The secretary, recovered from the ghost-shell trauma, said, "If he thinks you're wonky by the stuff he knows, what would he think if he heard about some of your dreams?"

"You okay?" Lee asked.

"Just feeling a little wonky," Jen said.

They finished their dinner with no further discussions about the strange happenings in town or in Jen's life. In the car, Lee opened his arms. "Come here."

Is this a command?

"No," the secretary said. "An invitation. Accept."

Jen scooted over to him.

They necked like teenagers. She had never cared for French kissing, but Lee's skills changed her mind. His tongue touches acted like a hotline to her lower insides. During a break, Jen traced her finger across the windshield and left a mark on the steamed surface.

"Do you think one of your men will knock on the window and tell us to go home?"

"No one would dare," Lee pulled her to him again.

As they kissed, that unbidden dream crept into her mind. Almost without thought, her hand moved down past his zipper.

Lee moaned.

Jen caressed the mass, bound by fabric, thin enough for her to feel the shape, heft, and length.

"Not like Miles," she murmured.

Lee stopped kissing her. "You called me Miles?"

"No. Did I? Pay no attention to me."

"Dummy!" the secretary scorned.

Lee adjusted his pants, took the keys from the top of the dashboard, and stabbed one into the ignition slot.

Jen noticed the LED panel above the radio indicating 10:00. *How long have we been parked?* The *Open* light on the side of the restaurant flashed off.

"I guess I should get back," Jen said.

"Right," he said in a half-snarl. "I've got a lot of work to do tomorrow. I'm expecting a conference call from the Feds. Gotta be sharp."

They rode in silence until the gas station around the corner came into view.

Jen put her hand around Lee's ample bicep. She pointed to the gas station where earlier they had kissed. "One for the road?"

"No," he said seriously. He turned sharply, stopping next to the tall metal apparatus with the word *Air* printed vertically. "At least ten."

He rammed the gear into park but didn't shut the engine off. He took her firmly and kissed her, touching his tongue to hers. When she was almost breathless, he pulled away slightly. "I'll work a bit harder to keep your mind on *me*."

Lee did just that. She couldn't think of anything other than his embrace.

"Now," he said, releasing her, "what's on your mind?"

"You," she answered, letting out a breath.

"Good. Now I'll take you home."

When they pulled into the drive, the house was dark.

Strange. She thought she had left a light on in the living room.

Lee escorted Jen to the front steps. Rex barked while she unlocked the door. Inside the entrance, the dog wiggled and wagged.

Lee pushed her gently against the door jamb and quick-kissed her goodnight. He stepped away and waited while Jen snapped on Rex's leash. "I'll do a quick walk around your house."

She waited on the porch step until he returned.

"Good night, Jen." Lee saluted with two fingers and headed toward the car.

She waved goodbye to him and walked Rex around the lighted yard. "Do your business, Rexie. I don't like being out here by myself." *Am I by myself?* "Brad?"

"Here," he said.

"Did you wait the whole time I was out?"

"No, I had some things to do. I thought Miles would be back by now."

Miles. "I hope he's okay."

"Nothing we can do." Brad materialized as a biker.

"Are you here for the night?"

"I promised Miles to stay with you."

He followed her into the house. She unsnapped Rex's leash from his collar.

"I'm going to bed." She paused on the stairs. "Good night, Brad."

"Sleep tight," he said.

Brad, seated on the couch, covered from head to toe in his motorcycle leathers and helmet, winked out of view like the flame on a birthday candle.

Can I sleep after all this? It will be Xanax tonight. For the fifteen minutes it took for the sleep assistant to do its thing, Jen reviewed the happenings of the preceding days, like rewinding a movie. Rodovich? Brad's description of the spiritual shed skin, Miles's trip to Union City, and her date with Lee. If those events weren't enough, would the Lust Dust sprinkled about Livonia courtesy of the Dark Forces make its way into her fortress? *No weird dreams, please.*

Jen slept a dreamless and peaceful night.

In the morning, on her way to the kitchen, she smelled the sweet Cavendish blend. Her smile built, and by the time she passed the living room, it had reached its full potential.

"Good morning, Miles."

Miles put his pipe down and stood up from the table. "Good morning, dear Jennifer."

She pressed against him. "Brad and I worried about you."

His arm circled her waist, keeping her near. "Thank you." He released his hold. "Nothing for concern. It took me longer to get to Union Town than I anticipated."

Jen moved to the cabinets. She turned her head toward him as she made the coffee. "Transportation problems?"

"Rather," he said. "I rode, invisibly, in the passenger seat of a Coca-Cola truck on its way to the Union City bottling plant. The driver must have been receptive because he sensed I was there. He kept looking at the seat. I know it made him uncomfortable. When he stopped for fuel, I got out. It took me hours to achieve my destination. Luckily, on my way back, the other truck driver I accompanied did not suffer from the same awareness."

"I could have driven you there."

"No. I don't know what awaits me when I travel. I won't expose you to danger. I must look into alternative modes."

"Trains and planes?"

"Trains, perhaps. What is a plane?"

"Flying. Aircraft with jets or propellers. You don't know about planes?"

"Ah, aeroplanes. Yes. Amazing things. I had an acquaintance, Sam Langley, who was interested in aviation. He built a flying machine that he claimed worked, but he crashed it on its maiden attempt. A very short time later, two Ohio men — brothers, I believe — tested their flying invention, and it worked. Flying held a fascination for me. I would like to have experienced flight."

"Oh, Miles! I would like to take you to a huge museum

outside of Washington so you can see what leaps we have made in aviation in the hundred years since you've...."

"Slumbered?"

"Yes. You would love the Space Shuttle."

"What's that?"

"Men and women fly into space. We've walked on the moon."

"Incredible."

"I will take you to that museum. The place will blow your mind."

Miles's face hardened with a serious expression. "I don't believe I'd want that again. It's how I met my demise."

"You remember?"

"Vividly. Two men unknown to me took me unawares, brought me to the carriage factory, and shoved me next to two other captives. One of the unknowns shot me from behind, and I assume the other detainees suffered the same fate."

Jen put her hand to her mouth and shook her head.

Miles stepped to her and ran his hand down her arm. "There, there. Don't be troubled. Things are what they are, and it happened over a century ago." He slid his hand up to her shoulders and caressed her. "Everything has a reason, my dear." He guided her to the little table and pulled a chair. "Here, sit down." His gaze caught hers. "I need to go away again. I'll likely be gone many days."

"Can't Brad go? He's a Paladin."

Miles pressed her hand to his lips. "It is not as easy to leave your domain as it was to enter. However, I must do what Brad knows is needed."

"How can Brad, a teen biker, be so brilliant? I don't understand."

Miles turned her hand and kissed the inside of her wrist. "Ah, a perfect arm. Although I don't understand why Brad is vital, I know his wisdom is unfailing. If we are to be saved from the Dark Side, it will be Brad who guides us."

"You really trust him, don't you?"

"Friendships form when individuals share danger."

"When must you leave?"

He took a long pull at the pipe, letting the cloud of sweet smoke roll into the room. "I'm afraid it needs to be this morning."

Jen inhaled the aroma. She no longer required him to smoke near the window. The scent was part of him now.

Miles tamped the tobacco from the pipe into the glass ashtray and restored the smoking items in the bureau drawer. Returning to the kitchen, he embraced her. "Try not to worry."

As he opened the door to leave, she extended her perfect arm and waved goodbye.

The jangling phone jarred her. Caller ID announced a call from Zelda. *Not now!* The ringing continued. Jen blew out air from her nose, dropped her head, and picked up the phone.

"Hello, Zelda," she said.

"I'm ready."

"For what?"

"Show and tell, honeykins. Are you free?"

Chapter Fifty-Eight

"I am. I'll be over in thirty minutes."

At the seer's house, Zelda served coffee to Jen. "Grandma told me someday the right time would come for the truth. I think you have made the time right. Remember Emma Caulfield?"

"Zelda and Miles's child?"

"Good, you're paying attention. Emma came to Livonia in search of her birth mother. No one knew Emma's biological parents here, so she never found out. She, unmarried, had her own baby, whom she named Earl Caulfield, and after baby number two, she went back to New York. Miles had made a name for himself here, and Jeezy vowed never to tarnish it or hurt her friend Virginia. But she kept track of Emma and her kids, Earl and Lucinda."

"Caulfields?"

"Yep, they took Emma's name. Earl beget Jasper, who beget Eldon, then Johnny. As in Johnny Caulfield, local ne'er-do-well."

"So, Johnny Cee is Miles's great-grandson?"

"There's more. Miles had a brother, Grant Hampton. He married an Owings gal, and they had a bunch of kids, who in turn had their own and so on. One of those great grandsons is Burleigh Ferguson."

"I don't believe it!"

"Believe it. Lee and Johnny Cee are related — some kind of second cousins once removed."

"Wait a minute. Why are you telling me all of this?"

"Because years ago, Miles Hampton was set up, killed, and blamed for murder, arson, and suicide. I see a setup happening to

Johnny Cee, and I won't let it."

"So why not go to Lee?"

"Lee loves me like a grandmother but doesn't take me seriously. He thinks I'm batty. Plus, Lee and Johnny have a history. They don't know of their blood relationship, but in elementary school, they became friends. In high school, they had a terrible fight, and Johnny kicked the crap out of Lee. Since then, they've clashed several times. I know Lee is a fine man, but he's still human. I believe he enjoys arresting Johnny, who didn't fare as well because of his upbringing."

"Wait. Johnny gets into trouble on his own."

"True. But inside, Johnny is a sweet boy, like Lee. Fate can be cruel. I tell you this so maybe you can work on Lee to give Johnny a break."

Jen sipped coffee. "Maybe Pam would help?"

"Wouldn't she have done so by now?"

"How do you know these things, Zelda? Can you prove them?"

Zelda whipped out a wad of printed sheets. "You have to base this on Granny's claim Emma was hers. The rest is right here in the Caulfield family tree."

Jen pored over the sheets, following the lines down to Johnny. "What do you think you can do for him?"

Zelda took back the papers. "I would be willing to pay for an attorney, but Lee has to do his part. The last time I saw Lee, he spoke of you." Her smile lit up her face. "I can tell he loves you."

Although Jen knew it, hearing about Lee's affection gave her an inner grin. She sat back on Zelda's couch, digesting the Caulfield data. "I could talk to Lee about Johnny."

"Good," Zelda said. "There's more."

"More about Johnny?"

"No, about Miles."

Jen sat up.

"I thought that would get your attention," Zelda said, raising her eyebrows.

Jen leaned toward her hostess. "Why do I get the feeling

you really do have some psychic ability?"

"Because I want you to. That's the real gift, to make someone *believe* you have abilities." Zelda waved her hand. "Psychic, Schmychic. Anyone who pays attention can be a seer. Grandma made a good living reading people. She said even though people look different on the outside, most of us are alike on the inside. Pull something out of your mind and say it to the client. Look at their eyes for a sign of recognition. It works. Trust me. And it's most effective on the hard cores, if you know what I mean."

"You think I'm hard core?"

"Hard? Nah, you're a kind soul. That's why you want to know about Miles."

You have no idea, lady.

Zelda rubbed her hands together. "Ready to bump it up a notch? Those Speigals have always been trouble. Remember when I said Jeezy had an arranged marriage to an older man, a pharmacist? Sometimes she delivered medicines and supplies to the wealthier clientele. One day she schlepped meds to Mr. Wolf Speigal and was directed into his study. He left her there to get money, and while she waited, she saw a typewritten letter next to the typewriter. The name Miles Hampton caught her eye. She read it and took it. To cover the theft, she opened the window, telling Mr. Speigal that she, being pregnant, needed fresh air to keep from fainting. A breeze blew through the window and scattered papers with each gust, even a few right into the fireplace. If Speigal suspected anything, he never acted on it."

"What did the letter say?"

"Here." Zelda unfolded a yellowing page. "Read for yourself."

Jen read the typewritten letter aloud. "MacCaffrey, send one of your best. It's time to fix Miles Hampton once and for all. He's been snooping around the factory and word is he's got enough evidence and witnesses to put us away in spite of who we have put in as chief. We don't own enough judges yet. I have a plan that will take care of those two witnesses, Hampton, the evidence, and the one at the Ratterlee factory. Send someone good with fire or explosions. Get a move on it, we don't have much time." Jen looked at Zelda and back down at the letter. "Signed W. Speigal." Jen thought for a second. "Why do *you* have this letter?"

"The day Jeezy took it, Abe Zeigler, the pharmacist— yeah, Gran's name was Zelda Zeigler. Can you imagine? She wanted to warn Miles, but he was out of town. Well, old Abe croaked that same afternoon from a heart attack, and she needed to make arrangements. A few days later when Miles returned, the explosion occurred and immediately Hampton was blamed. Jeezy couldn't come forward. She knew the police chief and mayor had been put in place by the Speigals. As a widow, she felt vulnerable and knew it would be dangerous for her and her kids. Not only would it not have done any good, Wolf Speigal could have had her arrested for theft. Fate prevented her from helping Miles. She figured Wolf Speigal phoned the hit men, and they got Miles when he came back to town."

Zelda took a breath. "After the explosion, Jeezy was such a mess she could barely function. She lost both her husband and the man she loved. She comforted Virginia, and while they hugged, they both sobbed. Virginia probably assumed Jeezy mourned for Abe, but in truth, she cried for Miles. By the time Gran got herself together, Virginia remarried and left town. She put the evidence away."

Jen sat for a moment biting her lip. "This letter. You say it's written by Wolf Speigal. Okay, it's on his business letterhead and it looks old. But it's not proof of a frame up."

Zelda laughed and did a sitting jig. "I was hoping you'd say that. I have more." She removed the letter from Jen's grip. "Shortly before Miles died, Livonia got a new doctor when Miles's father, Dr. Hampton, fell ill. Doctor Conrad Lambrigger and his bride set up housekeeping. Newly hired by the town council and on probation, Doctor Lambrigger was under close scrutiny from the crooked mayor."

"Do you refer to the doctor who owned this house?"

"You've been doing your homework. You must have dug deep for that small tidbit."

Miles pointed it out to me.

"In those days the town doctor also served as the coroner. Lambrigger functioned as the medical expert in the inquest of the deaths at the carriage factory."

"But—"

The seer put her finger to her head. "My abilities tell me you want to know about the bodies? They weren't burned because the newly formed fire department, headed by an Owings, turned out to be top notch, and dragged the bodies out before being destroyed. Anyway, Doctor Lambrigger certified he found bullet wounds in the back of the head for two bodies, and one to the temple on Miles. Supposedly, one of the policemen found a note nailed to the hitching post admitting to the murder, the explosion, and the suicide. The police said when the fire was extinguished, they investigated and found a gun near where the bodies had been."

"What?" Jen went stiff.

Chapter Fifty-Nine

Zelda's voice became grim. "Virginia denied the note, saying it was not Miles's handwriting and insisted nothing in his behavior indicated suicidal tendencies, but Doctor Lambrigger ruled it, as we know."

"That's preposterous!" Jen could hardly sit still.

"Hold your ponies, girl. Later as the doctor's practice grew, along with his family—Julia seemed to be pregnant frequently—he sold this house to Jeezy. Dr. Lambrigger, or Connie, what friends called him, had been an *up* kind of guy when he moved to Livonia, but after the inquest, he kept to himself. When Jeezy hung out her *Seer* shingle, guess who was her first customer?"

"Doctor Lambrigger?"

"Yep. Over the years, he visited, and as he grew older, he asked some questions, which made her suspicious. He asked about facing up to the wrongs in this life. Was he doomed to suffer in another life because of wrongs in this one? Jeezy couldn't resist. Knowing about a possible hit and putting two and two together, she used her *seer* skills and told me she sensed he had wronged someone who passed over."

Only Miles didn't pass over.

"Jeezy offered to hold a séance, but that frightened poor Connie. He didn't go for it. So, she gave him an option where he could write his wrong and an apology on a special piece of paper, one she provided, and showed him how to fold it after he'd written. He folded it and handed the message to her. Then they chanted and burned the paper in a fancy plate, sending the confession and regrets to the wronged one by the way of smoke."

Jen smiled. "But she switched the paper?"

"She did indeed. Voila!" Zelda held a folded sheet up for Jen's examination.

Jen took the sheet and unfolded it, the edges darkened and dirty from age. She read aloud.

"To Miles Hampton. The bullet hole was in the back of your head, like the others. I lied about that. I saw no gunpowder evidence at all. I am sorry for what I did to your family and to your reputation. The mayor told me if I wanted to keep this job, or get a job anywhere close, I would have to say what he told me. My wife was pregnant, and I needed the position. Please forgive me."

Jen put the Lambrigger sheet over the Speigal sheet. "Okay, you explained why Zelda Senior didn't expose the Speigal letter. But years later, when the Owings were running things, she could have shown this confession."

"No way. Lambrigger didn't die until he was really old. She couldn't out him like that. By the time the doctor died, Jeezy was getting on and didn't have the energy to face all the legalities. My own mother didn't shiv-a-git, so Gran gave the letters to me and said when the right moment presented itself, I could use them. I'm giving them to you."

Jen ran her finger over the papers. "Why don't you give them to Lee?"

Zelda shook her head. "I told you. Lee loves me, but he thinks I'm crazy and wouldn't believe any of this. He might believe you."

"He'd wonder where I got them, and it would come back to you again."

"Yeah, I thought about that. But you know what? I think you're sharp and you'll come up with a plan."

The two women sat for several minutes in silence.

Jen picked up the papers. "Has anyone important passed away lately? You know, from a rich, old Livonian family?"

"Rayma Harris, the widow of the president of the oldest bank here, just died. Why?"

Jen nodded her head as the plan jelled. "Did she leave an

estate? Cedar-chest-type stuff?"

"Probably. Big money, big house, old family. What are you thinking?"

"Did they have a lot of old books?"

"The house had its own library. I've been there many times."

"Do you think there are some books Chilly Milly might like?"

"Of course. All the old books find their way to the library. Young people don't want musty old books. They download to their electronic thingies. Are you going to tell me what you're thinking?"

"Aren't you the seer?"

"Hey, I have a certain amount of influence around town, you know. And with Lee, too."

"Hold on to your knickers, Zelda. I'll tell you. Do *you* have any old books that would interest the Livonia Collection here?"

"Sure. When I croak, the library will get them."

"Don't wait until you croak. Send out two tomorrow. Slip these papers in the pages and put the return address as the Harris estate. Include a note saying the books are meant for the Livonia Collection."

"And?"

"Mildred told me she personally inspects every page of books destined for the special collection. When she finds the papers, she'll make the connection and take the evidence to her brother, Paul."

"Who solves the old crime! Brilliant and sneaky. My favorite kind of plan. Oh, welcome to my club, Jennifer!"

Chapter Sixty

Once again, Brad appeared in the evening to spend the night invisible on the couch. Jen told him she would be out for the afternoon and night of the next day; perhaps he didn't need to come then. He assured her he would be waiting.

I can't ask Lee in after our date.

The next day, Saturday, Jen sang to herself as she dusted and did her chores. She needed to stay busy to keep the anticipation down to a manageable level. Not only did she have a date with Lee, a mystery date—not that she needed more mystery in her life—but she looked forward to seeing *Oklahoma*. And, he had told her they were going to eat afterwards at a very special place. She wondered what kind of funky name the restaurant would have this time.

As four o'clock loomed nigh, Jen put on her dark blue velvet pants suit accessorized with gold earrings and a necklace. Keith had been a generous gift-giver. Due to his good taste in jewelry, she had come away from the marriage with a large chest of high-end pieces. After the final mist of hairspray, she went to the closet door mirror and checked herself over.

Speaking aloud to the secretary, she turned this way and that. "I've lost some more weight. I look good."

"Watch out for the Pride Dust," advised the secretary.

"Good is good, pride or not," Jen said.

Before she became entrenched in the conversation, she heard a deep, rich rumbling in front of her house. She peeked out the curtain from the bedroom window. A red Porsche glided up the driveway, the engine revving.

Jen flew down the steps into the living room. She ran to

the door, answering the knock.

Lee smiled and kissed her cheek. "You look super."

"Thanks." She stepped back and gave him the once-over. "I like your jacket. Kind of tweedy."

"It's my professorial guise. I'm trying to impress you with my versatility."

"I'm impressed." She grabbed her purse.

As they walked out, she called out. "Keep watch, Rexie. Don't let the bad guys in." She handed Lee the front door key.

Lee paused. "That goes double for me, Rex. You are her protector when I'm not around."

While Lee locked the door, a little wave of guilt passed through Jen. *Rex, Miles, and Brad, plus the holy water.*

"Lee? Can I drive?"

"The Porsche?"

"What else?"

"Do you know how to drive a stick shift?"

"I had an old VW bug in college. I think my feeble brain can remember."

"Okay."

"That was too easy. Do you let anyone drive it?"

"No."

Here is the perfect opportunity to check out Zelda's theory.

Jen whipped around and grabbed Lee by the mid-arm. "You let what's-her-name-the-vet drive."

Lee's eyes widened. "What?"

"I know you did. I see it."

"Okay. So what?"

"Nothing. I just wanted you to know I know."

Lee pulled the car keys out of his pocket. "Here."

"So," she tested, "I will be the third person to drive it."

He nodded.

Damn, Zelda was spot on. This is fun.

Jen fired up the sports car. In reverse, she touched the gas pedal, rocketing it into the street. Easing the gear into first, she carefully guided the red darling down the street. "I don't know where I'm going. You'll have to give me directions."

"Turn right."

Within a few minutes, Lee had directed her into the parking lot of the high school. Dotted lights on the street-side marquee flashed *Oklahoma*.

"A high school play?"

"My cousin's daughter, Mary, is Ado Annie, like you. My cousin, Josh, watched some of the rehearsals. He said it was really good. Plus, I want you to meet my family." Lee got out of the passenger seat and opened her door. "And," he added as he locked the car, "I want them to meet you."

Oh, great. I hope they are friendlier than Mill-Dread.

It was early, and most of the auditorium seats remained vacant. Lee escorted Jen to the good seats. At the end of the row sat Mildred, a short, balding man, and another woman.

I'll see and be seen.

Lee whispered, "That man next to Aunt Mildred is Uncle Paul, my boss, Chief Owings. The lady on Uncle Paul's right is his wife, Marion. I'll introduce you."

"Can we do that later? Um…." She searched for a reason not to be introduced.

"Sure." Lee took her hand. "You're not shy, are you?"

"Well, not exactly. Maybe after the play." *And either I have built up my nerve or insisted on leaving.*

"You have more class than that," chided the invisible secretary. "You need to meet them."

Jen squeezed Lee's hand, an affirmation of the secretary's advice. "I'm assuming more of the family will be here after the play. Then I can meet them all."

"Right," Lee said. "Good thinking. See what great taste I have? I'm attracted to beauty and brains." He pressed her hand to his lips.

Jen remembered Miles kissing her wrist. *Will Lee comment on my perfectly formed arm?*

"Nice hand," Lee whispered.

Close enough.

The play came near to the quality of traveling troupes. At the end, as the audience stood and applauded the performance, Jen raised her voice so Lee could hear her. "That was terrific! What a talented bunch." She consulted the program for names. "Your cousin's girl, Mary, gave an impressive performance."

"They will love to hear that," Lee said above the thunder.

A group of people gathered outside the auditorium. The presence of Mildred, Paul, and Marion signified the others were Owings. Jen lifted her shoulders high. She adopted a smile and picked up her step.

Joining the group, Lee put his hand on Jen's shoulder. "Family, this is Jennifer Hughes. The *Jen* you've heard me talking about."

Lee's voice projected affectionate pride when he said her name. A wave of happiness radiated over her, which lasted two seconds. Mildred's polar response, "I've met her already," destroyed the pleasure.

The rest of the group greeted her with casual warmth.

Lee's smile encouraged Jen to breathe a sigh of relief. Then a gurgling sound from his stomach caught her attention.

"Are we ready to rumble?"

Lee patted his stomach. "For sure. Time for chow."

"A funky-named restaurant?"

He smiled. "They all have funky names. It's a tradition here in Livonia. Tonight, we'll eat dinner at the Oh! Wings! Barbecue Place."

"That's not a very catchy name considering the other places."

"Wait and see if you don't think it's clever. You want to drive again?"

They walked to the parking lot with his arm linked in hers. Nearing his red treasure, Lee buzzed the door locks open and gave her the keys. Jen sat behind the wheel, checking the equipment. The ignition gave the car a rich reverberation, like a promise of adventure from the engine. She eased the car onto the road.

"Make the first left," he said.

After a few turns, Lee pointed to a big house at the end of the street. "Pull in there."

The mailbox said: *Paul and Marion Owings.*

"Why are we stopping here?"

"Uncle Paul's specialty is barbecued wings. We're eating here tonight. You'll really get to meet my family."

Chapter Sixty-One

Paul Owings. Oh! Wings! Oh, great. Catchy.

Jen drove the car into the circular drive. By the time Lee came to her side, cars came one after another, parking near them. A lot of cars.

"Family?" Jen asked.

"Mostly, but Uncle Paul's position makes him important. There," he said, pointing to a Cadillac, "is the fire chief. And see that Jaguar? That's the mayor. There's Doctor Rafael Peters, and with him, his wife, Dr. Susan Peters, a dentist."

"The glitterati of Livonia show for a barbecue celebrating Mary Owings's dramatic debut?"

"A party for any reason. Uncle Paul's barbecue wings have become legendary. Now you'll be part of the legend."

I can think of more interesting legends. And I AM part of them.

"Come on," he said, taking her arm. "Time to shine."

Lee introduced her to everyone in attendance. Lee stopped Paul Owings as he carried a huge tray of uncooked wings to the patio. "Can we be of service, Uncle Paul?"

"Not unless your psychic friend here wants to tell me where my wife stored the beer. We can't find it."

Lee turned to Jen. "Can you help?"

Goose bumps formed. *Not fair. Taking me by surprise. Putting me on the spot.*

The secretary nudged her. "Get a hold of yourself and give them a clever answer."

Jen stood a little taller. "Try the beer locker in the garage."

"Ah!" Marion Owings said, coming up behind them. "Now I remember! I had Josh stack them in the garage fridge."

She looked at Jen. "Gee, you're good."

Mildred stopped next to Paul. She shot Jen a snake-eye glare. "Psychic. There's no such thing."

Mildred had rubbed Jen the wrong way from the first time they met. The Ice Queen's comment tipped the scales. She put her hand on her hip and spoke to Mildred. "Non-believer, eh? Then I guess you won't want the message from Daniel Shoemaker."

Mildred paled. Her ashen lips formed words slowly. "A message from Danny?"

"J-en?" Lee said, drawing her name out into two syllables.

Jen put her other hand on her hip. *Everyone is staring. I've ruined the party.* "I need to go home, Lee."

Lee wove his arm around hers to circle her waist. He took a step toward the door, pulling Jen with him.

"Wait," Mildred said, her voice barely audible. "What is the message?"

Jen halted the movement and turned back to Mildred. "He has heard your words, and he knows you've been true. He waits for you and wants you to wear the ballerina slippers on his birthday."

Someone in the gathering crowd muttered, "Bullshit."

Mildred nodded her head. "He waits for me." She bit her lip and rushed to the door. Paul shoved the tray at Marion and rushed after his sister.

Lee hurried Jen to the car. He didn't offer to let her drive.

"I'm sorry," Jen said, just managing to keep the flood gates closed. "I embarrassed you and upset your aunt."

He ground his jaw. "My aunt started it."

"You're not angry?"

"More like agitated. I would rather have had wings and beer with a bunch of laughing relatives and friends, but Mildred had it coming."

Jen reached over and took his hand, rubbing it against her cheek.

He kissed her wrist. "I'm still hungry, but I'm not in the mood to wait, so how about something from The Finger?"

"Okay," she said, ready to agree to anything at that moment.

Lee inched the Porsche back and forth from its tight spot between the other cars and roared over the grass to the road. "Jenny, I'm scheduled to meet with the Feds in Washington on Tuesday. Come with me. We'll leave around noon on Monday."

Alone with Lee. I'm supposed to see Miles's relatives Tuesday. In Manassas and Reston. Washington, D.C., is perfect. "Can I borrow your car while I'm there? I have some places I want to go."

"We'd have to take the Porsche. I couldn't let you drive the Crown Vic."

"Fine with me.

They stopped in The Finger's parking lot. As he helped her from the car, Lee kissed her shoulder. "Jen, we'll be in a hotel in Crystal City. You don't have any hang-ups about hotel rooms, do you?"

Hang-ups? Damn, I asked for that. Her eyes met his. "I am truly looking forward to sleeping with you."

Lee made a small gurgle in his throat.

Back at her house, Jen kissed Lee goodnight at the door several times.

Lee stepped back a few inches and caressed her chin. "I can't wait until we get to Washington. And I don't mean meeting the Feds. You'll like the hotel. Nice rooms, cozy, and private."

"Sounds good," Jen said.

As soon as Lee left, Brad materialized on her couch, not a slow build-up, but like she had seen on television shows like *I Dream of Jeannie.*

"Have you been there on my couch all night?"

"No," he said. "I walked in with you and your friend."

"Don't do that anymore. I don't like it."

"Hey, I'm here to protect you."

"I'm not sure I need you."

"You don't. Once you're in the house, you're pretty safe. That is, from the average evil. It's the Big Evil I worry about."

"But you don't know who that is," Jen said.

"No, and that's a major problem."

"You're the spirit guru. Don't you recognize another ghost when you see one?"

"I would if this person was a ghost. But it's a human hosting a high-up evil being."

"What the heck are you talking about, Brad?"

"Look, apples and oranges—departed souls as opposed to the Evil One."

"What do you mean by Evil One?"

Brad spread his gloved hands in the air. "Evil Incarnate. The Big Kahuna of Bad, see? The presence here in Livonia gathers souls to increase evil's power. It's not the Evil One itself, but a helper, kind of a lieutenant of the Evil Big Kahuna."

"Is this Big Kahuna the opposite of God?"

"Well, it's the opposite of good. The Evil One has sent its assistant, who is kicking ghost ass. Oh, excuse me. Okay. . .someone here in Livonia poses as an average citizen, but that's a disguise. His or her real day job is to suck the energy of spirits. What we don't know is why or what this energy will be used for. It won't be pretty. Miles travels to see what's going on around us. Now that he is a Paladin, he'll gather information and offer help to spirits if they need it."

"I only saw Miles for a few minutes this morning. He didn't tell me what he found in Union Town," Jen said.

"He didn't find anything. That's why he has to go farther. He just came back to check on you."

"I'm safe in this house. You said so."

"Yeah, but not safe from the guy who just left."

"I'm safe with Lee. What are you talking about?"

"Haven't you figured it out? When worlds collide, Jennifer. Miles can't stand you messing around with that Breather."

"Messing around?"

"Don't forget. I was outside waiting for you. I couldn't help but overhear... And Miles ain't stupid."

"Oh, God!" Jen clenched her fists. "I have needs, Brad." *Shit. Did I just say that?* Lately, words had a way of escaping her before she could get control.

"Needs. Right. But, Miles in his solid form could… I mean, after all, I'm rooting for my dude."

"Enough! Time for you to go," Jen said.

"No way. I promised Miles I'd stay nearby at night. And if I don't, it might distract him. You don't want that on your conscience, do you? He and I are working hard to find out what's building. So, here I stay at night until Miles completes his mission or until I have to go." Brad blinked out.

Jen stomped up the stairs. *Another mystifying twenty-four hours in Livonia.* She reached for the bottles of Xanax and Valium and turned each bottle in her hand. "No!" She sailed one bottle across the room, and it made a soft plop into the wastebasket.

"Two points," the secretary said. "Try the other one."

The second bottle followed the arc and landed with a plastic thud on top of its predecessor.

Jen slid one hand over another in a final brush-off gesture. "Bye-bye, boys." *I just got un-dependent from Keith. I don't need addiction as my new master.* She moved to where the wastebasket sat and gave it a light kick.

Eventually, she lapsed into the nighttime unconsciousness called sleep.

The next morning going down the stairs, she saw Brad's figure blink solid on the same spot she had seen him disappear.

"Hey," he said. "How're things with you this morning?"

"I'll be busy. I've got company coming."

"Oh, really?"

She noticed the accusation in his words. "Not that it's any business of yours, but my family is coming to dinner today."

"Sorry. I should stay out of whatever is going on between you and Miles."

"Yes, you should."

Brad touched his helmet and bowed before he melted dramatically, starting from the top of his head to the bottom of his black boots.

So, what exactly goes on between Miles and me?

"You have the hots for him," the secretary said. "And why not? In his solid form, he's a man with all of the benefits endowed to men. And he's dynamite gorgeous—the strong shoulders, handsome features, and a suave personality. Who else takes your arm and calls it perfection? You can't deny he cares for you."

I can't think of all this now. I've got a dinner to plan.

"Chicken," the secretary taunted.

"Roast beef," she said aloud, dismissing the conversation.

Chapter Sixty-Two

Shortly after noontime, Keith, Chrissy, Bobby, and James, Keith's younger brother, arrived together. James entered the living room last. He kissed Jen's cheek and stepped back, moving his head to one side, then another. "Mmm. Divorce looks good on you. You've turned into a fox, Jenny."

She tousled his curly blond hair. "Thanks. You haven't changed a bit. You still look like you're eighteen, with that peachy skin and baby-blue eyes. Do you shave yet?"

Jen had kidded James about being baby-faced since she met him.

"I'm all man," he said, coming close to her ear. "We're both free. Want to see my grown-up talents?"

Jen put her head back and laughed. "Are you asking me on a date? You live in Baltimore."

"I have a car."

Keith made a face and shouted at his brother. "Hey, are you hitting on my wife?"

Both James and Jen turned toward Keith and said simultaneously, "Ex-wife."

"We'll see about that," Keith protested.

Jen led the visitors into the kitchen, where she checked the oven temperature. James leaned against the doorjamb. "Seriously, are you seeing anyone?"

The room got tomb-quiet. Obviously, other people in the room wanted to hear the answer. Chrissy put her purse on the counter. "So, Mom?"

The Quitcher Bitchin' sign clattered to the floor. The noise caused a synchronized "Oh!" from the group. Rex wagged his tail.

    Miles!

Jen used the distraction to avoid answering the question. James retrieved the sampler and handed it to her.

"Thanks," Jen said, taking the sign. "You're such a nice guy."

"I know," he said, feigning innocence.

"So, what happened between you and Mona?"

"Uh," James twirled a golden lock. "It probably had something to do with a young cocktail waitress." He held his hands cupped in front of his chest.

"James! You divorced Mona over a busty cocktail waitress?"

"Mona divorced me."

"I don't blame her, but I'm sorry," Jen said, brushing a speck of dust from the Quitcher Bitchin' plaque.

"Ah, don't be," he said. "She was kind of a bitch."

"I don't believe for a second that you mean that. Mona and you are perfect for each other." She replaced the sign and offered appetizers and drinks.

James shrugged and reached for a rumaki. "These are good. By the way, this looks like a great house. Can I see it?"

"Help yourself. Pay close attention to the basement. I need to ask you some questions about what I can do with it."

"I'm your man. You can even ask me questions about architecture."

"Come with me, Uncle James," Chrissy said. "I'll give you the tour."

Bobby went with them.

Keith came to her and wrapped his arms around her waist as she browned the beef. "Can I help with anything?"

Jen cringed. She broke the hug and transferred the roast into the roasting pan. "No. But you can step aside so I can put the roast in the oven."

She set the oven timer. The visitors upstairs clomped on the steps. They tromped through the kitchen, and James disconnected the hasp on the basement door. He and Bobby and Chrissy thumped downward. She listened for comments, but no noise emanated from the dirt room underneath the kitchen. *No raccoons. Good.* In a few minutes, the clomping upward broke the silence. First, Chrissy, then Bobby, then James came into the room.

James reconnected the hasp. "Great house. Well built. The design is a perfect balance of proportions. But, man, that basement."

"Do you see why I want to modernize it? Can it be done?"

"Sure, it can. Nothing monumental. Have you consulted anyone?"

"Yes. The contractor who rebuilt my garage said it couldn't be done."

"Would you like me to measure today and draw up a few plans Monday?"

"If you don't charge too much. I know you're in the big leagues."

James took a kitchen towel from the counter and rubbed a spot of flour from her nose. "I'll think of some way you can pay me."

"James," she admonished.

The Quitcher Bitchin' sign hit the floor again. Rex wagged a little more vigorously.

Jen retrieved the sign. "Drafts."

"From closed windows?" James asked.

"Excuse me. I need to go into the pantry," Jen said, emphasizing the *pantry*.

She closed the pantry door behind her. "Damn it, Miles."

Miles appeared and seized her forcefully. He kissed her in a prolonged embrace.

When she could talk, she pushed him away. "Leave the plaque alone."

"I don't like him."

"And you don't like Lee or Keith either." *I wonder if Brad told him anything. No.* Miles was too much of a gentleman to ask

Brad for a report. "Have you spoken with Brad?"

Miles's eyes met hers. "Not yet. I've come here first."

"You have another assignment?"

"I'll be away for many days, but I had to see you first."

Jen put her head in the cradle of his neck. "Please be careful. I worry about you."

Miles stroked her hair. "Not possibly as much as I worry about you."

"I'm fine, protected by this house."

"What lies outside the house does not comprise my principal concern at this moment." He kissed her again and disappeared.

Jen grabbed a can of green beans and stepped out of the pantry.

"Who were you talking to?" Keith asked.

She swung the door wide. "Do you see anyone in there?"

Keith shook his head. "Besides being beautiful and fascinating, my darling Jennifer, I believe you are quite cracked."

Jen lifted her chin high and walked to the sink. "Cracks let the light in, Keith."

Chrissy and Bobby, who sat at the table with James, laughed.

James said, "On Monday, I'll make some drawings. I'll work with my main guy on what I'll need for materials. When you pick a drawing, I'll write up the necessary paperwork and file them for you at the county seat. When it's approved, what we need will be delivered, then a couple of construction guys will come here. We can do it in two days. If you can put us up here, I won't charge you anything but the materials."

Jen pointed at him. "*You* will work? I can't imagine you full of cement and dirt."

James's bow-shaped lips broke into a smile. "It's true. The construction guys usually do the work, but I'm willing to do a bit and get my hands soiled. I may need help showering."

"Hey," Keith said. "Cut that out. Why are you being so nice? You can't possibly think she'd be interested in you."

"Stranger things have happened. Let's just call it a birthday present for Jen."

"Her birthday is in three months."

"A present in advance. At least let me have a shot at her, brother."

"You don't have a chance. I'll pay for a motel for you and your crew. That's *my* birthday present to her. Okay, by you, Jen?"

"Absolutely! I can't wait to be able to use that basement."

The Quitcher Bitchin' plaque moved at a slant and then back to normal. Jen looked around to see if anyone noticed, but no one appeared to be aware. It meant Miles had stuck around for a few minutes but now took his leave.

The conversation at the dining room table went like a passed-around joint. Keith started with what interesting things happened at the law firm, then James talked about a recent design. Bobby talked about computers. Jen couldn't follow the terms regarding technology, but it didn't matter. Chrissy excitedly spoke about her chemistry and anatomy courses needed to become a radiology technician. At Jen's turn, she described her life in the lovely Victorian home, quelling the building terror of her words while relating the details of the fire and her great annoyance from raccoons. She didn't mention her relationship with spirits or the two attempts on her life.

After dinner, Jen served dessert. While the other diners ate their cake, she closed her eyes and remembered Miles's strong grip and the kiss that took her breath away.

Chapter Sixty-Three

In the morning, Jen packed her suitcase for the trip with Lee and brought it down next to the front door. She entered the kitchen to unload the dishwasher from the previous night's meal. Zelda called to say she mailed the books to the library. Jen smiled because their plan had been set in motion.

Mid-morning, she put Rex in the car and drove to the vet's office to board him. She wanted to get a good look at Dr. Ann-Marie Golden, Lee's emergency squeeze, but a tech-led Rex away before Jen could sneak a peek.

By eleven-thirty, she had everything ready for Lee's noon arrival. The knock on the door, however, was not Lee.

At first, Jen didn't recognize the woman standing in the open doorway. Her soft gray and blonde hair flowed over rosy silk-covered shoulders. "Mildred?" Jen said.

"May I come in?"

"Uh, yes. Of course. Please."

Jen showed Mildred into the living room and, with her sweeping hand, indicated a seat on the couch. Jen sat in a wing chair.

"I owe you an apology," Mildred said. "I owe many people apologies. Your words changed my life. I've been angry at the world since Danny's death. Now that I know… Thank you."

Mildred pulled a crushed linen hanky from her magenta pants pocket. The hanky's scalloped edge matched her outfit's color. She dabbed at her nose. A bar pin dangled little shoes over the blouse pocket.

Ballet shoes!

Mildred nodded, seeing Jen's eyes on the jewelry piece.

"Yes, these are the ballet slippers he said to wear." Her words stumbled out through the tears. "Today is his birthday. When we dated, he took me to a ballet, and I liked it so much, he gave me this to remember it by." She dabbed her nose. "You said he's waiting. Is there anything else? I must know. How long will he wait?"

Pins pricked at Jen's spine. "Um." The question had an ominous feel. *What is Mildred really asking?* "He'll wait for as long as he has to. But, Mildred, yours must be a natural death. You can't, um, help it along. If you do something like that, you go to a different place. You may never meet up with him then." *How do I know that?*

"Oh," Mildred said.

"And you know," Jen added. "Danny wouldn't want you to do anything like that."

"You're right. He wouldn't want anything to hurt me. I have missed him so much. Even after all these years, he's the first thing I think of in the morning and the last image I see when I shut my eyes at night."

Jen used an all-knowing Zelda professional tone. "He was a wonderful man."

Mildred scooted forward. "He was. You really have a gift. The night before he left, we were together. Really together."

"I know what you mean," Jen said.

"My upbringing discouraged that type of behavior, but I am so glad I did!" She wiped away tears. "I relive that night over and over. It has sustained me."

Aha! Zelda Silverstein may know how to fake Seeing, but she doesn't know everything about Mildred.

"That night we…were close, we vowed to always be together, even if one of us died."

They made oaths. Brad said we have to keep our oaths.

"Your psychic ability let me know Danny has honored his vows. That means the world to me. I'm in my seventies. I don't fear anything now. Thank you."

"You're welcome," Jen whispered. A pang of guilt slammed

her because she had told Mildred about Danny's message as a snide comeback.

Mildred stood and pushed the hanky into her side pocket. "I believe God puts people in the right place at the right time for the good of others. You are an instrument of good. I know why Burleigh thinks so highly of you. I've taken some time off. I'm spending the week at Arlington Cemetery."

"Is that where Dan Shoemaker is buried?"

"Yes. I've never been to his grave." Mildred headed for the door and got in her car. Jen followed and waited next to it.

Mildred rolled down the window. "When I get back, I'm retiring. Thank you again, Jennifer. God bless you."

The car drove away. The secretary gave Jen a hard smack. "Retiring! Who's going to get those books with the letters clearing Miles?"

"Oh, shit." She stood in the driveway trying to gather her thoughts when Lee honked his horn to get her attention. He greased the Porsche into the drive like buttering toast.

"I'll get your bags," Lee said, exiting the Porsche.

Jen walked into the house with him, still in a zombie-like state.

"You okay?" he asked.

"Uh, yeah. Bags. Near the door."

He eyed her at an angle. "You're not having second thoughts about going with me?"

"No, no. Believe me, I want to go. I *need* to go."

"Okay. Give me your keys, and I'll check the doors and windows. You don't look like you're completely together. You should get in the car."

She gave him the door key. *Oh, man. This is messed up. Zelda mailed the books. What can we do?* She slipped into the Porche's front seat.

In a few minutes, Lee took his place behind the wheel. "Ready?"

Jen nodded. *It'll work out. I'm going to enjoy my time with Lee.*

The car headed east toward the interstate. Lee pulled over near the town's limits to a lunch truck. A magnetic sign proclaimed *Uncle's*. "How about a corn dog?"

"Are you joking?"

"No, I'm in the mood for a good old-fashioned corn dog. You want one or two?"

"One, with mustard," Jen said.

She watched as he strode to the truck and conversed with the vendor. He returned to the car and handed her the steamy cornmeal-coated goodie, its stick wrapped in a paper napkin.

"No barbecue wings?" Jen said.

Lee stared at her with no expression. "What do you mean?"

"Uncle's? As in Uncle Paul? That man is undercover."

Lee transferred his corn dog to the other hand and stared at it. "Damn, you're really good."

Not really. You didn't pay for the food.

He pulled back on the road. She ate her corn dog in small bites, thinking about her conversation with Zelda. She rolled the empty stick into a paper napkin. "You knew Johnny Caulfield in school. Tell me about him."

"Why?"

"Curiosity. I want to know about your life. Humor me."

"If you insist. I met Johnny in sixth grade. He was, ah, mature for his age, like me, only he knew how to make the best use of his size."

"What does that mean?"

Chapter Sixty-Four

Lee took his attention from the road and turned his head toward Jen. "What do you *think* mature for his age means? We were in elementary school. The girls, sixth, seventh, and eighth graders, were all over him."

"You mean…?"

"Oh, yeah. And I benefitted big time. I got his extras, you might say. By the time we hit high school, Johnny had become a legend, and I was his sidekick."

"Sounds like you had fun in high school."

"Uh-huh. But Johnny had no father, only a no-good mother. He practically raised himself. One night he showed up at my house in a really cool convertible. My dad had gone fishing with Uncle Paul, and against my mother's protests, I hopped in. Johnny didn't own a car, and I didn't ask questions. He found a bum on a street corner and gave the guy money to buy us beer. After drinking a few cans, we went on a ride. Then, for no apparent reason, he picked up a couple of bricks and drove to a florist shop named Neilson's. I guess he had a beef with Neilson because he heaved those bricks at the windows."

"He sounds like a delinquent."

"Not really. I don't know what got into him that night, stealing wheels and breaking windows. Neilson, a distant cousin of my dad, identified him and me to Uncle Paul, who was just a uniform then. The cops found us and took us to jail. Dad bailed me out the next morning. When I got home, Dad sent Mom out of the house for the day. Uncle Paul and Dad had a *talk* with me. They insisted I give Johnny up as my friend. I refused. That's when Uncle Paul held me down, and Dad convinced me with his belt to walk the straight and narrow. Without Johnny."

"Your father and Paul beat you? That's *child abuse*."

"No, that's knocking sense into a fifteen-year-old asshole on his way to destruction. Johnny wasn't that lucky. He stayed at the city's expense for another day. I made a deal. I promised to break the friendship if they bailed Johnny out. I figured it would blow over, and we could be friends again later.

"When Johnny got back to school, he thought I'd blamed him for the whole mess and beat the shit out of me. I was still pretty sore from my *talk* with Dad and Uncle Paul, so I wasn't in good fighting shape. Plus, I was never a match for Johnny. He was street tough."

"So, you two have been enemies ever since ninth grade?"

"I don't consider him an enemy. He dropped out of school, got busted a couple of times, and left Livonia. I think he went to stay with some relatives in New York. He came back to town five or six years later. Our paths have crossed as cop and lawbreaker. He makes bad decisions, but he's not a bad guy."

"Isn't he in jail for kidnapping?"

"Arlene Holmes? That's the charge. Oh, he had her trapped in that motel, scaring her with predictions of violence from other people, but *he* wouldn't have hurt her. She doesn't want to press charges, but what he did is illegal, so Arlene has no choice. Her parents have her stashed at their vacation home in the Finger Lakes. I called her. She claims to be in love with him. He has that kind of effect on women."

Like Pam.

"I think he could help us get dirt on the Speigals, but he won't give them up. That's why we're keeping him in jail. And as long as Arlene's folks keep her sequestered and no one pays his bail, he'll stay there. At least until trial."

"Can't you help him? You know, make things easier for him?"

"I'd talk to him and do what I can, but he doesn't want to see me. I put money in his jail account, so he can get candy bars and the stuff he needs."

"Oh, Lee. That is so nice. Does he know that?"

"If he does, it hasn't made him want to deal with me."

"So, you'd give him a break if you could?"

"Sure. I'm telling you, he's not a bad guy. He's just been misguided. Why this interest in Johnny Cee?"

"Pam Caulfield thinks you're out to get him. Zelda wants to hire a lawyer."

"Zelda? That sounds like her. I'm surprised she doesn't have fifteen stray cats."

"*You* picked up a stray dog, remember?"

"Your point?"

"Zelda thinks Johnny's a good guy, too. It sounds like you have a lot in common with Johnny Caulfield." *Not to mention you're probably related to him.*

"Yeah, I guess we do."

After chit-chatting their way to Washington, they spent the rest of the afternoon strolling around the mall of the Capitol Building and caught the last hour at the Arboretum. At the hotel, Lee gave the porter the bags, and they walked a few blocks to an Ethiopian restaurant. After dinner, they returned to the hotel. Lee led her to the bar and ordered drinks.

He put his drink on a coaster. "You haven't told me about your childhood. Can I ask a few questions?"

"Okay," Jen said. "But first, I have one for you."

"What's that?"

She put her glass of wine down, making a clink on the table. "My question is: Why are we sitting here drinking?"

"Right." Lee pulled bills from his wallet, laid them down, and took her hand.

In the empty elevator, he pushed her against the wall and kissed her, rubbing his hips against hers. At the end of the kiss, she whispered, "Don't they have cameras in the elevators?"

He stroked his cheek against hers. "Who cares?"

The door glided open, and they headed to their room at the end of the hall. Lee turned on the bathroom light, grabbed her, and backed her against the opposite wall.

"You like wall kissing, don't you?" Her voice had a hint of laughter.

"I like kissing. Anywhere." He unfastened the top button of her blouse.

Jen started on his shirt as well. "Aren't you going to turn on the lights?"

"The bathroom light is enough." He took off her blouse and ran his finger along the cleavage of her breasts.

Jen kicked off her shoes as Lee guided her toward the bed. He slipped off his shoes.

"I can't see what the room looks like," Jen said, undoing her waistband.

Lee took off his belt and unsnapped his trousers. "Exactly. You don't need to see anything right now. You might detect a mirror, or ghost, or something that."

She kissed him. "Nothing will distract me."

Good," he said, reaching around to undo the back hooks of her bra. His trousers hit the floor. Sans clothing, he pulled back the bedspread and top sheet, then drew her down to the bed.

Jen gasped as he nuzzled her breasts. She didn't have enough air to moan. Lee guided her hand to his groin.

Her fingers explored him, and the photo of Johnny Caulfield popped into her memory. *I know they're related!* Even without light, she knew he was Johnny Cee's equal…*or better*.

Panting, he tore at the condom foil. "Put it on. Slow."

It had been over twenty years since she'd touched one, but Keith had never stretched the latex like this. Pulling the soft material downward made her insides twitch until she thought she'd die if she wasn't filled soon.

Lee embraced her and rolled on top.

"Now," she urged. "I can't wait any longer."

"Let's not hurry, honey. Enjoy."

"*Now.*"

Amid the stroking and filling, Jen couldn't think, only feel. In a very short time, she cried out so loud Lee put his hand over her mouth to muffle the cries. Soon he made his own muted groan.

Jen pushed herself against Lee's body while she allowed the sizzle to wind down. "It's been so long," her voice quivered. "I'm sorry."

"Don't be. It was the best I ever felt. Are you up for another try?"

She heard the smile in her voice. "Of course. Are you?"

Lee moved her hand to his groin. "What do you think?"

No quickie, this session. Lee took his time, kissing every spot on her he could find, fulfilling the promise he made to her at Chu Phly Pi's. And although the climax didn't reach the pinnacle the first round had achieved, the results pleased Jen highly. Sleep came easy that night.

Light penetrated through a crack in the curtains when Lee stretched his arm to turn off the annoying alarm. "Good morning," he said.

"Yes, indeed. A very good morning." She sat up and spread her arms, pulling happy muscles out as far as possible.

Lee snapped on the bedside light and bent over his luggage to retrieve his bag of toiletries. Jen, fluffing the pillows for support, leaned back and admired his body. She reviewed their nighttime activities, and, added to the sight of his body, she was ready for another course.

"Lee, what time is your meeting?"

He grinned. "I can't, baby. After I dress and grab a coffee, I'll have just enough time to catch the subway to make my meeting. And I don't want to short you. You deserve the best."

"No quickies. You only do longies?"

"That's right." He disappeared into the bathroom.

When Lee came out, he dressed and looked dashing in his suit, especially when he held the leather briefcase. He sat on the edge of the bed. "This ought to be interesting. I'm meeting with FBI and mob cops regarding the League of Learned Lawmakers." He stopped talking and pointed his finger at her. "I know you're taking the car today, so I'm telling you straight out . . . don't go near the League. Okay?"

Jen pushed out her lip. "You can't tell me what to do, you know."

"Yes, I can on this matter. It's not safe there. Understand? I'm not going to have anything happen to you." He scooted closer. "Honey, look at us. I'm happier right now than I can remember. Please. I can't stand the thought of you getting hurt or caught up in some legal mess. Promise me right now."

"I'm not planning on going near the League."

"Not good enough. Your word of honor."

Jen put her hands behind her head, not saying anything.

"Jennifer, don't play with me."

"You mean ever?"

"I'll cancel my appointment if I have to."

"No, don't cancel your Feddie appointments. I promise not to go near the League. I'm doing ancestry research today."

"Good." He breathed out. "That sounds safe enough." He took the valet ticket from the nightstand drawer and handed it to her. "Drive safely." He inclined toward her and kissed her.

She sat up and brushed her hand against his fly.

"No more of that now. I've got to stay sharp." He stood tall and saluted. "Have a good day. I'll call if I'm going to be past four o'clock, okay?"

Jen blew him a kiss and watched him leave, looking handsomely stalwart. She took her time dressing and enjoyed the hotel's continental breakfast. She had arranged to meet Winslow Hampton, Miles's great-grandson, in Reston at 11:00. The second descendant, Carvelle Huron, Miles's elderly granddaughter, had agreed to meet at 2:00. Jen gathered the photos she had seen at Zelda's house. The batty, but dear, lady had made copies.

In the car, she reviewed the GPS on her phone and then maneuvered through the city. Before long, she traveled on a freeway unclogged from the morning traffic. Having arrived early, she parked at a convenience store to wait until the appointed time. Jen practiced her questions. At precisely eleven, she pulled into the driveway of a neatly kept one-story suburban home. A man with graying hair, who looked a little like Miles, walked to the car.

"Ms. Hughes?" he said.

"Yes. I'm so glad to meet you, Mr. Hampton."

"Please, come inside." Winslow walked her to the front door and held it for her.

They both sat in the living room. Jen noticed a shiny brass badge and a name tag sitting on the table. The engraved name *Miles Hampton* darkly contrasted on the surface of the brass bar.

Jen picked up the items.

"Yes," Winslow said. "I thought you might like to see them."

Jen examined the metal insignia and the badge lovingly, turning them over and feeling their weight in her hands. Miles had worn these. Now she knew why Miles couldn't summon the items when he wore his uniform.

When she put them back on the table, her host's fingers drummed on the upholstered arm of his chair.

"All right," Winslow said. "Tell me why you're really here. Let me guess, you're an investigative reporter. Something has come up in that little town, and you're gathering background information. Or, you're a private investigator trying to win my trust by claiming to clear my ancestor's name. Once I trust you, then you start doing the real grilling."

Jen would have laughed, but this man believed the accusation. "Absolutely not. I want to know what happened to Miles's sons and grandchildren after he died."

The man locked eyes with Jen. "Why?"

Jen kept hold of the man's stare. *Go for broke. What have we got to lose?* "Because I bought the house Miles and Virginia built. Miles is still there. His spirit wants to know what happened."

"Why didn't you say so in the first place?"

"You believe me?"

"Of course. I speak to ghosts regularly. I attend séances and festivities for the departed."

"Tell me what you know about them—the spirits."

"I'm so glad you asked!"

Jen listened to the man's claim. He knew nothing of Innocents, Warriors, Paladins, or Lingerers. He did not mention Salients or Evil trying to swallow the energies of Floaters. His childish description of ghosts bored her after ten minutes. After that, she barely listened to his ravings. *This man's gone to LaLa-land. I wasted my time.* Jen looked at her watch. She lost motivation to ask questions about this man's knowledge of Miles and his family. Now noon, she wanted to leave.

She pulled out a plastic baggie from her purse. "I have something for you." *I might as well give him this for his time.* "Copies of photos." The copies Zelda had made of the old photos from the Rothberg's studio.

Winslow spilled the copies onto the table. "Where did you get them?"

"From the descendant of Miles's friend." Jen fished among the pictures and found reproductions of newspaper clippings and grainy newspaper photographs.

Winslow examined the copies, reading the captions Jen had written on the back based on the originals. The man's expression took on emotional wrinkles.

Jen snapped her purse shut. "I know Miles Hampton was innocent. Thanks for seeing me."

"Wait. Don't go just yet. My grandfather, Miles and Virginia's son, assured me of his innocence a long time ago. I wish there was a way we could wipe away the stigma, but I don't see how."

"Things have a way of righting themselves eventually, Mr. Hampton."

"Please call me Winn." He stood. "Maybe I have something for you." He left the room.

A few minutes later, he returned with a heavy ornate album. Inside were photos of Christopher and Timothy, Virginia, Damon Cisco, and family photos. Each succession of photos appeared more modern until the black and white images became color.

"This is wonderful," Jen said, turning the pages. "Thank

you. I so wanted to see photos of the sons." She studied the World War One military portraits of Christopher and Timothy, handsome, with an obvious resemblance to Miles.

After going through the book, Jen closed it and stroked its cover. "Could I borrow this for a short time?"

"I'm not comfortable loaning them. Um, perhaps I could send you copies?"

"If you'll go with me to the local office supply store, we can make copies right there. I'd be glad to drive."

Winn looked out the window. "In that Porsche? Sure. Will you peel out of the driveway?"

While Winn went to lock up and get his jacket, Jen held the brass nameplate and badge, pressing them against her cheek. She pictured Miles in his uniform, remembering the empty spots where these items should have been. She imagined the day she could sit down with Miles and let him look at the photos she had. She could call it *The Miles Hampton Collection,* like the *Livonia Collection* at the library. Then she thought about the letters that had been sent to the library. How would she fix that mistake? Somehow, she had to get Mildred to read through those books.

Jen and Winn got into the Porsche. Jen stepped on the gas, squealing the tires on the drive, sending errant pebbles in all directions. They found a Staples, and the young man behind the counter made short work of the copying. Jen paid, eagerly embracing the bag with her treasure.

After a short ride back to Winn's house, he got out of the car. She rolled her window down. "Thank you for your help and generosity. I'm headed to meet your relative, Carvelle Huron."

"I don't know her well. I've met her a couple of times at Cisco and Hampton reunions."

I guess it makes sense they go to Cisco reunions. Cisco raised Miles's boys. I wonder how Mr. Cisco felt when Christopher and Timothy changed their names back to Hampton.

Having less than an hour to make her appointment on time, Jen pressed the Porsche into what it did best. She roared down the highway. The adrenaline pumped through her system, vaguely dampened by her worry of a ticket. At two minutes after two, she shrieked the tires to a stop in front of the modest white frame house in Manassas. An aging lady with dark hair answered the door.

"Hello," Jen said. "I'm Jennifer Hughes. I have an appointment with Carvelle Huron."

"Come in." The lady opened the door wide. "Mother," she called. "Jennifer Hughes is here."

The woman at the door looked at Jennifer. "My mother is eighty-seven and sharp as a tack. She enjoys visiting with company. Won't you sit down?"

"Great," Jen said and sat in the living room.

Carvelle Huron, a petite, gray-haired woman, entered like a queen. She wore her coiffure pulled back in a twisted bun. Carefully applied makeup gave her an extra portion of elegance. Her dress, a flowing mid-length aqua-printed silk, suggested she would be attending a tea. Jen ogled Carvelle's gold necklace with the sparkling blue pendant and earrings to match.

"Good afternoon, Ms. Hughes," Carvelle said, extending her hand. Her voice, firm and soft, had the social graces of aristocracy.

"Hello," Jen responded. "Thank you for seeing me."

"How may I help you, Ms. Hughes?"

"Please call me Jennifer."

"Very well, Jennifer."

"Be honest," advised the secretary, "without the ghost stuff."

"Mrs. Huron, I bought the house built by Miles and Virginia Hampton. I found their wedding photo stuck behind a drawer. There was something about the picture that piqued my curiosity. Please, believe me, I'm not doing an article of any kind. I'm not investigating to get personal information on a legal case. I'm interested in what happened to Miles Hampton's family after his death. For my own curiosity."

Carvelle smoothed her pastel dress primly over her knee. "I've seen the house. I never met my grandfather, but I was close with my grandmother, Virginia. My mother suffered from melancholia. I lived many years with my dear grandmother."

Jen brought out the photos, the ones from Zelda and the ones she had just acquired.

"You have done some work here, Jennifer."

Carvelle picked up each photo and studied it, taking her time.

Among the photos, Jen spied one she hadn't placed in the pile; the one of Emma Caulfield, Zelda Rothberg's child by Miles. *How did that get in there?*

Carvelle took Emma's likeness from the pile and brushed the others aside until she found the photo of Miles's high school graduation portrait. She put them together. "Hmmm," she said.

Carvelle studied the two photos and nodded ever so slightly.

"I would like to hear about your grandmother, Mrs. Huron."

"Very well." Carvelle put down the photos and leaned back against the sofa pillows.

The petite size and commanding manner of this woman suggested a mix of Scarlett O'Hara and Eleanor Roosevelt, with a dash of Queen Victoria. The image strengthened when the lady called for her daughter to serve tea.

Carvelle folded her hands on her lap. "My grandmother, Virginia, was an exceptional woman. She fondly remembered Miles, her husband. Throughout her life, I did not hear a single word against him. I wish I had met him. The man I knew as Grandfather was Damon Cisco. He treated me well. I was not supposed to know, but he had a few ideas about Miles that were distinctly negative. Grandmother took care to shield me from adverse comments about her first husband. Despite her efforts, I knew Miles Hampton had been suspected of murder and corruption. Such a shame."

Carvelle paused when the tray bearing tea and madeleine cookies arrived. She poured a cup for Jen and one for herself. Jen glanced at pictures on the mantle. She rose from her seat for a closer look.

A cup gently clinked in the saucer. Behind her, Carvelle said, "That's me at my college graduation, and the other shows my husband and me at our wedding."

Jen brought the pictures of Carvelle to the couch and compared the image of young Virginia to them. The resemblance amazed her. Carvelle looked remarkably like Virginia, with high cheekbones, full lips, and a well-proportioned nose.

Carvelle found the picture of Emma and placed it next to her own college picture. The resemblance here was remarkable, too. They shared the same eyebrow arch and curly hair.

While sipping the tea and nibbling on the cookies, Carvelle recounted details of her life and memories with her grandmother and Damon Cisco. "Grandfather Cisco gave up police work when they moved to Pittsburgh. He became a silversmith. Although Grandmother freely talked of Miles out of her second husband's earshot, Grandfather Damon rarely mentioned him and, without a direct order, let everyone know Miles would not be discussed in his household. Grandfather Damon died when I was twelve, and Grandmother and I lived happily together until I left for college and then got married."

The woman studied the array of photos again. She sorted through the pictures. "I already have these."

"I got them from your relative Winslow Hampton," Jen said.

"Oh, the family embarrassment."

"He said he didn't know you very well, but why do you call him that?"

"My nephew knows me. I took care of him sometimes when he was a boy. We lived nearby at the time. A few years ago, Winslow had a stroke, which left him *not right*. He believes he speaks and cavorts with ghosts."

"You don't believe in ghosts?"

"Not at all," Carvelle said with enough emphasis that Jen did not doubt. "Well, Ms. Hughes, it has been a pleasure thinking back to my tender years. I hope I was of help to you."

Jen recognized the brush-off and was disappointed that she hadn't learned more. "Most certainly, Mrs. Huron. Thank you for your time." She gathered up the copied photos from Zelda Silverstein. "These are yours if you want them."

"Thank you. I'll take them. I don't know what will happen to my memorabilia when I die. My daughter isn't interested, and I doubt my grandchildren or great-grandchildren care."

"Too bad," Jen said. "I am truly interested, as you must have guessed by now."

"Goodbye, Ms. Hughes."

Jen left and hit the road for Crystal City, meeting stop-and-go traffic all the way. When her mobile phone rang, she knew it would be Lee wondering where she was. She answered, promising to get back as soon as possible. She breathed relief when she gave the car over to the hotel's valet. Lee was sitting at a desk near the window reading when she entered the room.

He rose and embraced her. "Let's go somewhere outstanding for dinner tonight."

She put her purse and package of photos on the bed. "No funky names? No wings? No corndogs?"

"I want *Chez* something, or *House of*. Something classy and expensive."

Jen raised her eyebrows. "Uncle Paul sounds generous."

"I don't think so. I get a $50 per diem for food when I travel on business. The appetizer needs to cost that much tonight, or it won't suit me."

"Are we celebrating?"

He put both his arms around her neck. "We could celebrate here first before we eat."

"I'm hungry, but celebrating sounds good."

Two hours later, they were starving and took a cab to *Nage* at the concierge's recommendation. Jen could hardly enjoy the food because she had seen the prices. Each steak cost more than Lee's food per diem allowance. And the rest of the meal was ala carte.

When they returned to the room, the bed had been remade.

Jen threw the two chocolates aside. She and Lee celebrated again.

The next day after concluding business with the FBI, Lee had a free day. They checked out of the hotel and visited a few museums. After dining at a moderately priced Cuban place called *Papa's*, they headed back to Livonia.

Jennifer relaxed in the Porsche's soft passenger seat. "What plan did you and the Feds hatch at your meeting?"

"You know I can't tell you that."

"Wait a damn minute. I'm the one who gave you the information about the League and the Currier in the first place. Now I'm cut out of the loop?"

"'Fraid so. But you have the gift, so figure it out."

Jen crossed her arms. "Okay, you will send an old fart incognito to check into the League. He'll flash his money around, and after a day or two, he'll ask about some action. Of course, you will have already established a computer identity, so as soon as the bad guys check on him, they will find him an irresistible customer. When he gets to the Currier, he signals and you all swoop in for the takedown."

Lee chuckled. "Oh, come on. You can do better than that."

"I don't need to. I'll find out on the evening news when it's over."

"Nope. This all goes down extra quiet-like because many senators, governors, and even an FBI biggie have daughters attending that school. The sting will go in and out with a whisper. No flashing cop lights, nothing noticeable."

"But how do you pounce on the baddies and the night girlies?"

"You tell me."

Jen sat quietly for a minute. "Big black cars…strategically placed in Livonia when Mr. X leaves the League."

Lee shook his head. "That's all you got?"

Jen leaned back into the buttery leather seat and closed her eyes. Mentally shutting out all noises and the headlights of the oncoming cars, she concentrated.

"Jen? Are you with me?"

"Okay, this is how it will happen. The FBI gets someone on the inside who learns the routine. A maintenance man. He wires the rooms the mob uses for their nefarious affairs. Mr. X makes his date, and when the time is right, you and the Feds, waiting at your secret hideout, quietly swoop in for the kill."

"Not bad. Wow."

"I'll figure it out. Actually, I'll harass you until I know I am right."

"Don't."

"Well, then give me a clue. Just an outline. No real details."

"You are right about the maintenance man who does windows for the cleaning company."

"Ah, yes," she said. Her pointer finger tapped her forehead. "He puts in audio and visual doo-dads that are so small—"

"Close. You are amazing."

"Psychic. Look, I understand the hookers are young and actually attend the school, but I can't figure out how this all happens under the noses of the legitimate students."

"The school has a building for guest rooms situated away from the dorm. I was only there once, but Marjorie took me to the suite her parents used when they visited. The hookers are roommates, and they cover for each other. It's a brilliant setup. The agent will wire all the guest rooms. And, since you've figured out this much, I'll tell you it's two Mr. X's."

"Double your pleasure, double your fun?"

"Double for protection in case they get caught. Double agents in case one girl drops out at the last minute. All we need is one girl. She gets immunity for information. If we can get both girls, even better. Maybe the swoop will be so quiet the real students never know what happened. But, when this goes down, it has one chance."

"So, what happens if both the girls drop out? The plan doesn't work? The two Mr. X's get freebies?"

"Jennifer? We speak of professionals here. Older, wiser gentlemen who labor to rid our fair country of mobs and mob-related crime."

"Um, hmm. Older and wiser, and who don't want a wild evening on the country's dime."

"Absolutely not."

He slowed for a tollbooth. As he rolled the window down, a five-dollar bill, caught by the draft, flew onto the dashboard. Lee grabbed it and shoved it into his shirt pocket. "Must be the change from the corn dogs the other day. It got stuck to the wrapper, and I remember it dropped behind the seat."

"Change? You *paid* for the corn dogs?"

Chapter Sixty-Five

Lee patted his breast pocket. "Of course. If I hadn't paid, it could be a tip-off for someone who watched. The first rule of undercover — keep it normal."

"Uh, yeah, right," Jen said. She flipped down the visor and selected a CD from the holder. *Air Supply. I love them.* She popped it into the player. They listened to music for the rest of the way home.

Pulling up in her drive, Lee shut off the ignition and turned to her. "I had a great time, honey."

"I did, too. Just what I needed."

"Have you changed your mind about letting me stay overnight at your house?"

"No," she whispered.

"Or mine?"

"No," she said in a half moan.

"We need to work this out." He grasped her face gently and caught her gaze. "I love you."

Her lips parted. Her own declaration of love almost escaped. "Oh, Lee. . ."

When she didn't say more, he released her face. "I'll get your suitcase."

She stepped out of the car while he got her things from the trunk. Jen paused at the front door. She clicked the lock, but instead of turning the handle, she leaned against the doorjamb.

"What are you doing?" he said.

"Waiting for my wall kiss."

He smiled. Several kisses later, Lee set her suitcase inside by the hall tree. As she followed him, she glanced toward the couch. A motorcycle helmet peeked out from the back.

Jen took Lee's hand and steered him back to the front door. "Good night. Thanks for a great time."

"I'll call you tomorrow."

When the sound of the Porche's engine fired up, Jen bolted the door. She turned. "Hello, Brad. All quiet in Livonia?"

Brad appeared next to her. "No, now that you've asked."

"No?"

"The baby has gone."

"The baby? The Innocent under the bleachers? Where'd she go?"

"Her mother came for her."

"You mean Abigale?"

"You know about her?"

Jen nodded, sadness washing over her. "I know that Abigale, a student at the high school, kept her pregnancy hidden and had her child under the bleachers. She left the poor thing to freeze. When the guilt became too much to bear, Abigale killed herself."

"That's about it."

Jen sat on the couch and hung her head. "That poor little baby. Has she been there since her mother left her to die?"

"Yeah."

"Why didn't the baby go straight to Heav—the Other Side?"

"Everyone who doesn't pass over has a purpose. The baby provided a safe place for the Floaters."

"Why did Abigale come now? You said once the spirit passes to the Other Side, they can't come back."

"I did say that, and it's still true. Abigale didn't pass over. She went somewhere else."

"Oh." The skin on Jen's arm was raised in little bumps. "She went to the Suicide Place. Sounds awful."

"The Suicide Place? Interesting title you have there, Jen."

"It's a part of Hell, isn't it? I mean, Abigale killed herself, and killing is a terrible sin, even if it's yourself. So—"-

"Whoa, whoa. Don't get so excited."

"Did you get to talk with Abigale? What did she say?"

"We communicated briefly. She went to The Healing Garden. Others, who work out their own troubles, offer help to suicides. When the suicide sufferers complete their tasks, they can travel to the Other Side. Abigale took her baby, our Innocent, with her."

"So, the baby completed her mission?"

"Yes, or her mother couldn't have taken her."

"Is the light gone from under the bleachers?"

"Really gone."

Jen left the couch and went into the kitchen. Regretting, she threw away Prince Valium and his minions, the Knights of Xanax. She worried about the dreams in store for her tonight. She hadn't had the chocolate dream for a while now. *Chocolate. I need some. If not a dream, at least to eat.* On her short trek to the freezer for a frozen Snickers, she noticed the light on the answering machine blinked. She hit the *play* button.

"Hi, Jenny. James here. I have your plans drawn up, and I faxed them to the county building department. I know they'll approve them, no problem. I'll order the materials and see you in a few days. Let me know you got this message. See ya."

Wow, that was fast. I'll call him in the morning.

Jen found a Snickers in the freezer and ate it at the little kitchen table. The grandfather clock chimed ten. Bidding Brad goodnight, she climbed the stairs to her bedroom.

After breakfast the next morning, Jen called James. He said he pulled strings to get the plans approved as soon as possible and told her the materials would arrive Saturday. He and two of his crew would be there mid-morning on Monday.

She should have felt elated at the prospect of having that nasty basement all fresh and cement-smelling. Instead, she felt empty. *Menaced. Naught will bode well.* "Jeez, now I'm thinking like Miles talks." *Where is Miles? Is he okay?* The image of a shed snakeskin formed. *No! No! Not Miles!*

"Stop it," the secretary commanded. "Pick up Rex, then do

something to take your mind off this ridiculous stuff."

While Jen waited for the vet tech to bring the dog, an attractive brunette approached the reception desk, chart in hand. *Dr. Golden, DVM,* was embroidered in blue thread letters on her lab coat. The tall, slender woman wore her hair pulled back in a simple bun. The loose lab coat did not conceal the lady's figure. Firm, uplifted breasts, trim belly and thighs, long willowy legs.

So, this is Lee's emergency squeeze. Pretty face. Tall gals want tall men. Like Lee. Great. She's hot.

The attendant brought Rex on a leash and said there was no charge as a favor to Lee.

Swell. I'd rather pay. I don't want Lee to owe that woman any favors.

Rex wiggled and put his front paws on Jen's thighs. She petted him and thanked the attendant. When she parked in front of the garage, the raw wood on the fascia caught her attention. She needed to do something about that.

She hadn't parked inside since the Rodovich attack. Any time she had to go in there, she kept the side door open and the big door fully up.

The weather had turned chilly, but not so cold she couldn't paint. Since Dave Blakely had apparently gone out of business, she would paint the trim herself.

The big door opened in a smooth motion. She assembled her materials, the stepladder, paint, rags, and brush, and searched for a big screwdriver to open the can.

Do I have a big screwdriver?

"Lee," answered the secretary.

Jen laughed. She reviewed their nights in Washington while she fished around the cabinetry, searching for an opener. Surprisingly, she found a metal tool used to open paint cans. Maybe it came with the paint. How many weeks ago? It seemed like years since the fire, the rebuild, and all the other unbelievable happenings in her life.

Paint can and brush in hand, she said, "No one can say I don't have an interesting life." She moved the step ladder to the outside and painted the fascia an almond brown.

Halfway down the length of the garage, she stepped off the ladder to rest. At the same time, Lee's Crown Vic pulled into the driveway. She pressed the lid down on the paint can as he and Grainger approached her.

Hi," Jen said to Lee as she wiped her hands with a paint rag. "Good morning, Detective Grainger." She hoped she hadn't emphasized *detective* even though in her mind she did, still stung by the man's caustic words.

Grainger shoved his hands in his pockets. "Um, sorry about that, Ms. Hughes. You don't have to call me detective."

"That is your title."

"I know. But to tell the truth, I'd rather you call me Ash. Lee and I being friends and all, and you and Lee... Save the title for official stuff, okay?" He put out his hand to shake.

Jen held back for a second and then extended her hand. "Even though you know I'm wonky and weird?"

He pushed his hand forward and took hers. "Yeah, even with all that. Lee likes you. That's good enough for me."

"Likes?" Lee said.

Jennifer smiled and gave Lee a hug. "Thank you, Ash. And please call me Jennifer. To what good fortune do I owe a visit from Livonia's finest?" She stepped away and picked up the paint can.

"To inform you that Rodovich has been located," Grainger said.

Jen wiped the rim of the paint can with the rag. "Good."

"Maybe not," Lee said. "Hikers found his body near Cumberland. We won't be getting any information from him."

"Oooh. So, you still don't know why Dave Blakely hired him to—"

Grainger shook his head. "We don't think Blakely did that. It's more likely to be Speigal-related."

"But—"

Lee held his hand up to speak. "Gut feeling. We think Speigal got Blakely to take on Rodovich as a worker. Dave might have had second thoughts, and when he heard Rodovich had the cops looking into his confrontation with you, he panicked and fled."

"So, you aren't any further into why I'm targeted?"

"No," Lee sighed. "We're still working on it." He turned to Grainger. "Can I have a word alone with the lady I *like?*"

Grainger smiled. "Sure. Take your time. I'll be in the car."

Lee conducted her inside the garage. "I've been thinking a lot about Washington. I know this isn't exactly the right place to discuss relationships, but damn it, Jen, I need to know how you feel. About me."

"What do you want me to say?"

Lee ran his hand through his hair. "You're kidding?" He locked eyes with hers. "I love you. Usually, that's hard for a man to say. But it's easy, especially after being together. It's clear to me what I want. So, what do you want?"

Jen searched her mind for the right words. She couldn't find them and the invisible secretary failed her. "I need some time," she finally said. "I haven't been divorced even a year yet. I'm not rushing into anything."

"Okay, I won't push you, but you have to know how you feel."

She nodded, hoping it would be enough for him.

Grainger stuck his head out the passenger window. "Hey, got a call. We need to go."

Lee kissed her. "We'll talk later. Be careful on that ladder. On second thought, wait two days. I'll come over on Saturday and do it for you."

"I want to do it myself. I'm practicing my independence."

"Independent. Great. Be careful."

She went to the back step, sat down, and watched them leave.

"Jennifer." A welcome voice came from behind the back door.

Miles! Jen scrambled to get up. She opened the door, and as she entered, Miles materialized.

"My return is well-timed, I see."

Did Miles hear the exchange in the garage?

Miles took her in his very solid arms and kissed her, not letting go, even after the kiss ended. "You have been away," he still held her.

"Uh," she stammered. "I spent a couple days in Washington."

"With him." It was a statement, not a question. "I came back twice to find our house completely void of life."

What am I supposed to say? Apologize for not being here?

"No," the secretary directed. "No more than you would to Lee. They both need to learn you're not moving to their music."

"Yes. I went there with Lee." She stepped back. "Have you spoken with Brad yet?"

Miles's face tightened. "Why? Has something occurred?"

Chapter Sixty-Six

Jen frowned. "You didn't notice the light over the bleachers is gone?"

Miles embraced her again. "Of course, I did. That is why I came here first. To check on you."

"Me? Why would you think—?"

"The evil focuses on you. I'm sure of it."

"How can you know that?"

"As my strength builds, so does my understanding of evil. I have become a Paladin, much to my loathing. I would happily have remained a Floater and stayed here with you."

Jen shook her head. "Not true. Because that's not who you are. You know what needs to be done, and you do it." She laid her head against his shoulder. "It's your most attractive quality."

"And that which causes me to depart when I truly wish to hold you and not let go." He pressed his lips against her neck.

A surge of electricity shot between her thighs. A soft moan escaped her lips.

Miles shook his head and stepped back. "I must go."

"I know," Jen said.

After he departed with a slow fading transformation, Jen sat at the little kitchen table and put her head in her hands. Soft fur rubbing against her leg relaxed her. "Rexie," she whispered as she ran her hand over his velvety ears. "You're such a comfort."

The living room clock chimed. "Lunchtime." She scooped a small amount of kibble into the dog's dish. "Maybe a sandwich will fill that empty feeling I have."

That empty feeling isn't from food shortage. No sandwich will satisfy that hunger. She stomped her foot. "Damn the Lust Dust!"

"Are you sure it's the Dust?" the secretary asked.

Jen ran to the fridge and took two Snickers out of the freezer, then returned to the table. "You're such a good boy, Rex. You can stay outside with me while I finish the painting. I don't need a sandwich. The chocolate will do."

As she finished the first candy bar, the phone rang. The ID indicated Chrissy. "Mom, can I come and visit for the weekend?"

"I'd love it. What's up?"

"Nothing much. I haven't spent much time with you since you moved. And, I just," she paused, "wanted to visit. I've concentrated on my schooling so much I've kind of neglected you and Dad. I know I said I wanted to be on my own, but sometimes I think about chatting and —"

"You've met someone and want advice."

"Wow. How'd you know that?"

Jen laughed. "I'm psychic."

"You must be. I'll see you Friday afternoon."

"Awesome!"

Jen put the phone back into its charger. *I doubt if I can help her. I can't sort out my own affairs.* She and Rex went outside to finish the garage.

After stroking the paintbrush on the last spot, Jen climbed down from the ladder and admired her work. She had to admit Dave had done a good job restoring the garage, improving the harmony between the buildings.

Rex clawed and moved back and forth at the side of the house.

"Stop it!" Jen shouted. "I know you want at the raccoons, but I won't have you digging out the foundation. Come, Rex."

The dog followed her into the garage, where she put away the materials and cleaned the traces of paint on her fingers with mineral spirits. She hadn't realized how much time she spent painting until she noticed the sunset.

"Now I'm hungry," she said to Rex as they approached the back door.

Not wanting to cook after working all afternoon, she

rooted in the pantry and brought out a can of chili. When the microwave dinged, she grated cheese and topped the bowl with sliced green onions. Adding crackers and a glass of Coke, the dish became a meal, satisfying her food appetite. The other need, the hunger Miles had stirred up, remained.

After dinner, she settled in front of the television and flicked through the channels, looking for something other than the news.

"If you please," Miles said.

She pressed the remote to turn off the television.

Miles sat next to her. "Thank you."

"I didn't think you'd come back so soon."

"Tonight grants me a rare opportunity to be with you."

"Rare? Why?"

"Brad leaves tomorrow."

"Why? Don't we need Brad here? You said he— I mean, what about the Floaters? Who will protect them?"

"Events have transpired indicating the completion of Brad's duty here. All of the Floaters in Livonia have advanced to Shields, Warriors, or better. Although still threatened by the Dark Forces, in their enhanced state, the spirits no longer need Brad's protection. That is why the baby could leave with her mother."

"Will Brad pass over to the Other Side?"

"Brad believes another area shelters a similar evil. He will go there to marshal the resident souls."

"Where?"

"In the Middle East, half-way around the globe. He wishes to say farewell to you. He will visit tomorrow."

"Does that mean you will take over whatever it is Brad does?"

"Yes. It also means I won't have time to be with you." Miles moved his arm around her shoulders. "Some time ago I had an opportunity to be close. Curse me for a fool, I spurned that chance. I have this night, dear lady. I won't let good fortune elude me again."

Miles stood, extending his hands toward her.

Jen placed her hands in his, and he drew her into a deep embrace. In a fluid movement, he slid her fully into his arms, lifting her. "Naught but air, sweet one." He carried her up the stairs.

In her room, Miles put Jen on the bed. As he kissed her neck, he unbuttoned her blouse and placed his lips on her shoulders. Jen unfastened her bra and allowed him to remove her slacks. He ran his finger under the lacy elastic of her panties before sliding them down, and relocated his kisses to her navel and its environs.

Miles disappeared for less than a second. Upon materializing, he wore no clothes. The lights filtering in from the hall shadowed his body. The soft glow defined the ridges of well-developed muscles from shoulder to thigh, broken by the curling golden chest hair and the amber silk of his groin. He stood next to the bed, his stance reminding her of the statue of David. That statue could not compare to this man.

Jen moved over and pulled back the covers. Miles slipped in next to her and gently rolled his chest over hers. He lifted her arms over her head. He kissed her. Miles's attentions, unhurried and thoughtful, both relaxed and excited her. She closed her eyes. Her mind, immersed in a dream-like state, invited the slow burn building within her body.

When Miles pushed apart her legs and entered her, the sensation was unlike anything before. His flesh brushed against her perfectly, producing the purest effect of pleasure. In a short time, she called out a high-pitched whine as sweet electricity zapped throughout her body, down to the smallest nerves in her fingers and toes.

Soon he cried out in a masculine groan, then rolled next to her.

When the liquid feeling of bliss settled, she inhaled a deep breath. "Miles! What? Did you change your size...um...as you moved...in and out?"

He cleared his throat with a small chuckle. "I have abilities I did not possess in my former life. It seemed like the right choice."

"You can change your size?"

"You have the proof. Not bad for a man exceeding one hundred and forty years, eh?"

"You made a joke. That's the first time I've heard you say anything humorous."

"Wouldn't a man being celibate for over a hundred years feel great joy after something so wondrous? Great joy yields good humor."

"Joke number two! I'm seeing a new side of you. And I like what I see." She rolled on her side and moved her hand to his chest. Pushing her fingers through his silky hair, she twirled a curl with her forefinger. "Maybe it's because you're naked, but you look different somehow."

"I am wearing my twenty-five-year-old body."

"You can change your age?"

"I just did."

"Could you take yourself down to, say, a baby?"

He swiftly swung her under him and put his lips to her breast. "Maybe a hungry one."

"Wow! Three jokes."

"But the truth is, no. I have to be able to remember how I was to summon the time frame. Plus, whatever age I choose, my mind stays the same, so I can't go back too far in my personal history."

Jen sat up and put her hand on his arm. "Oh, God. You didn't use…. Can I get pregnant?"

"You can't get pregnant by me," Miles said in a serious tone.

"But you are corporeal, like any man, so —"

"I don't understand the physical aspects of the spiritual world. I just know what leaves my body disappears. Let us say, I'm safe if I spit into the wind. Do not worry."

She put her head on his shoulder and snuggled close. "When you were with Zelda, didn't you worry about getting her pregnant?"

"It was my most fervent dream."

"Really?"

"If she carried a child, her father would have had to let me marry her, religion be damned. Right before I was to graduate high school, I attended a fencing tournament in New York City. While there, I finalized my business with a cousin who needed a partner for his second store in Brooklyn. I planned to borrow the money from my father, marry Zelda, and move to the apartment over the store. However, when I returned, she had left, ironically, for New York, where she decided to end our love affair."

"You didn't discuss this with her before you left for your tournament?"

"No. I wanted to have it all arranged before I asked her to marry me. A pregnancy would have helped, but I would have asked her no matter what."

Zelda made the sacrifice to save Miles's reputation. He could have saved hers by moving to New York. Neither one of them communicated their decisions. How sad. How awful. "Oh, Miles."

"Here now. Enough questions. Did anyone ever tell you how strange you are?"

"Only all the time."

"Well, then, woman, hold your tongue. Unless, you can think of something better to do with it. As your humble servant, I stand at the ready."

"Oh, no. I need a few minutes to let that wild ride sink in."

He laughed. "You do have a unique way with words. Shall we sleep now?"

"One more question."

"Very well."

"When I fall asleep, will you sleep, too? Or will it be nether sleep, and I'll wake up alone?"

"You slipped in an extra question. I shall sleep like a normal man. I may even snore. After all these years of nether-rest, I look forward to a genuine night's sleep. Especially with my arms around you, beautiful princess."

"Good night, then."

Miles inched closer and nuzzled her neck with his nose.

"Good night."

When Jen awakened in the morning, Miles still slept, snoring mildly. She touched his shoulder. He stretched his arms up and outward. Swinging his legs over the side of the bed, he stood. His well-formed body looked less strapping in the morning light.

She sat up and put her arms behind her head. "Back to your forties, I see."

"One can't stay young forever...." He disappeared for an instant and returned fully dressed. "Maybe I can be young once in a while."

"I'd prefer you to be my age." She rose and took clothes from the chest of drawers.

Miles folded his arms over his chest and leaned against the doorway.

Jen stepped into her panties. "I feel self-conscious while you watch me dress."

His lighthearted tone faded to its normal serious sound. "I am fixing your image in my mind. After Brad leaves, I don't know when I can see you again."

He followed her downstairs and let Rex out. She made her morning coffee.

When she opened the door to Rex's scratching, the dog wasn't alone. Brad was there, too. The figure, dressed in his leather motorcycle suit, gloves, and shiny helmet, stepped inside the doorway.

He said, "I couldn't leave without saying goodbye."

Jen embraced him and kissed the plastic helmet where his forehead would be underneath. "You be careful."

He laughed. "So, what can happen? I'm already dead."

"Snakes skins and all that?"

"Yeah. I suppose I could run into a posse of those bad dudes. But I've learned a lot in Livonia."

"What are your plans? What can you do in the Middle East?"

"I'll know when I get there. Maybe I'll call to let you know.

Tell me your phone number."

Jen recited her phone number.

He nodded. "I'll remember them. Jennifer, thanks for caring about me. I . . ." His voice caught. "Well, thanks."

Miles opened the door. Brad stepped out and he turned to Jen. "The protective wall around this house still works, but there's something here evil wants. I don't know what, but the Forces haven't figured out how to get it."

Jen put her hand to her throat. "Do you think they'll find a way?"

Brad shrugged. "Don't know. But even if you are safe in the house for now, don't let down your guard." Crossing the threshold, he disappeared.

Miles touched a finger to his forehead in a small salute and vanished too.

Setting aside Brad's departure and comments, Jen thought about Chrissy. Memories of the night before with Miles often trumped the anticipation of Chrissy's visit. Both happy events alternated in her mind, and she breezed through the day doing chores with an energy she hadn't felt for a long time.

The phone rang. Jen glanced at the caller ID before picking it up. "Hi, Pam."

"Hey. Feel like going to the movies tonight? It's a romance. Good reviews."

"Thanks, but my daughter is spending the weekend. She's coming this afternoon."

"How about Monday?"

"I don't think so. I'm having my basement done. Materials are to be delivered Saturday. The work should start Monday morning."

"Your basement? I thought the contractor bailed on you."

"He did. My ex-husband's brother is an architect. He's offered to bring a small crew to do the work if I pay for the materials."

"Really? That's pretty generous. From Baltimore?"

"Yes. James is a sweetie. He said it would only take a few

days."

"Okay, then," Pam said. "I'll give you a call next week. Good luck with your basement."

At four that afternoon, Chrissy knocked at the door.

"I grabbed your mail from the box," Chrissy said. "There's a package."

"Put it on the kitchen counter." Jen's arms coiled around her daughter. "I'm so glad to see you." Jen took the extended handle of the small rolling suitcase, and while Chrissy put the mail in the kitchen, Jen took the bag upstairs to the guest room.

Back in the kitchen, Jen served tea and cookies while Chrissy talked about school and her studies toward a bachelor's degree to become a radiology technician. Jen didn't ask questions but listened quietly like a mother should.

"I met someone, Mom."

"Tell me about him."

"Randall Smith. He's a doctor, half-way through his internship. We've been dating for three months, and it's becoming serious. He wants to take me to St. Louis to meet his family."

"Has he proposed?"

"No, but he says things like we could get jobs together in Seattle, or Houston. He's thinking about the future with me."

"Are you in love with him?"

"He says it to me, and I say it back. But, Mom, I don't know what love is. Tell me."

Jen sighed. "That's both hard and easy to explain. If you're in love, you should know it, but the fear of making a mistake can get in the way. Real love comes slowly. And it is difficult to discern love for lust. Let me ask you this. When you are, um, *close*, do you feel like your heart is going to stop at any second? Do you see fireworks? Does electric pleasure jump through your every synapse? When he kisses you, do your toes curl like a New Year's Eve horn? Do you have to gulp for air?"

"Mo-ther! I'm pretty sure you're not referring to Daddy. *You* have a *boyfriend*. Forget my stuff. Let's talk about you."

The heat of blush ran through her. Her mind whizzed with

the recent memories of lusty actions.

"Mom?"

Jen came out of her thought coma. "Oh, uh, sorry. What did you ask me?"

Rex started to bark. A car sounded in the driveway. Jen went to the front door and opened it. Lee took the pathway in giant strides.

"Hi," he said, marching into the living room. He gave Jen a quick kiss. "Destry, parked at the end of the street, radioed me you had a visitor. I thought I'd check it out."

Chrissy came into the ling room.

Lee approached Chrissy and put out his hand. "I bet you're Christine."

"I am."

"I'm Lee Ferguson."

Chrissy stepped back and looked him up and down. "Uh-*huh*. Mom was just talking about you."

Lee smiled at Jen. "Good things, I hope."

Chrissy cocked her head. "Sounded good to me."

She thinks I meant Lee. Well, I guess he could qualify. Skyrockets? Oh, yeah. Electric currents cascading through my wiring? Oooh, a regular zap-o-rama. Toe curling? Bent over like a hairpin. Yeah, he qualifies.

Lee grinned. "Great. How about I take you lovely ladies to dinner?" He turned to Jen. "Well?"

Chrissy turned to Jen too. "Mom?"

Jen revived from her mental review. "Huh?"

"Dinner?" Lee said. "Mexican? We could go to the Jolly Tamale. Fantastic food."

Jen shrugged her consent and looked at her daughter.

Chrissy made a face. "I've had Mexican three times this week."

"What's your pleasure then?"

"Ooh, how about Chinese? Mom?"

Oh sure, we can elbow our way through the spirits huddling at Chu Phly Pi's. What if Miles is there?

"Mom?"

"Jen?"

She wobbled her head for a second to focus. "Uh, sure. Whatever."

"Okay," Lee said. "That's settled. When do you want to eat? Now would be a good time. Since it's Friday evening, the place will fill up within the hour."

"Now's good for me," Chrissy said.

"Yeah," Jen said. *It might already be filled with ghosts. You just don't know it.*

After a quick walk for Rex and putting kibble in his bowl, Jen ran upstairs to refresh her makeup. She locked the front door and got into the Crown Vic with Lee and Chrissy.

The tinkling bell attached to the door rang as they entered Chu Ply Pi's Asian Kitchen. Once again aromas, like savory perfumes, greeted Jen.

Chu Phly grinned wide when he saw them and escorted them to the table. He winked at Jen and spoke in his fake accent. "How good to see you again, Miss Jennifer. You bring sister to Chu's." He bowed low and took Chrissy's hand. "Tell Chu you name."

"Christine."

"Ah, so. Jennifer and Christine. Twins? Chu double-blessed tonight."

"Oh, brother," Lee complained. "Just give us the menus, please."

"No menu. Chu make special just for you." He snapped his fingers dramatically and two black-clad Asian girls brought tea and a tray with noodles and colorful sauces.

"But this time, we pay," Lee said.

"If you insist, Lieutenant Policeman." Chu bowed at the waist and hurried away.

Chrissy reached for a noodle. "Detective?"

Lee dipped his flaky pasta strip into the red sauce. "Uh-huh."

"How'd you meet my mother?"

Jen kicked Lee under the table. She caught his eye and sent him a *please don't* look.

Lee took another noodle and looked back at Jen. "She might want to tell our story."

"I found a book with writing in it that looked like a loan-shark record. I called the police and Lee came out to pick it up." She thought it best not to mention Zemric's threats.

"Cool. So, what happened with the book?"

"They're still working on it, right, Lee?"

"That's right." Lee agreed. "Taste the yellow sauce, Chrissy. It's curry and saffron."

As Chrissy sampled the sauces, Jen rubbed her foot against Lee's leg in a *thank you*.

Chu returned with a new bowl of noodles. "Miss Jennifer, my mother has changed symbols around restaurant. You like to see?"

The symbols looked the same, but Jen understood he wanted to speak to her. She allowed Chu to help her up from the seat.

Jen and Chu went into the kitchen, where a small Asian woman stirred a large pot.

"Mother," Chu said in a non-accent, "this is Jennifer." He turned to Jen. "Jennifer, my mother, Su-Lin."

"Hello," Su-Lin said in a thick Chinese accent. "I so glad you talk with me. I see you aura change big since last time you here."

"Excuse me?"

Su-Lin raised her eyebrows and smiled at Jen. "You really good friends with spirits. Very close."

"What?" Jen asked.-

Chu scratched his nose. "She recognizes your aura, meaning you have an exceptionally close relationship with a spirit."

Where is this conversation going?

"Take control," the secretary advised.

Jen put her hand on the small woman's shoulder. "Su-Lin,

your symbols and rituals have made this place a haven for spirits against the Dark Forces. They appreciate your efforts."

Su-Lin smiled wide. She slowed her words. "Can I talk to them? You call some in kitchen? Yes?"

"It doesn't work that way. If they want to speak with you, they will appear themselves."

"You see many spirits here?"

"No. I can't see them unless they want me to."

Su-Lin stirred her pot. "You tell spirits Su-Lin want to meet, okay?"

"If I get the chance, I will. Um, I need to get back to the table." As he she left the kitchen she shuddered. *Is the restaurant a haven full of spirits I can't see? Could Miles be here?* Jen returned to the table.

Chu Phly lived up to his reputation regarding his creation. After the meal, they finished with almond cookies.

Just as Lee called for the check, his mobile rang. Lee scooted his chair away. "I need to take this outside."

Chrissy slid from the table, too. "I have to go to the ladies' room."

Now she was alone at the table. She looked around. "Miles?"

Jen jumped when a ghostly man dressed like a train conductor appeared next to her. "He's not here. Do you want me to find him?"

"No. Uh, thank you. I just wondered."

When the old gentleman faded away, she turned around.

Lee stood behind her with a thunderous expression. "What are you doing? Calling for Miles Hampton? In the restaurant?"

"He isn't here."

Lee sat down. "He isn't anywhere, Jen. Isn't it enough that you think your house is haunted?"

Jen put her palm up. "I don't want to discuss this."

"I know I said I didn't care if you thought you communicated with ghosts, but I do, and we need to talk about it."

"Not now."

Lee folded his arms over his chest. "Soon."

A black-clad young woman brought the check in a leather holder. Lee opened his wallet and took out a credit card. When Chrissy returned, he stood and held her chair and sat staring at Jen.

With leftovers carefully boxed and bagged, the three of them walked to the car and rode home silently. Lee took Rex outside while Jen put away the left-over cartons.

"Mom," Chrissy said. "The two of you are awfully quiet. When Lee comes in, I think you need to talk. Plus, I'm dead tired."

Lee brought Rex in and hung the lead on the hook near the front door.

Chrissy approached Lee. "Thank you for a lovely dinner. I'm bushed, and it's time for me to go upstairs."

"Great to meet you," Lee said. "Good night."

Lee and Jen sat on the couch. He cupped her chin. "Look, I love you, and I've made it clear I want us to be together. Just you and me. That means no one else. No spirits, or goblins, or zombies, or any*thing*. You've got to get over this Miles Hampton notion."

"You don't know what you're asking." Jen pulled free of his hold and looked away.

"I'm not asking. I'm giving you a choice."

She clenched her teeth. "What? I stop believing something I know to be true so you can be my boyfriend?"

"Not a boyfriend. Husband. But I can't and won't deal with this spirit crap." Lee put his hands on her shoulders and turned her to face him. "Put the ghosts out of your mind." He snapped his fingers. "Like that! Poof! Gone. See how easy?"

"Get out." She walked to the door.

Lee shook his head and sighed. "Is that it? You throw me out and we part? All for some damned criminal who's been dead for a hundred years?"

Jen opened the door. "He's no criminal. Never say that again."

Lee grabbed the door handle and closed it. "He left a

confession note. The Inquest proclaimed suicide, plus guilty of murder. I've read the reports."

Jen put her hands on her hips. "The note wasn't from him. Don't you recognize a frame when it stares you in the face? A setup from corrupt city officials, including the police chief?"

"Is that what you think?"

"I believe it."

Lee blew a breath. "You're not going to give up on this spirit stuff, are you? I don't know if I can compete. I just don't know." He let himself out.

Chapter Sixty-Seven

Right after breakfast the next morning, the construction materials came. Jen told the men to stack the blocks, bags of cement, wood and the rest on the side of the garage. Two hours later, the rental company delivered the cement mixer and the tools James had ordered.

Surveying the items, Jen smiled at her daughter. "I'm so pumped. I'm finally going to get that nasty basement fixed. Bless your Uncle James. I can count on him."

"He's a sweetie, Mom. Too bad Aunt Mona divorced him. I couldn't believe it."

Jen shook her head. "It surprised me, too. They were so in love. Indulging in matters of the flesh can sure mess up a good relationship."

The invisible secretary gave her a shove. "Maybe you should think about that yourself."

"So, my dear daughter, what would you like to do this afternoon?"

"How is that outlet mall on the interstate?"

They spent the day strolling through the stores and appreciating the finer aspects of discounts. A late lunch at an all-you-can-eat soup and salad bar kept their appetites at bay until later that evening. At nine that night, they stopped at The Finger for takeout chicken.

At home in the kitchen, Chrissy pushed the mail to the side on the counter to make a spot for the bag of chicken and fixings. After polishing off her third piece, she wiped her hands. "I had a great time today. I wish I didn't have to leave tomorrow, but I have a big test Monday and need to get back."

Jen hugged her daughter. "Too bad you have to leave early. Will you come again soon?"

"I will. Maybe Bobby will ride with me next time. He spends a lot of time with Dad playing golf."

"Golf? When did Keith go back to golf?"

"When he started feeling lonely on the weekends. He's taking karate lessons during the week too. Mom, I feel sorry for him."

"His choice. And you have no idea the favor he did me."

They hugged goodnight and went to bed.

The next morning after breakfast Jen walked her daughter to the car. "Good luck with your test."

"And my man," Chrissy said.

"Be careful, honey. I mean driving and loving."

"You be careful, too. I hope you work out your relationship."

"With Lee?"

"Is there someone else?" When Jen looked away and didn't answer, Chrissy said, "Mom! You have a second guy? Oh, sweet. Tell me."

"Nothing to tell really." *Certainly not something you would understand.*

Chrissy clucked. "Nuh-uh. Liar, liar, pants on fire. You have another boyfriend."

"Not exactly. Just someone…who is hardly here. He floats through now and again. Spirited, but nothing substantial." She smiled at her truthful cleverness.

"What does that mean?" Chrissy turned the ignition.

"A relationship that has no future." *Jeez, it's true.*

"And Lee?"

"That connection may have a potential future." She stepped back from the car.

"I like him, Mom."

Jen waved until the car turned out of sight. She gave Rex an ear scratching. "Come on, Rexie, we'll work in the garage for a few minutes."

She organized her gardening tools. A car crunched in the driveway. Thinking Chrissy forgot something, she hurried out.

Mildred Owings emerged from her white Cadillac.

"Hello," Jen said.

"I just stopped by to say how much I appreciate your help. I'm back from my trip to Washington. I feel so much better about life…and death."

"Are you still thinking of retiring?"

"I already have. I cleaned out my office and turned the library over to my assistant."

Distress hit her like an arrow in the back. *The books with the letter and confession! How will they be discovered? Miles will never be cleared.* "But you can't leave the library!"

"Why not?"

"The Livonia Collection. You can't let that go. It's important."

Mildred put her hand to her chest. "Of course. You must have received another message from Danny. He understands the collection will languish without someone devoted to keeping it up. He would want me to continue the history of the city. We used to talk about the importance of keeping history for our town's future people. Oh, Jennifer, thank you so much. I'll talk to the new librarian tomorrow and volunteer to work on the collection. Now I can dedicate all of my time to what I like best." She smiled. "Your messages from Danny have given me back my life."

Liar, liar, pants on fire.

Mildred hugged Jen and kissed her on the cheek. She got back in the car, and with a smile and a wave, backed out. She rolled down the window. "You are wonderful."

Does Lee still think I'm wonderful?

Jen took Rex into the house. The ticking clock amplified the quiet. "Alone," she said, and wished she had company. She missed Chrissy. She missed Lee, Miles, and even Brad.

Early the next morning, Jen woke with dread. As she sipped her morning coffee anxiety plagued her. *I wonder when James will be here.* The dread she experienced earlier coalesced. The scream of brakes and the vision of blood ripped into her mind. "James!" she cried out. "Oh, my God!" She grabbed her purse, locked the doors, and ran to her car. She pulled into a space near the emergency entrance of the hospital. An ambulance, lights flashing and siren blaring, squealed to a stop at the double doors.

As Jen reached the ambulance, the EMT's lowered the stretcher and clicked the wheels in place. Bloody bandages hid most of the man's face, but Jen recognized James by his blond curls.

"James!" Jen said rushing to the stretcher.

"Ma'am," the lead attendant said.

"I'm family," she snapped.

"Mona?" James whispered.

"No, honey, it's Jen." She glowered at the EMT and ran alongside the stretcher.

James moaned. "I want Mona."

"Ma'am," the attendant warned. "Step away."

Jen stopped but called out, "Okay, sweetie, I'll get Mona."

A doctor and two nurses hustled to the stretcher, directing the EMT's to a room. Jen watched as the doors closed behind them.

A hand cupped her shoulder. Lee turned her to face him. "You know that guy?"

"He's my brother-in-law. I came as soon as I realized something was wrong."

"How could you know that?"

Jen put her hand on her cheek. "I just knew James was in trouble. What happened, Lee? What kind of accident?" Movement outside caught her attention. A black van slowly drove to the side of the hospital. From where she stood, she could see another set of double doors. The attendants unloaded two more stretchers, this time both completely covered with sheets with large bloody patches staining the fabric.

"No accident," Lee said. "I came here to investigate, to see if I could question the survivor. Two surveyors saw the victims' truck pursued by a larger truck that tried to run them off the road. When the smaller truck made an evasive turn, the big truck came back and rammed them down an embankment. The big truck didn't have a license plate. We're looking for it. The only one to survive is the driver. He or one of the dead guys must have had an enemy."

A nurse walked by holding a clipboard and slowed as she passed. "Hi, Lee."

A mental image told her they had once been intimate. She flushed. *Jealousy?* Jen checked the nurse's hand. *A wedding band. Good.*

"Can you find out what's happening to James?" Jen asked, pointing to the nurse.

"Sure. Hey, Florence, wait a minute." He followed her into a glass-walled office.

Jen trailed them at a distance and waited, watching the activity behind the enclosure of the nurses' station. Lee talked with Florence and another nurse. One of the attendants came in, and they conferred with him.

Lee returned. "They're X-raying him now. They don't know for certain what injuries he has, but so far it looks like broken ribs, broken arm, and facial lacerations. They need to do more testing for internal injuries. Lucky that he had his seat belt on. One guy didn't and went through the windshield. The third man's head was crushed with a toolbox stored behind the seat."

Jen angled her head, trying to gather her thoughts.

"Try not to worry. Although this is a small hospital, our people are top-notch. We have almost everything a big hospital has. The patient is in good hands."

"Thanks. I need to sit down."

"Come with me." He led her down a corridor to a door that had a small metal sign reading: *Conference.* He flicked the lights on. Taking her purse, he set it on the long table. After a pause, he put his arm around her and led her to a pair of upholstered chairs in the corner. "You okay?"

"Yes."

He pressed his lips into a fine line. "I've been considering what you said about Hampton being framed. I did some research and you could be right. I looked over some documents we have on file, and a few things felt fishy. Aunt Mildred told me you did extensive research about the background of the house and Hampton, and all. Well, I understand it now."

"You do?"

"Work with me here, Jenny. I understand that you got a psychic bulletin saying Hampton had been framed. And, you in your quest for fairness, want his reputation, and his *memory* to be cleared of wrongdoing. So, it's his *persona* you feel, and want to protect. I accept that. I'm not jealous of a persona."

"No, Lee. It's *him*, Miles Hampton. I see him and talk with him." *And we've even made love.*

"No, you don't. He's not flesh and blood like me. Hampton is a memory. He can't hold you or kiss you. You can't put your hand on his body." Lee placed her hand on his fly. "He doesn't have this."

Oh, yes, he does. And his can do tricks.

"Why are you smiling?" Lee said.

"Miles is real. As real as you."

"Okay," Lee said, running a hand through his hair. "Tell him to speak to me. That way I can tell him to get the hell out of our lives. Call him. Right now."

"I can't!"

Lee glared, nostrils flaring. "Because he's not real."

"Lee!"

"When he appears to me, then I'll believe."

"Be careful!" warned the secretary. "Don't try to explain."

She stood. "I'm not going to ask him to appear to you. Believe what you want."

Lee stood, too. They walked to the door. "That's it, then?"

"For now. Please excuse me. I have calls to make." She headed down the corridor and looked back. He stood where she left him. She didn't look back again and headed for her car. *Lee is such a shit.*

"No, he's not," the secretary said. "He's a good man. You're driving him crazy. He loves you and wants to get married. You need to figure out what he means to you. Are you willing to lose him for Miles? Has Miles professed his love for you? You said it yourself. What kind of future do you have with Miles?"

Leave me alone. I'll think about this later. I need to make my calls.

In her car, she called Keith. Keith, normally cool-headed, stammered and groped for words to question her further. "Can I stay with you while James is in the hospital? Until I know he will be okay?"

"Of course. Maybe Mona can stay as well. Call her, then call James's office. Let me know what time to expect you at my house. We can go to the hospital together."

Later that afternoon, Keith and Mona arrived. Jen had the bedrooms ready. She put Mona next to her, and Keith down the hallway.

When they entered the intensive care ward, James lay in a bed beyond the glass wall. He was attached to multiple tubes and wires. The doctor assigned to his case was called to talk to the family. In response to Keith's and Mona's questions, he listed six cracked ribs, a concussion, a fractured right arm ulna, and a hairline fracture of his collarbone.

Mona tugged at Keith's elbow. "Let's go in to see him. I really need to touch him and talk with him."

Jen waited in the hallway since only two were allowed at his bedside. After a few minutes, Keith joined her. "He's going to be all right. What a relief."

"Thank God," Jen said. The view behind the glass wall of the ICU made her smile. Mona was busy covering James' face with kisses.

"You know," Keith said taking Jen's hand, "James is getting another shot at happiness. How about you and me? You could come back to our house. Redecorate, refurnish, re-do, whatever your heart desires. I just won a big case and got a huge bonus. We can take a luxury cruise. Anything you want. What do you say, honey?"

Jen could barely think. Now the evil trying to get to her had spilled over to her family. Even if she considered going back to Keith, which didn't appeal to her at all, she would be bringing unknown dangers with her. She shook her head. "No, Keith."

"Give me a good reason why we can't patch this mess up."

Jen clenched her jaw then released. Her reason to stay apart went much deeper than her fear of bringing evil to her family. Words flew. "I have made my own life and have no desire to go back to the country club scene or work on the charity teas with those snooty wives. I don't want to join the book club and talk about recent best-sellers." *Sleep with you? Ha! I like creepy Livonia, where evil tries to work its tendril fingers into my protected house. Where the handsome detective woos and charms me. Where my ghost lover makes me feel like I'm going to explode when he. . . But, jeez, where I've had two attempts on my life? Baltimore, safe, maybe. Livonia, unpredictable. Keith, or Lee and Miles?* "No, Keith. I like it here."

He sighed. "We'll talk about it later sometime."

Jen reflected on the last few months and smiled. *No, we won't.*

Chapter Sixty-Eight

Keith and Mona stayed a full week while James recuperated enough to go home. Keith, Mona, and James went back to Baltimore the day he was released from the hospital. The house seemed extra empty after the visitors left. Jen had not heard from Lee, and resisted the urge to call him. The only call she received came on Wednesday, when Keith let her know Mona and James had moved in together. Every so often, she looked at the phone and debated calling Lee. One of those phone-stares surprised her when it rang.

"Hello, Jennifer?"

She didn't recognize the voice. "Yes?"

"It's Brad."

"Oh, um, Brad. Good to hear from you. Uh. . ." She didn't know what to say.

"I'm in Syria. And I'm taking down some real evil types."

"You're killing people?"

He laughed. "No. I'm gathering evidence, tipping off the authorities, and learning stuff to help the world get rid of some really bad dudes."

"Oh, good. Everything is okay with you?"

"Yes. I wanted to tell you because... Well, Jennifer, you're the closest thing I have to a mother, and I—"

"I know. Consider yourself my son. Thanks for letting me know you're doing something important. Brad, I'm proud of you. Any mother would be." She could sense his satisfaction, even if he didn't say anything.

"Thank you," he practically whispered. "How's our friend?"

"I haven't seen or heard from him since he left with you."

"Yeah, I saddled him with a lot of responsibilities. He's the kind of man who will see to them all the way. You'll hear from him as soon as he can. You know that. Listen, I'd better go."

"You'll be careful, right?"

"What could happen?" He laughed. "I'll be careful. Can I call you again some time?"

"Sure. Let me know you're, uh, still with us."

"I will. I have to get this phone back to the guy I borrowed it from. It's gonna cost him plenty for the call."

"You asked someone to use a phone?"

"Uh, not exactly. I lifted it. But I'll put it back and try to find some way to repay him."

"Okay, Brad. Keep up the good work. I'll be thinking about you."

"Thanks, Jennifer. Thanks for everything."

"Bye, Sonny boy," she said, and hung up.

Thursday afternoon she went shopping. Before she returned home, she saw a pastry shop bordering one side of the town center and decided to treat herself to cake and coffee at *Sweet Spot.* She sat at a small table near the window where she could see the other businesses flanking the town plaza. Just across the small park she a neon sign flashing *the Jolly Tamale,* the place Lee had offered to take her and Chrissy. A red Porsche rumbled to a stop in the diagonal parking lines in front of the restaurant.

Lee got out of the car and walked to the passenger side. He opened the door and extended his hand to a woman. Jen recognized the veterinarian. The lady wore a soft white sweater dress that clung in all the right places. She was tall and trim, with her dark hair curling onto her shoulders.

Jen's stomach squeezed together. Acid oozed, burning. She put down the bite of pastry on the fork. As the couple walked toward the entrance of the restaurant, the woman slid her arm around Lee's waist. Although Lee didn't put his arm around her waist in return, he didn't remove her arm.

Jen lost her appetite. She went home.

The next day dragged. Jen tried to put the image of Lee's date out of her mind, but it crept back repeatedly. With no appetite, she barely ate all day.

In the afternoon, Lee called. "Jen, can we talk?"

"Yes. Whenever."

Later that day, a car pulled into the driveway. She peeked out the curtain to see an unfamiliar black sedan. When the doorbell chimed, she left the lock chain attached and cracked the door open. Two dark-suited men stood on the step.

The taller man said, "Ms. Jennifer Hughes." He flipped a leather holder with a shiny gold badge. "I'm Agent Fleming, and this is Agent Boyles. We're with the NSA. We'd like to talk to you."

A jolt of fear swept over her. "No thank you. Not today."

"Ms. Hughes." One of them increased his volume. "We could open the door and take you for questioning by force."

"What do you want?" she shouted.

"Just talk. We have some questions about someone who called you. Don't make this hard on yourself. Just some questions."

She thought about Keith. *I don't want to call him, but he'd know what I should do.*

"You can handle it yourself," the secretary scolded. "Let them in. If you need Keith, then you can call the louse."

Jen unlatched the chain. "Just some questions?" She opened the door a few inches. "Come in."

Jen continued to back away until she reached one of the wing chairs.

Without invitation, the two men sat on the couch before her bottom touched the cushion. "What's this about? It's dinnertime. Couldn't this wait?"

Fleming smiled at his companion.

Boyles nodded his head. "It's when most people are home. This concerns a certain fellow who likes you enough to call from far-off lands."

The three of them turned at the sound of another car. They

remained silent as steps clattered up the walkway. Jen jumped up at the knock and checked the window. She opened the door.

"Hi," Lee said. His expression turned into a questioning frown as he stared at the two suits in the living room. He bypassed Jen and confronted them. Lee fished out his leather holder, keeping it in his hand. "I'll show you mine if you show me yours."

The federal agents stood.

Jen moved closer to Lee. "How do you know who they are?"

"I don't. But it's not hard to tell they're Feds. The suits, the dark car, the look." He flipped open the flap of leather, showing his shield.

Boyles and Fleming pulled their identification cases out in a synchronized motion, like a kind of wallet ballet. After a moment of inspection, the three men re-pocketed their badges.

"What is this about?" Lee asked.

"It's between us and the lady," Fleming said.

Jen shook her head. "You boys, sort it out. I'm going to make some tea."

"Please don't, ma'am," Boyles said with a more respectful tone. "If you say he can be here for the interview, we don't mind."

Jen sat back down. "Okay. Tell me why you are here."

"You had a phone call yesterday evening. Tell us about the man known as Brad."

"Brad? What about him?"

"Tell us everything you know, starting with his name. Is Bradley his first name? What's his last? Where is he from, and how long have you known him? Describe the man."

Jen swallowed hard. "I don't know much. He's a nice young man named Brad. I think it's his first name, but I haven't a clue regarding a last name. He called basically to say hello."

"He only called you. It had to be more than just a hello."

"Just hello, and I'm okay, that's it."

"Ms. Hughes," Boyle said. "Don't provoke us. You wouldn't like it. Concealing vital information is a crime."

Jen focused, quietly listening. She noticed their ease with each other and the times they finished each other's sentences. Obviously, they had worked together for a long time and had become close. Both men wore wedding bands. "Is concealing infidelity a crime?" she asked.

Boyles sneered. "What?"

Jen looked at him with a hard stare. "I recall my ex-husband, an attorney, laughing about infidelity being still officially against the law. So, if you, Mr. Fleming, aided and concealed Mr. Boyles's illicit affair, then you would be breaking the law, not to mention hurting an unsuspecting wife."

Bingo! The flash of guilt in each man's eyes confirmed Jen's accusation. *Zelda was right-on! Wait, this is too easy. Not right.*

"What are you talking about? We are here to get information from you," Fleming said.

"Really? And if you, Mr. Fleming, think you are covering your friend's back, and that he will protect you some time, think again. You need to watch your own back. You can't trust him."

Fleming turned to Boyles. "What does she mean?"

"I don't know," Boyles said.

Fleming shot his partner an ugly look. "That unsigned memo circulating the office about the misuse of funds hinted at me. That was you, wasn't it?"

"Hey!" Boyles protested. "She's fishing."

"Uh-uh," Lee shook his head. "You're interviewing an incredible psychic. This lady sees things. She's really gifted."

The invisible secretary laughed. "Madame Jennifer, Gifted Seer. We'll have to get you your own sign and give Madame Zelda a run for her money!"

Shut up. Shit. Am I turning into Zelda Silverstein?

The room went quiet.

"Look," Jen said. "I'll cooperate as best I can. I have nothing to hide, and neither does Brad. And then you tell me what you are about, agreed?"

The agents exchanged scowls, looked at her, and nodded.

Jen nodded, too. "I never saw Brad's face, so I can't describe him. He wore a motorcycle outfit with the helmet closed."

Boyles shook his head. "Come on. You never saw his face? From what we've seen, he wears fatigues, a hat, sunglasses, and a scarf over his nose. Many soldiers keep their noses and mouths covered because of the sand."

Jen spread her hands. "So, you haven't seen his face, either. Look, I can't believe he did anything wrong. Brad is a good boy and definitely not a liar. He'd never give you bad evidence. I'm sure of it. He's only been gone a few weeks, but I got the impression he has already tracked down a few terrorists and given the information to United States officials."

"True," Fleming agreed. "We've received some valuable data."

Jen folded her arms over her chest. "Then what's the problem?"

"He has technology vital to our national security. We need it."

She made a face. "What technology?"

The men exchanged looks. They both glanced at Lee, who sat on the edge of the cushion.

Boyles leaned in as if to whisper. "He has some kind of apparatus rendering him invisible. We want it."

Jen's tongue wouldn't work for a second, the time it took to wonder how she could answer truthfully. "I promise, I know nothing about an invisibility apparatus. Actually, I doubt if Brad has a machine that can do that. You must be mistaken." *But I know they're not.*

Boyles licked his lip. "We have examined security tapes. He gets into offices undetected and leaves notes signed Brad. Sometimes we can see him, but other times, all we see is—well, like a drawer opening and paper coming out and then a pen writing. Sometimes doors don't open or close when he enters or exits. We've had experts examine the words on the notes. They say the writing indicates a young, under-educated male. But everything he writes is accurate. He even told us of an ambush planned on a dignitary's limousine."

She raised her chin. "Why don't you just sit back and let Brad do his thing? Forget the technology. He wants to help, so allow it. If you try to contact him, or catch him, *which you won't,* you'll piss him off, and he'll go away." Once again, the room fell quiet.

Lee stood. "Okay, fellows, I guarantee if Ms. Hughes knew anything else, she'd share. Do like she said and lay off this Brad guy. He sounds like an ace in the hole if you ask me. Don't *F* it up for our country. Time to go."

Boyles and Fleming stood. They walked stiffly to the front door.

Jen walked with them. "Work it out, you two." She pointed to Boyles. "Stop cheating on your wife. Since there's nothing more, I can tell you I don't expect to see you again."

She opened the door, and they left.

When she came back to the couch, Lee opened his arms with an invitation. She sat down and leaned into the embrace.

Lee kissed the top of her head. "Oh, honey. NSA? Invisibility apparatus?"

"Yeah," she said, pushing closer to him. "Silly, huh?"

"Silly with most people, but you. . . I never know what's going to happen next. Um, do I want to know about this Brad guy?"

"He's a kid, nothing to worry about. It's nice to see you here. I didn't know if —"

"I felt bad about the way we parted at the hospital. I let things get to me. I drove by and saw you had company. By the way, Tuesday night, the gig at the Currier went down."

"It did? So quietly?"

"I told you it would be low-key. No one in town got a hint. The prostitutes sang like nightingales. We got the headmistress, the accountant, some mob staff, and all of the working girls. The staff will give us information about other businesses in return for lighter sentences. We really cleaned. Thanks to you."

"Oh, that's why you're here, to thank me?"

"I'm here because I love you, and I missed you."

"Oh yeah? Then how come yesterday —"

"Annie called me. We had lunch. Damn! Will I ever have a secret from you?"

Yeah. Worry about that. "Not ones that will affect my happiness."

"If you know I had a lunch date, then you also know I didn't enjoy myself."

Jen watched his eyes. "And you refused her offer to sleep together." She saw the flash.

"Yes, I refused. I don't want anyone else. I only want you."

"To sleep with."

"To be with," he countered. "I love you."

"I love you, too." She kissed him. They slid over the couch cushions, kissing. Jen broke it off and took a breath. "Let's go upstairs."

His eyebrows hiked up. "Here?"

"Yes, but hold on just a minute." She hurried into the kitchen. Taking the Quitcher Bitchin' sign off the wall, she put it face down on the counter. *If Miles comes, he will see the Crown Vic in the driveway and notice the sign down. He won't go upstairs. I hope.*

Chapter Sixty-Nine

The next morning as Jen headed downstairs to make breakfast, she reflected on the night before. The lovemaking was good, very good, electricity zapping and her toes curling like a New Year's Eve noisemaker. Yes, indeed. And Lee was here. All the time. Solid, breathing, eating, sweating, real.

In the kitchen, the Quitcher Bitchin' sign was back on the wall.

Miles had been here.

A tornado of panic whirled through her. A surge of adrenaline, like a near-miss when driving, pulsed its heat.

"So," the secretary began, "Lee is here. He is solid, and he sweats. Remember?"

I remember.

She picked up the coffee canister and loaded a new filter in the basket. As she poured the water into the tank, Lee treaded on the stairs.

"Coffee will be ready in a few minutes." Two slices of bread went into the toaster.

"Thanks," Lee said. "I can only stay for ten minutes or so. I have to get back and change clothes. Agents are coming this morning to do a post-conference on the Currier take-down."

"Okay." She took cups and saucers from the cabinet. In the allotted minutes, Lee had his coffee and toast, kissed her cheek, and said goodbye, promising to call later.

She made two more pieces of toast. What first smelled like bread burning, she recognized the smell of Cavendish.

"Miles?" She got the ashtray from the cabinet and put it on the table.

He appeared. "Suffer no unease. I nether-slept on the couch until I heard you come down this morning."

She let out the breath she'd been holding. "Thank you for your consideration."

Miles pulled out a chair from the small kitchen table. "I almost materialized to talk to him."

Oh, God!

"I would have asked his intentions toward you."

"I can tell you his intentions. He's asked me to marry him."

"And?"

"And I didn't say yes."

Miles took a long, thoughtful drag on his pipe. "What are *your* intentions?"

"I'm not ready to get married. Ever since I gave up college in servitude to Keith, I've been a stick in the mud. I'm really living now. I told Lee I love him. And I do, but not enough to give up what I've gained. I'll be Lee's girlfriend and let him stay over now and again."

"And me?"

"How often am I to see you? Once every few weeks?"

Miles sighed. "If that often. My work—"

"Right. Your work. And someday, you'll finish your work and pass over."

Miles held his pipe and shook his head. "I doubt if my work will be done any time soon."

"What if your name and reputation are cleared?"

"That is not why I remain here."

"How do you know?"

"Brad said I would realize my purpose, and I have. I am to protect the wandering souls from being used by Evil and train them to fight the Dark Forces. I won't be here in Livonia for long periods of time. However, when I am here, I want to be with you."

Jen cast her gaze to the floor. "I want that, too." She tightened her jaw. "I don't understand it, but—"

Miles reached over the table and took her hand. "Don't try

to understand it. What is, is."

"You might want to know Brad called me."

"I trust he is making headway on the other side of the globe."

"You wouldn't believe how much."

He took another long pull on his pipe. "I must go. I will try to see you again as soon as I can. I hope at that time you are — "

"I know," she said.

He tapped the ashes into the ashtray and put the pipe in the bureau drawer.

"Adieu." He kissed her acclaimed symmetrical hand.

Jen returned to the table and sat, staring at the wall. She tried to sort out what had happened during the last week: Chrissy's visit, the disagreement with Lee, the truck crash with the deaths and James's injuries, the discussion at the hospital, her visitors, Lee's lunch with the veterinarian, the NSA agents, last night with Lee, and this morning with Miles. She didn't know how long she sat, but Rex, bumping her on the knee with his nose, brought her out of the recollective stupor.

"Oh, Rexie! I'm sorry. I haven't let you out. You must be turning yellow." She ran to the door and opened it, leaving the door ajar, trusting him to return because the phone rang.

The phone's identification feature indicated Mildred Owings. "I must see you. May I come over right now?"

Jen consented. Within fifteen minutes, Mildred arrived carrying a folder. Jen invited her into the living room and offered her a seat.

"Coffee, Mildred?"

"No, I need to talk to you." She tapped the folder. "While I was away, the library received two books destined for the Livonia collection. I found them on the desk I requested in the archival room." Mildred spread open the folder. "These were in the books." She put Dr. Lambrigger's yellowed hand-written confession on one side of the folder and the typewritten letter to McCaffrey asking for hit men on the other side.

Jen looked down at the papers as if she'd never seen them

before. She looked at Mildred, not asking questions but waiting for an explanation.

"My brother, Paul, is the cautious type. He is reluctant to spend the money budgeted for forensics to pay for experts on antiquities and writing. But he will order the assessments on my say-so."

Jen still didn't say anything and hoped she wasn't turning red with guilt.

"I think you know something about these," Mildred said.

Oh, shit. Snagged.

Chapter Seventy

Jen sat still and said nothing, formulating multiple reasons excusing her guilt.

Mildred handed her the yellowed paper. "Please, concentrate. I need your opinion. I have full faith in your reading. Tell me if it's real."

Jen strained to keep her expression calm. Swallowing hard, she put the paper to her cheek and closed her eyes. "Uh-huh," she said for effect. "Hmmm," she added and ran her hands over the piece. "Let me see the other letter."

Mildred solemnly handed her the other piece from the folder.

Giving this sheet the same treatment, Jen bit her lip in deliberation. She returned the two papers to their spots on the open folder.

"Well?" Mildred stared at Jen.

"Miles Hampton was framed."

"Really?"

"I'm certain of it. As if he told me himself."

"I knew I could rely on you." Mildred closed the folder. "With your word, I wonder if I should still have Paul call the experts. They check ink and paper and other indicators of age. Do we need them?"

"Yes. Have the experts examine the papers. Just in case someone challenges the authenticity."

"It's not like anyone's future is on the line for this information," Mildred said.

"Please! It's important that Mi — Mr. Hampton's innocence be proven. I mean, the city officials did him wrong. It ruined his reputation and hurt his family. You know the value of history. History must be accurate. At all costs." Jen took a breath.

"I absolutely agree. I'll tell Paul to contact the experts."

Jen started to sigh in relief but caught herself. She escorted Mildred to the door. "Thank you for your belief in me."

"Thank you for sharing your abilities. If you get any more messages—"

"I'll contact you immediately."

When Mildred backed out of the driveway, Jen puckered and blew out a long breath. "Is it too early for a glass of wine?" *Why do I ask questions aloud like that?*

"Because," the secretary said, "in this house, you never know if someone will answer you back."

Jen smiled. She went into the kitchen and checked the refrigerator, then the freezer, realizing a Snickers bar had no timetable. She pulled two from the bag.

Smacking the frozen bar on the counter, it cracked into pieces. One of the bits sailed against the tile backsplash. Fearing ants, she rushed to find the chocolaty morsel. Behind the recipe books, a brown paper corner peeked out from its wedged position. She removed it and discovered the parcel Chrissy had brought in when she visited. Jen took the package to the little table.

Savoring small bites of candy, she looked at the return address. Carvelle Huron. After undoing the tape, she unwrapped the brown paper from an old leather-bound book. Once white, the fine-grained leather had turned creamy, like an exquisite pearl.

On the first page, calligraphic handwriting pronounced this book to be the property of Virginia Felice Carvelle. Jen held in her hand the personal journal of Miles's wife. A slip of paper floated to the table from the back of the book.

"Dear Ms. Hughes. This is my grandmother's story. As you can see, I am her namesake. None of my family members care about their heritage. But you did. Perhaps the words within will help fill the gaps you so eagerly sought when you visited me. Warm regards, Carvelle Huron."

Jen pushed the candy away. Part of her yearned to see what

Virginia wrote, but another part stayed her hand. A violation of privacy? Would her attraction to Miles be affected by becoming close to Virginia, the person most intimate to him? How could she know until she read the words? She put the book on the table and took Rex for a walk.

They walked for an hour. When she returned, Jen slid the journal into the row of recipe books. She needed to think about reading it. A diversion would help. *I should call Zelda Silverstein.*

"How's things?" Zelda asked.

"I heard the library received books with data of historical importance."

Zelda cackled. "I see. Dating the lead detective has many benefits."

"Many." *I'll let Zelda think I got the information from Lee.*

"So, the old Iceberg retired. Good thing she decided to volunteer for the archival collection."

Jen agreed. "I understand Paul Owings has arranged to call in experts to verify the artifacts."

"Ah. And he'll probably ask his cousin, the editor of the Livonia Beacon, to publish the findings. I can see the story now — Chief Owings, Champion of Justice, for the past, present and future."

"I don't care if it makes the chief look good, Zelda. I want Miles vindicated."

"Yeah, me too. He had a bad deal. If only he could know."

"He'll know."

"If you say so. Whatever. We know he was innocent."

They said their goodbyes.

Jen eyed the spine of the pale leather journal aligned with the backs of her recipe books. It didn't feel right to read it. Not then.

She looked around the kitchen, assessing what needed attention, but the phone rang.

"Jennifer?"

This time she did recognize the voice. "Hi, Brad. Borrow someone else's phone?"

"Yeah. Everything okay in Livonia? Things have gotten too quiet here. Not good."

"Don't explain. You need to know I had visitors from the NSA recently. They think you have an invisibility apparatus. Of course, I laughed at such a notion. They've seen you disappear on their security tapes. I guess their cameras can get defective."

"Hmm. I'll have to leave notes in the sand from now on."

"I'm sure they'll know about it after this call." Lee had warned her that the phone might be tapped. "You know?"

"I get it. You don't mind if I still contact you?"

"Of course not, Brad. Although it's not fair for the guy who *loans* you the phone."

"True." His voice increased in volume. "Hey, Feds, since you're listening, please take care of the charges in light of the good information I have. I'm on the trail of one of the high-ups. As soon as I find him, I'll leave my note."

"In the sand?" Jen asked.

"Yep. No more sneaking into offices. I don't want you to be harassed. An invisibility apparatus! I should be so smart."

"Oh, Brad. You're smart and good. Have I said how proud I am of you?"

"Yeah, the last time. I don't mind hearing it again." He took on the louder voice. "Feds, leave Jennifer Hughes alone. If you bother her again, I'll stop helping you." He paused. "Okay, Jen, done for now. Bye."

She wondered what Brad meant about things getting quiet there and why he linked that to Livonia. She wished she could question him about it. She stopped him from explaining because she didn't want the ghost aspects of her life to go public. She thought for a few minutes. Even with a bugged phone, the Feds had no way of tapping all the phones Brad could borrow. If he was careful and put the phones back, he could call someone else. She'd have to think on that.

The call from Brad offered her a brief distraction. Her line of sight moved to the row of books on the counter. Temptation to examine Virginia's life overwhelmed her. She grabbed the book and headed for the couch.

Leafing through the pages, Jen concluded Virginia had not kept a daily journal and only noted important events. The first account recalled her sixteenth birthday when she received the book as a gift.

Jen turned pages, reading events that would be important to any young girl. The first page that stopped her began with *Today I met Zelda Rothberg. I already adore her and know we will be best friends forever.* After a few more pages, *Zelda has traveled to New York but promised to be back.*

The next attention grabber stated *Zelda came home. We attended a fencing tournament. I watched a fencer all in white move like poetry. He won. Zelda introduced me. When he took off his face mask, I fell in love. Miles Hampton. The name, like honey, rolls off my tongue. I boldly gave him my card.* The next annotation of interest said *Today, Zelda took her vows of marriage. She cried, but I'm sure they weren't tears of joy. Poor dear. Abraham is older and ugly! She wouldn't tell me why she agreed to her father's choice. I know there must be a good reason.*

Most of the subsequent passages involved Miles, how he called upon Virginia and asked to court her, the family's esteem, and her deepening love.

The paragraph that hit Jen between the eyes commenced, *God, please forgive me for my heinous falsehood. I couldn't take the chance he would meet someone at his college. When Miles came home for Christmas break, I told him we had to get married. He, being a true gentleman, agreed. He immediately asked my father for my hand.* The following entry said: *All of the invitations have been sent. I told Miles I must have lost the child, for I had been ill for a few days. I offered to let him out of the marriage. He said he would not embarrass me, and the wedding would continue as planned. I lied twice, but I swear! I will never lie to him again.*

After that, *My wedding day! How many people attended our ceremony! Both Zelda and I wept with happiness. With my dowry and what Miles's father has pledged, we can build a house.*

Jen closed the book and pressed it against her chest. *Tears of happiness. Two women, two ways of loving one man. Zelda sacrificed her life to protect Miles's reputation and future success. Virginia tricked him, making him quit college.*

Jen put the book on the coffee table and got the box of old photos she had gathered. Putting the portraits of Zelda and Virginia together next to the journal, Jen compared the faces. Both fair and attractive, with similar hairstyles, white batiste dresses, same photo studio backgrounds. Jen concentrated on the images. She sensed personalities and feelings.

"Stop it," the secretary commanded. "It does no good to discover this history. Let it be."

Jen gathered the photos and put them up, returning Miles's wedding picture to the drawer. But she had to finish the journal.

She flipped to the next entry of interest. *Miles has become a policeman.* Then inserts regarding the birth of their children. Another was: *Miles is brilliant, solving so many crimes. He has been offered detective status.*

Jen turned the pages until she stopped at *Miles is dead! I know he didn't die by his own hand. The newspapers say he committed crimes. Many people in the town decry the claims, but the inquest has rendered the opinions. My dear, beautiful love. What will I do without you? Zelda's Abe has died. We grieve together.*

Months passed without comment until: *Damon Cisco has been so helpful throughout this ordeal. I know he is lonely since his wife died. He is good with the boys. He won't discuss the appalling claims against Miles, but I'm sure he can't believe them.* Months later: *Damon still attends our needs. He has told me he will look after us for as long as we need. Bless him.* And then, about a year later: *Damon has asked me to marry and wants to move to Pittsburg, where he has a good job offer. Many of the people in Livonia treat me and the boys like we have leprosy. I have accepted.*

Most of the entries after that were one-sentence descriptions of her mundane life, concerts, sons' achievements, and the adoption of the boys by Damon Cisco. As Jen flipped through, she went back to one when the words, *back to Livonia,* caught her eye.

I brought the boys back to Livonia to attend Mother's funeral. When I visited Zelda, she introduced me to one of her boarders, a young girl from New York named Emma Caulfield. As soon as I met the girl, I immediately saw the composite of Miles and Zelda. I looked at Zelda. She said nothing but nodded her head. When Emma left, Zelda put her hand up, meaning I should not ask questions. I asked one — did Emma know? Zelda said no, and those who knew the truth were sworn to secrecy. I will never see Zelda again.

So! Virginia knew. And she held it against Zelda. *Miles, the criminals weren't your only enemies.*

Jen wiped a tear and put the book away in the utensil drawer. As she closed the drawer, she heard the masculine voice she knew so well.

"I have but minutes to be with you."

"Hello, Miles." She moved to him and put her arms around him more as a protective gesture than a romantic urge. "You can't stay for just a little while?"

"Unfortunately, no. I must make contact with another paladin in Virginia."

"You mean you have to travel?"

"There is no other way of communicating."

"How about using the telephone? Brad does."

"But he calls here. I need a network. Other than that emergency call for you, I have not used a modern phone."

"I can think of two people who would love to help. They have phones."

"Explain."

"The cook at the Asian Kitchen wishes to help. And, I can think of a gentleman in Reston, Virginia, who already believes he communicates with spirits. He goes to meetings with other spirit lovers. I'm pretty sure these people would help you with your quest to defeat the Dark Forces."

He led her to the couch. "Elucidate, please."

Jen told him about Su-Lin and her wish to work with the spirits, then described Winslow Hampton, his great-grandson.

"You could arrange this for me?"

"Yes, but not my phone, from a pay phone. Lee, your least favorite detective, showed me an old working phone at the drug store. It still has its booth. The drug store owner keeps it for sentimental reasons."

"The drug store on Main Street?"

"Yes. You know it?"

Miles's shoulders sagged. "The drug store once owned by Abraham Zeigler."

"Zelda Rothberg's husband?"

Miles looked at her with a questioning expression. "You know of him?"

"I do," she mumbled and closed her eyes, thinking of all the information she had learned. "Wait here for a minute." Jen ran upstairs and threw a few traveling items into a canvas bag. Returning to the kitchen, she said. "Come with me, Miles." *Two women made mistakes with you. I'm going to help you.*

She grabbed her purse. "Rex! Let's go for a ride." She locked up, and the three of them — Jen, her darling ghost, and the dog — got in the car.

Chapter Seventy-One

Jen parked in the small lot in front of Chu Phly Pi's Asian Kitchen. Leaving Rex in the car, she gave instructions to Miles about her plan.

Inside the restaurant, a few early supper guests dotted the dining room. Chu Phly met her at the door with a bow, greeting her in his heavy faux accent.

"May I speak with your mother?"

"Certainly," he said softly in plain English. He led her into the kitchen.

Su-Lin stood, barely seeing over a large soup pot. Four dried won-tons sat on the counter next to a huge cellophane bag stuffed full of uncooked pastas.

"Mrs. Chang," Jen said.

"You call me Su-Lin. We friends."

"Su-Lin, do you still wish to help the good spirits ward off the evil ones?"

"Yes."

"I want you to meet someone, a ghost."

As arranged, the kitchen door swung open by itself. Su Lin gawked at the swinging door as it gently stopped in the jamb. Miles materialized behind the small woman and came to her side.

"Su-Lin, this is Miles Hampton."

Su-Lin turned. She scowled and shook her head. Then she touched his arm and poked him in the chest.

"Ha. Door open itself. Trick. You not ghost. You real." She looked at Jen, crestfallen. "Why you bring this man here?"

"He's really a spirit. I promise."

She picked up a heavy metal spoon and pointed it at him.

"You spirit? Prove."

Miles faded away slowly and returned with equal speed.

Su-Lin grabbed her chest. "Ahhh." Her knees buckled. Miles caught her before she hit against the steel counter.

Jen touched Su-Lin's neck to check her pulse. "Seems okay, but, gee, maybe this wasn't such a good idea."

Su-Lin opened her eyes and pushed Jen's hand from her neck. "You real! What you name?"

"Are you all right? I can call nine-one-one," Jen said.

The woman threw Jen an exasperated look. "No call." She stared at Miles. "Who you?"

Miles helped the small woman to her feet, steadied her, then let go. "I am Miles Hampton, and very pleased to make your acquaintance."

"Yes, yes!" Su-Lin wiped her hands vigorously on her apron. "You," she turned to Jennifer, "told me spirits stay here for refuge. Now I meet them? All? How can Su-Lin help?"

Jennifer gave Miles a quick glance. Reluctance loomed in his return look. She patted Su-Lin's hand. "Maybe you can meet more spirits later. They are shy." She swallowed and took a short breath. "I know it sounds strange, but Miles might want to use your telephone now and then."

"Not strange. Anything you want. I knew long time ago I would help get rid of evil."

Miles took the lady's hand and put it to his lips. "Thank you. For now."

"Good," Jen said. "That's done. We have some traveling to do. Goodbye, Su-Lin."

The old woman waved. Jen and her invisible companion left through the swinging door.

In the dining room, Jen said a quick goodbye to Chu. No explanations. If Su-Lin wanted to share the information, she would. Jen left the Asian Kitchen and started the car. When she turned out of the parking lot, Miles materialized in the front seat.

"Thank you for your support," Miles said. "You are a woman of many talents."

"I think that may be quite a compliment coming from a man of your era."

"An accomplished woman transcends any era."

"Oh, come on. You Victorians suppressed women. Like, when did women get to vote?"

"Women vote?" He laughed at his joke.

"You know we do. How many women had jobs during your time? Did Virginia drive?"

"If Virginia wanted to drive, she would have been behind the wheel. One could describe my wife as being determined. Little stood in the way of obtaining her desires."

If you only knew. Although she read Virginia's journal account, she wanted Miles's side of the story. "You mentioned you attended college."

"I attended the university in New York on a fencing scholarship."

"Fencing. You must have been very good."

"Humility prevents me from bragging. However, my only defeat came from a gentleman from Heidelberg." Miles ran his finger down his cheek. "He had the scar."

"What did you study from your scholarship?"

"Medicine. I planned to take over my father's practice."

"What happened? Why didn't you finish?"

"I finished pre-medical studies. Before the medical training began, I married Virginia."

"Forgive my questions, but you loved Virginia so much that you withdrew from college?"

"I cared deeply for her."

Jen didn't comment for a moment. "Zelda?"

Miles turned his face toward the car door window. After a pause, he said, "My love for Zelda never left my heart. Even to the very last. I saw her face in my mind before I...."

Jen forced herself to watch the road. "And me?"

"I care deeply for you, Jennifer. I owe my present success to your efforts. Your company offers me the comfort I need. And, pleasure. You provide welcome, delightful, warm harmony in a confusing circumstance."

"I need to think about that."

"Indeed, my dear."

Chapter Seventy-Two

Jen and Miles drove to the historic drugstore with an antique but working payphone, where she called Winslow Hampton and made arrangements to meet with him the next day. She returned to the car and headed in the direction to find the interstate highway toward northern Virginia. Heavy traffic slowed their progress. As the light outside faded, she steered into a motel a few minutes from Winslow's home.

"We'll spend the night in this motel."

"Explain motel."

"A combination word meaning a hotel catering to motorists. Usually, cars can park in front of the rooms for easy access. This motel chain allows pets."

"Amazing," Miles said.

"Wait here. Invisibly." Jen went into the office to register. She returned and started the car. "I got a room here. I'll go through a drive-in and get dinner. Rex won't mind eating a burger."

Later, with food bags in one hand, and overnight pack in the other, Jen opened the motel room door. Returning to the car, she clipped Rex's leash for a quick walk on a grassy area.

Entering the room, she saw Miles sitting on a chair next to the drawn curtains.

"My dear," he said. "I've explained your importance to me. Perhaps you don't realize the magnitude of your service in general. Brad has traveled to an area where he believes evil has taken over those who inflict terror. He feels this is the first step of a larger campaign. My task here is to unite the spirits and prepare them. When the escalation occurs, we will be ready."

"What escalation?"

"Ah. That confounds us. We know naught of future details, but I work to establish a network of training, recruiting, and establishing centers to offset the Dark Forces. Your efforts have assisted me, not only offering needed solace, but now you transport me and provide networking communications. Brad sensed your importance immediately. Through you, we have a chance at defeating whatever the Dark Forces build."

"I don't want to think about Dark Forces. I have enough on my plate."

"I understand. Your detective has professed his love and proposed marriage."

"I love him, too, but I'm not ready to commit. I couldn't promise to be faithful. Not with you around."

"Then Fate has revealed my destiny regarding you."

"Oh, no, it has not. I'll let you know when I want you to bow out." Jennifer locked her eyes on his. "It looks sleazy, I know. One woman with two lovers. One she loves and one she can't resist. Jeez, I've become quite the tart."

"That is not so, and I'll soundly thrash anyone who says it."

"I just said it."

"Then, I must thrash you. Right now."

Miles took her by the hand and led her to the bed.

After her sound thrashing, Jen fell asleep in Miles's arms.

In the morning at ten, she pulled into Winslow Hampton's driveway.

Winslow came out. "Please come in." He bent and petted Rex. "Bring him too. I'm so glad to see you again."

Jen sat on the couch with Rex by her knee. "I'll come right to the point, Winslow. At our last conversation, you told me you spoke with ghosts."

"I do. I belong to several organizations involved with spiritual manifestation. Good spirits, of course. We have nothing to do with the bad sort."

"So, spirits manifest themselves to you?"

Winslow looked down to the floor. "No, not exactly."

"What exactly, if you don't mind telling me."

"We talk to them in hopes that they'll contact us. We organize séances, graveyard rituals, and practices that convey our desire to communicate. We want them to know we are waiting."

Jen took a breath. "Would you like to meet your great-grandfather and help him with an important mission?"

"Miles Hampton?" Winslow rushed to the mantle. He brought back a framed photo, the picture of Miles when he made detective, the same one used in the old newspaper to defame his reputation and honor.

"My great-grandfather," Winslow said. "I can meet him? When? I can't believe it. Oh, my!"

"Calm down," Jen pointed, directing him to sit. "Are you sure you can handle it?"

"Of course!"

"All right then."

Winslow grabbed a lighter and ignited a candle sitting on the coffee table. He sat and took both of Jen's hands, interlocking his fingers with hers. "Oh, spirit of Miles Hampton," he said pleading with a distorted voice.

Jen broke her hands free. "Cut it out, Winslow. That's not what we do."

He put his hand to his mouth. "Really? Maybe that's why they don't answer us."

"Look," she snapped. "Sit tight. I don't know. . . maybe this isn't a good idea."

"It is! Really. I'm fine. Please call him."

"Miles," Jen said.

Miles materialized into view, standing tall and proud in the uniform of the framed picture. Winslow's mouth opened and shut and opened again.

"Winslow, may I present your great-grandfather."

Winslow stood slowly and extended his hand to shake. Miles accepted the greeting and, holding Winslow's elbow, led the man back to his seat.

Jen hopped up from her place on the couch. "You two

have some things to talk about. I'm taking Rex for a walk. A long one." She picked up the dog's leash and left.

Fifteen minutes into the walk, Jen's cell phone rang. "Hi, Lee."

"Everything okay? I went to your house. Not only you weren't there, but Rex didn't bark."

"I'm fine. I'm in Reston, visiting, um, a friend. I'll be back tonight."

"Good. I worry about you, honey. I'll see you when you get back."

"Thanks, Lee."

She clicked off. *Okay, secretary, I'm sure you have something to say.*

"Only don't beat yourself up over being with Miles. He's phenomenal. Luckily, I'm along for the ride. And what a ride!"

Oh, great. "You're the one who talks sense. You have no advice about me sleeping with Lee and Miles?"

"When you're ready to give up Miles and commit to Lee, you will. If you were a man, no one would think twice about a relationship with two lovers."

Thanks.

Jen pulled Rex's leash and headed back to Winslow's house. He let her in. "You fellows have a good time while I walked Rex?"

Miles smiled. "We did. You should return home. Winslow will take me where I need to go. I'll stay here for a while and make my way back to Livonia."

"Goodbye, Winslow," Jen said. "Thanks for helping us."

The man beamed. "I can't wait to be of service. Drive carefully."

Miles walked her to the front door and kissed her hand.

"I hope I see you before too long," Jen said.

Miles sighed. "I fear it may be a long time, but as soon as it is possible."

Jen put Rex in the car and drove back to Livonia.

When she pulled into the drive, she picked up her mail

and found the newspaper on the front step. As she put the paper on the kitchen counter, the headline caught her eye.

Jen read the article, which consumed the entire front page. "A Century-Old Mystery Solved," claimed the *Livonia Beacon*. Miles had his day. According to the newspaper, distinguished citizen and librarian-renowned, Mildred Owings, discovered two historical documents that gave evidence of Miles Hampton's innocence. The work described the forensic nature of the search pursued by Paul Owings, Chief of Police. The article spotlighted the already legendary brother and sister team. The *Beacon* called them heroes. Jen didn't care who got the credit. She and the Gifted Seer had pulled it off.

Jen called Zelda.

"I guess you saw the local rag," Zelda said.

"You have such a colorful vocabulary."

"I calls 'em as I sees 'em. I knew Paul would use it to his best advantage."

"I never asked about this," Jen said, "but do we elect the police chief here?"

"Nah. We only elect the mayor. But Paul Owings will be chief as long as he wants. Can you guess why?"

"Because the mayor is Paul's first cousin, and Paul is an excellent chief. Plus, most of the Livonia folks love the mayor."

"You're no fun," Zelda complained. "But now that we've cleared old-dead-and-gone Miles, we need to clear young-alive-and-here Johnny Cee. I'm going to get him a good lawyer and pay his bail, and you're going to work on Lee to find evidence to clear him."

"Okay, Zelda, but I talked to Lee and he said there's no bail for Johnny. In Lee's opinion, with the incriminating evidence against him, it's a slam dunk. The court fears Johnny will flee, and they need him to testify against the Speigals. He's not cooperating, though. Plus, as long as he's in jail, he's safe because the bad guys know he hasn't said anything."

"We need to talk to that boy."

"We?"

"Yeah. I'm old and weird. Johnny won't enjoy a visit from me. But you still have *it*, kiddo. He might take to you and listen."

Jen groaned. Only a few days ago Keith offered a return to country-club, book-of-the-month, suburban life. And what did she decide instead? Livonia, unpredictable and exciting. Now the town's palm reader wanted her to visit the county lock-up to convince a petty criminal to spill the beans on the mob? Maybe she should contact Pam.

A sudden chill hit her.

"Better leave that one out of the picture for now," the secretary said. "Let Pam do her own thing about Johnny."

Zelda's voice grated, "Jennifer? Still with me?"

"Uh, yeah. I'm still here. No promises about visiting the county jail, though."

"You'll do what's right." The gifted seer cackled and said goodbye.

Jen sat on the couch. "Rex!" The dog trotted over and sat with his head positioned under her hand. She petted him. "You are the one male who knows when to keep your mouth shut and just be there for me."

Rex's ears went up. He ran to the front door when a car pulled in the drive. She peeked through the curtains at the white Crown Vic and rushed to open the door.

Lee didn't get the time to knock. "Hi." He put his hands around her waist and pulled her close. "I missed you."

Jen placed her cheek against his shoulders. "I missed you, too."

Lee backed away and held her chin in his palm. "What's wrong?"

Jen turned her face from his hand.

"Hey! I can tell there's something bothering you." He tipped her chin up to capture her gaze. "Come on." His tone changed to a tease. "Come sit on your Uncle Lee's lap. You can tell him all your troubles. He's got candy. You like candy, don't you?"

Jen smiled and shook her head at him.

"See there? I made you laugh. That's one trouble down. Tell me what's happening."

Jen motioned him to the couch as she took a seat. "Zelda's getting Johnny Cee a good lawyer. I'm supposed to talk *you* in to digging for evidence to help him."

Lee ran his fingers through his hair. "I've already done that. He's in trouble for kidnapping, and Johnny was the last one to be seen with Sal Zemric as they left the motel."

"The motel Johnny took Arlene Holmes to? If Johnny left the room with Arlene still there, how could it be kidnapping?"

"Johnny told Arlene she was in danger if she went out. That's a form of kidnapping."

Jen shut her eyes. "He kept her there because he knew she *was* in danger. Wait! Can you get a hold of Arlene?"

"Why?"

"You need to talk to her. Tell her Johnny's in jail and what's going to happen to him."

"What's that going to do?"

"Trust me, Lee."

"Well, I guess I can call her." His cell beeped, and he checked it. "Gotta go now."

Jen walked him to the door and enjoyed the lingering goodbye kiss. She wished his visits could be longer but understood that he came by when he could. His stopovers, even the brief ones, gave her a bit of security, especially appreciated with the dark, vague threats looming over Livonia.

Chapter Seventy-Three

The article about Miles in the Beacon had caused a stir in the community. The next day the mayor wrote a public apology to the remaining Hampton family, calling the false charges a *miscarriage of justice* and inviting the town to attend a ceremony to lay a wreath at Miles's grave.

Jen hadn't even thought about Miles having a grave. It wasn't that she didn't know he was dead, but...damn.

For three days the newspaper ran articles about historic wrongs and reports of momentous Livonian events forgotten by current residents. Speculations about the carriage factory explosion ran rampant, as if the town had been awakened from a quiet slumber. Lee stayed busy working on the Johnny Cee case, looking for Dave Blakely, and residual paperwork from the Currier. She missed his short visits. He called her several times a day to check.

Jen awoke in the morning when a newspaper hit her front door. Working through her usual routine with Rex, she came into the kitchen, made coffee and toast, and commenced reading the *Beacon's* latest historic rumination. Today's article remembered Livonia's World War One heroes.

She read until the articles made her yawn. She needed a distraction. Miles was away, and Lee only called. Maybe she should bake something. Something chocolate. Brownies. They fixed everything.

"No, they don't," advised the secretary, "but they taste great. A weak substitute for sex."

Jen got busy.

In the afternoon, she recognized the sound of the Crown

Vic. Then the metallic thud of two doors shutting. Lee and Ash.

Lee's greeting, "Hey, Jen," preceded a hug.

"Hello, Detective Grainger," Jen said.

Ash grimaced. "You know you don't have to call me that. I didn't mean to be such an ass. So, won't you just call me Ash?"

I don't know. Even though he was an ass, he is Lee's friend. "Okay, Ash." She turned to Lee. "What's up?"

Lee smiled. "I called Arlene like you said. Her folks lied to her. They told her Johnny took off to Mexico with a woman. I laid out the whole story. She left the cabin and visited him in jail. Not only is he going to give up everything he knows about the Speigals, but Arlene will testify she went with him willingly. Her parents had coerced her into saying Johnny kept her there, but she is going to help him, especially when she can account for his whereabouts at the time of Zemric's death. We have another winner here, Babe. Thanks to you."

"Anything else happening? Crime in the streets and all that?"

"Nothing," Grainger said. "I've never seen it so quiet in Livonia. It's almost scary. Like the quiet before a storm."

A chill ran through her. Brad had said the same thing. Rex interrupted her thought with a bark and a growl. After his barking intensified, Jen heard the doorbell.

Lee answered the door. "Ms. Caulfield."

Pam shifted her purse and a shopping bag as she entered. "Nice to see you, too."

"Hi, Pam," Jen said, shushing Rex.

Pam looked at her watch. "I hope you don't mind me stopping by. I was in the neighborhood, and we hadn't been together for a while."

Lee's cell phone chimed. When he rang off, he gave Ash a head movement, meaning they had to leave. The look on his face gave Jen a pang of concern. She followed him to the door.

Lee bent close to her ear. "Dispatch just told me Dave Blakely wants to give himself up, but only to me and Ash." He hurried after Ash, who had taken the driver's seat.

"Everything all right?" Pam asked. "A visit from the local constabulary doesn't look good in the neighborhood."

"No problems, really."

"Great. I hoped it might be tea time," she added in a British accent.

"Good idea. What kind of tea do you fancy? Ooh, I have a marvelous tea I saved from my trip aboard the Queen Mary. It's made just for the ocean liner. Shame on me for filching it, but what can I say? Everyone has a streak of larceny now and then."

Pam smiled wide. "Yes, we all do, and I'm glad to hear you're not perfect. I'd love to try that tea. Who knows, maybe in the future, you and I can travel together on a cruise."

"You're in a good mood," Jen said on her way to the stove to heat the kettle.

"You bet I am," Pam said, consulting her watch. "Since you have confessed your wickedness, what sinful thing have you to offer with the tea?"

"Are pecan brownies with semi-sweet chips for frosting iniquitous enough?"

Pam laughed. "Absolutely not. Let me tell you about iniquities!"

"Okay then," Jen said. "Let's do this tea thing right." She set a kettle on the stove. In the dining room, she took out her good china. By the time the Country Roses teapot had warmed under the tap, allowing the hot water to acclimate the pot for tea, the kettle whistled. While the tea steeped, Jen cut four gooey brownies and placed two on each plate.

Pam pointed at Rex, who had been making low growls. "Jennifer, I'm allergic to dog hair. Can you put him in the other room?"

"Okay. He's usually so friendly." When Jen returned, she put the plates on the dining room table. "For you, Lady Pamela, the finest my realm has to offer."

Pam took her place and put the folded napkin on her lap. "How ironic. You dub me royalty, but it is you who shall be queen."

"Queen Jennifer. It has a good sound."

Jen poured the tea. Perfect, it needed nothing more. Eaten with a fork, the brownies seemed even more decadent.

After a few moments of silence, Pam dabbed at the corners of her mouth. "Jen, I thought maybe this would be more difficult, but I believe things have fallen into place. When something should be, it will be and becomes whole."

"What?"

"I originally selected Arlene Holmes. Those rich spoiled types are easy prey for the Johnny Caulfields of the world, but after I saw how easily I could manipulate her, I started to worry. The Great One needs someone compliant, but with a strong character, someone who doesn't frighten easily."

"What are you talking about?"

"I wasn't impressed with you at first. And after you invited me in, I didn't need you. But, after I tried to get rid of you, not only once but twice, I gave you a harder look. You seemed to be a lightweight, but the ghost in the house didn't scare you away, and I don't know how you clobbered those guys who lit your garage. I worried a little when you started fucking that idiot cop, but I was convinced you were the one when you stood up to Rodovich."

Jen's napkin fell to the floor. She focused on Pam. "I don't understand."

"Listen. Today in your basement, The Great One will come. And you will house His Essence. Once you and the master combine, you will be queen. First of Livonia, then the country, and after that, as we unite our forces with the ones in Syria, we'll rule the world. We've worked hard for this. Me and the lieutenants before me, for over a hundred years." She checked her watch. "Today. Soon!"

Jen pushed the chair from the table and stood. "You're crazy, Pam. You better leave."

Pam rose from her chair. "You want this, Jen. It's why you got rid of the ghost. We know he left."

"You knew about Miles?"

"Of course. We couldn't get into the house, and he couldn't get out without your help. When you wanted to buy this house, I had to make that contract work. I needed you to invite me in, so we could be ready for the Ascension. The fact you turned out to be the perfect vessel was a divine bonus."

"Oh, my God. Get out." She stomped her foot. "Leave this instant. Never come back."

"You invited me in, remember? Once summoned, always invited. Miles failed to tell you that, didn't he? I'm not sure how you ditched him, but thanks. Not that he was any threat to us, that stupid Floater, but sometimes the goody-two-shoes spirits pick up on our ways. He might have warned you about us. Of course, he couldn't have done anything to stop us."

"I want you out of here," Jen yelled.

"Nope. Hey, I'm offering you the world, Jen. It's wonderful." Pam put the paper bag on the table and pulled out a small handgun from her purse. "Embrace it." She screwed a cylinder on the end.

Jen took a step backward and stared at the gun. "Who are you?"

"I was nobody until the old hag who had been the second came to me in New York. My father, a pathetic underling, worked for one of the biggest mob families. Poor Dad didn't have the stones to move up in the firm, but I had aspirations. When Anjeena arranged for me to get a position in charge of the Speigals here in Livonia, I jumped at it. Anjeena knew she had little time left and many things needed to be done. I agreed to take her essence and complete the plan. You wouldn't believe the power." Pam pulled her shoulders up and let out a celebratory breath. "I, young and strong, would be the second until we could prepare a soul for the Ascension."

"The Ascension?" Jen looked around, wishing Rex was there. "Who's ascending?"

Pam's face became serious. "We do not speak the master's name." She looked at her watch. "In seventeen minutes, the name will be Jennifer Hughes, Queen of the Dark Forces and Ruler of the World."

"You've got to be kidding." Jen put up her hand, but her gaze never left the gun's muzzle.

"I'm not kidding. We must get you ready."

"We?"

"I share my body with Anjeena,"

"A ghost?"

"Not really, but a good enough description for the uninitiated. Soon, not only will the Great One emerge, but once inside you, will rule the world."

Jen stiffened and stood tall. "No one is entering me."

Pam grabbed Jen's shoulder with her free hand. "Don't screw this up, Jennifer. Whether you like it or not, the Great One will enter your body." She tilted the gun to check her watch. "In less than ten minutes." She gave Jen a hard push toward the basement door. "Get your ass down to the cellar."

"What if I don't move from this spot?"

Pam cocked the gun, aimed it at the wall, and pulled the trigger. Jen jerked at the *pfft* it made. The Quitcher Bitchin' sampler went flying.

Pam blew on the barrel for effect. "If you won't cooperate, I'll shoot your knees, drag your ass down the stairs, and do everything myself. The Great One won't mind a little pain. But it's today or another four hundred years, and in a different location. So, Bitch-Woman, move!"

With one hand, Pam held her bag and moved the gun sideways, with the other indicating the basement door.

Jen shook her head. "I hate it down there."

"For Christ's sake, get going," Pam said through clenched teeth.

Jen crossed her arms over her chest. "You're calling on Christ?"

"Yeah, kind of funny, eh? See, there, Arlene would have cried and begged. You have moxie. No question, you're perfect for our needs and a wonderful liar. I actually believed you when you denied knowing Sal. That bastard got his. I assume you found his book and turned it in. I suspect you had something to do with locating Arlene, too." Pam moved behind Jen and shoved her to the basement door. "Open it."

Jen undid the hasp and pulled at the door. She flicked the light switch to illuminate the stairwell and took careful steps down the wooden risers, keeping a hand on the wall for support. She turned when she felt the hard-packed sand of the basement floor.

Pam rotated the weapon as a command for Jen to face forward and walk ahead.

"So, you work for the Speigals?"

"Of course not. I had all the dirt and made the Speigals do *my* bidding. I had stuff on the Ratterlees, too. I paid Johnny to get Arlene to stow the CD in her safe deposit box as my control over the families. I heard the cops got it. I'll bet you had a hand in that. Shit, of course, it was you. And, wait a minute, you got the goods on the Currier School, didn't you? Miles? No, I don't buy that at all. But you'll tell me all your little secrets. Once you become ours, that clever side of you will come in handy."

"So, Johnny Cee works for you?"

"Nah. He was good for one thing. Oh, was he good! But even as dumb as he was, he smelled a rat and got Arlene out of town. Zemric was on Johnny's trail to align against me, but I fixed him. When Arlene left, I panicked." She grinned and shook her head. "What irony. There it was, right in front of me. You! Looking all suburbanite and silly, but in reality, strong and crafty. Perfect."

"Wait, all that stuff about the Speigals blackmailing you and making you work for them was for pity? So, I'd back you up to the cops if you got caught?"

"Bingo." Pam glanced at the sand and smiled.

The crack in the middle of the floor expanded into a lopsided oval, looking much like a huge dirt vagina. It opened, and greenish slime oozed from raised earthen lips.

Pam watched the seepage flow and smiled. "See why I couldn't let you cement over this spot? This plot is the center of the Indian ritual grounds. It had been left untouched until that stupid Miles bought it and built his house here over a hundred years ago. We tried to stop him, but he had been so well-respected the city thought they owed him a variance to the land. Then, after we got rid of him, we intended to get the place condemned. But he still had a few friends who wanted to keep the house for its beauty. Even in modern times, this place has its defenders, so we took a different tack. A new owner. There you were, ripe for the taking, and we took you. Here, put this on," Pam said and pulled two pieces of shiny cloth from the bag. She handed Jen one of the cloths.

Jen unfolded the fabric to find a shawl, white satin trimmed with golden symbols and arcane designs. Pam slipped her own shawl over her shoulders. She shook the pistol for Jen to put on hers. "Do it."

Jen fumbled with the garment, taking as long as possible. A greenish glow emanated from the floor vagina, sending forth a light so bright Jen averted her eyes.

"Ah, my master," said Pam. "Have patience. I have not yet prepared the heir."

Chapter Seventy-Four

Jen faced Pam. "What are you going to do with me?"

"This first." With one hand, Pam removed handcuffs from the bag. "Put it on."

"No," Jen said.

Pam's lips pushed into a hard line. She pressed the muzzle against Jen's shoulder. "I *will* hurt you."

Jen slipped the handcuff on her own wrist.

"Now the second," Pam sneered, pressing the gun harder. Jen closed the other cuff.

Pam backed up a step. "Next, I say the incantations and then the transfer kiss. The timing has to be perfect." She checked her watch. Pam stiffened and listened to a blast of raspy noises as a huge wave of green-gold light spurted from the hole. "I'm not ready, Master."

The light surged upward. Pam spoke words in a strange language. She chanted and gesticulated, ever clutching the gun. The light engulfed Pam for a second and disappeared into her body. Rays of light emanated from her nostrils and ears.

Pam gripped Jen's arm and pulled her close. Gravelly, unintelligible words escaped Pam's light-bearing lips.

Pam's head turned robotically. She smiled. Light rays beamed from her mouth. "And now the kiss," she rasped.

The Pam-thing grabbed Jen by the neck. Jen wrenched away and brought her hands up with as much force as she could muster, smacking Pam in the face with the cuffs. The Pam-thing shrieked and pushed Jen against the earthen wall. As she leaned in for the transfer kiss, Jen kicked her hard. Pam's eyes widened, and light escaped her open mouth. In a tenth of a second, Jen saw her chance. She butted her head against Pam's forehead, then, with her hands, pushed Pam against the dark dirt corner. A loud chattering and a blur of fur moved in the thin light. The Pam-thing groped at her back with her free hand, and when she turned, her face twisted into surprise and fear. A huge raccoon had leaped onto her and hung on.

"Jen! Help me! This body can't take the double essence for very long. Put your mouth to mine. Or die." Pam pulled the trigger. The lizard part of Jen's brain made her duck away. The silenced gun made a hissing plop launching the bullet into a dirt wall. The raccoon grasped Pam's neck with its opposable thumbs. She writhed and squirmed with the raccoon still attached. "Jen, kiss me. You will be queen!"

"No!" Jen said, staring at the gun's muzzle. She swallowed hard and pushed Pam aside with all she had.

Pam's body shook and quivered. Spasms rippled her face. She screamed. A few beams of light escaped where the raccoon had scratched. The raccoon stiffened and fell.

Jen backed away, flattening against the nearest wall. Neon-green light shot like a pressurized fire hose from Pam's body. The light bounced around the room, illuminating the basement like a green bonfire.

Jen hurried up the steps, but at the top, she turned and watched the light. As the seconds passed, the glowing decreased. The glaring rays faded into specks floating and wafting in the air. The dirt vagina constricted to a thin crevice. The light softened, like neon glitter filling the atmosphere, lightly falling on the dirt floor and over the unmoving body of Pam Caulfield. A furry mound lay under Pam's shoulder.

Jen ran into the kitchen and put the hasp back on the basement door. She grabbed her cell phone and called 911. When the operator answered, Jen fumbled for words. "Someone has collapsed in my basement." Her next call was the speed dial to Lee. What could she say to him? That was easier. "I need you here right away." She didn't give him time to question and rang off.

Now that she'd made the calls, she became painfully aware of the handcuffs. "Where would Pam keep the key?" Jen rifled through Pam's leather satchel. She found a small brass key that fit the lock on the cuffs.

Jen shook off the handcuffs. She stuffed the white shawl back into the shopping bag and shoved the cuffs into a utility drawer. She stumbled into the living room and sat on the couch, hyperventilating. Lightheaded, the room spun. She closed her eyes. When she opened them, Miles stood over her.

He embraced her. "There, there. Are you all right?"

"Not really," she said in a small voice. His touch, strong and firm, was what she needed. "I'm so glad you came back to Livonia."

"Winston is willing to drive me where I'm needed. You should see what is happening outside. Dark spirits run about the streets howling and crying, lamenting the death of their leader."

Jen pressed into his shoulder. "Yeah," she whimpered in a staccato voice. "I think they've all become whores of combat."

Miles laughed. "Hors du combat. Yes, they seem to be out of commission. And I suspect you had something to do with that."

Two vehicles slammed to a stop in Jen's driveway as Lee arrived with the ambulance. Miles faded. "I need to go to the Asian Kitchen. Winston is waiting at the corner gas station for me. Your detective is here. I trust you will be in good hands." He disappeared.

The two emergency techs and Lee banged on the front door, and Jen let them in.

Lee eyed her. "What's going on?"

"Pam Caulfield." Jen pointed over her shoulder. "She's in the basement."

Jen hurried to the kitchen and undid the hasp. The EMTs eyed her. She made a face regarding the door. "In the basement. We have raccoons."

The two techs raced down the steps.

Jen half-fell, half-sat on a kitchen chair.

Lee descended a few steps into the stairwell. "Guys?"

Voices carried up the stairs. "No pulse. Let's defibrillate." After a few moments, the EMTs shouted, "Clear!" A few seconds later, someone said, "Again. Clear!" This was repeated once more.

Minutes later, both techs carried Pam's limp body up the stairs and onto the stretcher.

"Lee, there's a gun down there," the lead tech said as he opened a sheet to drape over the corpse.

"A gun?" He turned to Jen. "Yours?"

"No. Pam was talking crazy. She held a gun on me and tried to make me kiss her." The secretary gave her an internal smack. *I'm not lying.*

Jen pointed to the shreds of plastic frame scattered across the floor. "She shot my sampler, then made me go into the basement with her. I think she would have hurt me, but a raccoon jumped on her, and she collapsed."

Lee made a puzzled face. "In the basement. She held a gun on you and demanded a kiss? Why didn't you just kiss her?"

"I didn't *want* to."

"That's my girl." He lifted the sheet covering Pam's face and said to the EMTs, "What do you think?"

"You know we can't pronounce death or diagnose, but I'd say heart attack. She's got scratches but no serious indication of foul play. Check with the M.E. tomorrow. Oh, and there's a dead raccoon down there, too."

When the EMTs departed with the body, Lee sat across from Jennifer, who handed him Pam's purse and the shopping bag.

He pulled out the shawl. "This looks like what she had on."

"Yeah, twin day at Jennifer's house," Jen said, looking into the living room. "I wish you hadn't left earlier."

"We went to get Dave. He claims he and his family had been held by gunmen all this time. This morning the guys left, taking the keys to his truck. Dave was trying to hotwire it when we got there. The cabin didn't have a phone. It wasn't Dave who called us. We don't know who it was."

I know who arranged that call. Pam had to get rid of Lee and Ash.

"I told you my story," Lee said. "Would you like to tell me what happened here?"

"I just did. Pam came over after you left. We had tea." She walked to the dining room and pointed to the remnants on the table. She put her hands on the teapot. "See. It's still warm."

Lee touched the pot and nodded.

Jen grabbed the teapot and the dish of brownies and brought them into the kitchen. "After tea, Pam insisted I put on the shawl and go into the basement. When I refused, she pulled that gun on me."

"We'll check it for prints," Lee said.

"You won't find mine this time."

"Good." He pointed to a chair at the small table. "Finish your story."

Chapter Seventy-Five

Jen sorted out what Lee would believe. She gave him details but failed to mention being handcuffed. In the last few months, she had become skilled at what not to say. "In the basement, Pam said some funny words and then announced she was going to kiss me. I tried to push her away against the corner. That must be where the raccoons get in. Anyway, I shoved her backward, and a big raccoon jumped on her. She screamed and carried on, then fell on the ground. I ran up here and called for help. That's all I can tell you."

The secretary gave a contented grunt of agreement.

Grainger entered the kitchen. "What's going on?"

Lee waved Ash in. "Pam Caulfield is dead. The EMTs think it's from a heart attack, but Jen here says she died from the want of a kiss."

Jen slapped the tabletop. "Lee!"

"Uh-huh," Grainger said. "One kiss today, wedding bells tomorrow."

Jen paled at the mention of their first meeting at the liquor store.

"Hey," Lee said, switching to a firm professional voice. "There's a gun in the basement. Will you bag it and handle the paperwork?"

"I'll get the evidence kit from the car," Grainger said and left.

Lee reached for a brownie. "Straight, right? No weed? Because even for you, this situation is weird."

"I haven't done weed since college." She pinched off a piece of a brownie. "Besides, marijuana ruins the taste of a good brownie. It's better to smoke it. But you probably know that. Cops get the best stuff."

Lee popped the rest of the treat in his mouth. "Look, I'm involved, so I'm going to let Ash work this case."

"Involved?"

"Yeah, well, you're my lady. Milady. The lovely princess Jennifer. My girlfriend."

"Girlfriend? Talk about downgrades. From Queen of the World to princess, to girlfriend."

Lee moved to where she sat, kneeled, and kissed her hand. "You're the queen of my world."

He backed away and brushed the utility drawer with his hip. The handle caught the leather badge case he wore on his belt, and the drawer came open. "Sorry," he said and turned to close it. He pulled out the handcuffs. "Oh, Queenie!"

"Someday, I'll tell you the story behind those cuffs, but for now, I want to take Rex and get out of here for a while."

"That's a good idea. You look pale. I think Uncle Paul will give me a few days off. After all, Johnny Cee is spilling the beans about the mob, and I just dropped Dave Blakely off at the station. I need to finish some paperwork. You pack a bag, and I'll pick you up later. We'll go to my house."

"Your house? That isn't exactly what I had in mind."

"To pick up the Porsche. Then we'll drive until we find a place we like. How's that?"

She nodded, and he kissed her forehead.

Ash Grainger and two uniforms inspected the basement and returned with the dead raccoon and the gun.

Before he left, Ash patted her shoulder. "Relax."

She hoped that meant he didn't suspect her for Pam's death.

Alone, Jen tidied up the place and packed a bag for a few nights. Miles had said the atmosphere in Livonia had changed. Maybe she imagined it, but *things* felt better.

Her phone rang. It was Brad. "Hi, Jen. You ruined a big birthday party."

It took her a few seconds to understand. Brad couldn't say it straight because her phone most likely had a bug. "Oh, yeah. Guess I did."

"I ruined one too. Great, right?"

"Huh-uh. Um. What's going on with you?"

Brad chuckled. "Not much now. I have a few things to finish here. The bad guys left are just the little evils."

"Any plans?"

"I'll wander around. Always new souls to meet. I might call you now and then."

"I look forward to it, my traveling son. Take care of yourself."

"Thanks, Mom. Watch out for yourself, too." He clicked off.

She thought about Brad's words. When the Master Evil couldn't be born from the basement's glowing vagina, it went across the globe. She would really like to hear Brad's story. Whatever the scenario, Brad had foiled that entry. The world was relatively safe. For how long?

Late that afternoon, Lee returned. When Jen let him in, he looked shaken.

"What's wrong?" Jen asked.

Lee sat on the couch. "I closed the door to my office so I could get the paperwork done. I looked up, and a man stood there. He introduced himself as Miles Hampton."

Jen put her hand to her throat and sat next to him. "And?"

"I'm sorry I didn't believe you." He ran his hands through his thick hair. "He told me about the house and the things you did for him."

Jen felt faint. "He did? What things?"

"Your kindness, helping him find information, setting up a network, a center, someone to help him. He is grateful for all of your guidance and ideas. You even bought him his pipe! He said there was more, but I should let you tell me."

Oh, Miles. Ever the gentleman. Thank you.

"You know what else? You told him you loved me. He

said we should get married."

"You know what that means," the secretary said. "Miles has stepped away from you."

"Jen? Let's get married. I can get another job. We'll move and put all of this behind us."

Jen looked around the room. She loved the house. And the house loved her. It had protected her, given her psychic powers. Through the voice of the secretary, the house had become her voice of reason. But, two attempts on her life, a restaurant full of ghosts, the business in the basement with Pam. Yeah, she could leave. She stared at Lee. Handsome, smart, loving, and great in bed. Yeah, she could marry him and be happy.

"Okay," she said.

"Okay? To what, exactly?"

"Let's get married. We'll sell the houses, and you get a job somewhere else. I'm pretty sure once I leave this house, I won't be psychic."

Lee shook his head. "I'm a good detective on my own. I just want you to be my wife. No psychics need apply."

Rex ambled over to them. Lee scratched behind the dog's ear. "Are you two ready for a road trip?"

Jen nodded.

As they drove through town, they spotted Zelda Silverstein. Lee pulled to the curb.

"Hey, you two." She pointed to Rex. "Excuse me, three. What's up?"

Jen hit the button to lower the window. "Can you recommend a real estate office? I believe the Speigals won't be around much longer."

Zelda grinned wide. "Sounds like Johnny Cee got chatty. But why do you want a real estate office?"

"We're putting our houses up for sale," Lee said.

Zelda put her forefinger to her head and closed her eyes, going into her *seeing* pantomime. "Ah, yes. Jennifer, I see a tall, good-looking man in your life. Your long, happy life."

"What else do you see?"

Zelda tapped the space between her sagging breasts. "Me, buying that Victorian. I've always loved it. Don't know why I didn't do it before."

I know why. The house wasn't ready for you.

Zelda shuddered. "The dirt floor in the basement has to go, though."

Jen nodded emphatically. "Make me an offer on the house. You'd be surprised what I'd take for it."

"I'm a rich old lady. I'll pay you what it's worth, honey."

"Sold!" Jen said.

Zelda backed away and saluted.

Wow. I wonder if Zelda will meet Miles. What a hoot. That house might make her truly psychic.

Lee headed the Crown Vic toward his house. He transferred their bags to the Porsche and tapped the small seat in the back for Rex to jump in. Jen leaned back into the soft leather. She barely noticed the rumble of the engine or the fact they headed north. She thought about all the rage, lust, greed, and violence. The effort to overcome the problems had made her strong.

All that has happened to me in the last few months. Incredible. Who would believe it? What a great book it would make. *Yes! I'll write a book starting with the purchase of the house. I'll include every mind-boggling detail. Of course, I'll have to change names.*

She came out of the trance when the car lurched with Lee braking hard to avoid a black cat in the road. Jen noticed the old graveyard on her right where one of the headstones leaned, allowing the light to shadow on the name *Livonia Grainger*.

There! I'll start with the town and call it Livonia.

The End

Patricia is a former art teacher and high school librarian. She lives in South Florida with her husband and three dogs. She writes short stories, novellas, and novels, mostly fantasy and Sci-Fi. She has also written three Romances, a Sci-Fi, a Victorian, and a Contemporary. Her stories revolve around action and deep relationships, allowing the reader to watch the scene unfold as if present. Patricia is active in three critique groups and often helps new writers learn the ropes. She is an active member of the Florida Writers Association, Mystery Writers of America, and Romance Writers of America.

When not writing, Patricia enjoys painting watercolors and drawing in several media. Currently, she is learning illustration techniques for future books. Her frequent travel provides opportunities to check off bucket list items and sometimes inspires new stories. She is a voracious reader and loves a good book talk.

Check out her Facebook page at Carpewordum@gate. net.

www.ingramcontent.com/pod-product-compliance
Lightning Source LLC
Chambersburg PA
CBHW020928020726
47495CB00002B/393

9 798891 260146